Me and My Sisters

Me and My Sisters

SINÉAD MORIARTY

PENGUIN
IRELAND

PENGUIN IRELAND

Published by the Penguin Group
Penguin Ireland, 25 St Stephen's Green, Dublin 2, Ireland
(a division of Penguin Books Ltd)
Penguin Books Ltd, 80 Strand, London WC2R 0RL, England
Penguin Group (USA) Inc., 375 Hudson Street, New York, New York 10014, USA
Penguin Group (Australia), 250 Camberwell Road,
Camberwell, Victoria 3124, Australia (a division of Pearson Australia Group Pty Ltd)
Penguin Group (Canada), 90 Eglinton Avenue East, Suite 700, Toronto, Ontario, Canada M4P 2Y3
(a division of Pearson Penguin Canada Inc.)
Penguin Books India Pvt Ltd, 11 Community Centre,
Panchsheel Park, New Delhi – 110 017, India
Penguin Group (NZ), 67 Apollo Drive, Rosedale, Auckland 0632, New Zealand
(a division of Pearson New Zealand Ltd)
Penguin Books (South Africa) (Pty) Ltd, 24 Sturdee Avenue,
Rosebank, Johannesburg 2196, South Africa

Penguin Books Ltd, Registered Offices: 80 Strand, London WC2R 0RL, England

www.penguin.com

First published 2011
2

Set in 11/13 pt Dante MT Std
Typeset by Palimpsest Book Production Limited, Falkirk, Stirlingshire
Printed in Great Britain by Clays Ltd, St Ives plc

A CIP catalogue record for this book is available from the British Library

ISBN: 978-0-241-95058-6

www.greenpenguin.co.uk

For Mike

Once upon a time there were three sisters . . .
    and a brother who lived in a tree

1

Julie

We stood under the tree, peering up. Even though it was only five thirty in the afternoon, it was pitch dark.

'Uncle Gavin!' the triplets shouted. 'Happy nearly Christmas!'

Nothing.

'GAVIN!' I roared at my brother.

'The name's Willow,' the tree replied.

'Oh, for God's sake – Willow, then.'

My brother's face appeared over the branch. 'That's better.' He grinned.

'Can we come up?' the triplets begged.

'I'm not sure there's enough room, guys. Why don't we do it one by one?' Gavin suggested.

'How are you doing up there?' Harry, my husband, asked.

'It's surprisingly comfortable,' Gavin replied.

'Really? Well, I think you're stark raving mad. It's freezing.' Harry rubbed his gloved hands together.

'It's OK if you have the right gear,' Gavin assured him.

While Harry lifted Liam up to his uncle's makeshift tree-house, I tried to talk sense into my brother. 'You've been up there a week now. Don't you think you've made your point?'

'Julie, until they agree to cancel the clubhouse expansion and save this tree, I'm going nowhere. You have to stand by your beliefs. The problem today is that people are apathetic about everything. Money is the new religion. You'll thank me when your kids are older.' Wagging his finger at me, he added, 'Remember, Julie, we do not inherit the Earth from our ancestors, we borrow it from our children.'

'He has a point,' Harry said.

'Don't encourage him,' I hissed.

'This is so cool!' Liam shouted down at his brothers.

'My turn! My turn!' Luke was impatient to get up.

I turned back to the tree. 'Seriously, Gavin, you have to stop. Mum and Dad like coming to this golf club. They've practically lived here since they retired and they're freaking out because you're making a holy show of them. Why can't you go and save a tree in the Amazon? Why do you have to do it half a mile from their house at their golf club?'

'My name is *Willow*, Julie, and all I'm doing is trying to get people to think before they act. Ripping down a two-hundred-year-old tree is unacceptable. My mission is to save it.'

I sighed. There was no point in talking to him when he was like this. Gavin was an impressionable and very passionate twenty-three-year-old. I was a cynical, exhausted, thirty-nine-year-old mother of four boys whose only mission in life was to get a full night's sleep. It had become the Holy Grail: I truly believed that it would be the answer to all my problems. If I could just get one uninterrupted night, I'd find my old self again.

Gavin was the youngest in the family by a significant amount – my mother thought she was starting early menopause when the pregnancy symptoms kicked in. With three much older sisters, Gavin had grown up completely indulged and spoilt by our mother and mercilessly teased by us girls. He was now a man-child: he wanted to 'save the world', just as long as it wasn't too far from his mother's home cooking and laundry service.

His naïveté had made him an easy target for 'Forest', a twenty-nine-year-old seasoned eco-warrior whom Gavin had befriended while working in a music store after finishing his finals last summer. Since meeting Forest he had begun spouting on about people killing good trees to print tabloids and how he was now an Earth warrior, and recently he had insisted that we call him 'Willow', which caused much hilarity among us sisters. Our parents, however, were not amused.

'UP, UP,' shouted Tom, my eighteen-month-old, from his buggy.

I leant down. 'No, pet, you're too small.' He smiled at me and touched my face. I kissed him. My little accident. My little pet.

'I want to live in a tree with Uncle Gavin for ever,' Leo said.

'It's Willow, little dude,' Gavin called.

'I want to live in a tree with Uncle Willow.' Leo tugged at my sleeve.

'When you're eighteen you can go and live in a shagging cave for all I care,' I replied.

'Cool! Can Liam and Luke come too?' The triplets did everything together.

'Hell, yes – and you can take Tom as well.' Harry laughed. 'Look on the bright side, Julie. They're four and a half now, so only thirteen and a half more years till they move out.'

'Oh, that'll fly by.' I smirked.

Harry tried to keep a straight face. 'Well, exactly. I mean, the last four and a half years have only felt like –'

'Five centuries.' I giggled. Laughter was the only thing that kept me sane – there was often a slightly manic edge to it, these days. Laughing and reading were my saviours, although there hadn't been much time for either in the last few years. 'Come on, kids, we have to go – we'll be late for mass.'

'*Muuuu*mmy, I hate mass, it's so boring,' Liam huffed.

'Don't say "boring",' Leo scolded him.

'Or Santa won't come,' Luke reminded his brother.

'Right, we're off. I presume you're coming down for Christmas dinner in Mum and Dad's tomorrow?' I asked Gavin.

'Yeah, I'll be home about three.'

'OK. Well, have a good night. Here, I bought you this – you might as well open it early.' I handed my brother his Christmas present. It was a fleece that I'd bought in the Great Outdoors. The guy in the shop had told me it would keep you warm in Antarctica, so I figured it would do just fine in suburban Dublin. My younger sister Sophie had already kitted Gavin out with the best camping equipment money could buy.

'Thanks, sis.' Gavin smiled. 'See you kids tomorrow. I hope Santa comes.'

'Mummy said he can change his mind until the last minute,' Leo told him.

'Bit harsh, Julie.' Gavin pulled his new fleece over his head.

'They drew all over the kitchen dresser with ketchup,' I explained.

'Ah, I see. OK, boys, be good for your mum and dad and say hi to Jesus.' Gavin's head disappeared behind a branch.

'Do we really have to go to mass?' Harry asked, as we walked back to the car.

I turned to him. 'The last time we went to mass was last Christmas. I don't think once a year is too much to ask.'

'You're right. It's just, you know, they'll be running riot in the church.'

'It's a children's mass so it'll be more relaxed. Come on, let's get it over with.'

We piled into the car. Well, let's be honest here: it's practically a van. After the triplets were born I had reluctantly waved goodbye to my pink Mini Cooper and bought a people-carrier. I hated it. It screamed, 'My life is over. I am a slave to motherhood. I am a dowdy, stay-at-home mum who has no life outside the home. I am boring, permanently exhausted – to the point where I am quite likely to fall asleep in the middle of a conversation – overweight, badly dressed, ignorant of all current affairs and any affairs that don't involve celebrities in the old issues of *Hello!* that I read in the doctor's surgery, where I frequently find myself, most recently for the nurse to remove a pistachio nut lodged in Liam's right nostril.

My waist went missing in 2005 and hasn't been seen since. As I'm turning forty next year, the chances are slim that it will be recovered. I had high hopes of finding it *circa* 2008 when the triplets turned three and I was beginning to see a chink of light at the end of a very dark tunnel. I even began exercising again . . . until I found out I was pregnant with Tom and my waist entered the Bermuda Triangle, never to be seen again. Family packs of KitKats and Hobnobs replaced carrot sticks and low-fat hummus.

4

Having two thin, toned, beautifully dressed sisters does not help. You'd think I'd find it motivating, but I actually find it annoying, and thinking about their small neat waists makes me eat even more. When we go out to dinner and they order steamed fish and green veg, I order battered cod and chips. It's completely irrational, but their self-control and discipline wind me up and I become the extreme antidote, much to the dismay of my misplaced waist.

We shuffled into a pew towards the back of the church. While Tom sat calmly on my lap, the triplets shuffled, fidgeted, pushed each other, thumped each other and kicked each other. Harry and I ignored them until they climbed on to the back of the pew in front and shouted, 'Hello, Poohead,' at an elderly woman trying to pray. Harry pulled them back and ordered them to sit still.

The couple beside us had two daughters, who were playing angelically and very quietly with their dolls. The mum smiled at me – a 'God love you, you poor cow' kind of a smile. I had seen it almost daily since the triplets were born. When they were small and I'd take them out in the ridiculous triplet buggy I'd had to order online from America, women would stop me and ask, 'Are they really triplets?'

'Yes.'

'All boys?'

'Yes.'

They'd say how sweet the babies were and then they'd walk away muttering, 'Could you imagine anything worse? How does that poor haggard woman feed them?' Answer: badly and irregularly. 'How does she bathe them?' Rarely. 'How does she get them to sleep?' Never at the same time – look at my eyes.

I cuddled Tom closer. At least one of my kids was well behaved. When I found out I was pregnant with him, I freaked. He was the accident that happened when I forgot to take the pill due to exhaustion. Three weeks later, with my head down the toilet, I realized my mistake. My first reaction was 'FUCK!' My second reaction was '*FUUUUUUCK!*'

When I finally wrapped my head around it, I thought, OK, well, it's obviously going to be a girl. I'm going to get a little angel girl like my niece, Jess, who sits quietly and never raises her voice. Finally I'll get to buy pink, and instead of playing football, wrestling or engaging in a home-made version of *kung-fu* that involves causing maximum harm to the other person, I'll get to play Princess.

'It's a healthy boy,' they announced, when Tom was born. My first reaction was 'FUCK!' My second reaction was '*FUUUUUUCK!*' But it turns out that Tom is my saviour. He was the sweetest baby and is now the sweetest toddler. Sometimes I secretly hope he's gay so he can be my buddy. We can go for coffees and he can advise me on what to wear, and we can gossip and go to chick-flicks together.

I foolishly told Harry this one night and he was decidedly unimpressed. Men seem to think that having a gay son somehow emasculates them. Honestly, I'd love it if he was. I wonder is it OK to pray to God on Christmas Eve for your baby son to be gay?

'Earth to Julie.' Harry shook my arm. 'The boys have gone AWOL.'

My head snapped around. 'What were you doing?'

'Praying!'

'With your eyes *shut*?'

'Yes.' He put his hands up. 'I know, incredibly stupid of me. Can you see them?'

I looked right and left. Nothing. Then I saw movement in front of me. Oh, God, they were in the manger.

'Manger!' I hissed.

Harry followed my eye line, and groaned. 'Rock, paper, scissors.'

'No way,' I protested. 'You took your eye off the ball.'

'You were daydreaming.'

'OK, go on.'

Harry did paper and I did rock. Damn. I stood up, handed Tom to his dad and gingerly made my way up the side of the church to the altar. I could see the three *amigos* rolling about in the straw at the back of the life-size manger, squealing with glee. I could hear furious mutterings from the pews around me.

'Disgraceful!'

'Where are the parents?'

'Running wild!'

'Those children have ADHD.'

Not for the first time – and I'm not proud of myself for this – I thought about disowning them.

By the time I got to the manger, Luke was lying in it and the other two were trying to wrestle him out so they could get in. When they saw me, they jumped in and dived under the hay. I had no choice: I dived in after them. Thus ensued five minutes of me trying to rugby-tackle them on to the floor, but I only have two arms. I managed to get Leo and Liam under each one, but Luke escaped. Eventually a middle-aged man, who was watching all this with much amusement, came to my rescue. He hauled Luke out and followed me and my red face to the back of the church, where Harry was waiting with Tom strapped into his buggy, ready to leg it as soon as I got there.

I thanked the man, and when we got outside I turned on Harry: 'Why the hell didn't you help me?'

'Because Tom just puked all over me!' He pointed to his vomit-spattered coat.

'I hate my life,' I cried.

'Is Santa not going to come now?' Leo asked.

'No, he bloody is not. I'm furious with you. Why can you never behave yourselves?' I lashed out.

'Sorry, Mummy.' Liam's chin wobbled.

'Sorry, Mummy.' Leo's eyes welled up.

'Sorry, Mummy.' Luke was bawling.

'It's OK, boys, Mummy didn't mean it.' Harry glared at me. 'Of course Santa's coming. Now, come on, let's get home and get you ready for bed.'

I looked at Tom. He smiled and threw up all over me.

2.00 *a.m.*

'Jesus *Christ*.' Harry threw down the screwdriver.

'Calm down, it can't be that hard.' I peered at the instructions for the zillionth time.

'Well, then, why don't you assemble it?'

'Sesus, sesus.' Tom gurgled.

'Great. Now he's cursing.' I sighed.

'What?'

'He's trying to say "Jesus".'

'Yes, Tom, good boy, it's Jesus's birthday.' Harry nodded to his baby son.

'Bit lame.'

'Can you please stop criticizing and help me?' Harry demanded.

'I am helping. I've been holding the instructions for two hours and handing you all the right nuts and bolts in between cleaning up Tom's vomit and changing his pyjamas.'

Harry got up to stretch his back. 'Right. Let me see those instructions again.'

I handed him the sheet of white paper, densely covered with diagrams. 'Remind me again why we thought it was a good idea to get the boys a life-size sleigh in a country where it rarely snows?'

'Because I know they're going to love it – and, besides, these wheels are supposed to be attached to the bottom so they can sleigh all year round, even in the summer.'

'Isn't that a bit dangerous?' Harry held up one of the wheels. It did look quite big.

'It's OK, there's a brake. Here it is.' I held up a piece of steel.

'Where the hell does that go?'

I shrugged.

An hour and a lot of cursing later, we finished assembling the sleigh. It looked fantastic.

'Well done! It's gorgeous – they'll be thrilled.' I handed Harry a well-earned beer.

'Never again, Julie. Next year they're getting something that comes ready-made.'

'I thought you'd be good at putting things together because of your job.'

He was incredulous: 'I'm a computer programmer, not a carpenter!'

'I guess Joseph would have come in handy tonight so.' I grinned. 'I bet Jesus's presents were all perfectly put together.'

Harry laughed.

'Sesus,' Tom cooed.

I checked his temperature. It was finally down and he hadn't got sick after the last bottle I'd given him an hour ago. I pulled him up on to my lap. 'Do you think Tom's going to know Santa isn't real now that he's seen us assembling the sleigh without any sign of a bearded man in a red coat coming out of the chimney? Do you think we've ruined Christmas for him?'

'Julie, he's eighteen months old. He can't even speak, not to mind process who or what Santa is. He'll be all right – I don't think he's going to become a serial killer because he saw me making a sleigh.'

'Well, I hope not. I love them believing in Santa.'

'Me, too, and I want them to believe for as long as possible.' Harry picked Tom up from my lap and gave him a cuddle.

Harry's mother had died when he was only three years old and his father was a very strict, stern schoolteacher. When Harry was four he had asked Santa Claus for a bike. His father sat him down and told him that Santa didn't exist and there was no money for any bike. That year he'd got new shoes for Christmas. His childhood was officially over. Because of this, Harry wasn't at all strict with our boys and sometimes I found myself wishing he was a bit stronger on discipline. I understood that he didn't want them to experience the same coldness he had from his father, but the boys were a bit wild and needed to be reined in.

I was delighted last week when Harry lost his cool and bellowed at them because they poured honey into the keyboard of his laptop and then Super-Glued it closed. But for the most part I was the 'bad cop' to Harry's 'good cop'. Sometimes I think the triplets are only ever going to remember me shouting at them. My vocabulary from dawn to dusk consists of 'Stop it', 'Get down', 'Share', 'Get off him', 'Stop hitting him', 'Don't do that', 'I'm warning you', 'You're in big trouble' and, for the last month, 'Santa's watching you.' Every day I wake up and vow, Today I will not raise my voice. And within ten minutes of being awake I'm hollering like a fishwife. I'm surprised I don't have permanent laryngitis.

We finished wrapping the little presents for their stockings.

'I wonder what Louise's news is?' I said, as I put a small racing car into Luke's. My older sister Louise, who lived in London, had texted yesterday and said she had some news to tell me on Christmas Day, but when I rang her to find out what it was I just got her voicemail.

'Boyfriend?' Harry suggested.

'She didn't sound excited, so I don't think that's it.'

'Probably not. She's pretty scary. I can't imagine guys are queuing round the block to go out with her.'

'Hey! That's not fair. Louise is great – she's just very focused.'

'I'm a fan of Louise's, but I wouldn't want to go out with her. She can be a bit icy.'

'She just doesn't suffer fools – and she's very successful. For some reason men find that intimidating.'

'Julie, we're simple creatures. We want to be with a woman, not a woman who acts and thinks like a guy, which is what Louise does.'

'Maybe she's got a new job.'

'I thought she'd just been made senior partner at the law firm.'

'Oh, yeah. Maybe she got head-hunted, then.' I stifled a yawn. 'Well, whatever it is, I'll have to wait until tomorrow to find out.'

'You mean today. It's after three a.m.' Harry pointed to the clock.

'Oh, God, let's get to bed quick. The boys are bound to be up early.'

'Are Sophie and Jack coming to your parents for dinner, too?'

'Yes.'

'Great,' Harry drawled.

'Come on, you like Sophie and you just have to ignore Jack.'

'It's difficult to ignore someone who takes over every conversation.'

'He's not that bad, just a bit over the top.'

'He's an arrogant tosser. I swear if he tells me how much money he made this year, I'll deck him.'

My brother-in-law, Jack, was an incredibly successful hedge-fund manager. He had told Harry and everyone else 'discreetly' last Christmas that he had earned four million that year. Harry, who had earned a tiny fraction of that, had almost choked on his wine. Jack had then insisted on taking Harry for a spin in his brand-new Maserati, which was parked beside our people-carrier. When they'd arrived back, Jack had made a big show of giving Sophie her 'real' present – apparently the Jimmy Choo boots she'd got that morning were only a token. Louise had rolled her eyes at me across the room while Dad muttered, 'Gobshite,' under his breath. Jack had produced a large Tiffany's box. Inside lay an incredible platinum-and-diamond chain with a big diamond S on the end.

I'll never forget the look on Harry's face. He'd given me a Tiffany's box that morning, and inside was a lovely silver chain and a round silver pendant with J inscribed on it. I was thrilled and had shown it to my sisters when we arrived, but I knew Harry now felt belittled. Ever since then, all hope of the two brothers-in-law being friendly was gone. Jack had always been showy, but in the last few years he had gone to another level. Harry, who liked most people, couldn't stand him. I knew Dad wasn't keen on him either, but he tried not to show it out of loyalty to Sophie. To be honest, I thought Jack was a bit of an idiot, but I tried to like him for Sophie's sake.

I hung up the stockings on the fireplace and stood back beside Harry. Three big stockings, for Luke, Liam and Leo, and a mini-stocking at the end for Tom. I was suddenly overcome with love for my four boys. My little men. I fought back tears.

Harry put his arm around me and kissed my cheek. 'We're very lucky.'

I nodded, the tears now rolling down my face.

We tucked Tom up in his cot and collapsed into our bed. I was asleep before my head hit the pillow.

5.50 a.m.

Three hours later, I was woken by a stocking smacking me on the head. 'SANTA CAME!' the triplets squealed, bouncing up and down on our bed.

'It cannot be morning already!' I croaked.

Harry looked at his watch. 'Well, it's dawn.' He leant over and kissed me. 'Merry Christmas, Julie.'

'Come on, Mummy! Come and see! Santa brought us a real live sleigh! It's so cool.' The triplets pulled at my arm until I stumbled out of bed.

'Erry Issmas, Mummy.' Tom clung to my leg.

I bent down to pick him up and we all headed off to go sleigh-riding around the hall.

2

Louise

I hated being delayed. My plane to Dublin had been held up and there didn't appear to be any good reason for it. It was infuriating. The flight wasn't leaving until nine thirty, so I wouldn't get to the hotel until eleven and I had at least two hours' work to do. Thank God all the Christmas presents were organized. I had ordered all the children's things from Hamley's in November and the adults' from Selfridges. They'd been gift-wrapped and delivered to Mum and Dad's house.

I poured myself a coffee – my second of the day: I never drank more than two, it dehydrated me – and sat down at an empty table in the lounge. I avoided eye contact with the man sitting at the table opposite me. He'd been trying to catch my attention since I'd walked into the Gold Club lounge and I was determined to ignore him. I didn't feel like being chatted up. Not tonight. I had too much on my mind. Besides, he wasn't very attractive and he had a beer belly. I never went for men who were unfit or overweight. They were clearly lazy, unhealthy and unfocused.

I couldn't imagine a life without exercise. It cleared my head in the mornings and gave me a physical and mental high. Over the last few months exercise had kept me sane as I tried to work out what to do with the mess I'd got myself into. I was still shocked when I thought back to that day. It was so unlike me to lose control. What an idiot I had been. I sighed, sipped my coffee and forced myself not to wonder how my family was going to react to my news. I didn't want to think about it any more: I was worn out.

Julie thought I was addicted to exercise and she might have been right, but at least it was a positive thing to be addicted to. I wished she'd start working out. She really needed to lose her baby weight and start taking control of her life. The triplets were a nightmare and she was always too tired to discipline them properly, which was hardly surprising considering she survived on a diet of chocolate biscuits and left-over fish-fingers.

Last winter she'd rung me crying because she couldn't fit into her fat jeans – her skinny ones were long gone – and I'd spent ages creating a detailed schedule of what she needed to do. I had typed up a day-to-day meal plan for her and given her an exercise regime that she could fit easily into her chaotic life. But it didn't last. She said she had tried really hard for four days, but then the boys got expelled from summer camp for cutting off a little girl's ponytail during the arts and crafts class and Julie had turned to chocolate for comfort. When I suggested she could have tried to eat carrot sticks and nuts instead she'd told me to 'Shove your carrot sticks up your arse,' and slammed down the phone.

It wasn't that I didn't see it was tough for her – the triplets were a real handful – but I did think that if she managed her time better she'd be able to fit everything in, including more sleep, exercise and some time for herself. I was just trying to help.

My youngest sister, on the other hand, had far too much free time. I couldn't understand how Sophie wasn't bored out of her mind. How many pedicures can you have? She had only one child, Jessica, and a full-time housekeeper-childminder. Sophie was always perfectly groomed and she looked great, but I found it incredible that, with all her spare time, she never seemed to read the paper or even watch the news. She was completely clueless about current affairs – all she seemed to read were fashion magazines. Her life consisted of tennis, beautician, hairdresser, and endless coffee mornings talking rubbish with other bored, wealthy housewives. When Jessica started play-school last year I suggested Sophie should get a part-time job or go to college and do a course, but she looked at me as if I was mad and asked, 'Where on earth would I find the time?'

I was tempted to say, 'How about in between your skinny latte and your blow-dry?' but Julie kicked me under the table, so I shut up.

It also bugged me that Sophie never, *ever*, asked me about work. I didn't have a family, and my career was a huge part of my life. I had recently become only the second woman ever to be made senior partner at Higgins, Cooper & Gray. It was a really big deal. I got front-page coverage in the *Law Gazette*, the *Law Journal* and *Legal Week*.

I asked Sophie about Jessica and Jack all the time, and listened to her going on about Jessica's talent as a ballet dancer, the pros of an Aga versus a gas range and how Jack was making millions, but she never once asked me about my job. She was only interested in finding out what cool new restaurants were opening up in London and if I'd seen Priscilla Haddington – some kind of 'It girl' socialite who lived in my apartment block.

The thing that shocked me most, though, was the money issue. Five years ago Dad had sold his business, just before the bottom dropped out of the economy. His timing really was impeccable. With the money he made he gave all four of us €80,000 each, a 'rainy-day fund', he called it. I had ordered Gavin to hand his over to me to look after because I knew he'd waste it otherwise, and when Julie had asked my advice on how to invest hers, I'd offered to look after it for her. The money was really important to her. They weren't well off and she really wanted to send the boys to a private school. I was delighted to be able to tell her last month that her money was now worth €92,000.

When I was doing that for Gavin and Julie, I had called Sophie to see if she wanted me to invest hers too, but she said she'd given it to Jack. When I asked what he was doing with it, she said she didn't know and got really huffy when I said I thought it was ridiculous to have no idea where your own money was or how it was being invested. Considering how successful Jack was, she reckoned it was in pretty safe hands, she snapped.

The flight was finally called and we were able to board the plane at nine forty-five so I got to my hotel, as predicted, at eleven o'clock. I never wanted to stay at home with Mum and Dad – which Mum strongly resented: I found it claustrophobic. I'd been living on my own since I was eighteen and I liked my own space.

I worked on my laptop for two hours and collapsed into bed at one. I set my alarm for seven. I wanted to go for a run, have a nice long soak in the bath, finish reading the Grogan file and check on my apartment before heading over to Mum and Dad's. The two-bedroom apartment in a development near UCD was the first investment I had made fourteen years ago when I got my first big bonus. It was just before property prices in Ireland went through the roof. I never had any problem renting the place, but I only let it to mature students or lecturers. I didn't want younger students trashing my pension property.

I tossed and turned for ages, trying to figure out the best way to drop my bombshell at Christmas lunch. Eventually I fell into a fitful sleep.

At two thirty the next day I pulled the rental car into my parents' driveway and took two deep breaths. Here we go . . .

Mum rushed to the door to welcome me. We gave each other an awkward hug.

'I'm delighted to see you,' she said, ushering me into the lounge. 'Look, all your presents are here. They were delivered four weeks ago. I never heard of anyone buying presents in November, really and truly!'

'I had a busy December so I just wanted to be organized.' I tried not to snap.

Ignoring me, Mum continued, 'Well, you're the first here. Sophie and Jack were popping into his parents' house this morning and Julie's late as usual. Now, let me look at you.' She held my shoulders and peered into my face. I braced myself. 'You look tired, Louise. Working far too hard, I've no doubt. You need to get out in the fresh air and join a tennis club or something,' she suggested. 'You won't meet any nice men locked up in your office.'

'I went for a run this morning, Mum. I'm getting plenty of fresh air.'

'Running is a solo sport – you won't meet anyone doing that.'

'I'm happy being single,' I reminded her for the hundredth time.

'No one is happy on their own.'

'Maybe I'm just a freak of nature.'

'Don't get smart with me, young lady.'

'I'm just –'

Thankfully, before we ended up having yet another argument about my lack of desire to get married, Dad came in. He kissed me on the cheek. 'Welcome home, Louise. How's the corporate world?'

'Busy, thanks.'

'She's overdoing it as usual,' Mum said, picking up a bottle of wine. 'Now, sit down and have a glass of red before Julie arrives and the madness begins. Those children are completely out of control. They need a firm hand but Julie and Harry are walkovers.'

'Ah, you can't be shouting at them all the time. They're just lively.' Dad defended the boys.

'Boys need discipline.' Mum wagged a finger at Dad. 'Maybe if you'd been stricter with our Gavin we wouldn't be in this mess.'

'I'm not the one who spoilt him rotten all his life,' Dad muttered.

I decided to interrupt them. 'What time is Gavin coming?'

'Apparently he's going to grace us with his presence at three.' Dad fiddled with his tie.

'Mortified, we are.' Mum sniffed. 'We're the laughing stock of the golf club. Can you imagine how humiliating it is to have everyone looking at your son, your only son, living up a tree?'

'I wouldn't mind if he was protesting against child slavery,' Dad said, between gritted teeth. 'I told him I'd plant ten trees to make up for it. He says, "Dad, would the birth of ten babies replace me if I was murdered?"'

I suppressed a smile. 'At least he believes in something. Most young guys are out getting drunk every night.'

'Easy for you to say. You haven't been here,' Mum remarked

pointedly. 'You haven't had to listen to his eco-this and eco-that for the last six months.'

'If you're tired of listening to it, tell him to move out,' I suggested.

'And live where?' Mum asked. 'Sure he can barely boil water – he'd never survive on his own.'

'That's because you do everything for him,' Dad growled.

'Us girls had learnt to cook and do our own laundry by the time we were sixteen,' I reminded my mother. 'You never let Gavin do anything for himself. Maybe it's time you did.'

'Isn't he up a tree by himself?' Mum retorted.

'Yes, but you're bringing him casseroles and clean clothes every night,' Dad said.

Mum stiffened. 'What am I supposed to do? Let him starve? Let him wear dirty underpants?'

'It might make him grow up a bit,' I said.

'He's not tough like you. He's very sensitive,' Mum told me.

I bristled. 'You can be sensitive and self-sufficient at the same time. He's twenty-three, for God's sake. Stop mollycoddling him.'

'He's different from you, Louise. You've always been independent. The first chance you got you ran away to England and we hardly ever see you now. I don't want that for Gavin. I'd miss him too much.'

'I didn't *run away* to England. I took up a place to study law at Cambridge. I can see what a disappointment that must have been for you.'

'Now, now, you know your mother and I were very proud of you getting into Cambridge,' Dad said.

'Of course I was proud.' Mum pulled her cardigan around her. 'I just don't understand why you can only come home once a year and why you can't stay with your own mother when you do.'

I sighed. 'We've been over this a million times. It's not personal, it's just that I'm forty-one and I like my own space. I don't think it's such a terrible thing.'

'Noreen Ryan's daughter's forty-three and she always stays with her when she comes back from New York. She doesn't seem to have claustrophobia.' Mum took a noisy sip of her wine.

Thankfully, before it could escalate further and end up with me saying something I'd regret, Julie and her gang arrived. I rushed outside to say hello.

'Merry Christmas,' Julie said, hugging me.

'Thank God you're here.'

'What's she giving out about?'

'Working too hard, lack of a man and staying in a hotel.'

'Home sweet home.' Julie laughed.

'Nice ears,' I said, smiling at her red sparkly reindeer antlers.

'Hold on.' She pressed a button and the ears began to sing 'Rudolph The Red Nosed Reindeer'.

'You should have married Santa Claus.' I grinned.

'He's a bit old for me, but he might suit you!'

'Thanks a lot.'

'Here you go, Mrs Claus.' She fished a second pair of antlers out of her bag and plonked them on my head. 'It'll help get you into the spirit of the day.'

Harry came over, carrying Tom. 'Hi, Louise.' He kissed my cheek. 'How has your morning been?'

'A lot more civilized than yours, I imagine.'

'Don't talk to me.' He groaned. 'I'm exhausted already.'

He looked it. Since they'd had the triplets, Harry and Julie had aged ten years. Julie looked knackered too, and she'd put on more weight.

The triplets were running around in circles in the garden, wrestling each other to the ground. 'GET UP!' Julie roared, pulling Liam out of a puddle. 'Look at you. You're covered in mud and I went to all the trouble of dressing you up.'

They were wearing jeans and navy jumpers. Each jumper had a different picture on it – a Santa, a Rudolph and a snowman – which was now caked with mud.

'Say hello to your auntie Louise,' Harry told them.

'Hello, Louise,' one of them said – I could never really tell them apart. They all had brown hair, which made it difficult.

'Hello, Cheese,' another said.

'Hello, Keys,' the third said, as they all giggled.

Harry turned Tom to face me. 'Say hello to Louise.'

He beamed and said, 'Kello, Ouise,' in the cutest little voice. I kissed him.

'Well, at least one of them is semi-normal.' Julie sighed.

Harry shivered. 'Come on, let's go in. It's freezing out here. Louise, would you mind taking Tom while Julie and I grab the triplets?'

I carried Tom inside. He grinned at me, then vomited all over my dress.

There was a knock on the bathroom door. I opened it and Julie stood there, holding a packet of baby wipes. 'Oh, God, Lou, I'm so sorry.' She handed me some wipes. 'He's just getting over a little bug and I thought he was fine. Look at your beautiful dress!'

'It's fine – it's not new or anything,' I lied. It was brand new, expensive and I really liked it.

'I know you're lying, but thanks. I really am sorry. Last year you got apple juice spilled all over you and now this.'

'Forget it, it's done.' I rubbed the last bit off and prayed that a good dry cleaner would be able to eliminate all stains and vomit smells.

Julie sat down on the side of the bath.

'Apart from Tom's tummy bug, how are things?' I asked.

'Same old story,' she said. 'Honestly, Lou, you were so wise not to have children. It's like bloody Groundhog Day. I can't wait for them all to be in school so I can do something constructive with my life.'

'Are you still managing to read?' I asked. Julie had always been the most voracious reader I knew. She used to get through three books a week – anything she could lay her hands on: history, science, politics, religion, spirituality, sport, psychology. It was incredible, and yet she hadn't done particularly well in school or college. She wasn't interested in exams. She just liked reading for reading's sake.

'Less than I'd like, but I'm still managing a book a week. I can now read while cooking, cleaning, doing laundry and eating. Anyway, I'm much more interested in your life. How are you? Are you even more manic now that you've been promoted?'

I nodded. 'I didn't think it was possible, but my workload is even heavier. It's all good, though, and my new office has a view of the Thames and Big Ben.'

'Wow! Mind you, it's no more than you deserve after twenty years' devotion to that firm.'

'It's nice to be recognized,' I admitted.

Julie's head snapped up. 'I can't believe I nearly forgot to ask you! What's the news you said you had?'

I put my hands over my face.

'Oh, my God, Lou, is it that bad?'

I peered out from between my fingers. 'Brace yourself, Julie. You're not going to believe this. I –'

'Julie! Are you in there?' Mum barged in and stood glaring at Julie, hands on hips. 'If those children do not behave, I'm locking them out in the garden.'

'Where's Harry?' Julie asked.

'Harry doesn't seem to think there's anything wrong with his children pulling all the decorations off the Christmas tree, but I do!'

'OK, I'll be down in two minutes,' Julie promised.

Mum grabbed her arm and marched her downstairs. 'Julie, in two minutes my tree will have fallen down and killed someone.'

I sat down and exhaled deeply.

3

Sophie

'Merry Christmas, darling.' Jack handed me a big Cartier box.

I opened it and screamed.

He grinned. 'Happy?'

'It's incredible.' I took out the watch and held it up to the morning light. 'Oh, Jack, it's stunning. Thank you.' I turned to kiss him.

'A Cartier Tank Française eighteen-carat white gold and diamond bracelet watch for my beautiful wife.'

He helped me put it on and I watched the diamonds sparkle as I moved my wrist. I couldn't wait to show it off at Victoria's next coffee morning; she'd be green with envy. She'd wanted one of these for two years and had been dropping loads of hints to Gerry, but so far he'd ignored her. Mind you, he had given her a new Land Rover LRX Concept last year, which I admit I envied.

'Was the watch horrendously expensive?' I asked Jack.

He nodded. 'But who cares? I had a bloody great year and money is there to be enjoyed.'

'I just love it.'

'Well, I can think of one way you can thank me.' He rolled over and climbed on top of me. I wasn't in the mood for sex, but I could hardly refuse him after such an amazing gift. Thankfully, it was all over in five minutes and Jack fell straight back to sleep. I lay and admired my present.

There was a soft knock on the door. 'Come in, sweetheart,' I called. Jessica rushed in and climbed up on to the bed. Her cheeks were flushed.

'He came, Mummy! Santa came and he left me so many presents! My room is full up.'

I hugged her. 'Of course he came. You're the best four-year-old girl in the world. Now, come on, show me your new toys.'

'Daddy, are you coming?' she asked.

'Ssh, he's asleep,' I said. I took her hand and we ran across to her bedroom.

For the next hour we played with all her new things. I'd gone a bit mad and bought her everything she'd ever shown an interest in. I loved spoiling her. She was such a sweet, gentle little girl and so easy to mind. When I looked at what Julie had to deal with, I thanked God for Jess. I honestly didn't know how Julie did it. No wonder she always looked worn out and had lost her easy-going personality. She'd been constantly tired and grumpy since the triplets arrived. She'd started getting her life back to normal when they were about three, but then she fell pregnant with Tom and completely lost it. She cried for most of the pregnancy. I felt so sorry for her. It was as if she'd just given up and accepted that her life was over, which it pretty much was with four boys under five. I shuddered just thinking about her day-to-day life . . . and she had no childcare!

'Mummy, did Santa come to you?' Jess asked.

'Santa only comes to children, but look what Daddy bought for Mummy.' I showed her my watch.

'Oh, it's so pretty and shiny.'

'That's because of all the diamonds.'

'When I grow up I'm going to marry a prince who buys me diamonds,' Jess said.

I looked at my beautiful daughter with her long curly blonde hair and big blue eyes. 'I think you're going to have lots of princes wanting to buy you diamonds and that's a very good thing.'

She giggled and then asked to put on her new party dress. I'd bought her a red velvet one with a net skirt underneath to give it body. It had smocking across the chest and a white collar and cuffs. It came with a matching red velvet cape and beret. I loved dressing Jess up: she was like a little doll and looked beautiful in everything. Now she twirled around in her new dress.

'There's my princess,' Jack said, coming in freshly showered. He picked her up and kissed her.

'Daddy, Santa came!' Jess told him.

'I can see that.' Jack winked at me. 'I think Santa must have had a separate sleigh for you. He seems to have bought you everything in every shop. Come on, let's have some breakfast.'

We headed downstairs to the kitchen where Mimi, our Filipina housekeeper, had left everything laid out – a large fruit platter, natural yoghurt, granola, pumpkin-seed bread and sugar-free jam.

'Mummy, can I have a hot chocolate because it's Christmas Day?' Jess asked.

'No, honey – I'm sorry, but you know it's bad for you.'

'But I had it in Ella's house yesterday.'

'Well, Ella's mummy shouldn't have given it to you.'

'She didn't. It was Lilly.'

Lilly was Mimi's sister. They had both come to Dublin from the Philippines in search of work. I'd hired Mimi and one of the other mums at Jess's Montessori school – Naomi, Ella's mother – had hired Lilly.

'Lilly was wrong to do that. Hot chocolate rots your teeth and makes you fat. Now, here you go, here's a nice carrot juice.'

'Please, Mummy, it's Christmas.'

'Go on, Sophie, give her the chocolate,' Jack said indulgently.

'You're the one who always comments on other people's kids being fat or having bad teeth. Do you want Jess to end up like that?' I asked him.

He sighed and shrugged his shoulders. 'Your mum's right, Jess. It's not good for you and we want you to grow up to be as beautiful as Mummy.'

Jess looked upset. I went over and put my arm around her. 'I'll tell you what – if you drink your juice, I'll give you a treat.'

'What?'

'A chocolate rice cake.'

'OK,' she said, and proceeded to drink.

'You know, Jess, I fell in love with Mummy the first time I saw her,' Jack said. 'She was the most gorgeous girl in the room.'

'Did she have a princess dress on?' Jess asked.

'I think princess dresses tend to have more material than that one. It was red, short and very sexy.' Jack grinned at me.

'Jack! She's four.' I tried not to laugh.

'I love red,' Jess said.

'And you're beautiful in it,' Jack assured her.

'Mummy is too.'

'Yes, she is. But to be honest, Jess,' Jack leant in conspiratorially, 'Mummy is stunning in everything she wears, and even more so when she's naked.'

'Jack!' I giggled as he kissed my neck.

Jess laughed with us. 'I'm so happy you love Mummy. Rose's daddy doesn't love her mummy any more. He lives in another house by hisself.'

'I know, angel, and I know you're sad for Rose, but she'll be fine. Her mummy and daddy still love her the same as before,' I assured Jess.

Jack kissed her head. 'Jess, you never have to worry about Daddy going to live in another house. He loves you and Mummy way too much for that. There's nowhere else Daddy wants to be but here. I have a beautiful family, a big house and money to spend on having fun.' He winked at me.

'And buying presents,' Jess added.

'Yes, baby, lots of presents for you and Mummy.'

'Hurrah,' Jess and I said in unison.

While Jess ate her rice cake, Jack reached out to pour some honey over his yoghurt. 'So, dinner with the in-laws this year. That should be fun.' He smirked. 'Has Gavin come down from the tree yet?'

'No, he's still on his crusade. I had Mum on the phone for an hour yesterday, ranting about it. I don't blame her, though. It is embarrassing for them in the golf club.'

'He needs to get a real job. As soon as he starts earning proper cash, he'll leave all that eco-crap behind.'

'He's just finding his way in the world. Try not to wind him up – he's very passionate about it.' Jack had a tendency to slag people and sometimes he took it a bit too far.

'Is Louise home?'

'Yeah, she flew in last night. She's staying at the Four Seasons.'

'And Julie and Harry are going to be there too?'

'Yes.' I took a bite of pineapple.

'It'll be lively.'

'It's better than going to your parents' house and having to talk about surgery for hours.'

'True. My dad and Roger are terrible bores.'

'Thank God you didn't become a surgeon too.'

'I didn't have the brains.' Jack's mood immediately darkened.

It never ceased to amaze me how much it bothered him that he hadn't got enough points in his Leaving Cert to study medicine at university. No matter how successful he was or how much money he made, it still really got to him. Aged eighteen, as soon as he'd received his exam results, he'd run away to New York. He was ashamed and knew that he was a disappointment to his father. Roger, his older brother, had already finished his first degree and started his surgical studies when Jack took off.

'Jack,' I said, 'look around. *You* are the successful one in your family. They don't earn a tenth of what you do.'

'I suppose it's not bad for a kid who never went to college and started as a runner on the New York trading floor.'

'The same guy who then worked his way up to become a partner in the GreenGem hedge fund and was sent to Ireland to set up an office here,' I reminded him.

'Just think, if it hadn't been for the low corporate tax regime in Ireland, I may never have moved back here and met you.'

'It's lucky for you you did! Not only did you bag yourself a stunning wife but look at what you've achieved. Look at how much money you've made.'

'Ah, yes, but I'm not saving lives like my father and brother.'

Jack wagged a finger at me. 'I should donate it all to medical research. Maybe then they'd respect me.'

'Over my dead body! Let them live in their superior little medical bubble. It's a hell of a lot more fun in the hedge-fund world.'

'That's my girl.' Jack hugged me.

'Hug! Hug!' Jess said, jumping down from her chair to join in.

I slipped into my new black Prada dress and the very high, very cool Christian Louboutin boots Jack had brought me back from New York last week. I looked in the mirror and I liked what I saw. I was the thinnest I'd ever been, a small size eight, and I was thrilled. Every time she saw me, Louise told me I was too thin. As the eldest, she seemed to feel she had to boss us around the whole time. She was always telling Julie to manage her time better and to lose weight, and ordering me to stop dieting and getting so much Botox.

Julie did need to lose weight – she needed to lose at least two stone – but it wasn't Louise's place to nag her. As for the Botox, I'd looked ten years younger since I'd started getting it two years ago. It was completely addictive and I loved the way my forehead was now line-free. Louise said I had that frozen-face look but, honestly, at this stage in my life I just ignored her. She was always bossing me about something – I should get a job, go back and study, manage my own money . . . Why? I didn't want to get a job – I didn't need one. I had never been academic, so why would I want to go to college? And as for managing my own money, I hadn't a clue about investing and interest rates and all that stuff so I'd given it to Jack.

Thank God Jack had come along when he did. At thirty-one my career as a model was seriously drying up and I'd just broken up with Dominic Beaufort – he'd dumped me for a twenty-two-year-old who modelled for the same agency. I was so humiliated. I'd been with Dominic for two years, and when he'd taken me out to dinner to 'discuss something' I'd presumed he was going to propose . . .

I'd met Jack three weeks later at the opening of a new nightclub I was helping to promote. We'd flirted, swapped numbers, and I was determined not to let this one get away. He was better-looking and wealthier than Dominic. He'd only been back in Dublin a month – I was incredibly lucky to meet him that night or I'm sure he would have been snapped up by someone younger and prettier. Thankfully, it had all worked out for the best.

Julie once joked about how I only went out with rich guys. She was right. I did. When we were growing up I'd looked around me. Louise was super-bright, independent and ambitious. Julie was really content – she had her friends and her books and she was very happy. I, on the other hand, was never happy. I was always looking for something else, something better. The one thing I had going for me was that I was good-looking. That was it. I wasn't smart, or sporty, or popular, but I was pretty. So I used it to its full advantage. I made a career of it and got a rich husband too.

The bonus with marrying Jack was that I really loved him. He appeared very confident, but he had an insecure side because of his horrible family. We had our insecurities in common – his were about not being clever enough and mine were about losing my looks because they were all I had. That was why I starved myself and got Botox and fillers. I knew it was important for me to hold up my part of the deal. Jack married me because he loved me, but also because I was good-looking, thin and glamorous. I married him because I loved him and because his money made me feel secure and allowed me to have the kind of lifestyle I'd always dreamt of. Being Mrs Jack Wells made me feel powerful. It gave me status. I loved the way shop assistants fawned all over me. I loved staying in five-star hotels wherever we went. I loved having designer clothes, fabulous diamonds and a big car. It might seem shallow to some people, but I got a high from it. It made me feel important, the way some people's jobs make them feel important.

'Ready, darling?' Jack came into the dressing room with Jess. He was wearing the new caramel cashmere coat I'd bought him.

'The coat looks great.'

'Thank you. My wife has impeccable taste.'

'Yes, she does.' I turned around to show him the dress. 'Do you like it? It's new.'

'I like it very much and the boots are hot.'

'You look beautiful, Mummy,' Jess said.

'And you're adorable.' I kissed her nose.

I put Jess's cape and beret on her and we headed off in Jack's new Aston Martin. It was his Christmas present to himself.

As we walked up to his parents' front door I reminded him that we were only staying for an hour. 'We have to be in Mum and Dad's by three. I promised we wouldn't be late.'

'Don't worry, Sophie. An hour here will be plenty for me.' Jack rang the bell.

William, his father, opened the door. 'Greetings of the season. Don't you look lovely, Jess?' he bellowed. 'Sophie. Jack.' He peered over our heads and turned to Jack. 'New car, I see.'

'Yes, it's an Aston Martin. I remember you telling me it was your favourite car,' Jack said.

'Nice to look at, but far too ostentatious to own,' his father replied, and I watched Jack's face fall.

'I think it's fantastic,' I piped up, full of false cheer. 'It drives like a dream. You should take it for a spin, William, you might enjoy it.'

Jack's mum, June, came over and hugged Jess. 'Merry Christmas, Jessica. You look very nice.'

'Happy Christmas, June,' I said, leaning in for her to air-kiss me.

'Oh, my goodness, how on earth do you walk in those things?' She stared at my boots. 'They're awfully jazzy.'

'You have to suffer for fashion,' I said, fixing a smile on my face.

We went into the lounge where Jack's brother, Roger, and his wife, Fiona, were sitting at a chessboard with their daughter, Grace. She was two years older than Jess and in a different league intellectually. She'd been playing chess since she was three. Roger was leaning over the board in his navy blazer, explaining a move, while Fiona, in her simple but stylish black trouser suit and flat pumps, watched, beaming proudly. I always felt overdressed when I met them.

'Hi, everyone. Happy Christmas,' Jack said. They barely looked up.

'We'll be with you in a minute. Grace is just about to beat her daddy at chess,' Fiona explained.

'What's chess, Mummy?' Jess asked me.

I bent down to whisper in her ear, 'It's a game for people with no personality.'

'How are things, Dad?' Jack asked, sitting down beside me on the couch.

'Excellent, thank you. I've just been asked to speak at the American College of Cardiology convention in Florida next month.'

'Sounds great. Congratulations.'

'Checkmate!' Grace squealed. 'I did it! I beat Daddy!' She jumped up and down.

'She really is an extraordinary child,' June, the proud grandmother, said to me. 'They're taking her to be tested for Mensa.'

'Mensa is a society for the brightest people in the world. Your IQ has to be in the top two per cent of the country,' Fiona explained to me, her dim-witted sister-in-law.

'I know all about it, Fiona. My sister Louise is a member.'

'What?' She was clearly shocked that I could possibly have a genius for a sister.

'Yeah,' I said, deliberately casual. 'Louise has been a member since she was a kid.'

'What does she do?'

'She's a lawyer,' Jack said. 'She studied law at Cambridge and got a first, didn't she, Sophie?' he boasted, on my behalf.

'Yes, she came top of her year.' I squeezed his hand.

'We're hoping Grace will go to Harvard,' Fiona replied.

'And no doubt she'll become an arrogant bore like her parents,' Jack muttered. I forced myself not to laugh.

'Will you have a drink, Sophie?' William asked.

'Thank you. A glass of white wine would be lovely.'

He handed me a large glass and I gulped some down. It was going to be a long hour.

'So how are things with you, Roger?' Jack asked.

'He has just been made master of obstetrics and gynaecology at the Royal College Hospital,' William said, patting his elder son on the back.

'That's great. Well done.' Jack went over to shake his brother's hand.

'And Fiona has been promoted to head of radiology at RCH,' Roger said proudly.

'They make an incredible team, don't you think?' June asked me.

I could think of many words to describe them – smug, self-obsessed, snobbish – but 'incredible' wasn't one of them. 'Congratulations, Fiona,' I muttered.

'Thank you, Sophie. How's everything with you?'

'Great, thanks.'

'Still doing the stay-at-home-mother thing?'

'Yes.'

'I must say, I do admire you stay-at-home girls. There's no way I could sit around the house all day. I'd go completely insane. The lack of intellectual stimulation would kill me. Besides, I couldn't imagine not earning my own money.'

'Well, Fiona, Jack earns enough for a hundred wives, so I don't find it a problem.' I smirked at her. Jack grinned at me.

'Why don't we open presents?' Roger suggested, before a catfight broke out.

'Santa brought Daddy a new car,' Jess announced.

'Yes, I can see that,' Roger said. 'It's always easy to tell when you've had a good year, Jack. You're never shy about displaying it.'

'Jack had his best year ever,' I bragged. 'He's a genius at what he does.'

'I think you were being a little casual with the word "genius" there, Sophie,' Roger said.

'Who else do you know makes that much money?'

'Genius has nothing to do with money.' William snorted. 'Anyone can make money, but very few people can save lives.'

I wanted to punch him on the nose. Here we go again: 'We surgeons are gods, you know . . . We stop people dying . . . We make the difference between life and death, blah blah blah.' I was sick of hearing it.

'Let's do the presents. Sophie and I have to leave soon.' Jack cut across his father's lecture on the wonders of surgeons.

Jack was incredibly generous with his money. He loved buying presents and had put a lot of thought into his family's Christmas gifts. He knew Roger and Fiona liked opera so he had bought them flights, accommodation and tickets to the Rossini Opera Festival in Italy in August.

Roger read the itinerary. 'Thanks, but unfortunately we won't be available. I've got a conference in Mexico in August. I'm the keynote speaker.' He handed the envelope back to Jack. 'You guys should go. You never know, you might actually enjoy opera.'

I wanted to shove the envelope down his throat. What an ungrateful bastard. Jack was crestfallen.

'Oh, my goodness, Jack, this is far too generous,' June said, opening her envelope. 'Look, William, he's bought us a weekend at the George V in Paris.'

'Bit over the top, don't you think?' William boomed. 'No need to spend all your money in one go, son.'

Jack gritted his teeth. 'I'm not, Dad. I wanted to treat you and Mum. I know she's always wanted to stay in that hotel and I've had a good year so I thought it'd be a nice present.'

'It is, dear,' June said, patting her younger son's arm. 'It's a lovely surprise.'

William snorted.

Jack looked like thunder as we carried on with the presents. Roger and Fiona had given us a chess set – 'so you can teach Jess and expand her mind'. And they gave Jess a hundred-and-fifty-piece jigsaw, 'because Grace is doing three-hundred-piece ones'.

I had bought Grace a Burberry raincoat with wellingtons to

match. Fiona looked at them and fished around in the bag for the receipt. By the time we left I almost had lockjaw from the fixed smile I'd worn.

'Thank God that's over.' I laid my head on the headrest in the car.

'I can never do anything right. I'll never be good enough.' Jack thumped the steering-wheel with his fist.

'Maybe you should stop trying so hard. You always get knocked back.'

'They're my family. I'd like them just for once to bloody well acknowledge that I'm a success, not a disappointment.'

I put my hand gently on his arm. 'Jack, they're never going to do that. You have to let it go.'

He sighed. 'I know you're right. It's just so frustrating. I've always been second best and I'm sick of it.'

'They're so arrogant with their master-of-the-hospital this and head-of-department that, and their weird Mensa child. Who the hell wants to be like them? They're miserable. Grace is a freak. Who wants to play chess all day at six years of age?'

'Mummy, does the African American Queen dance on the stripy dance-floor with the White King?' our own little genius asked from the back seat.

Jack and I looked at one another and roared laughing.

4

Julie

I never got a chance to find out Louise's news: just after I came downstairs to drag the boys away from the Christmas tree, Sophie and Jack arrived and I didn't get Louise on my own again. I was dying to know what it was. Even though she looked perfect as always – gorgeous wrap dress, bobbed black hair immaculately blow-dried, her makeup subtle but artfully applied – she seemed really freaked out, and Louise was never fazed by anything. She was the most capable person I knew. That was why I had asked her to look after the money Dad had given me. I'd known she'd invest it wisely and after three years it was already worth €12,000 more than it had been when I'd passed it over to her.

I was going to use the money to put the boys through private school. Harry earned enough to cover our mortgage, bills and day-to-day living, but we'd never be able to afford a private education for four on his salary, so I really needed that money. I'd worked it out – at €2,000 a term, by three terms per year, by six years, by four children, it would cost €144,000. And that was just the fees: it didn't account for any extra-curricular activities or uniforms or school trips. I really needed to make Dad's money work, and I knew Louise was the best person to help me do it.

I tried to catch her eye so we could sneak out for a minute, but she avoided me. I'd have to grab her later, when the others were distracted. We sat down in the lounge to give out the presents to the kids and chaos ensued. While we weren't looking, Luke took a strawberry cream from the box of Milk Tray, decided he didn't like it and squashed it into the DVD player. Leo and Liam thought this was great fun, and by the time I noticed, half of the chocolates had been crushed into the DVD player. I yanked the boys away and made them sit on the other side of the room while I surreptitiously tried to scoop the melted sweets out of the machine. I knew Dad would freak if he saw the mess. He was very proud of his new 37-inch flat-screen TV and recordable DVD player.

Thankfully, he was distracted by the present Jack and Sophie had given him and Mum: a weekend trip to Spain to play on the Valderrama golf course. They were delighted.

'What a wonderful gift! Oh, my goodness, we'll have a ball. You're so good, Jack, thank you.' Mum got up to kiss her favourite son-in-law.

Harry, who was gingerly giving Tom another bottle, hoping it wouldn't end up all over him, rolled his eyes.

'Far too generous, Jack. Above and beyond. Thank you very much,' Dad said, looking a bit embarrassed.

'It's nothing,' Jack assured him. 'I've had a pretty spectacular year and we wanted to get you something special. When you make crazy money, you might as well enjoy it.'

'You're both so kind.' Mum kissed Sophie too. 'What did your husband get you?'

Sophie showed her the watch. Mum gasped. 'It's magnificent.'

'He really spoilt me today.'

'What was last year's diamond necklace? A trinket?' Harry grumbled.

I pinched his arm. 'Ssh.'

'He can't hear me, Julie. He's too busy telling your parents how much money he made.'

'He can't help being loaded,' I reminded my husband.

'Do you think Jack had a good year?' Louise whispered, failing to suppress a grin.

'I'm not sure, Louise. It's very hard to tell,' Harry drawled, getting up to change Tom's nappy.

'I know – he's so subtle.'

'The watch is pretty incredible,' I said.

'It's completely over the top.' Louise snorted. 'They live in suburban Dublin, not Beverly Hills. You could clear the debt of an African country with the money he spent on that.'

Sophie got up to take Jess to the toilet and Jack went to talk to the triplets. He was good with the boys: he knew how to talk to them on their level.

Mum came over to where we were sitting. 'Did you hear what they gave us?'

'Yes, it's great,' I enthused.

'I've always wanted to play in Valderrama. And look,' she pointed to the brochure, 'they've booked us into a suite. Can you imagine? It must have cost a fortune. Sophie did well for herself, marrying someone so generous. She's so successful.'

'At what exactly?' Louise asked. 'Spending her husband's money?'

Mum frowned. 'At everything she does – at modelling and at her marriage. You might take a leaf out of her book. She knows how to get a man and keep him happy. Jack adores her.'

'Come on, Mum,' Louise said, 'you don't measure someone's success by the size of their husband's wallet. It relates to personal achievement.'

'And some people put far too much emphasis on career success and not enough on romantic success,' Mum snapped.

Mum and Louise had always fought. I think Mum was a bit intimidated by her eldest daughter. Louise had been difficult to parent when she was a teenager. She was constantly challenging Mum on everything and she never backed down: Louise was always right. She'd been fiercely independent and unemotional. From the age of about thirteen, Louise hadn't needed parents. At school she'd made all her own decisions and waged all her own battles. She'd mellowed a bit as she got older, but her relationship with Mum had always been fraught. In fact, the only person who really saw her softer side was me: we were close in age – there were only twenty months between us – and we wanted completely different things from life so there was no competitive edge. We'd also shared a bedroom growing up, so she'd got used to confiding in me.

Thankfully, she also listened to me, and her Christmas presents for the boys were very welcome. She'd bought them the full set of Peter Rabbit books by Beatrix Potter.

'Boring!' Leo said.

'Rabbits are for babies.' Liam pouted.

'That's not a present,' Luke announced.

'Yes, it is,' I hissed. 'Say thank you to your auntie Louise.'

'Books are not presents.' Luke dug his heels in.

'Yes, they are,' I reminded him. 'Say thank you, now.' I gave him my do-not-mess-with-me-or-you-will-never-watch-TV-again stare.

'Thank you,' he mumbled.

There was no lack of enthusiasm when Sophie gave them her present. But it left me in a rage. I had asked her repeatedly to get the boys something small because we had no space, but she had produced three remote-control monster trucks. I know I shouldn't get annoyed about my sister's generosity but, unlike her, we didn't have a playroom so the bloody trucks would end up in the TV room or the kitchen. She always does it: every year she has to buy the biggest, most over-the-top presents. It drives me nuts. We know Jack's loaded. We get it.

'Monster trucks!' the triplets shouted. 'AWESOME!' They ripped the boxes open and began to play with them straight away, crashing them into Mum's sideboard. Meanwhile Jess sat quietly in the corner playing with the Sylvanian dolls I'd given her. Every now and then a truck would hit her leg and she'd retreat even further into the corner. She was terrified of the triplets.

The door opened and Gavin strolled in, smelling strongly of natural body odour.

'God, you stink,' Louise told him, as he hugged her.

'You really do,' Sophie agreed. 'I'm not sitting beside you until you wash.'

He looked to me for support. 'Sorry, you do smell nasty,' I admitted.

37

'Great to see you too, girls,' Gavin exclaimed.

'Get up the stairs, have a quick shower and change before dinner. It'll be ready in ten minutes,' Mum told him. 'I've laid out some clothes for you and bought the nice shower gel and moisturizer that you like.'

While our eco-warrior washed, we girls went into the kitchen to help Mum. I brought Tom with me.

'Sophie, that dress is so stylish. What make is it?' Mum asked.

'Prada,' Sophie said, nibbling a carrot.

'You look like a super-model in it. I swear you get younger looking all the time.' Mum was unaware of Sophie's fondness for Botox. She didn't believe in cosmetic surgery, and honestly thought Sophie's reverse-ageing was due to expensive creams.

'Yes, Sophie, how do you do it? How do you manage to look so young?' Louise asked, as Sophie glared at her. 'I'm sorry, are you frowning at me? It's hard to tell.'

'Our very own Benjamin Button.' I laughed.

'I don't know what you're laughing about.' Mum waved a fork at me. 'You could take a leaf out of Sophie's book. I know you're busy with the boys, but you need to smarten yourself up, Julie. Women have to keep themselves in shape or their husbands start looking around.'

'Gee, thanks, Mum. So not only do I look like crap but Harry's going to leave me now too.'

'I'm only saying –'

'Mum!' Louise cut across her. 'Julie's doing her best. Give her a break.'

'I know I need to lose weight. I know I look a hundred and fifty and I know my clothes are permanently covered in yoghurt or banana, but that's my life right now. There's no point wearing expensive clothes. They'd get wrecked.' As if to demonstrate the point, Tom rubbed his snotty nose into my jumper.

'Why don't you get one of those au pairs and give yourself a break?' Mum suggested.

'Where the hell would she sleep? The triplets are in the big bedroom and Tom is in the box room. We don't have space for an au pair.'

'There's no need to get het up. I'm only trying to help.' Mum turned to drain the Brussels sprouts.

But you're not helping, I thought. You could help by offering to babysit once in a blue moon. You could try not to look so horrified every time I call in with the kids. You could stop nagging me about my weight. You could stop telling me how perfect Sophie is and how beautiful her house and her clothes are. You could stop telling me that my kids are out of control. You could stop telling me that I should have had my Fallopian tubes tied after the triplets . . .

I tuned back to the conversation.

'Honestly, Julie, you're lucky Harry's parents are dead,' Sophie said. 'Jack's family are a nightmare. They're so bloody superior. I hate going there. That bitch Fiona always tries to make me feel like a loser because I don't work.'

'She's just been made head of radiology at RCH, hasn't she?' Mum asked.

Sophie rolled her eyes. 'Oh, yes, we heard all about it. And Grace is getting tested for Mensa. When I told them about Louise being a member they nearly fell over. They couldn't believe that I – bimbo – had a genius sister.'

'I hope you told them she went to Cambridge,' I said.

'Of course I did.'

'And that she's a partner in Higgins, Cooper & Gray.'

'I forgot that bit. I can never remember the name of the company.'

'I've only been there twenty years,' Louise muttered.

'Oh, you know I can never remember names.' Sophie waved her wine glass in the air.

'Did they see your watch?' Mum asked.

'No, I took it off. I didn't want them to say anything rude about it. They were so mean about Jack's car. Have you seen it? It's an Aston Martin DB9 Volante. It's so cool – it's like a James Bond car!'

'Wow, that's great,' I said, willing myself to be happy for her and trying not to compare it to my horrid people-carrier.

'She can remember some names, like Aston Martin DB9 Volante,' Louise whispered, and I tried not to laugh.

'I'm sure Jack would let Harry take it for a spin,' Sophie said. 'He'll probably insist on going with him, though. He's very protective of it. It's only two weeks old.'

I knew that Harry would rather cut his eyes out with a blunt knife than go for a drive with Jack in his 007 car. 'Maybe later,' I said tactfully.

The door flew open and a very red-faced Dad came in with Leo and Liam attached to each leg and Luke on his back. 'Can we eat soon? I'm starving. These fellas have me worn out,' he said.

'It's ready now.' Mum handed him the carving knife as I pulled the boys off. I bribed them with sweets and a new *Ben 10* DVD. We'd hopefully get half an hour of peace to eat while it was on.

We all helped bring out the food and sat down at the table, with the newly washed and fragrant-smelling Gavin. Just as we were about to tuck in, the doorbell rang.

'Who could that be on Christmas Day?' Mum asked.

'Oh, yeah, Mum, I forgot to tell you,' Gavin said, stuffing a forkful of food into his mouth as he stood up. 'Forest is coming for dinner – he had nowhere else to go and I knew you wouldn't want anyone to be alone on Christmas Day.' He rushed out to open the door before Mum could tell him exactly what she thought of that idea.

Forest came into the room and dropped his knapsack on the floor. If Gavin had smelt bad, Forest was ten times worse. After a cursory hello, he squeezed in between Sophie and Jack, while Louise and I tried not to laugh. Sophie took out her perfume and sprayed herself and most of Forest's head.

Dad handed him a full plate. 'Get that into you, son. You look like you haven't eaten in years.'

'Thanks, Mr Devlin, but I'm a strict vegan like Gavin.' We turned to look at Gavin, who quickly swallowed the large slice of turkey in his mouth.

'Give that here.' Mum grabbed the plate, scraped off the turkey and ham and handed it back with just Brussels sprouts and roast potatoes. She did the same with Gavin's.

Forest dived in. 'This tastes very good, Mrs Devlin. I've been surviving on a diet of nuts and berries.'

'Where was that?' Dad enquired. 'The Gobi desert?'

Harry choked on his wine.

'Actually, no, although that is somewhere I would like to visit. I've been tree-sitting in the UK, in the New Forest. I just came home for a few days to regroup.'

'Are you not worried that the tree'll be murdered while you're back here?' Dad wondered.

'No. I've left my sister in it.'

'Your parents must be delighted to have two tree-sitters in the family.' Dad winked at us. 'Gavin, maybe you could persuade one of your sisters to do a relay with you in the golf club. I'd say Sophie's your best bet.'

'Dad!' Gavin warned him.

'Is it something you'd like to get involved in?' the oblivious Forest asked Sophie.

'Excuse the pun, but you're barking up the wrong tree there, mate.' Jack roared laughing.

'Would you consider yourself an observant person?' Louise asked Forest.

'Absolutely, never miss a trick.'

'And you think that Sophie here is a likely candidate for tree-sitting?'

Forest looked Sophie up and down. 'Obviously she currently worships the false god of materialism, but the environmentalist lies within us all. It may be buried deeper in some, but it's there. It just needs to be set alight and nurtured.' Forest took a long sip of his wine.

'Excuse me,' Sophie retorted. 'I do not worship a false god. If anyone here is worshipping a false god, it's you – the god of bad hygiene.'

'Could you all show a little respect for my friend?' Gavin snapped. 'What happened to Christmas goodwill? Seriously, give the guy a break.'

'Amn't I feeding him and giving him wine and a roof over his head?' Mum huffed.

'What do you call a militant vegan?' Jack asked Forest. 'Lactose intolerant.'

We all laughed – except Forest and Gavin.

'How many carnivores does it take to change a light-bulb?' Forest retorted. 'None. They'd rather spend their lives in darkness.'

'*Touché.*' Gavin high-fived his smelly friend.

'What's for dessert?' I asked, having decided to change the subject.

'Home-made trifle,' Mum said. Turning to Forest, she asked, 'Do you people eat trifle?'

'It depends on the ingredients. What have you made it with?' Forest asked.

'This fella has a death wish,' Dad whispered to me.

Mum leant across the table and eyeballed Forest. 'It's made with a secret recipe that my grandmother handed down to me and I have no intention of divulging it to you or any other tree-huggers who cross my threshold. Now you can eat it or you can sit here and be quiet. I don't want to hear another word about your ideas or causes. I blame you for putting the mad notions into my son's innocent head that have led to him living up a tree in my golf club.' Mum waved a serving spoon in Forest's face. 'I want you to tell him to get down from that tree and stop this nonsense.'

'I'm sorry, Mrs Devlin, I can't do that. Did Gandhi stop? Did Martin Luther King stop? No, they did not.'

'He's not heading up a movement in the golf club car park. It's hardly an international incident,' Louise pointed out.

'It's all part of peaceful civil disobedience,' Gavin said. 'If Rosa

42

Parks had given up her seat to that white passenger in Alabama, we might not have ended segregation.'

'Rosa Parks!' Dad buried his head in his hands.

'I blame you too.' Mum poked Dad in the back. 'I told you all those years ago not to join Amnesty International. They're a very aggressive bunch.'

'Jesus, I gave them a monthly donation, Anne, I didn't set myself on fire.'

Mum turned to Gavin. 'Will you please stay away from that tree? You're down now. Just stay at home.'

'I can't, Mum. I committed to saving it and I'm not giving up. You can't go around bulldozing two-hundred-year-old trees.'

'Stay strong, brother,' Forest said.

'Can we please talk about something else?' Sophie complained.

'Actually, I have a bit of news,' Louise said. We all turned to face her. 'I'm pregnant.'

5

Louise

Well, that certainly got their attention. I thought Mum was going to have a heart attack on the spot. She turned bright red.

'What did you say?'

'I'm pregnant. Due in April.' I licked the custard off my spoon.

'Congratulations.' Julie jumped up and came over to hug me. 'Why the hell didn't you tell me earlier?' she whispered.

I ignored her. I knew that Julie would be the one to catch me out. I had to stick to my story.

'Wow.' Sophie leant over and squeezed my hand. 'Good for you.'

'Dude, aren't you a bit old for kids?' Gavin asked.

I put down my spoon. 'No. Lots of women have children in their forties now.'

'Excuse me,' Mum interrupted. 'What do you mean you're pregnant? You never told us you were seeing anyone. Are you also going to tell us you're married?'

'No, Mum, I'm not married and there is no man. At least, not any more.'

'Did you misplace him?' Dad enquired.

'No, he didn't want a baby, so we broke up,' I lied.

'You mean to say he left you when you told him you were expecting?' Dad asked.

'Yes.'

'The bastard,' Harry said.

'Oh, God, Lou, that's terrible.' Julie put an arm around me.

'I'm fine, really. I don't want him to be involved. He's a total plonker.'

'Why'd you shag him, then?' Jack asked.

'*Jack!*' Sophie glared at him.

'That's just not good enough, Louise.' Mum was getting wound up now. 'I don't care what type of a "plonker" he is, he has to take responsibility for his child. A baby needs a father. George, you'll just have to go over to London and talk to this individual.'

I jumped in before Dad started booking flights. 'He lives in New York and no one is going to speak to him. I don't need him and neither does the baby. He's made it clear that he doesn't want children. This was not supposed to happen but it did and I've decided to keep the baby. I'll be raising her on my own.'

'Her?' Julie asked.

'I'm having a girl.'

'You lucky thing,' Julie said.

'Julie!' Harry gave out to her.

'I can give you lots of gorgeous girl clothes. Jessica only wore half of what I bought her,' Sophie said.

'Thanks.'

'Do you want me and Forest to go to New York and sort this guy out for dumping you?' Gavin asked.

I looked at Gavin's baby face and his stick-thin, dreadlocked friend, and smiled. 'No thanks, Tony Soprano, but I appreciate the offer.'

'How long were you seeing this individual?' Mum asked. She was staring at me with her MI5 eyes. Thank God I'd prepared all my answers.

'Only a few months. It was nothing serious, just a fling, really.'

'How could an intelligent woman like you get yourself into a situation like this?' Mum wondered.

'Too much alcohol,' I told her truthfully.

'Jesus, Louise, at your age.' Dad shook his head.

'I'm not proud of it, Dad, but it happened and I'm dealing with the consequences.'

'If you're due in April you must be five months now,' Julie said. 'Where's your bump?'

'Here.' I flattened my wrap dress against my tummy to show it.

'Very neat.' Sophie was impressed. 'You're so fit, you'll hardly put on any weight. I bet you lose it really quickly after too.'

I saw Julie look down at her stomach and wince. Harry reached for her hand.

'What's the father's name?' Mum asked.

'It doesn't matter because he's never going to be involved. You need to forget about him.'

Mum banged the table with her hand. 'Do you think your daughter will forget about her own father?' She was getting worked up. 'Do you honestly think she won't be damaged by this? It's dysfunctional, Louise. He has to be involved, whether he likes it or not.'

'My dad wasn't around and it didn't affect me,' Forest volunteered. 'You don't miss what you don't know.'

'Well, that makes me feel much better,' Dad said. 'All going well, in a few years' time my granddaughter will be babysitting trees in the New Forest.'

'There's a lot worse she could be doing,' Gavin said.

'Like what?' Dad wanted to know.

'Drugs, robbery, murder.'

'We live in suburban Dublin, not Baghdad.'

'What are you going to do about work?' Mum asked me.

'What do you mean?'

'You can't work ten hours a day and do all that travelling with a baby.'

'Why not?'

'Because it's unrealistic, Louise.'

'I've booked her into a crèche that's open from seven a.m. to seven p.m. Monday to Friday. It only closes on Christmas Day and Easter Monday. My cleaning lady's going to pick the baby up if I need to work late. She'll stay over when I have to travel and cover me on weekends when I need to go into the office. So everything is under control.'

'When are you planning on seeing the baby?' Mum barked.

'Most evenings and weekends.'

'Louise!' Mum was exasperated. 'Babies don't slot into your life, they turn it upside-down.'

'Amen to that,' Julie agreed.

'Jess didn't change Sophie's life,' I countered.

Sophie shook her head. 'Well, that's not entirely –'

Jack interrupted his wife: 'It's true. Your life doesn't have to change. You just need to hire good staff and pay them well,' he assured me.

'How much maternity leave are you going to take?' Julie asked.

'Three weeks.'

'WHAT?' Julie, Sophie and Mum exclaimed.

'Meredith Baker, the only other female partner at the firm, took three weeks. I can't be seen to take any more. Besides, she seemed to cope just fine. She never comes in late, never leaves early and just gets on with it, which is exactly what I plan to do.'

'But you can't leave a three-week-old in a crèche,' Julie said, emotional at the thought.

'Of course you can. It's not like I'm leaving her in a dump. It's a very exclusive crèche with properly trained maternity nurses looking after the small babies. It's a one-nurse-to-two-babies ratio until they're a year old and then it's one-to-three.'

'I think Julie's right,' Sophie said. 'Three weeks is very early to leave a baby. You won't want to be away from her. You'll want to spend more time getting to know her.'

'Don't be *ridiculous*. You cannot leave a three-week-old baby in a crèche!' Mum wagged a finger in my face.

I glared at her. 'Yes, you can. I love my job and I have no intention of giving it up or slowing down or taking a back seat or any of those things women always do when they have kids. I'm going to continue as normal, just like Meredith.'

'Does this Meredith you think so highly of have a husband?' Mum asked.

'Yes, she does.'

'I thought so.' Mum looked triumphant.

'I need to use the bathroom,' I said, hurrying out of the room before we ended up having a blazing row.

Mum had a habit of rubbing me up the wrong way. She was always trying to fix me and tell me how to live my life, how to make it better, how I needed a man to make me happy, how a career was not enough . . . She just couldn't let go. She couldn't accept the fact that I was different from her. I didn't need mothering. I didn't need a husband to make me happy. I was perfectly capable of looking after myself. I always had been.

I went upstairs and lay down in the old bedroom I'd shared with Julie. Our beds were still there, side by side.

'I knew I'd find you here,' Julie said, a few minutes later, coming in and sitting down on her bed. 'Come on, Lou, what the hell is going on? I know when you're lying. How did you really get pregnant?'

I looked at the ceiling and took a deep breath. 'Remember when I went to Venice with work to celebrate the company's fiftieth anniversary and they announced that I was being promoted to senior partner?'

'Yes – I was so jealous because I've always wanted to go to Venice.'

'Well, I hadn't expected to be made senior partner so soon. I thought I'd have to wait at least one if not two more years so I was taken by surprise – and you know how I hate surprises. Anyway, I was thrilled obviously and I ended up drinking too much champagne, way too much.'

'Oh, my God, did you have sex with your married boss?' Julie gasped.

I shook my head. 'Worse. I slept with one of the other guests at the hotel. I don't even remember his name and, to be honest, even the sex is a bit hazy. I was the drunkest I've ever been.'

'Lou! That's so unlike you.'

'I can't believe it either. I do one stupid thing in my life and, *bam*, I get pregnant.'

'Boris Becker in the broom cupboard at Nobu has nothing on you. What about the next morning? Where was the guy?'

'Gone. He left a note that said, *"Ho avuto una grande notte. Grazie."*'

'What does that mean? "Great shag, thanks"?'

'More or less. I think the literal translation is "I had a great night. Thanks."'

'So even if you wanted to find him you couldn't?'

'Nope.'

'Louise Devlin, you're a slut.' Julie started laughing and I joined in. It was such a relief to laugh, a relief to have told them all, for my secret to be out, for my pregnancy to be announced. By the time Sophie came to find us we were almost hysterical.

She sat down beside Julie. 'What's so funny? Come on, fill me in. You're always leaving me out.'

'Louise is a dirty slapper.' Julie giggled. 'The baby's father is some random bloke she met in a hotel in Italy and she can't even remember his name.' She and I roared laughing again.

'No way!' Sophie looked shocked.

'Unfortunately it's true,' I admitted. 'But Mum can never find out. Ever.'

'I won't tell her, I swear. Are you OK about it?' Sophie asked.

'Yes – it was a really reckless thing to do, but I'm fine about it.'

'Are you excited?' Julie asked.

Was I excited? Not in the way other women seemed to be. Not in the way both Julie and Sophie had been when they were pregnant. Not glowy and bloomy and running around buying baby clothes at six weeks pregnant. In fact, I hadn't actually realized I was pregnant until fourteen and a half weeks. My periods were sometimes irregular, so I wasn't worried when I skipped a few. But after three months of no periods and feeling sick and tired all the time, I went to my doctor expecting him to tell me that it was the onset of menopause. When he told me I was pregnant, I nearly fell off my chair.

I could not believe it. How the hell could I be pregnant after a stupid one-night stand? I knew it was that night because I'd been feeling too sick since then to have sex. There was a man, Daniel, whom I dated and had sex with whenever he was in town. He was an old client of mine who lived in Monaco but came to London every six weeks on business. Whenever he was in town we'd get together. I liked it. No strings attached, no expectations, no drama.

I'd been on the pill for twenty years, partly to regulate my periods and also as contraception. But when I arrived in Venice I realized I'd forgotten to bring it with me. I wasn't expecting to have sex, so I didn't worry about not taking it for a few days. Big mistake. Huge.

When I'd found out I was pregnant, I'd planned to have an abortion. I was forty-one, single and married to my career. A baby was not something I craved. I had never felt broody when I saw other people's babies. I hated it when I went to visit someone with a newborn and they thrust it into my arms for a 'cuddle'. I didn't want to hold their baby, which smelt of vomit, pee and quite often poo. I used to count the seconds until I could hand it back. I didn't find going to baby shops and looking at tiny clothes fun. I always sent my secretary, Jasmine, to buy the presents.

I'd seen so many women give up their jobs and their lives for their children, and for what? The kids didn't thank you. They didn't appreciate it – frankly, they didn't give a shit. When I looked at Julie's life I shuddered. She had gone from being an attractive, fun, bubbly, outgoing person to a shadow. She was always exhausted, she never had any time to herself, she looked awful, she was cranky a lot of the time, and for what? The triplets didn't care. They'd never be grateful. They just took it for granted that their mother was there to feed them, clothe them, bathe them, read to them, play with them, drive them around, love them, protect them and mind them.

I kept hearing women say, 'I'm so glad I gave up work and devoted myself to my children.' Why? Why are you so glad? How do you know it made any difference whatsoever? If you had worked part-time or even full-time, would they have turned into sociopaths? Probably not and you wouldn't have lost your identity, your personality and your sanity in the process. Sophie had probably the best life of any mother I knew and she was boring. It's a harsh thing to say about your sister, but she was. All of her spare time was spent focusing on looking good. And she looked great, but she had very little to talk about. She had no outside interests, no hobbies – working-out with a personal trainer is not a hobby.

There was no way in hell I was going to give up my life so I decided to have an abortion. I went to the clinic fully intending to go through with it – until the ultrasound. The doctor explained that they had to do one to confirm the pregnancy, check the size of the foetus, get a picture of the ovaries and uterus and rule out any problems like an ectopic pregnancy. When I looked at the screen I expected to see a blob. I didn't. I saw a baby with legs and arms, a face and a little nose. I stared at the screen in shock. I hadn't expected that. It was a real miniature person.

I was shaking when I left the room and told them I'd changed my mind. I went straight into the nearest bar and drank a large gin and tonic. I know you're not supposed to drink alcohol, but the child was conceived in a vat of champagne so I figured one more wouldn't do it too much harm. I'd taken a half-day off work to have the procedure, so I walked through Hyde Park and tried to come to terms with my decision. A baby . . . me, Louise, having a baby . . . the least maternal person in the world . . . lawyer . . . career woman . . . *mother*?

6

Sophie

I don't think I've ever been more shocked in my life. Louise pregnant! It was the least likely thing to happen. She didn't have a maternal bone in her body. And to think it had happened when she was blind drunk. It was so out of character. Louise didn't drink much because she didn't like losing control and she hated the way hangovers made her lethargic.

Yet here she was, five months pregnant at forty-one after a drunken shag, and planning to go back to work when the baby was three weeks old.

'Lou, I think you need to be more realistic about your maternity leave,' I suggested. 'Having a baby is tough. It's really hard going. You'll be physically and mentally exhausted.'

'She's right. The first four months are a bloody nightmare. You're leaking from everywhere, your brain is fried, and if someone says boo to you, you fall apart,' Julie agreed. 'As capable as you are, even you can't just give birth during a coffee break and carry on with your meetings.'

'My job is very stressful. I'm used to intense situations. I'm used to pressure. I'm used to being up all night working. I'm used to multitasking. How hard can it be?'

I looked at Julie. We shook our heads.

'It's the hardest job you'll ever have,' Julie explained.

'I'll be fine. Everything's organized. I've got a night nurse booked for the first six weeks to get me over the hump and to train the baby to sleep through the night. All the books say that if you get the baby into a good routine by six weeks, they'll be good sleepers for life.'

'Routine!' Julie screeched. 'Good luck with that.'

'I'm not having triplets, Julie. Look at Sophie. She had an easy time with Jessica.'

'She doesn't work and she had a full-time nanny and a night nurse,' Julie said. 'With no job and all those staff, of course she found it easy.'

I tried not to let the comment get to me, but it did. It really bugged me the way my sisters dismissed me. They always assumed that my life was easy. That all I did was sleep in late and get my nails done. I knew Julie had had a much harder time because she'd had triplets and Tom, and they never really slept, but it hadn't been plain sailing for me either. Just because I didn't talk about it didn't mean that I hadn't struggled with being a new mum. I had. No one knew how badly, not even Jack. I pushed the memories away.

'What are you going to tell the baby about her dad?' I asked Louise.

'Just the truth.'

'Come on, Lou, you can't tell a child that her dad was a one-night stand you can't even remember,' Julie objected. 'You'll have to think of something nicer, less honest.'

'Like what?'

'What about telling her that you fell in love in Venice, but her dad died tragically in a car crash?' I suggested.

Louise and Julie looked at each other and burst out laughing. It was like being a kid again, sitting in their bedroom while they laughed at me. I hated being the youngest girl. I always felt left out. When I came along, Mum moved Louise and Julie into the same room and they had shared it until Louise went to Cambridge. I'd slept in the small room next door. When Gavin arrived, fourteen years after me, the attic was converted into a bedroom for him.

Growing up, I'd hear my sisters talking and laughing through the wall, but whenever I went in they'd kick me out and tell me I was too young to listen to their conversations. I'd stomp back to my room and try to listen by putting a glass up against the wall.

When Louise went to college, Julie and I had become a bit

closer, but then she had followed Louise to England and they had seen a lot of each other while I stayed at home and modelled. I'd got closer to Julie when she moved back to Dublin and got married, but when she had the triplets she kind of disappeared for a few years. And when I'd tried to include her in my group, it had been a disaster.

I'd invited her to a girls' dinner about six months after the triplets were born. She'd arrived an hour and a half late. Her breast milk had leaked through her blouse. She was wearing one brown and one black shoe and she had yoghurt in her hair. When I served the main course, a spinach, pear and walnut salad, she asked if I thought she was a rabbit and proceeded to eat the entire basket of olive spelt bread, which none of the other girls touched.

She drank four glasses of wine, while everyone else sipped half a glass. Because she was so sleep-deprived, the alcohol went straight to her head. She rudely commented on the fact that no one was eating or drinking and said we were all 'ridiculous stick insects', before passing out, face down, at the table. I hadn't asked her back.

The women I hung around with were all like me, stay-at-home mums. We took care of our appearance – worked out, watched what we ate and liked a nice life-style. I didn't see anything wrong with that, but Julie did. I actually think she was jealous because we all had full-time help and no money worries. But she had always said she wanted a big family and she had four healthy sons. She and Harry seemed happy, so I didn't understand why she had a problem with me having money. Besides, I was always buying her kids presents and offering for Mimi to go over and clean her house. But she'd always said no. I didn't know why: her house was a mess and she needed a good cleaning lady. The one she had, Gloria, was fifty-eight years old and suffered from arthritis.

Gloria did nothing. She sat on her bum while Julie made her cups of tea, all the while complaining about her stiff joints and her useless husband, who was banged up in prison for trying to rob a post office. The only thing she seemed to do was the ironing. I called in to Julie one day to find her on her knees cleaning the oven, while Gloria was sitting on the couch watching *Loose Women* and absentmindedly rubbing the iron over one of Harry's shirts.

I told Julie she needed to manage her staff better, but she just glared at me and said Gloria wasn't 'staff', she was a friend. I pointed out that she was a friend who was getting paid eleven euros an hour to sit on her arse. Julie said that Gloria was the only person she could leave all four kids with, and therefore the most important person in her life. The only time Julie could ever properly relax when she was out was if Gloria was babysitting. Unfortunately, Gloria was only able to look after the boys occasionally because she was too busy watching TV in her other employers' houses. People had always taken advantage of Julie. She was far too nice.

It's not that I was mean to my staff. I treated Mimi very well, but I never made the mistake of becoming her friend. Once you crossed that line you were screwed. I'd seen it a million times with friends who got too close to their nannies or housekeepers. They'd start asking for loans of money, days off, extra holidays, sick days . . . They'd start telling you their problems and expecting you to solve them. Olive, a good friend of mine, had a housekeeper who asked if her daughter could come over from Hong Kong, stay in her room and go to college here. Olive agreed to it. When the housekeeper came back from the airport, she had her sister and her niece with her too. Olive ended up having to put them all up until she could find jobs and accommodation for them. I told Mimi when I hired her that I didn't want any family members coming to live with her in my house. If they wanted to come over, they had to get their own place. I was very good to Mimi: she had her own little apartment within the house – a bedroom, bathroom and a small lounge with a TV and computer. I gave her my old clothes, shoes, handbags, even some jewellery that I no longer wore, and I paid her more than any of the other housekeepers were paid. It was a win-win situation: everyone was happy. Gloria wouldn't have lasted two minutes in my house. I didn't want a new friend: I wanted a clean house.

'Come on, Sophie, don't look so pissed off. I'll take your

suggestion on board,' Louise said. 'I'm just not sure about the car-crash ending.'

'Why don't you keep it close to the truth, but make yourself sound less like a slut?' Julie suggested. 'You could tell her that you met her dad at a conference in Venice, which is true, that he was gorgeous, also true, and irresistible – she's the living proof of that. Explain that you had a weekend of romance and passion in Venice, but that her dad hadn't left any number or address or surname. That you just knew him as Giovanni. That's a nice Italian name.'

'Not bad. I may use that. But can I remind you that the baby hasn't even been born yet, so I won't need to come up with a story for at least three or four years? I've got plenty of time to figure something out.'

'What are you going to do about Mum? You know she's going to keep at you about the father being involved,' Julie said.

'If I was you I'd pretend I was really upset,' I said. 'If she thinks you're devastated about being dumped and are just doing your best to get on with it and to put the relationship behind you, she'll back off . . . for a while.'

'Good idea,' Louise said. 'Anything to get her off my case.'

I felt a bit sorry for Mum. I knew she yearned to have a better relationship with Louise, but my eldest sister never let her in. She kept her firmly at arm's length. Mum didn't know how to handle Louise. She was so intelligent, strong-willed and capable, she could be a bit overwhelming at times.

Louise was impatient and dismissive of people who were weak or indecisive or not very clever. Sometimes she made me feel like a total idiot, especially when she talked about business or current affairs. I had no interest in either. I never had had and I never would. They bored me. I'd much rather talk about fashion or interior design or new restaurants or which celebrities were dating each other. I didn't want to talk about boy soldiers in Africa. I didn't want to talk about which bank shares were up or down. It bored me rigid.

Louise thought my life was frivolous but I thought hers was empty and lonely. All she did was work. She never even had time to spend all the money she earned. She had a stylist who knew exactly what she liked and came to her apartment three times a year with a wardrobe already picked out. Where was the fun in that? Shopping gave me such a high – I loved it. The buzz I got when I found the perfect dress was amazing.

Louise only took two weeks' holidays a year – one week she spent at an ashtanga yoga retreat in Majorca and the other in New York, going to art galleries and the theatre; she never went to musicals – she thought they were rubbish. I smiled to myself. I wasn't sure how many worthy plays she'd be seeing when the baby arrived.

'So, do you have a name? Knowing you, you've probably registered her birth in advance,' Julie said.

Louise laughed. Julie was the only one who got away with slagging her. 'Clara Rose Devlin.'

'Clara's lovely,' I said.

'Not sure about Rose.' Julie wrinkled her nose.

'It's after her dad,' Louise said.

Julie and I looked at each other. 'What?'

Louise grinned. 'Mr X left a rose on my pillow the morning after the night before, and seeing as I don't know his name, I thought I'd put "Rose" in.'

We all roared laughing.

Louise rolled on to her side. 'God, it feels good to laugh. I've been so uptight the last few weeks trying to get my head around deciding to keep the baby and then having to tell Mum and Dad. And now, when I go back, I'll have to tell the senior partners at work.'

'How will they react?' Julie asked.

'Badly. My boss will be shocked. I just need to make sure he knows that I'm not going to be any less committed. Thank God Meredith has shown how a woman can do the mother thing and continue to be a ball-breaker.'

'Thank your lucky stars it's not triplets. The only balls I break these days are Harry's, and it's not sexual.' Julie sighed.

'Did you have much sex when you were pregnant?' Louise asked.

'Jesus, do you not remember how big I was, Lou? I could barely walk after five months, so the answer is no.'

'What about you, Sophie?'

'We kind of continued as normal until I got very big towards the end.'

'What's normal?' Julie enquired.

'I don't know – two or three times a week.'

Julie sat bolt upright. 'Twice a *week*! Jesus! Harry's lucky if he gets it once a month. Do you really still have sex that often?'

I nodded. I didn't tell her that sometimes I'd rather watch TV or just cuddle and talk. It wasn't that I didn't like sex with Jack – he had a great body and we had always been very compatible in bed – but sometimes I just wasn't in the mood. But I was worried that if I said no he'd look elsewhere. I knew Jack wouldn't want to cheat on me, but over time if you kept saying no to sex, a man would start looking at other women. I'd seen the husbands who'd had affairs and I knew that the main reason they cheated was because their wives didn't want to have sex with them and the husbands were sexually frustrated. There was no way that was going to happen to me. Jack was going nowhere.

'I'm meeting Daniel next week and I'm gagging for some sex – it's been months. Do you think it's weird to have sex with someone when you're pregnant with someone else's baby?' Louise asked.

Julie wrinkled her nose. 'I think it is a bit.'

'It's not as if you're ever going to see the biological dad again, so I think it's OK,' I told her.

'I'm with Sophie,' Louise said. 'The father's not in the picture so I'm entitled to have sex.'

'I miss great sex,' Julie admitted. 'I don't have the energy for it any more. Sometimes I fall asleep when we're doing it. Harry finds it really insulting. I've told him it's nothing to do with him or his technique, just exhaustion. I really should make more of an effort, though. My underwear's an absolute disgrace. I bet you two have gorgeous stuff.'

'I just buy Elle Macpherson underwear in bulk,' Louise said. 'It looks good and I find it comfortable.'

'I didn't even know she had an underwear range – they certainly don't stock it in M&S. What do you wear, Sophie?' Julie asked.

'La Perla mostly,' I admitted.

'Oh, God, their stuff is amazing. Right, that's it. I'm ditching the grey knickers and I'm going to make more of an effort.'

'Just be careful you don't get pregnant again,' Louise warned her. 'You've done enough to assist the repopulation of the world.'

'Don't even joke about it.' Julie shuddered. 'Honestly, girls, if I got pregnant again I'd kill myself.'

'What about you, Sophie? Would you like to have more?' Louise asked me.

'I've stopped taking the pill,' I lied. 'I know Jack would like a boy. So, if it happens, it happens. But I'm happy enough with just Jess. I don't really mind if we don't have any more children.'

The door opened and Gavin threw himself down on the bed beside Louise. 'I knew you witches would be up here. What are you talking about?'

'Underwear.'

'I go commando,' Gavin informed us.

'Too much information,' Louise said.

'Does sexy underwear really matter to guys?' Julie asked.

'Hell, yes. There's nothing worse than ripping a girl's clothes off to find big granny pants or hairy legs. I really hate hairy legs.'

'I haven't shaved since August,' Julie confessed.

'No guy likes gorilla legs. Sort it out.'

'Aren't you eco-warrior types into that *au naturel* stuff?' Louise said. 'I thought hairy armpits and hairy legs would go down well with you.'

'Hairy armpits are the biggest turn-off,' Gavin assured us.

'How can someone like Forest, who smells like a sewer, have a problem with hairy legs?' I asked.

'No guy wants his girlfriend to be hairier than him. Trust me.' Gavin grinned.

'Enough about hairs, it's making me feel nauseous.' Louise groaned.

'I cannot believe Miss Kick Ass Career Woman is having a baby,' Gavin said.

Louise punched his arm. 'Have some respect for your elders.'

'I can't wait to see it.'

'See what?'

'You as a mother – it'll be classic.' Gavin whooped.

'What do you mean?'

'Come on, Louise, you're a control freak. Babies puke, shit and cry all the time. You're going to flip.'

'No, I won't. I'll just be organized and have good help.'

'Whatever you say, sis.' Gavin winked at Julie and me.

'So when are you going to stop this save-the-golf-club-tree campaign?' Julie asked him. 'You're driving Mum and Dad mad.'

'I'm trying to save the planet from extinction.'

'Seriously, Gavin, grow up,' Louise said. 'If you really want to save the planet, do something worthwhile, like join Greenpeace or the WMO.'

'WM who?' Gavin asked.

'Oh, for God's sake, don't you know anything about climate change?' Louise shook her head. 'The WMO is the United Nations' World Meteorological Organization. It was established in 1950 and currently has 189 member states.'

'How do you know?' Gavin asked.

'I had a client who was involved.'

'Is he the guy who got you pregnant?'

'No, he is not.'

'So who is this guy?'

'I know Mum sent you up to spy on us and try to extract information, but it won't work,' Louise warned him. 'What did she bribe you with?'

'Fifty quid.'

'I'll give you a hundred if you tell her I'm really upset about the guy dumping me and I really don't want to talk about it – ever.'

'Hundred and fifty.'

'A hundred, Gav, or I'll tell your hairy friend Forest that you eat meat every time he turns his back,' Louise said.

'OK, deal.'

'Speaking of Forest, where is he?' I asked.

'He's showing the triplets his tattoos. They are seriously impressed.'

'Fan-fucking-tastic. Where the hell is their father?' Julie wanted to know.

'Harry and Jack are racing the monster trucks in the hall, and it's getting seriously competitive.'

'And Mum thinks I need a man to complete me!' Louise exclaimed.

7

Julie

Thank God Christmas is over. The triplets go back to school tomorrow. If they get kicked out of this Montessori, I'm booking a one-way flight to Brazil. They were asked to leave their previous school in May for trying to flush Laurel and Hardy – the school's rabbits – down the toilet. Mrs Robinson said in all her years as a teacher she had never seen such complete disregard for animals. She had only just arrived in time to save them. She told me the rabbits were completely traumatized, as were the other children in the class and that the boys were not welcome in her Montessori any longer. I begged her to keep them. I said I'd buy two new bunnies, send Laurel and Hardy to counselling, whatever it took. But she showed us the door. I cried all the way home. It was the first school they'd gone to and they'd only lasted five months. They'd been in the new one for three months, and so far, so good – thankfully, Mrs Walsh had no pets.

The last week of the Christmas holidays was proving to be an endurance test. Trying to keep four boys entertained while the rain pelted down every day was a nightmare. Harry practically sprinted out of the door to work after New Year leaving me alone with the children for five whole days.

I called in to my parents one afternoon, just to say hello and kill an hour. Their faces fell when they opened the door and realized it was me with the kids. After ten minutes – during which Liam had knocked his drink on to the floor and Luke had eaten Leo's biscuit, which resulted in Leo wrestling him to the ground and kicking Dad in the shin – Mum stood up and said she and Dad had to go out.

'Do we?' Dad looked surprised.

Mum glared at him. 'Do you not remember that appointment we have?'

'Oh, yes, of course, the appointment.' Dad rushed off to get his coat.

'What appointment?' I asked Mum.

'Oh, em . . . we have to see the man about fixing the front gate,' she said, whipping the cups off the table and into the dishwasher.

'Shouldn't he be coming here so he can see the gate?'

'Oh, for goodness' sake, you can't expect everyone to come to you all the time.'

'But how can he tell you he can fix it if he can't see it?'

'Because I'm taking a picture of it.'

'That's ridiculous, Mum,' I said, becoming suspicious.

'Stop fussing, Julie.' She left the room to get her coat.

When Dad came back in I asked him about the appointment. 'Where do you have to go?'

Dad fiddled with the buttons on his coat, avoiding eye contact. 'Oh, well, we just have to meet some people up in the golf club to, um, discuss, uh, fundraising and that.'

I jumped up, hustled the boys out of the door and into the car without saying goodbye. I was furious. I hardly ever called in. I'd been desperate to get out of my house for one measly hour. I never stayed long because I knew they found the boys full on, but now they were *lying* to get rid of me. These were my kids, their grand-children, and sure they were lively, but they weren't that bad. The boys were great, sweet and funny and, yes, OK, energetic, but it didn't make them pariahs to be avoided at all costs.

I put the key into the ignition and tried not to get upset. Mum rushed out to the car. 'Are you off, then?' she asked, looking guilty.

'You're obviously very busy with your special *appointment*, so I'll leave you alone.'

'Why don't you call in with Tom when the boys are back in school?'

I didn't want to fight with her in front of them, and I knew she'd tell me I was being paranoid if I accused her of faking an appointment. 'Yeah, maybe, I'll see,' I said, and drove off.

There was nowhere to go. My parents were lying to me to avoid having me in their house. None of my friends wanted me calling in with four boys. Sophie never invited me over – she said it was because Jess was afraid of the boys, but it was also because she was a control freak and hated her house being messed up. I drove around aimlessly. It was lashing rain so I couldn't even take them to the park. Eventually, I gave up and went home.

Two days later I called over to my next-door neighbour, Marian. She was back from her Christmas holidays. If it wasn't for her, I'd have gone insane. She had four children: Brian, five; Oscar, four; Molly, three; and Ben, six months. She was the only person who ever asked me over with my kids. The mothers at the Montessori always ran when they saw me. They were terrified I'd invite their kid over to play, then they'd have to invite my three back. Last year I'd had six different children over and not one of the mothers invited my triplets back, so I'd stopped. As Marian says, 'Fuck it, they have each other to play with.' Marian is slightly unhinged, curses like a drunken sailor and shoots from the hip on everything. I love her to bits.

She opened the door in her pyjamas, Ben on her hip and a cigarette hanging out of the side of her mouth. Marian, like me, had lost her waist. She only got dressed when absolutely necessary and often brought the kids to school in her pyjamas.

'Can you believe this fecking weather?' she asked. 'Why do we live in this country? It's a dump.'

'Eckin, eckin,' Tom said. I put him down and sent him in to play with Molly. She treated him like a live doll. The last time we'd called in, I'd found Tom dressed in one of Molly's princess costumes – glittery high heels, tiara and all – having his makeup applied. This consisted of Marian's red lipstick being smeared all over his lips, cheeks and eyes. He was delighted with all the attention.

'How was Christmas?' I asked. Marian had gone to stay with her mother-in-law, who lived in a little village twenty miles outside Galway.

'Nightmare. I don't do country. Who the hell wants to live in the arsehole of Ireland with one shop that opens when the owner decides to drag herself out of bed? Considering she's about three hundred and ninety years old, it's closed most of the time. The stuff is ancient and covered in dust. I actually found a tin of powdered eggs. Powdered eggs, Julie! They ate them in the Second World War.'

'That's bad.'

'I said to Greg, "If you expect me to come down here next year and listen to your mother moaning at me about my cursing and calling my kids 'wild animals', you can fuck right off."'

'What did he say?' I couldn't help laughing.

'He said, "At least my mother cooks." Now, you know my mother hasn't cooked since 1979 when my dad left. We had pizza for Christmas dinner last year. But as I said to Greg, I'd rather eat pizza than overcooked, dry turkey and Brussels fucking sprouts. Which is exactly what his mother, Dawn, tried to shove down my kids' throats. You can imagine how that turned out. They all started gagging and spitting the sprouts on the carpet. I thought Dawn was going to have a heart attack, but no such luck.'

'What did you do with the kids all day?'

'Wandered the streets. Anything to get out of the house. I've never had so much fresh air – who the hell wants fresh air when it smells of cow shit? The kids kept crying and begging me to go home, but Greg said we had to stay. He's worried his mother's getting old and she won't be around much longer . . . That woman will be around for the next millennium. She's like the bloody Duracell bunny.'

'What about when it rained?'

Marian took a long drag on her cigarette. 'We spent a lot of time in the pub next door with the kids eating crisps and drinking Coke, which made them hyper, but at least we weren't under Dawn's feet.'

The great thing about Marian was that she always made me feel better about my parenting skills. She let her children drink

Coke and eat unhealthy food, she smoked in the house, she cursed, she shouted at them and would admit openly that they drove her mad at times. She was honest to a fault, which I found very endearing.

'I'm just going to close the door.' She got up and pushed the door to her small playroom shut.

We could hear all the children inside causing havoc. Marian didn't care if they made a mess or kicked balls against the walls or jumped up and down on her couch. Brian and Oscar were pretty full on and she was happy to let them be as boisterous as they wanted. It was heaven for me to call over – I didn't spend the whole time giving out to the triplets or trying to discipline them.

Marian went to put the kettle on. 'Is it too early for wine?' she asked.

I looked at my watch. It was eleven o'clock. 'I think so.'

'OK, I'll put a drop of brandy into the coffee instead.' She got the cups out. 'Tell me, how was your Christmas?'

'It was OK, but I'm wrecked. Tom's waking up every night because he's teething. And I can't wait for the triplets to go back to Montessori. They have so much energy.'

'Amen to that.' She handed me a cup.

I took a sip. 'Jesus, Marian. It's rocket fuel.'

'Sorry, wrong cup. That one's for me.' She handed me the other. 'There's only a tiny bit of brandy in that.'

I tasted it. It was fine.

'How were your sisters? Did Sophie get a Ferrari for Christmas this year?' Marian asked. She didn't like Sophie. They had only met a few times, but they rubbed each other up the wrong way. Sophie had called in to see me last year after her holidays and Marian was there with her kids. Jack had taken her to the Burj Al Arab – the seven-star hotel in Dubai – for her birthday. She wanted to show me the brochure and tell me all about it. At the time, Marian was heavily pregnant and even less tolerant than usual.

While Sophie described the hotel, Marian flicked through the brochure.

'It was incredible, Julie, I swear I've never seen luxury like it,' Sophie gushed. 'You have your own butler twenty-four hours a day. Every time you turn around someone's there to offer you food, drink, magazines, a cool face-cloth . . . whatever you need.'

'It sounds like heaven.'

Sophie yawned. 'It was, but I'm exhausted. The flight was delayed two hours, so we didn't get home until midnight and I had to bring Jess to school at nine.'

'So, after a week's holiday, you only got eight hours' sleep last night, poor you.' Marian snorted. 'You do realize that Julie has had no sleep for the last week? All her kids have had the vomiting bug.'

'Oh, Julie, that's awful,' Sophie said. 'Poor you.'

'And she's still got the chest infection she's had on and off for the last six months,' Marian continued.

Sophie looked at me. 'You never told me that.'

'It's fine,' I said. 'I'm fine. It's just been a crappy week. Now, tea or coffee?'

'Just water, thanks. I've got a session with my new personal trainer.'

'Is he good?' I asked.

'Brilliant. Total slave-driver, but very effective. You should think about hiring him – he's not too expensive. The fitter you are, the more energy you'll have and then you won't get run down. I haven't been sick all year.' She flicked her long honey blonde hair off her face. Then, looking at the chocolate biscuits on the table, she added, 'You know, Julie, sugar is a disaster. Maybe you should try to cut out biscuits and chocolate from your diet. They're false friends. After the initial sugar rush, they completely drain you. The best things to eat for energy are slow-releasing carbohydrates, like porridge and oatcakes.'

'It doesn't seem to be working so well for you. You're exhausted after eight hours' uninterrupted sleep,' Marian said sharply.

Sophie glared at her. 'Why are you so hostile? What's your problem?'

Marian leant across the table. 'My problem is women like you, with your staff and your ten holidays a year and your stupid-looking jeeps to ferry one kid around in, telling women like me and Julie, who have no help, husbands who have taken serious pay cuts in the last year, and a shedload of kids, to hire personal trainers and cut down on sugary foods. Chocolate is the only thing that gets me through the bloody day. If I wasn't eating Dairy Milk at seven a.m. to get an energy rush, however temporary it may be, I'd probably stick my head in the fucking oven.'

Sophie stood up, manicured hands on hips. 'And tell me, Marian, who forced you to get pregnant four times? Who made you have more children than you can cope with or afford? No one. *You* decided to have a big family. *You* decided to keep having children when you probably shouldn't. So why don't you stop trying to blame other people for the situation *you* created? And if I want to encourage my sister to be healthier and fitter so that she can cope better with her boys, I'd appreciate it if you kept your nose out of it.' She grabbed the keys to her Range Rover, got up and stormed out. That was the last time they'd seen each other. I figured it was best not to try to nurture that particular 'friendship'.

I put my brandy-coffee down. 'No, Marian. Sophie didn't get a Ferrari for Christmas. She did get the most incredible diamond watch. But the big news is that Louise is pregnant.'

'Louise the lawyer?' Marian had never met Louise, because Louise hardly ever came home from London, but she'd heard me talk about her.

'Yes. She's going to bring the baby up on her own, no dad involved.'

'Probably better off. Greg's no bloody use at all. The only thing he does when he comes home is cause chaos. Last night I had them fed, bathed and in their pyjamas, calmly watching TV, by seven thirty. I sat down for the first time all day. Then he came in from work and started wrestling them, throwing them up in the air, totally winding them up and making them hyper again. But after five minutes he'd had enough and wanted his dinner. Obviously the kids wanted to carry on playing and climbed all over him until Greg got pissed off and shouted at them to calm down!' Marian leant back in her chair and took a long drink of her strong brandy-coffee. 'I give up.'

'Do you think we'll ever get our lives back?' I asked.

'Not really, no.'

I groaned and rested my forehead on my hands. 'I miss my old life. I miss having a waist and remembering what day it is. I miss having clean clothes and furniture. I miss having conversations that don't get interrupted every thirty seconds. I miss my name – I'm Luke's, Liam's, Leo's or Tom's mum now. I miss sleep. I miss talking to Harry about things that don't involve arrangements, the children or where our money goes every month. I miss the freedom to walk out of the door and not have to think about what calamity is going to happen while I'm gone. I miss going to the cinema and not having to check my phone every ten minutes to make sure the babysitter hasn't called. I miss high heels. I miss earning my own money. I miss people thinking I'm fun to talk to, instead of coma-inducing. I miss reading the newspapers in bed on Sunday mornings and going for breakfast at three in the afternoon . . .'

'STOP!' Marian put her hand up. 'If you don't, I'll end up slitting my wrists.'

'You're right.' I sighed. 'Let's be positive. Between us we have eight healthy children.'

'And . . . we have a roof over our heads,' she added.

'And . . . food to eat.'

'And brandy.'

'And our health.'

'And . . . I can't think of anything else,' Marian wailed.

Later that day I sprinted out of the house to the hairdresser. My brown hair had gone grey when I was only twenty-seven, so I'd been colouring it for years. The grey roots were showing through after the holidays and I really needed to sort it out. It was bad enough to have lost my figure so I sure as hell wasn't going to be grey, too. I had asked Gloria, my cleaning lady – who did no cleaning at all, really – to come and look after the boys for two hours. She couldn't so, in desperation, I had bribed Gavin to look after them by promising to give him the money to plant two new trees. He finally agreed to come down from his own tree to help me out.

'Thanks, I really appreciate it,' I told him, as he put his backpack on a chair.

'It was hard to say no, you sounded so desperate.'

'See my hair?'

'Not a good look.'

'How come you don't smell bad and are all freshly shaven?' I leant towards him and sniffed. 'And . . . Hold on a minute, you're wearing aftershave! What's going on?'

He blushed. 'Nothing.'

'Oh, my God, have you met someone at the tree? Are you seeing one of those older golf ladies who bakes you the cottage pies? Is she a cougar?' I giggled.

'Jesus, Julie, give me some credit. They're all Mum's age. Believe me, none of that lot are cougars, although the captain's wife is pretty fit.'

'Tell me it's not her! That would push Dad right over the edge.'

'I'm not shagging the captain's wife.'

'So why did you blush? Who are you seeing?'

'No one. Well, not yet anyway.'

I tapped my watch. 'Gavin, I need to go and get my hair fixed so that I don't look like a homeless person. I don't have time for you being coy. Spit it out.'

'OK, OK! Forest's sister, Acorn, is back home for a while. She's just finished up a three-month stint helping out with the Stop Heathrow Expansion campaign. She's been hanging out with me in the tree and sitting in it when I need to go home to shower and stuff.'

'Please tell me she doesn't look like her brother.'

'Give me some credit.'

'Does she have his personality?'

'If you mean is she as passionate about saving the climate, then yes.'

I groaned. 'Why can't you go out with a nice normal girl who doesn't feel the need to save everything?'

'She looks a bit like Angelina Jolie.'

'Now it's making more sense.'

'And, yes, before you ask, she washes regularly.'

'What do they call having sex in a tree? Is it the mile-high club or the tree-high club?'

'None of your business.' He laughed. 'And we haven't even snogged yet. We're still getting to know each other.'

'Haven't plucked up the courage yet?'

'I'm working on it.'

I put my hand on his shoulder. 'She may look like Angelina Jolie, but you look like a young –'

'Don't say it.' He squirmed.

'Jason Donovan.'

'Julie!' He covered his face with his hands.

'Jason was really good-looking in his day. We all fancied him in *Neighbours* – even Louise.' I sniggered.

'Stop talking right now.'

'OK, I won't torture you any more.' I ruffled his surprisingly soft clean hair. 'What's Acorn's real name?'

'That *is* her real name. Her mother's kind of a hippie.'

'You don't say! Does she know your real name isn't Willow?'

'No, and I'd like it to stay that way.'

'The Willow and the Acorn . . . It sounds almost romantic. Have Mum and Dad met her?'

'No, and I'm not planning to introduce them any time soon.'

'Kind of hard to hide someone in a tiny space up a tree?'

'They're not exactly regular visitors. They only come down late at night to tell me I'm a gobshite.'

'Well, they have a point. They spent a lot of money on your education and now you're tree-sitting.'

'This is the first time I've felt really passionately about something. The environment is our future.'

'Gavin-Willow, you've felt passionately about loads of things – starting with Spider-Man, Nintendo, the guitar, Limp Bizkit, Destiny's Child and then the *Matrix* movies. Remember when you started wearing Sophie's long black leather coat everywhere and asking us to call you Neo or Morpheus depending on the day? So you see, little bro, this is definitely *not* your first obsession.'

'Thanks for the reminder. Don't you have to get off now – before you go completely grey?' He hustled me out of the door.

'OK. Don't let the kids out of your sight. Tom is silent but deadly – he puts everything he can find into his mouth and could easily choke to death. Keep a close eye on him. Don't let the triplets near the washing-machine or the DVD player. They've already broken them both twice.'

'It's cool, Julie, just go and do your thing. I have it all under control.' Gavin waved me off.

As he was closing the door, I added, 'No visitors – I don't want you shagging Acorn in my bed. You're here to babysit.'

'Goodbye.' He shut the door in my face.

Half an hour later, I was sitting peacefully in the hairdresser's, my head covered with hair dye, a pile of magazines in front of me and a nice cup of sugary tea in my hand. Bliss.

My phone rang. I glanced down. It was Gavin's mobile. I picked it up, heart sinking. 'What's up?'

'Uhm, I think you need to come home, sis,' he said. I could hardly hear him – there was a commotion going on in the background.

'What happened?'

'OK, don't freak out, but there was kind of a fire, but not a bad one.'

'JESUS CHRIST! Are the kids all right?'

'Oh, yeah, totally, no injuries at all. They're just getting a bollocking from the firemen.'

I hung up, ran out of the hairdresser's – dye still in my hair – and drove home like a maniac. When I arrived, there was a fire-engine outside the house and I could see the triplets sitting in the front, pretending to drive it, under the supervision of two firemen.

'What the hell?' I asked Gavin, as he handed me a bewildered-looking Tom, who was naked and wrapped in a blanket.

'The triplets got the tomato ketchup and poured it all over Tom, so I had to give him a bath to wash it off. Then they found matches and kind of lit a fire in the TV room. The neighbour saw smoke and called 999.'

'Which neighbour?' I asked.

'The guy who looks like he wants to kill someone.' Gavin pointed to Mr Ryan. He lived in the house behind us and hated us. The triplets were constantly kicking their football into his garden and climbing up on to the back wall and shouting, 'Stinky bum,' at him.

I could see him pointing at me and heard snatches of his conversation with the chief fireman: 'Out of control . . . savages . . . need a firm hand . . . mother can't cope at all . . . no parenting . . .'

The chief walked towards me. 'Are you the mother?'

'Yes.'

'Your house is fine. Not much smoke damage at all, mostly just a bad smell, but that'll go in a few days. However, the rug in your lounge has seen better days.' He pointed to it on the road behind him. There was now a large black hole in the middle.

'I'm sorry –'

He held up his hand. 'No need to apologize, madam. I can see you've got your hands full. You can't watch children twenty-four seven. Now, I've given the boys a stern talking-to and I don't think they'll be playing with matches again any time soon.'

'But I don't understand where they got them. I never have matches in the house – I'm not completely insane.'

Gavin looked sheepish. 'I think they might have been mine.

73

They were in my backpack. They must have found them when I was washing Tom.'

'Jesus, they could have all been killed,' I hissed.

'I know. I'm sorry.'

'Look, these things happen,' the fire chief interrupted us. 'On a positive note, we didn't have to use any water. We put it out with fire blankets so there's no water damage. To be honest, Mrs . . . ?'

'Nichols,' I said.

'Mrs Nichols, your main problem is your very angry neighbour. I'd steer clear of him for a few days, if I was you.' He added, in a whisper, 'And you might want to choose your babysitters more carefully.'

'Thank you very much – and, again, I'm so sorry about all this,' I said, wiping the dripping hair dye off my face with my sleeve.

The chief called the triplets down from the truck and lined them up in front of me. Their faces were tear-stained. I bent down to kiss them.

'What do you say to your mummy?' the chief asked.

'Sorry, Mummy,' they said solemnly, in unison.

'What will you never, ever play with again unless you want to go to prison?' he asked them.

'Matches or any kind of fire,' they chimed.

'Now, be good for your mother,' the chief said. He patted their heads, climbed into the fire-engine and drove away.

I turned to the arsonists. I was at a loss for words.

'Mummy.' Liam tugged my arm. 'Are you super-cross?'

'Are you the crossest ever?' Leo asked.

'Are you infinity cross?' Luke wanted to know.

Before I could answer, Mr Ryan came marching towards me. 'Mrs Nichols, I'd like a word.'

'Not now, dude,' Gavin said, blocking his path. 'You can come back later and rant when their dad's home.' He pulled me and the boys into the house and closed the door.

The hall stank of smoke. I sank down to the floor and started to cry.

8

Louise

My office phone flashed. 'What is it, Jasmine?'

'It's your mother again, Louise.'

'Tell her I'm in another meeting.'

'I did, but she said it was an emergency and she won't hang up until she talks to you.'

Mum and I used to speak about once a month, but ever since I'd told her I was pregnant she'd been stalking me. This was the fourth time she'd rung this morning.

I picked up the phone. 'Hi, Mum, what's up? I'm really busy.'

'I don't care how busy you are. I'm calling to see how you're getting on. I want to make sure you're looking after yourself and the baby.'

'I'm fine, the baby's fine. It's all good.'

'Are you taking it easy? Have you cut down on your workload? You know that stress is very bad for babies – they can sense it. The more uptight you are when you're pregnant, the more difficult the baby will be when it's born.'

'Mum, I'm not stressed, I'm just very busy.'

'Have you spoken to the baby's father yet?'

I gripped my desk. 'No, Mum, I haven't, and I'm not going to. I told you, he doesn't want to know. Forget about him.'

'How can I? Every child needs a father. You'll have to make him see that he needs to be involved.'

'I don't want him to be involved. He's an idiot.'

'Why on earth did you go out with him, then?'

The last thing I wanted was to get into a long conversation with my mother about the baby's dad. I needed to get her off the phone and off my back. I remembered Sophie's suggestion at Christmas to pretend I was heartbroken. She was closest to Mum and was by far the best at handling her. I'd give it a go.

'Look, Mum, I liked him, but he dumped me and I was really upset for a while, but I'm over it now. I don't want to think about him because it brings back bad memories. I'm trying to move on, so please stop talking about him. It's hard for me.'

'I'm sorry if I've upset you, pet. I'm just thinking of the baby.'

I took a deep breath. 'I know, Mum, but it's my problem and I'll deal with it when I'm ready. I just can't go there right now, it's too raw.' I cringed as I said the words.

'That's understandable. I'll say no more about it for the time being. But you'll have to deal with it at some stage.'

I punched my fist in the air – *yes*! Good old Sophie. 'Thanks, Mum, I'd really appreciate that. I have to go now. Talk soon.'

'Don't work too hard.'

I hung up and leant back in my chair. Thank God I had my mother off my back. I had enough to deal with in work without grief from her, too. My boss, Alex Sutton, had not taken the news of my pregnancy well. At first he'd thought I was joking and refused to believe me until I took off my jacket and showed him my bump.

'But you always told me you didn't want children. I don't understand.'

'It's a long story,' I lied. The last thing I wanted to admit to my boss was that I'd got so drunk I'd slept with a stranger and used no protection. 'But I'll be raising the baby by myself and I assure you it's not going to affect my work. I've got my childcare well organized. I'll be taking three weeks off in April to have the baby, but I'll have my phone and laptop with me at all times and I'll be back in the office before you've noticed I'm gone.'

Alex pushed his glasses back up his nose. 'That's what you all say and then the child is born and you go all cooey and want to run home early to play with it.' He wagged a finger at me. 'I stuck my neck out for you, Louise. It was because of my repeated recommendations that you were made senior partner so early. This was not what I expected at all.'

I swallowed hard. 'Alex, it's fine. I love my job and I'm very good at it. I know you pushed for me to be made partner and I won't let you down. Look at Meredith. She hasn't skipped a beat.'

'Meredith married someone who is always there. Stewart gets home at five every day and if the child is sick, *he* takes the day off work to look after it. Are you planning on getting hitched?'

I shook my head.

'Perhaps you should consider it.' Alex's face was like thunder.

'Look, Alex, it's just about being organized, which I am. I've got the crèche booked and a back-up childminder if the baby gets sick or I need to travel. I've worked my arse off for twenty years at this firm, and I have no intention of taking my foot off the pedal now. Trust me.'

Alex looked directly at me. 'Don't let me down, Louise. I'm counting on you for the Hollywell case. If I see any signs that you can't keep up the pace, I'll have to ask Dominic Rowe to step up. It's too important to risk.'

I gritted my teeth. 'I'm fully aware of how important the case is. After all, I'm the one who persuaded Simon Hollywell to hire this firm. I'll manage the pace just fine.'

'Make sure you do,' he said, walking out.

I closed the door and sat down. My heart was pounding. I'd known Alex wasn't going to be thrilled about my pregnancy, but I hadn't expected him to threaten me with Hollywell. I owned that bloody case. I'd heard through the grapevine that the billion-dollar computer technology corporation Micropack was looking to buy the Hollywell Limited games company for $485 million. I had personally got in touch with Simon Hollywell and persuaded him to let Higgins, Cooper & Gray advise them on the sale. It was complicated because forty-nine per cent of Hollywell was owned by Games4us2play. They had shareholders located in four continents, making it a very complex transaction. I was working with multiple parties across the world to get a handle on the key commercial and legal issues. It was a huge case and we were billing hundreds of hours. I was determined to lead it to a successful conclusion and bask in the kudos that would follow. I was damned if that snake Dominic was going to get his hands on it.

Within an hour, the entire office knew I was with child and I had a stream of people coming in to congratulate me. They all seemed shocked, especially my secretary, Jasmine. She stood in my office, staring at me open-mouthed. 'Are you really pregnant?' she asked.

'Yes.'

'Wow.'

'Yes.'

'Are you happy?'

'Yes.'

'Is it true you're raising the baby on your own?'

'Yes.'

'It's not easy. Believe me, I know.'

I smiled stiffly at her. 'I'll manage.'

'Well, if you need any advice, I'm bringing up three alone, so I can certainly give you tips.'

'Thanks.'

'Do you want to ask me anything now?' she asked.

'Yes. Can you get me the Hollywell file? I want to review it.'

She sighed and went to get it.

In the canteen at lunchtime, Dominic Rowe sidled up beside me. It was as if he could smell blood. I knew he would like nothing better than to get his hands on the Hollywell case while I stayed at home breast-feeding. He was currently a junior partner and was extremely ambitious. I didn't like him and the feeling was definitely mutual. He spent most of his time ingratiating himself with Alex. They both played golf and bored me to death in meetings about birdies and eagles. Dominic was from a blue-blood family – his father was a member of the House of Lords and seemed to own half of Sussex. He had gone to Eton, then studied law at Cambridge. Although he was short, squat and not very attractive, he had very high self-esteem and the sense of entitlement that seems to go hand in hand with a privileged background.

He'd been a member of the incredibly exclusive Harrington House Golf Club since he was twelve. Alex had been trying to get into the club for years and it was through Dominic's connections that he had finally got his membership. I'd felt sick when he told me. With this one well-planned manoeuvre, Dominic had Alex in his debt, which was a very powerful position to be in. Dominic was a spoilt, over-indulged, back-stabbing, two-faced fake, but he was clever – and excellent at manipulating people. I needed to watch my back.

'Well, well, well! Aren't you a dark horse, Ms Devlin?' he said, smirking.

'What do you mean?' I eyeballed him.

'Come on, it's the talk of the office. Louise Devlin, career woman, is pregnant. So, who's the father?'

'None of your business, Dominic.'

'You're going to bring the baby up alone?'

'Yes, I am.'

'Very brave of you.' He swept his auburn hair off his large forehead.

'Thanks.'

'With your workload, I imagine it will be very difficult.'

'I'll manage – I'm very resourceful.' I took a sip of my water.

'Alex is concerned about the Hollywell deal.'

I froze. 'He has nothing to be concerned about. It's completely under control.'

'Well, don't worry.' Dominic patted my arm. 'When it all gets too much, I'll be here to pick up the slack.'

I stood up. 'Thanks, Dominic, you're very sweet. If I'm stuck for a babysitter, I'll give you a shout.'

'I didn't –'

I cut across him: 'Don't take too long over lunch. We have work to do.' I turned on my heels and left the canteen.

The patronizing little shit. He was already after my job. I'd have to work harder than ever to prove to Alex that this baby wasn't going to make me less dynamic, sharp or focused. I pushed away the seed of doubt in my head. It was all about being organized and staying on top of things, both of which I was very good at.

That evening while I was at home finishing off some emails, my phone rang. It was Julie.

'I need help,' she begged. 'I've just weighed myself. I've put on five more pounds. I have to lose it. I'm forty this year. I will not be forty and fat.'

'You're not fat.'

'I've gone from a size twelve to a sixteen. I feel fat.'

'It's all just excess weight. If you focus, you'll lose it quickly.'

'Tell me how.'

'I gave you a detailed plan last year. Do you still have it?'

She snorted. 'Louise, I'm lucky if I can find myself among the piles of laundry, toys and general chaos.'

I suppressed a sigh. For the last four years Julie had called me every January, crying because she'd put on weight, and every time I'd sent her a weight-loss plan that she'd ignored. 'OK, I'll do another for you tonight and email it over. But if you really want to lose weight, you have to follow it properly. No cheating.'

'I promise I'm going to do it this year. Do I have to eat vats of spinach and cabbage? LUKE, GET THAT OUT OF YOUR NOSE.'

I held the phone away from my ear. Conversations with Julie always included a lot of shouting at the boys. 'No, you just have to stop eating rubbish. You need slow-releasing carbohydrates.'

'Sophie's always banging on about them.'

'She's thin,' I pointed out.

'She doesn't eat anything, slow-releasing or not. Did you see

80

her on Christmas Day? She ate three Brussels sprouts and a small slice of turkey.'

'I agree she's too thin, and there's no point starving yourself because you'll crack one day and end up bingeing.'

'What type of exercise should I be doing? Everyone says Pilates is great for toning up.'

'It is, but you need to mix it with cardio.'

'I can't afford to join a gym. CURTAINS ARE NOT ROPES – STOP SWINGING OUT OF THEM.'

Thank God I'm having a girl, I thought. 'You don't need to join a gym. I can send you a Pilates DVD and a cardio one. When Tom goes for his nap, do half an hour cardio and half an hour Pilates. You just need to get more organized so that you can focus on your weight loss.'

'It's hard to be organized with four kids. *If* Tom goes for a nap, I usually try to catch up with the laundry or tidy up, or else I pass out face down in my own bed because I'm so tired. GET OFF ME! I'M TRYING TO HAVE A CONVERSATION WITH MY SISTER. GO AND ANNOY YOUR DAD.'

'Losing weight and keeping fit aren't easy. It's hard work and you need to be disciplined.'

'You're right. I'll try, but I'm not like you and Sophie with your incredible self-control. I seem to be missing that gene.'

'Well, be happy as you are and stop asking me to help you lose weight.'

'But I'm not happy being this big. This time I really want to be thinner. I have to drop two dress sizes before my fortieth in June.'

Julie *was* different from me and Sophie. She'd never been driven like us. She'd drifted through school, popular, happy, laid-back. Then she'd gone to college and decided to study social science because it had so few lectures each week. She'd had lots of fun and scraped through her exams, having done the minimum amount of study. After college her best friend, Linda, had moved to London, so Julie tagged along, not having any idea what she was going to do. When she went to a recruitment agency to find work, she'd got on so well with the owner, Sylvie, that she'd been offered a job.

Julie didn't even have to go looking for Harry – they'd met when he'd come to the agency looking for a new job. Julie was the agent assigned to him, and they'd hit it off immediately. When she'd wanted to get pregnant, she'd conceived the triplets straight away. That was Julie all over.

'If you follow my diet and exercise plan, you'll drop two dress sizes by June.'

'Brilliant. You're a star. I'll definitely do it this time. Anyway, enough about me. How are you doing? Are you feeling OK?'

'Yeah, fine. I've had to stop doing ashtanga because my bump is bigger, but I'm swimming every morning and finding that really good. I'm hoping to keep it up all the way through.'

'How long do you swim for?'

'An hour.'

'Bloody hell! Are you sure that's safe? DO NOT THROW THAT CUP.'

'I checked it out. Swimming is the best exercise to do when you're pregnant. I feel great after it, totally energized.'

'You're an amazing woman. Did you tell your boss yet?'

'Yes. Not a good reaction.'

'Yikes.'

'The vultures are circling, ready to pounce on my job if I screw up.'

'You'll be fine. You've never put a foot wrong in your life . . . with the obvious exception of the one-night stand that resulted in pregnancy.' Julie giggled. 'Is Alex still cute in that Alan Sugar kind of way – small, grey-haired and crinkly with a twinkle in his eye?'

Julie had met Alex once, years ago, when she lived in London, and through a haze of white wine had found him attractive.

'He looks like Alan Sugar's beardless brother and, no, he is not cute in any way whatsoever.'

'Look, I'm a full-time mum, I fantasize about anyone – I even had a sex dream about George Bush, and I think he's gross.'

'Jesus, Julie!'

'I know. But at least I only dream about one-night stands, as opposed to actually having them.'

'I wish mine had been a dream. I now have Mum stalking me.'

'Well, clearly you gave an Oscar-winning performance on the phone today. She told me you were very upset about the nasty boy dumping you and she was giving you some space.'

'Alleluia!'

9

Sophie

I stepped out of the shower on to the warm bathroom tiles and dried myself. After moisturizing carefully with the new Crème de la Mer body cream, I shook my hair out of the shower cap, put in some heated rollers and applied my makeup. The good thing about modelling was that it had taught me how to do my own hair and makeup like a pro. I'd learnt all the tricks of the trade and it was a great asset.

I finished with some lip-gloss in a neutral shade and moved into the dressing room. I studied the rails of clothes. I wanted to look smart and stylish, but not as though I'd made too much of an effort.

I was going to Victoria's for a coffee morning. She was an incredible hostess – even a coffee morning turned into an event. I pulled on my new black dVb jeans. I loved them because they were low rise and made my bum look tiny. I put on really high black Gucci boots and, after trying on ten different tops, I decided to wear my black Alexander McQueen draped cashmere-blend jumper. I finished off the outfit with a Zac Posen chain-trimmed jacquard jacket. I inspected myself in the mirror. Perfect – cool and stylish with a modern twist. The jeans made my legs look really skinny. I was thrilled. I put on my new Cartier watch, my diamond stud earrings and my Tiffany necklace with the diamond S that Jack had given me the Christmas before last.

When I got downstairs, Mimi was ironing Jack's shirts.

'Morning! How are you?' I asked.

'Good, thanks, and you?'

'Fine, thanks. Listen, Mimi, when you're doing the grocery

shopping today could you pick up some fat-free yoghurts and skimmed milk for me? Thanks.'

'You need drink normal milk. You too skinny.'

'Mimi, I've told you before, you can never be too rich or too thin!'

'You skin and bone now.'

'I know and I love it!' I smiled at her as she tut-tutted. 'Can you pick Jessica up from Montessori today and give her lunch? There is wholemeal pitta bread and celery, red pepper and carrot sticks in the fridge. She can have them with organic hummus and a pro-biotic yoghurt with raisins, apricots and prunes for dessert.'

'Can she have treat today?' Mimi was always trying to get me to give Jessica sugary things. She thought kids should be allowed chocolate biscuits and sweets. But I wanted Jess to have a really healthy diet, so her skin would glow, her teeth would be white and she'd be naturally slim. She was allowed to have sweets at parties, but only a few. I know Mimi thought I was a total Nazi about it, but I only wanted the best for my daughter and I was determined for her to look as gorgeous as she possibly could.

'She can have a small bowl of unsalted microwave popcorn after her lunch,' I said, as I left for my coffee morning.

On my way to Victoria's, Mum called. 'Are you alone?'

'Yes, I'm in the car.'

'You have to talk to that brother of yours.'

'Has he not come down from the tree yet?'

'No, he has not. I'm mortified. It's been three weeks now and I'm at my wit's end. Your father won't discuss it. He said it's bad for his blood pressure. Just thinking about it makes him turn a dangerous shade of red.'

'Don't get yourselves too worked up. It's just a phase. He'll get bored. Remember when he decided he wanted to be a photographer and went around taking black-and-white photos of flowers and half-open doors and unlaced shoes? It only lasted a month. This'll be the same. Just let him get it out of his system. Besides, Gavin is too fond of his creature comforts to stay up there much longer. I'll

call him later and talk to him. I'm on my way to Victoria's for coffee.'
I wanted to get Mum off the subject of Gavin. We'd discussed him
at length yesterday and the day before.

'That'll be nice. Doesn't Victoria live in that enormous house
overlooking the sea on Countess Road?'

'Yes. The views are incredible. Her husband, Gerry, just sold
one of his many companies for thirty million. Can you believe it?
I'd say Victoria's got loads of incredible new clothes. She always
looks amazing.'

'So do you.'

I smiled. 'Thanks, Mum, but she's in a different league. She has
her own personal hairdresser, who also does her makeup and
comes to her house at least three times a week.'

'Seems a bit over the top.'

'I suppose so.' It did sound excessive, but she looked fantastic.
I'd never seen her with a hair out of place. She had a stylist who
flew to London, Paris and New York with her every season to see
the new collections, so she always had the latest fashions. She was
five foot five and a size six. Everything looked incredible on her.

Mum added, 'You don't need that kind of help because you do
your own hair and makeup like a professional and you're always
immaculate. What are you wearing to this?'

I described my outfit.

'It sounds gorgeous. You'll be the most stunning by far. I wish
Julie would take a leaf out of your book. She was such a pretty
child, with her lovely brown curly hair and those big brown eyes,
but she makes no effort any more. She does herself no favours the
way she goes about in those baggy, shapeless clothes with no
makeup on.'

'She's swamped with the kids, Mum.'

'I had four children myself, remember, and you can't let yourself
go. If you don't look after yourself you start to lose your self-
esteem and get depressed. I saw it happen to lots of my friends.
You have to drag yourself out of bed and go for walks and put
your lipstick on. It's not easy – there were many days when I just

wanted to stay in my pyjamas, but I didn't. I forced myself up and out. Life with small children is not easy, but you have to be strong and keep your pecker up. I'll have to have a word with her.'

'Be careful, Mum, she's pretty defensive about it. Maybe you should wait until the triplets go to national school next September and she has more breathing space.'

'There's no time like the present. She's only defensive because she knows she needs to take care of herself.'

'Try to be subtle.'

'Aren't I always?'

Julie was clearly in for one of Mum's pep talks. I thought about warning her, but decided against it. I didn't want to get caught in the middle. 'OK, Mum, I have to go, talk to you later.'

I hung up and waited for Victoria's electronic gates to open. They swung back, revealing the curving driveway up to the three-storey red-brick house and spectacular sea views. Victoria's housekeeper opened the door and showed me into the drawing room. I was the first to arrive. A fire was blazing in the huge hearth. Victoria's best china was out and she had lovely little pastries from Chez Max. My stomach grumbled. I was hungry, but there was no way I was going to eat any of them: there were a million calories in each one. The only person who would eat them was Saskia and that was only because she'd throw them up later. Her bulimia was the worst-kept secret in town.

'Hello, sweetie.' Victoria walked in to greet me.

She was wearing a beautiful grey short-sleeved wool-blend Roland Mouret dress and Marc Jacobs grey suede ankle boots – I'd seen them both in *Vogue*. Her skin was golden-brown from her recent sun holiday. It didn't matter what I wore, she always looked better than me. No matter how much effort I made and how pleased I was when I left the house, I always felt inferior to her when I saw her. She was perfect. 'You look amazing, Victoria,' I said.

'Thanks. This is great for just throwing on in the morning. It's so easy.' She pulled at the two-and-a-half-thousand-euro dress casually. 'And these boots are so comfy.'

I looked down at the six-inch heels. They didn't look remotely comfortable, but Victoria always wore really high heels to make her look taller and even more like a model.

'So, how are you? How was Christmas?' she asked, perched on the edge of her sofa. 'I haven't seen anyone. We only got back from Barbados ten days ago and it's been hectic. Thankfully, the boys are back in boarding school so I can breathe again.'

Victoria was Gerry Ward's second wife. He had two teenage sons from his first marriage, but they spent most of their time in boarding school, much to her delight. She and Gerry had one son together, Sebastian. He was four and very sweet. He was in the same Montessori as Jess, which was how I'd met Victoria. Jess and Sebastian got on well together and often had play-dates.

'Oh, my God, show me that watch.' Victoria's eyes homed in on my wrist. She grabbed it and held it up. 'Well, I see Jack had a good year. Was that your Christmas gift?'

'Yes, he really spoilt me.' I smiled.

'Gerry got me this.' She shoved her hand under my nose. There was an enormous pink diamond on her finger.

'Wow, it's beautiful.'

'Apparently there are only ten in the world.' She admired her ring. 'We're lucky girls to have husbands who spoil us. Behind every rich man is a happy wife.'

'Amen to that.'

Victoria lowered her voice, even though we were the only people in the room. 'Did you hear about poor Annabelle?'

'No! What happened?' I asked, worried that she was unwell.

'Frank's had to take a seventy-per-cent salary cut and he had most of his savings in bank shares, which are now worth nothing. They've had to cancel all their holidays. She's had to trade in her Porsche Cayenne for a 2002 Hyundai. They've had to give up their membership to Green Gates golf club and they may have to sell their house.'

'Poor Annabelle – that's terrible. But at least Frank still has his job. Hopefully things will improve next year.'

'Maybe, but they'll never get their social standing back.' Victoria stood up to welcome Paula, Saskia and Daniella, who had arrived together. 'I was just telling Sophie about poor Annabelle.'

'It's just awful.' Daniella shook her head. 'She has to cut back on everything. We'll hardly see her any more. She's not in the golf club or the gym. She won't be coming skiing with us in February or to Marbella for the summer. She said all charity balls and lunches are out, too.'

'Why don't I have a dinner party and invite them?' I suggested.

'Do you think that's a good idea?' Victoria asked. 'It could be embarrassing for them. All our husbands are doing so well and Frank isn't. They might feel awkward, especially if we're talking about skiing and sun holidays and all the things we do that they can't any more.'

'Oh, you're so right, Victoria,' Saskia said. 'Annabelle would hate it. She'd feel so left out.'

'Won't she feel more left out if we don't include her?' I asked.

'No,' Victoria said firmly. 'It's best to leave her alone for the moment. They don't need our charity.'

'It's not charity, it's a dinner party.'

Victoria laid her hand on my arm. 'Sophie, trust me, it's a bad idea. I've known Annabelle for a long time. She doesn't want us calling and inviting her to things. She needs space so she can figure out how to cope with this disaster. Now, Paula, tell me, how's your extension coming along? Did you go to that kitchen place I told you about?'

I sat back and let them talk. They had all gone to the same exclusive private school together and had known each other for years. I'd only met the others through Victoria. On Jessica's first day in Montessori, Victoria had come over and admired my brand-new red Moschino coat that I'd bought in London the week before. She was wearing an incredible Donna Karan sleeveless black shearling jacket.

She was so glamorous that I was flattered when she befriended me and included me in her group. Jack got on well with the husbands and we'd all gone skiing in St Moritz last year. It was Victoria who had persuaded me to take a villa in Marbella last summer. I liked being part of her group. They were stay-at-home mums and liked nice clothes, jewellery and holidays – the things I loved, too.

Sometimes I wondered if we talked about clothes and cars and houses a bit too much, but I enjoyed their company. Besides, I couldn't talk to Julie about shopping and decorating because she had no money, and Louise always made me feel like an airhead if I wasn't discussing politics or business. But I honestly found those subjects depressing and boring. I'd much rather talk about the new Miu Miu collection than the Taliban or stocks and shares.

After I left Victoria's I went to pick up Jack's suits from the dry-cleaner's. On my way back to the car I heard someone call my name. My maiden name.

'Sophie Devlin, I don't believe it – you look fantastic.'

I turned around and came face to face with Denise Fuller. I'd been in school with her but hadn't seen her for years. She'd aged a lot, very lined around the forehead and eyes – she could have done with some Botox. 'Hi, Denise, long time no see. How are you?'

'Great, thanks. Mad busy but all good.'

'What are you up to, these days?' I asked, noticing she wore no wedding ring. In fact, she had on no jewellery at all.

'I'm a scriptwriter for the BBC. I'm based in London, but I'm over for a month working on a one-off drama for RTÉ television.'

'That sounds really interesting.'

'Honestly, Sophie, it's the best job in the world. I feel so lucky to love what I do. I literally jump out of bed in the morning . . .' The more she talked, the more animated her face became and the less old she looked. It was as if she was lit up from the inside when she talked about her job. 'You get to work with the most amazing people. I'm also just finishing up a screenplay, which I'm hoping to get made into a film.'

'You were always really good at writing,' I said. 'I remember your essays being so much better than anyone else's.'

She laughed. 'Thanks. It's my absolute passion. How about you? What have you been up to?'

'Oh, well, I'm married and I have a little girl, Jessica, who's four.'

'That's great, congratulations.'

'Oh, thanks. She's really sweet. I'm very lucky.'

'Do you work?'

I shook my head.

'So you're at home all the time?'

'Yes.'

'Is it enough?'

'What do you mean?'

'Is being at home full-time enough to fulfil you? You know, does it feed your soul?'

I felt flustered. 'Well, I don't know. I'm just really busy looking after Jessica and Jack and the house and all of that.' I sounded a bit lame.

'Well, you look great. Obviously your life agrees with you. I'd better fly. I've a meeting in ten minutes.'

I watched her go, slowly climbed into the car and leant my head back on the seat. My life seemed so dull compared to hers. She was so full of passion and enthusiasm for what she was doing. When was the last time I'd felt that strongly about anything? If I was honest, it was when I'd bought that Jason Wu dress for the Breast Cancer Ball in October. But had it fed my soul? What did that even mean?

I called Julie.

'Hi, Sophie.'

'Does being a mum feed your soul?' I asked.

'Are you drunk?'

'No. I just met Denise Fuller, who was in my class in school. She's a scriptwriter now. You should have heard her, Julie – she's so passionate about what she does. She said her job feeds her soul. What feeds yours?'

'My soul hasn't seen the light of day in four and a half years. It's so deeply buried under the stress of my day-to-day life I think it may have been crushed to death.'

'What do you feel passionately about?'

'Sleep.'

'No, seriously, come on.'

'Sophie, I haven't got time to ponder whether my soul is fed or not. There are a lot of days when I don't get time for a thirty-second shower. Giving my soul a three-course meal is low on my list of priorities – it's on a par with getting my legs waxed because then Harry might think I want sex.'

'Do you think being a full-time mum is enough?'

'Enough for what? Enough to drive you round the bend? Enough to make you insane with love and pride one minute, rage and shame the next? Every time I hear about a woman expecting twins or triplets, I cry because I know she'll not come up for air for years. And when Angelina frigging Jolie was wandering around with a twin hanging off each boob, looking beautiful, I wanted to scream.'

'Maybe I should do something for charity.'

'To hell with charity! Come and babysit for me once a week – I'll be your charity. Let me describe my morning to you. It began at two a.m. when Leo woke me up to tell me he'd had a scary dream. At three thirty Luke did a poo and needed his bum wiped. At five Liam came in to ask me if God was bigger than a crane – yes. A house? Yes. A castle? Yes. A tree? Yes. A monster truck? YES! At six, Tom woke up and refused to go back to sleep. I then spent two hours chasing the triplets around, trying to get them to sit down and eat breakfast. Two bowls of Rice Krispies ended up on the floor. It took a further forty-five minutes to wrestle them into their clothes, during which one jumper and one shirt were ripped. We arrived to Montessori half an hour late. I got a bollocking from their teacher. When I got home I had to clear up all the breakfast things. While I was doing that, Tom went into the bathroom, drank some shampoo, went into my bedroom, climbed on to my bed and vomited everywhere. I now have to go and collect the triplets from school and think up ways to keep them entertained for the next eight hours. So, as you can probably tell, my soul, if it's still alive, is very badly neglected. I'm hoping to get reacquainted with it when the boys are eighteen.'

'But I'm not as busy as you. I have more time on my hands, so maybe I should do something else.'

Julie sighed. 'Sophie, your life looks pretty perfect to me and you seem very happy. Just because you met someone who loves their job doesn't mean your job as a mum and wife isn't important. Everyone is fulfilled in different ways.'

'You're right. Thanks, Julie.'

'I've got to go – if I'm late to pick up the triplets Mrs Walsh will probably call the police.'

Julie was right: I was happy. So what if shopping gave me the high that careers gave other people? Everyone had different passions. I liked my life just the way it was. I reached into my bag and popped Wednesday's pill into my mouth.

No more babies.

10

Julie

Gavin had called and invited himself over for breakfast. As it was Sunday, the triplets were still in their pyjamas, watching *Ben 10: Alien Force*, and Tom was playing on the floor with his Lego. Harry and I were actually able to have tea and toast in relative peace. I had thrown a sweatshirt over my fleecy pyjamas and pulled my hair back into a clip. Harry went to answer the door to Gavin, but arrived back with two people – Gavin and a younger version of Angelina Jolie. She was stunning in a totally natural way – which is actually unnatural, because so few people are. She had no makeup on and was wearing skinny khaki jeans and a plain grey sweatshirt, but she was drop-dead gorgeous. Harry was positively ogling.

'You might want to stop drooling,' I whispered, handing him one of Tom's bibs.

'Julie, this is Acorn.' Gavin introduced us.

I shook her hand. Shit, why hadn't I got dressed this morning and put on makeup? I felt like a wrinkly old hag. 'Very nice to meet you. Come and sit down. Will you have tea or coffee?' I asked.

'Coffee, please. We didn't get much sleep last night.' She looked at Gavin and giggled.

Oh, God, could this get any more depressing? They had obviously been having sex all night. New, steamy, rip-the-clothes-off-each-other sex. I remembered that . . . vaguely.

Acorn peeled her sweatshirt off to reveal a tight vest-top and a pair of big, round, perky boobs.

I glanced at Harry. I think his heart had stopped. Angelina Jolie was his ideal woman and here was a younger version, with bigger boobs, sitting in his kitchen. I poked him in the ribs. 'Harry! Pour the coffee, will you, please? I'm going to put on more toast.'

'Thanks, Harry.' Acorn smiled, as my lovestruck husband handed her a mug.

'So, who's minding the tree this morning?' I asked.

'Actually, it looks like the new clubhouse development is going to be shelved. The captain's wife, Mrs O'Connor, came to the tree last night with a lasagne and told me they can't raise the funding. A third of the members haven't paid their subs this year, so we should know in the next few days if it's been cancelled.'

'I know two people who will be very relieved,' I said.

'Yeah. Dad may even speak to me again in daylight.' Gavin snorted.

Acorn sniffed the air. 'Julie, is something burning?'

'No, that's the lingering smell from the fire that the triplets started when Uncle Gavin here was babysitting.'

'Dude, seriously?' Acorn turned to her boyfriend.

'It was an accident. I've apologized a million times.'

'Our very own arsonist.' Harry finally found his voice.

'You're a real comedian,' Gavin drawled.

'Morning.' Marian opened the back door and strolled in, wearing her dressing-gown. I felt better – she looked even worse than I did. 'Sorry to barge in but we're out of milk.'

'No problem, I've loads. Will you have a cuppa?' I asked.

'Will I have a cup of coffee and avoid going back to the chaos in my house? That's a definite yes.' She grinned.

'Hey, Marian, how's it going?' Gavin asked.

'Shite, as usual. How's the tree-hugging?'

'Good, thanks.'

'Is it true you've changed your name to "Blade of Grass" or "Tree Stump" or something?'

'It's Willow, actually, and this is Acorn. She's also, as you would say, a tree-hugger,' Gavin told her.

To Acorn, Marian said, 'Honey, you look like a super-model.

What are you wasting your time up a tree for? Get yourself a decent name and an agent. You could be the next Bond girl.'

'Climate change is all I care about,' Acorn said.

'Fuck the climate. With God-given assets like you have, you should be making millions and living a life of luxury. Do it while you're young and your boobs can still fight gravity.'

'How's Greg?' Harry asked.

'Greg's a wanker.'

'Right.' Harry took a sip of his coffee.

'Who's Greg?' Acorn asked.

'Marian's husband.' Gavin grinned.

'He arrives back from his conference in Miami last night and tells me he's worn out and needs to go straight to bed. I've been on my own with the kids all week, I've had no sleep and he wants a nap!'

'What did you say?' I encouraged her. I wanted Harry to hear the things Marian said to Greg: it made him think I was the best, sanest wife ever.

'I told him if he lay down on the bed, I'd set the fucking thing on fire.'

Gavin and I roared laughing. Harry and Acorn looked shocked.

'Bit extreme,' Harry said.

'In case you hadn't noticed, I don't do subtle.'

'How many children do you have?' Acorn asked.

'Four. It's three too many.'

'I think it's so cool that you both have big families,' Acorn enthused. 'I want to have loads of kids – maybe four of my own and adopt four more. It'd be amazing to have twins or triplets, and I definitely want to breast-feed for the first two years like my mum did.'

Before I could give Acorn some gentle advice about *never* wishing for triplets, Marian jumped in. 'Honey, you need to listen to me very carefully. Raising one child is difficult enough. Raising three at the same time is hell. I know you see these celebrities in magazines with their five, six, seven kids looking blissfully happy. I can assure you, these women are not blissful. They are out of their minds with stress and most of them are popping Prozac like Smarties. As for breast-feeding your children for two years, unless you want to see those perky tits swinging around your ankles with toothmarks all over them, don't even think about it.'

Acorn began waving her arms in a circle. 'You have a very negative aura. You should try meditating. Your stress levels are dangerously high.'

'Meditation! Do you have any idea what it's like raising four kids on your own with no help? Most days I don't get the chance to pee.'

'Look how calm it is in this house. Julie and Harry seem to have it sussed,' Acorn said.

Marian and I caught each other's eye and laughed hysterically. 'This house went on fire last week,' Marian reminded her.

'You happen to have called in during the twenty minutes we get per day when the kids watch TV at the same time without trying to kill each other. Just wait another minute or two and you'll see it kick off,' I put in.

As if on cue, we heard a bloodcurdling roar as Luke was shoved backwards through the TV-room door by Leo and Liam. He landed on Tom, who screeched.

'Boys,' Harry barely raised his voice, 'behave yourselves. Now come and meet Gavin's friend. Her name is Acorn.'

'Like from a tree?' Luke asked.

'Exactly,' Acorn answered.

'Mummy said people with names like trees are silly,' Leo piped up.

'No, I did not,' I spluttered.

'Yes, you did,' Liam reminded me. 'Remember when Uncle Gavin changed his name to Willow and you said he was a silly-billy and that he should have got a real job after college and not live in a tree like a bloody squirrel?'

'That's lovely language to use in front of them.' Harry glared at me.

'LIAM!' I scolded. 'Don't curse.'

'I'm not. I'm just saying what you said.'

'I can see your boobies,' Luke said, staring at Acorn's cleavage.

'Dude, have some respect.' Gavin nudged his nephew's shoulder.

'Marian said babies kill boobies,' Leo said.

'Fucking right they do,' Marian replied.

'Marian, I'd really appreciate it if you didn't curse in front of the kids.' Harry frowned.

Marian stood up, holding a carton of milk. 'Don't worry, I'm going before I corrupt them.' She winked at Harry. Turning to me she asked, 'Are you around tomorrow to take the monsters to the park?'

'Sorry, I'm meeting Sophie for a play-date.'

'I thought she hated the boys.'

'She doesn't hate them, she just finds them boisterous, and her Jessica is a bit scared of them.'

'Jess needs to toughen up – she's afraid of her own shadow,' Gavin said. 'It'll do her good to spend more time with the boys.'

'OK, let's do something on Tuesday. I'll give you a buzz. Thanks for the milk.' Marian turned back to close the door. 'I'll take my negative aura and my foul mouth home.'

'She just gets madder every time I see her,' Gavin said.

'I don't know how Greg puts up with her,' Harry commented.

'She has a very dark aura. She needs to do a negative-energy cleansing before it's too late. You should encourage her to do some positive visualization exercises.' Acorn looked upset: clearly Marian was a bad case.

'I don't know any cleansings. Can you give me one?' I asked. I had a feeling my aura wasn't too shiny either.

'Sure. Visualize yourself in a shower of light, and watch it pouring down to you from the sun. Let the rays wash over you, cleansing all the negative energy around you. Then visualize that light pouring into your body through the top of your head, cleansing you of any negative energy. See the negative energy pouring out of you through the soles of your feet into the Earth, where it will be transformed into love. It's the same way that trees transform carbon dioxide into oxygen.'

'I'll be sure to tell her that.' I'd try it myself tomorrow before I went to Sophie's to see if it worked.

The next day, as I stood in the shower, I closed my eyes and visualized the light shining through me. But just as I was getting to the part where the bad stuff goes out through my feet I heard a crash. I grabbed a towel and ran to the kitchen. The triplets were nowhere to be seen. They had somehow managed to push the heavy wooden kitchen table on to its side and all the breakfast dishes – glasses, cups and plates – lay smashed on the floor. Tom was sitting in the middle of the mess, looking bewildered. I picked him up, made sure he wasn't cut or hurt, and roared, 'GET OUT HERE NOW!'

The triplets shuffled out of their hiding place, heads down.

'Sorry, Mummy, it was an accident,' Luke said.

'How could pushing the table over be an accident?'

'We were trying to see who was the strongest of us and none of us could push it over. When we all did it together, it worked,' Leo admitted.

'You've broken everything!' I knelt down to pick up the pieces of my delft and tried not to cry. 'I've told you a million times not to push things over or break things. I'm so sick of this shit.'

'Don't say "shit",' Liam reminded me.

'SHIT, SHIT, SHIT!' I shouted, like a petulant child, and stormed off to get the Hoover.

I had arranged to meet Sophie in the park near her house. It had a good section for older kids and a toddler area, too. We were going to let the children play there and then take them for an early tea in the Italian restaurant behind the park. But five minutes after we arrived it began to rain.

'The weather in this stupid country is a joke. Let's go. My boots are going to get ruined,' Sophie complained. They were grey suede with high heels.

'You should have worn something more practical to the park.'

'They match my outfit. In any case, I don't want my hair to get wet – Jack's taking me out later.'

'Where do you want to go?' The obvious place was Sophie's house, which was close by, but I knew she wouldn't want my boys running around her perfect home.

The rain got heavier. Sophie put Jess's hat on, pulled her grey-suede jacket over her head and cursed. 'I suppose we'll just have to go back to my place until it stops. It can't last long.'

When we got to her front door, she ordered everyone, including me, to take our wet shoes off. She didn't want mud on her cream Italian marble tiles. I noticed she didn't take her own shoes off. She wiped them on the mat and led us into the kitchen. When we were all inside, she locked the door to the hall and the one to the pantry. The children were now contained in the kitchen and the playroom.

'Now, boys, I want you to play nicely with Jessica and don't be rough with her or her toys or I'll be very cross. OK?' Sophie said.

The boys seemed a bit frightened. 'OK.'

'Promise?'

'We promise.'

'All right. Now off you go and play.'

'Can we have a treat?' Leo asked.

'No. Treats make you hyper. Just go and play,' Sophie told him.

'If you're good, I'll get you a treat on the way home,' I promised him.

'Can we have Maltesers?' Luke asked.

'Maybe.'

'Can we have Rolos?' Leo asked.

'We'll see.'

'I want crisps,' Liam told me.

'Fine. Just go and play and we'll talk about it later.'

'You're not really going to give them all that junk, are you?' Sophie asked.

I shrugged. 'I know you're into all your organic stuff, but sweets are the only bribe that works for me, so don't give me a hard time about it.'

'You're just making more trouble for yourself. Sugary foods make them even harder to manage. You should reward them with unsalted popcorn or yoghurt-covered rice cakes.'

'Jessica is a saint. I can't believe those are her treats. The boys would freak if I gave them rice cakes.'

'I've never offered her sweets, so she doesn't ask for them.'

'Well, she's obviously got her mother's self-control.'

'I hope so. Latte?' Sophie asked.

'Love one.'

'Skimmed milk OK?'

'Sure.' I didn't like lattes with skimmed milk, but Sophie thought full-fat milk was the devil's juice.

The kitchen was like something you'd see in a magazine. There was nothing on the surfaces. No post, newspapers, socks, toys, bottles, beakers, vitamin jars, crumbs, half-eaten crackers . . . The only things you could see were a state-of-the-art kettle and a coffee machine.

'I'm thirsty,' Luke said, as they all trooped back into the kitchen.

'Ask Sophie nicely for a drink,' I told him.

'Auntie Sophie, can I have a drink?' he asked.

'I've got goat's milk or water.'

'Yuck.'

'Do you have any apple juice?' I asked.

She shook her head. 'It's full of sugar and rots kids' teeth.'

'Smoothies?' I tried.

'God, no, they're just as bad. Fruit juice is full of sugar. You shouldn't let the boys drink it.'

'I hate water,' Luke grumbled.

'Have some milk,' I said, pouring him a glass of organic goat's milk.

'I don't like this – it tastes weird.' He put down the glass.

'I'm thirsty,' Leo said.

'Milk or water,' I said.

'The milk is yucky,' Luke assured him.

'I don't want yucky milk or water. I want juice.'

'Juice is bad for your teeth,' Jessica explained to her cousin, as she sipped her goat's milk. 'Do you want to have yellow teeth that fall out? No. Well, you mustn't drink any juice.'

The triplets began to chase each other around the kitchen. Sophie ordered them to stop and ushered them back into the playroom, which was a shrine to princesses. Everything in it was pink and sparkly. I could hear the boys bashing around, giving out that the toys were only for girls. Tom, meanwhile, sat on the floor happily chewing my handbag strap. Jessica finished her milk and gingerly went to see what chaos her cousins were creating in her beautiful playroom.

'Do you have any biscuits?' I asked my sister. 'I'm starving. I didn't have a chance to eat lunch.'

'Come on, Julie, you know I never have chocolate or biscuits in the house.'

'I thought Jack might have a secret stash somewhere.'

'Nope. I have hummus and carrot sticks, no-fat yoghurt, apples or blueberries. Or some pumpkin-seed bread.'

'No wonder you're so thin – there's nothing to eat here. Can I at least have some sugar for my latte?'

'I only have Sucralose. It's zero calorie.'

'Fine.' I put two large spoonfuls into my watery latte, while Sophie sprinkled a few grains into hers. 'Did I tell you I met Gavin's new girlfriend, Acorn?'

'No! What's she like? Does she really look like Angelina Jolie?'

'Better.'

'Wow. Is she thin?'

'Stick. And she has great boobs. Harry spent the whole morning staring at them.'

'I wish I had bigger boobs,' Sophie admitted.

'The ones you've got look good in that top.'

'Only because I'm wearing a push-up bra with those silicone inserts.'

'I wish mine were smaller. I keep thinking they'll shrink when I lose weight.'

'Jack's a boob man – I think he'd like it if mine were bigger.'

'Maybe if you ate something they'd grow.'

'There's no way I'm putting on weight. I might get a boob job when I'm forty.'

'For my fortieth, I'd like a face-lift, boob reduction, liposuction, a tummy tuck and for Super Nanny to move in with me.'

'It's only a few months away now. Are you and Harry going to do something special to celebrate?'

'He's promised to take me to Paris. I honestly cannot wait.'

'Who's going to look after the boys?' Sophie pointedly didn't offer.

'Marian said she'd take the triplets and I'm going to ask Mum and Dad to have Tom.'

Sophie looked relieved. She was obviously worried I'd planned to ask her. I smiled at the idea of the triplets moving in with Sophie and Jack for a weekend of Evian and rice cakes.

'It'll be great for you to get away. You deserve a break.' Sophie sipped her coffee.

'We actually haven't been away on our own in five years.'

'God, is it really that long?' She was genuinely shocked.

'Yes. We definitely need it.'

'I can give you a list of really cool restaurants and places to shop.'

'Great.' I knew that Sophie's recommendations would be really expensive Michelin-starred restaurants and designer boutiques. Harry and I would be on a tight budget. I just wanted to eat in local cafés and drink carafes of wine. I had no interest in shopping; French women were unnaturally thin. They invented the word *petite*, for goodness' sake. Regardless of how many no-fat yoghurts I ate, *petite* was never going to apply to me.

'There's an amazing little boutique just off rue St-Honoré –' Sophie stopped mid-sentence as Jess rushed over to her, tears streaming down her face. Shit!

'Mummy, the boys are breaking all my toys,' she bawled.

I ran into the playroom, hoping to hide some of the damage before Sophie saw it. But they weren't there. They were in the utility room, staring at the washing-machine, which was making very strange noises as soapy water gushed all over the floor.

'I'm going to kill you,' I hissed, as my socks sloshed about in the water. Sophie came rushing in behind me.

'Aargh!' She backed out in her now soggy suede boots.

'What the hell have you done?' I asked, turning the washing-machine off before it flooded the house.

'We wanted to wash Jess's tea set and her dolls, so we put them in the washing-machine.'

Sophie came back, barefoot. 'Jesus Christ! Look at this mess. They've broken the bloody washing-machine. It's top-of-the-range – I had it imported from Germany. This is why I never want your kids in my house – they break everything. They're completely out of control.'

'Look, I'm sorry about the machine, but I can't watch them every second of the day.'

'And my floor is ruined and my boots are wrecked and it's just a bloody mess. They're wild.'

'No, they aren't. They're just curious and lively. Boys need to be running and climbing and exploring.'

'Not in my house, they don't. They can do it somewhere else. They're never coming here again.'

'Jesus, Sophie, calm down, it's just a bit of water. I'll mop it up.'

'Don't tell me to calm down. It's an inch of water, my daughter's china tea set is broken, most of her dolls have lost limbs and the washing-machine is banjaxed.'

'I'll pay for the bloody washing-machine and I'll get Jess a new tea set.'

'Your children have no respect for other people's property. They're just like you.'

'What the hell is that supposed to mean?'

'Come on, Julie, you were always borrowing my clothes and losing them, or bringing them home torn or with cigarette burns in them. You've no regard for other people's stuff and neither do your kids.'

'Actually, Sophie, I borrowed Louise's clothes. I never borrowed yours because I could never get close to them. You always locked your bedroom door.'

'What about my cream suede jacket that you borrowed and gave back to me covered in red wine stains?'

'Are you still banging on about that?'

'It cost me four months' wages. I'd only worn it once.'

'It happened fifteen years ago – get over it! You're a selfish cow.'

'I am not selfish. I care about how I look and like to have a clean and tidy house but that does not make me a cow.'

'Your house is like a bloody museum. I'm afraid to sit down in case I get a tiny speck of dust on something. You need to lighten up, Sophie.'

'And you need to get your shit together, Julie. You used to be the prettiest of all us sisters. Stop letting your children rule your life. Stop using them as an excuse for everything. Go on a diet, exercise, lose weight, put on some makeup and get some decent clothes. Stop moaning about it and talking about it and just bloody *do it*.'

'You try looking good with four boys! You try putting makeup on with triplets pulling at you and dropping your mascara into the toilet.'

'Punish them and they won't do it again.'

'It's not that simple.'

'It's not that complicated.'

'If I punished them every time they did something naughty, they'd live in the bloody bold room. You can't keep punishing kids. They need some leeway – they need to be allowed to express themselves. I can't keep them on a leash.'

'Maybe you should try. They need a firmer hand.'

'You don't know anything about it. You're too selfish to have another child and give poor Jess a playmate. You don't want your perfect life interrupted by a screaming baby. You don't want anyone or anything interfering with your ten holidays a year and your yoga.'

'That is total bullshit. Jack and I are trying for another baby and I am not selfish.'

'When was the last time you did something for someone else?'

'Today! When I had you and your boys back to my house, and look what happened.'

'Well, you won't have to worry about that ever again. Send me the bill for the washing-machine.' I grabbed my bag, picked up Tom and pushed the triplets out of the door.

It was only when I got to the car that I realized none of us had our shoes on.

When Harry got home late that night, I told him about the fight.

'Can't say I'm surprised,' he said, taking his tie off and throwing it over the chair beside him.

'What do you mean?'

'Sophie likes things to be perfect. Having the boys running wild in her house is her idea of hell.'

'It's not as if we're there every day. We haven't called into her in months. I only ever go there with Tom. She avoids the triplets like the plague.'

'I agree she's high maintenance, but she's generous in other ways.'

'What? Buying oversized presents for Christmas and their birthday?'

'Well, yes, and she has offered to send Mimi over to clean the house, but for some reason you keep saying no.'

'I don't want to owe her anything. I don't want her having done me any favours. She'll just throw it back in my face if we ever have a fight – like the bloody suede jacket she keeps bringing up.'

'What make was the washing-machine the boys wrecked?' Harry asked.

'I don't know – some fancy German one.'

'God, it'll probably cost a fortune to fix.'

'She won't let me pay for it. Sophie's not like that.'

'We should, though. Our kids broke it.'

'I know, but there's no way Sophie's going to send me a bill. She's selfish with things, not money. Besides, she'll probably just throw it out and order a new one.'

'It's the principle of the matter. I don't want Jack slagging me off about my kids trashing his house and him having to pay for it.'

'If he does, ignore him.'

'I try to.'

'He's not the worst, he's just a bit –'

'Of a tosser?'

'Yes, but Sophie said his family are really patronizing to him and that they consider him a failure so I think he's probably insecure.'

'He hides it well. It must be buried very deeply underneath that over-confident exterior.'

'I suppose all that financial success would give you a bit of a swagger.'

'I wish I could spoil you more. Get you a nanny and buy you nice jewellery.'

'The best thing you could do to spoil me is take the boys out on Saturday morning and give me a lie-in. That would be the best present ever.'

'It's a deal. But I do wish I earned more, so you could have some help.'

'Look, Harry, you do the best you can and I think you're brilliant. We have everything we need. Besides, there is light at the end of the tunnel. The triplets will be going to proper school next year from nine until one thirty, with the option of after-school care until five thirty. It'll be bliss.'

'Money would make things easier, though.'

'It doesn't necessarily bring you happiness. I think Sophie's life is really empty. She has far too much time on her hands. She's obsessed with her appearance, her clothes and her car. It's all about status, not about real life. Mind you, she looks great, doesn't she?'

'God, no. Her face is strange because of all that crap she injects into it and she's far too thin and bony. I like a bit of flesh on my women.'

'Well, you've certainly got that here.'

Harry put his arm around me. 'You're gorgeous and sexy.' He bent down to kiss me.

'Are you angling for sex?'

'It's been ages and I'm horny as hell.'

I giggled. 'OK, let's go before you start humping bus stops.'

Harry grabbed my hand and sprinted towards the bedroom.

Five minutes later he was fast asleep with a happy grin on his face and I was wide awake, trying to avoid the wet spot.

I couldn't sleep. I kept going over my fight with Sophie. I got out of bed and crept into the kitchen. I took out my phone to text my sister, but there was a message from her already: Sry I freaked. Dont wry bout washg mchn, is working fine.

That was the thing about Sophie. She wasn't a sulker. She didn't like any tension or bad feeling in her life. She liked everything to be sorted out and in its rightful place. I knew she was lying about the washing-machine being fine, but if I paid for it to be fixed, it would become this big thing – and Sophie wanted the quarrel to be over. She wanted the whole day to be in the past.

I wrote back: I'm sry too. Feel awful for shouting.

She texted back immediately: Lets 4get whole thing.

And I knew that would be the last I heard of it. Sophie's slate was wiped clean. It was good because, of course, I didn't want to continue arguing with her, but some of the things she had said had really hurt. I know I'd said awful things too, but I was feeling pretty crap about myself and her comments had stung. Mind you, she was right: it was up to me to take control of my life and my weight. It was up to me to find myself again.

I made some tea and logged on to the computer. I went to www.mumskeepingsane.com. It was my guilty pleasure. I loved the chat rooms and reading the things other mothers said. I always felt less lonely, less of a bad mother and less of a bad person when I read how much other people were struggling. I'd never posted any comments, but tonight I felt the need to write, so I began to type.

Threescompany was the name I chose for myself.

Hi, Mums,

This is my first time posting anything. I just wanted to know if any of you were feeling the same way. Despite having four children (four-year-old triplets and an eighteen-month-old – all boys) and never having a minute to myself, I feel lonely all the time.

I have a lovely husband and my children are healthy. I have nothing to complain about, but I find myself crying almost every day. Sometimes everything just gets on top of me. I didn't sign up for this. I didn't get married to end up drowning under a pile of laundry. Who the hell would apply for the job of wife and mother? Can you imagine the ad?

WANTED: female slave. No salary, no bonuses (fyi, husbands, sex is not a bonus when you're exhausted). No promotions, no sick days, no holidays, no medical care, no life insurance, no pension. Job involves cooking, cleaning, tidying up twenty times a day, washing, changing sheets, ironing, bathing and wiping arses – not just your own kids' but their friends' arses too. It will also require you to be a nurse, counsellor, maid, chef and peacemaker. You will also need the persuasive powers of a UN mediator to convince your kids that broccoli is not a tasteless, fuzzy, dry, grass-like food: it is delicious not to mention nutritious. You will not get any breaks – cigarette, coffee or even toilet. You will never be alone – even if you do eventually make it to the toilet, you will always have company. There is no personal space in this job. All of your belongings are now open to being dribbled on, sucked, chewed, bent, pulled, broken and, on many occasions, flushed down the toilet. Your clothes will be covered with food – carrot stains never wash out – and snot. Your sleep will be interrupted every night – a type of torture favoured in Guantánamo Bay. You will learn to sing songs over and over again until your head splits . . . And NEVER expect to be thanked, patted on the back, encouraged, cheered on or praised. You will, however, be criticized, moaned at, shouted at, told you are the worst person in the world, screamed at, screeched at, and have toys thrown at you. Sometimes you may be kicked, thumped and, on a very bad day, even spat at.

Would you apply for this job? What sane person wouldn't run screaming in the opposite direction? And yet that's it, that's a mother's lot. And you know what really bugs me? It's that my husband thinks women are born with a mummy gene. That 'motherhood' comes naturally to us. It's bullshit. We're not born with a special gene or chip or whatever it is – well, I certainly wasn't. I literally just stagger through each day trying not to kill my children or myself.

I love my boys. They are brilliant and funny and sweet, but sometimes (quite regularly, if I'm being honest) I want to walk out the door and leave them. Just for a day. I think if I could walk away for twenty-four hours, I'd be OK. I'd find sanity again.

I used to be quite pretty. I had shiny, bouncy, curly hair, big brown eyes and clear skin. I was never thin, but I wasn't chubby. I was just a little curvy, in a good way, in the right places. Now my eyes are smaller, due to lack of sleep; my hair is limp due to lack of care (I have to wash it during my ten-second shower and rarely get time to rinse the shampoo out properly); and I'm curvy in all the wrong places.

I had an argument with my sister today. She's gorgeous and slim and wears amazing clothes and has one perfect daughter. She told me to stop using my kids as an excuse. She said if I wanted to lose weight I just needed to stop talking about it and bloody get on with it. And she's right. But every time I decide to do it, something happens. One of the triplets breaks an arm, or they get chickenpox, or flu, or a chest infection, or expelled from school, or my little guy gets an ear infection, or is up all night teething, or falls out of his cot . . . and I'm too tired to exercise that day so I put it off until the next . . . and on it goes.

I'm turning forty this year and I keep looking at my life and thinking, Is this where I want to be? Is this how I want my life to continue? Is this how I want to look? Where did I go? Who am I?

11

Louise

I'd been really uncomfortable all day in the office. Not big, pregnant, waddly uncomfortable, but sore in my vagina. It hurt to sit down. I felt as if I was sitting on big lumps. I had no idea what was going on. My body was spreading in every direction, but this was obviously something else.

When I got home I had a shower and tried to see what was going on. But it was impossible as my belly was in the way. So after towelling myself dry, I got out my hand mirror and had a proper look.

Aargh.

There were big red lumps everywhere. The whole area was completely swollen. What was it? Were they cancerous? Was it a sign that the baby was coming early? Was my vagina infected? What the hell was going on?

I called Julie.

'Can I call you back?' she asked.

'*No!* Do not hang up,' I barked.

'OK, hold on . . . BOYS, I NEED TO TALK TO LOUISE. PUT THE TV ON AND MAKE SURE TOM DOESN'T SWALLOW ANYTHING DANGEROUS. IF HE STARTS CHOKING COME AND GET ME. OTHERWISE DON'T COME NEAR ME . . . I'm listening, Lou, shoot.'

'I have just discovered big lumps all over my vagina. It hurts when I sit down and it's all swollen.'

'Gross.'

'Yes, it bloody is. What is it? Is it normal? Did you get it? Is it pregnancy-related or am I dying?'

'I never got lumps down there and I don't know anyone who did, or certainly no one who admitted to it. Do they look like boils?'

'What does a boil look like?'

'I dunno – big and red and throbby, I suppose.'

'No, they're not angry-looking. They're just big and lumpy and disgusting.'

'I bet you Marian would know. I'll call her and ring you back.'

'No – you'll get distracted with the kids and call me back in five days' time. Give me her number. I'll conference her in.'

'Cool, can you do that?'

'Yes – get her number for me.' Julie read it out and I dialled it.

Marian answered: 'No, I am not interested in getting better rates from some telephone company in Outer Mongolia. Stop fucking ringing me at night-time with your bullshit offers. If you don't take me off your list of people to torment, I will come over there to Delhi or Mumbai, or wherever the hell your call centre is, and poke your eyes out.'

'*Marian!*' Julie shouted. 'It's me.'

'What number are you ringing me from?' Marian asked.

'It's my sister Louise's. She's got you on conference call from London.'

'God, sorry – I thought you were one of those telesales people.'

'Hi, Marian, sorry to bother you, it's Louise here.'

'The genius who got pregnant?'

Julie coughed nervously. Clearly Marian knew a lot more about me than I did about her – except her obvious aversion to tele-marketeers.

I wanted to get on with it. 'Julie said you might be able to help. I've just discovered lumps all over my vagina and I don't know what the hell is going on.'

'Jeez, Louise, get to the point, will you?' Marian cackled.

'Sorry – I just need to find out what it is and Julie thought you could help.'

'Have you heard of it before?' Julie asked her neighbour.

'Damn right I have. I had the same bloody thing when I was

expecting Brian. I thought they were tumours. I made Greg take a look and he was white when he came back up. He thought I was a goner too. Three weeks to live, tops. We're in the obstetrician's office the next day and we're both crying. The doctor starts laughing and tells me it's varicose veins in my vagina.'

'What?' Julie and I said at the same time.

'I know. Can you believe it? Varicose veins down there. So the good news is you're not dying.'

'What happens? Do they go away? Do they shrink? How the hell do I get rid of them?'

'The bad news is that you're going to have them until the baby comes out. Sometimes they get worse, sometimes they get a bit better. But they won't go until you give birth. Also, just in case you were planning on having sex, don't let any man near them. If they see those big yokes, they'll never want to have sex with you again. Greg didn't go near me until after Brian was born. To be honest, it suited me fine. Some women get really horny when they're pregnant but I never did – and nor did anyone I know. I actually think it's a myth invented by men to make us feel even worse than we already do when we don't want to have sex with a bloody bowling ball in our stomach.'

'I was about as randy as a corpse.' Julie whooped.

'I'm gagging for it,' I admitted.

'Really?' They both sounded stunned.

'Yes.'

'Well, please hop on a flight and put Greg out of his misery. I haven't got the fucking energy . . . STOP THAT RIGHT NOW!' Marian roared. 'I've got to go. Molly's just put an M&M up her nose.'

'Thanks for your help. 'Bye,' I said, as the phone line went dead.

'I told you Marian would know what it was,' Julie said.

'I owe you one, Julie. Marian is absolutely certifiable, but at least I know the lumps are not serious or permanent. I'll call you tomorrow after I've seen my obstetrician to confirm the diagnosis.'

*

I sat in the obstetrician's office, typing furiously on my BlackBerry. I glanced at the clock. Damn, I had a meeting in twenty minutes. Just as I was getting up to harass his secretary, Jonathan Bakewell called me in. We sat down face to face in his vast room.

'How are you feeling, my dear?' he asked.

'Big, fat and sweaty. Pretty revolting, really.'

'The third trimester can be difficult. But you're into single figures now – only six weeks to go.'

'Thank God for that. Look, Jonathan, something's bothering me. I seem to have lumps all over my vagina. I've been told it's probably varicose veins. Is that possible?'

'Climb up on the bed and let's take a look.'

I got undressed and covered myself with the sheet while I was examined.

'It's nothing to worry about,' he assured me. 'Now pop your clothes back on and we'll discuss it.'

'Is it varicose veins?'

'It would appear so, yes.'

'Aren't you supposed to get those in your legs?'

'In some cases women get them close to the vulva during the latter stages of pregnancy.'

'There must be some way to get rid of them?'

'They'll disappear once the baby is born.'

'In the meantime, I'm stuck with them?'

'I'm afraid so.'

'But they will definitely go once the baby is out?'

'Yes.'

'I suppose I should be grateful for that at least.'

'In the meantime try to sleep on your side and keep your legs raised as much as possible – it takes the pressure off the lower half of the body.'

'Can't you just take the baby out now and put me out of my misery?'

He smiled ruefully. 'You only have a short way to go. We're scheduled for your elective Caesarean at thirty-nine weeks. You're doing very well. Try to enjoy these last weeks. I'd like you to rest as much as possible.'

'If I get much bigger I won't be able to walk.' I sighed.

'Have you thought about a birth partner? Perhaps your mother, or a friend?'

'I'm used to doing things on my own. Besides, it's a brief procedure – I don't need a team of cheerleaders.' I glanced at my watch. 'I have to go. Thank you, Jonathan. I'll see you in a few weeks.'

'Try not to work too hard – you need to put those feet up.'

Yeah, right! As if I could tell Alex I was taking some time off to put my feet in the air because the veins in my vagina had swollen up like lemons. I rushed back to work and got to the meeting a minute late. I squeezed into a chair in the corner of the conference room. Dominic leant over and asked loudly if I needed a glass of water. Six heads – all male – turned to look at me.

'No, thank you.'

'You're a little flushed.'

'I'm fine.'

The truth was, my heart was racing. I'd had to run most of the way back from the obstetrician's and I was feeling a bit dizzy. But I was damned if I was going to show any weakness.

'Can I continue?' Alex asked brusquely.

'Absolutely.' I nodded.

'Right. I need all of you to work on the following shareholders at Games4us2play. We need to get everyone on board by the end of the month. You're going to have to fly over, meet these people face to face and get them to sign. Do not come back here without signatures. Dominic, I'm sending you to Singapore. Richard, I need you in Chicago, Lee in Cape Town and Louise is going to Buenos Aires to deal with the biggest shareholder, Eduardo Rodriguez. By all accounts he's a cantankerous old bugger and he's talking about pulling out of the merger. If anyone can get him to sign those papers, it's Louise.'

My heart sank. Buenos Aires, shit.

As if he'd read my thoughts, Dominic said, 'I don't think Louise can fly long distance at this late stage of her pregnancy. It's danger-ous, isn't it? I can fly directly from Singapore to Argentina. It's no problem.'

The snake. I wanted to put my fist in his mouth.

Alex looked at me. 'Is this going to be a problem, Louise?'

I fixed a smile on my face. 'Of course not, Alex. Thanks for your concern, Dominic, but it's a bit over the top. I am perfectly capable of flying to Buenos Aires to use my significant experience and persuasive powers to get Rodriguez to sign off on the deal. You just make sure you get the guys in Singapore to do the same. We don't want any loose ends.'

'Excellent. I knew I could count on you.' Alex was clearly relieved.

When I got back to my office I rang my obstetrician and explained the situation.

'It's not ideal, Louise,' Jonathan said. 'Long-haul flights at this stage of the pregnancy are not encouraged. When do you go?'

'In four days.'

'Come in and have your blood pressure checked the day before you fly. If it's high, you'll have to cancel the trip.'

'You don't understand – I have to go.'

'Louise, you're about to have a baby. Your priorities have changed.'

I hung up and rubbed my eyes. I was tired. I'd slept badly the night before. Why did everyone presume my priorities were going to be different? My career had always been my main focus and that wasn't going to change. I was sure I would like the baby and want to spend time with her – but that was what weekends were for. Work was my buzz, my high, my drug of choice.

I decided to book the flights myself. I didn't want Jasmine giving me a lecture about flying in the third trimester . . . I had to go to Argentina and that was that. If we could wrap this deal up before I had the baby, I'd go out on a high. I needed to prove my place as senior partner and this merger was my golden opportunity.

After booking the flights, I slipped off my high heels and raised my feet while I studied Eduardo Rodriguez's file. I wanted to know everything about him and his business background so I could get him on board as quickly as possible. He was the biggest shareholder and the one who could cause the most trouble.

'Louise – Louise . . . wakey-wakey.'

'What?' I lifted my head. Dominic was grinning at me.

Damn! I'd fallen asleep on my keyboard.

'I hope you're not going to nod off when you're with Rodriguez.'

'I wasn't sleeping. My keyboard was acting up. I was checking it,' I snapped.

'You have dribble on your chin.'

I wiped it off with my hand. 'Did you want something, Dominic?' I asked the weasel.

'I was going to ask you how you thought I should sell the deal to Chen Koh when I'm in Singapore. Apparently he's getting cold feet. But you obviously need a nap, so I'll come back later.'

'Have you studied his background? His previous business practices? Has he ever been involved in a buy-out before? How did he react? What exactly will he gain financially from the take-over? Does he have a family? Dependants? How is his health? What are his hobbies? His passions? You need to understand him completely before you meet him.'

'That's all very obvious. As Alex considers you an expert negotiator, I thought you'd have some special trick or manoeuvre.'

'You don't need tricks. You need to be prepared, persuasive and, most of all, convincing. Businessmen at his level can smell bullshit at twenty feet. They don't like being manipulated. That's the key. Convince, don't manipulate.'

'Hardly rocket science.' Dominic walked towards the door. 'I'll let you get some sleep.'

I thumped my desk. Of all the people to find me passed out on my keyboard, why had it had to be him? It would be all over the office. There was no way he wouldn't use it against me. Shit. I really didn't want Alex to hear about it. Where the hell was Jasmine?

She was supposed to stop people barging in unannounced.

I stuck my head out the door and saw her rushing back in.

'Where have you been?' I snapped.

'Sorry, Louise, Sam forgot his inhaler so I had to bring it to school for him.'

Jasmine and her bloody kids. She was always popping out for something. I was furious. 'The next time I'd appreciate it if you informed me first.'

Jasmine sat down at her desk and began to type. Without looking up she said, 'I was going to tell you, but you were fast asleep. I decided not to disturb you.'

I went into my office and slammed the door. This was not me. Louise Devlin did not fall asleep at her desk. I slapped my cheeks and jogged up and down. I needed to get my energy back. The jogging didn't last long, my boobs and my bump were too big.

Why hadn't I had that abortion? Why had I decided to have this baby? It was beginning to seem like a really bad idea. I had no control over my body. I had no control over my energy levels. I had no control over my sex life.

When Daniel had come to London from Monaco for New Year's Eve, I'd had to tell him I was pregnant. He'd looked horrified until I'd assured him it wasn't his. His relief had been almost palpable. But he wouldn't have sex with me. He said it would be too weird while I was pregnant with someone else's baby. I told him the father was not in the picture, but he still refused. I almost begged him because I wanted sex so badly, but he said no. He told me to call him when 'the kid is out and you're back to normal'.

Now I was big, bulky and tired, with a lumpy vagina and no sex on the horizon. Who the hell wanted a baby? It sucked. I needed reassurance. I decided to talk to my role model, Meredith Baker. Our paths rarely crossed as she specialized in employment law and was based on the other side of the building. I squashed my swollen feet into my shoes and went to find her.

'Hi, sorry to disturb you, Meredith, I wondered if you had a minute.'

She stood up. She was slim and toned, her hair was shiny, her makeup was perfectly applied, her nails were manicured and she was wearing a black dress with killer heels. She looked like I used to.

'Hi, Louise. Congratulations.' She nodded to my bump.

'Actually, that's the reason I'm here. You seem to have managed to have a baby and get straight back to work seamlessly. I'm planning to do exactly the same thing. I want to be back after three weeks and I just wondered if you had any advice.'

'What does your husband do?'

'There is no husband and the father won't be around.'

'You'll need staff – a cleaner who will also grocery-shop and cook, and a nanny for the child. If one is sick, the other will cover for her. You need to ignore all those women who drone on about breast-feeding and staying at home for the first year to have that special bond – it's bullshit. A happy mother means a happy home. I'd go around the twist at those awful mother-and-baby groups singing "Humpty Dumpty" like a brain-dead corpse. Who said having children means you have to give everything up? Children should slot into your life, not the other way around. Obviously you have to make some adjustments, but there's no need to go over the top.'

I beamed at her. She felt exactly the same as I did. A true kindred spirit.

'When I was a month old my parents went to Australia for six weeks,' Meredith continued. 'My mother had no guilty feelings. She said she couldn't wait to go away. She was exhausted, she needed a holiday. My parents had a very healthy, happy marriage because they put themselves first. I don't have any abandonment issues and I have an excellent relationship with my mother. Giving up your job, your looks, your hobbies, your sanity and your happiness will not make your child love you more. It will, however, make you love yourself a lot less and that's where the real problems start and marriages break up.'

'You're so right,' I exclaimed. I wanted to kiss her. 'I keep hearing how my life will be turned upside-down, my priorities will change and I'll want to stay at home. But I could think of nothing worse than being cooped up in my apartment with a baby all day.'

'Perish the thought. Honestly, I enjoy my weekends with Hermione, but I'm always relieved to get back to work on Monday. This job keeps me motivated and stimulated.'

'I totally agree. So all I need is good help?'

'Reliable childcare with back-up.'

'I've put the baby down for the Kensington Academy crèche and my cleaning lady said she'll cover any days the baby is sick. She'll also pick her up if I'm in work late or travelling.'

'What about her other cleaning jobs?'

'I said I'd pay her double on the days I needed her to cover for me. I presume babies don't get sick that often, so it should be straightforward.'

'It sounds like you have it sorted. That crèche is supposed to be fantastic. I'd advise you to have one more back-up person, though. Get a really good babysitter, a student – someone studying paediatrics would be ideal. That way even if your cleaning lady lets you down, you won't be stuck. Let's be honest here, Louise, the other partners have stay-at-home wives to sort this stuff out. They never have to think about their children. We have to do it all ourselves. If I took a day off every time Hermione was sick, I'd have been fired by now. You can't do it. At our level you have to be focused, flexible and available twenty-four seven. If we want to play with the big boys, we have to play by their rules.'

'I already have junior partners snapping at my heels, desperate for me to have the baby and take a step down so they can grab my place. I've worked too long and too hard to get here. I'm not giving it up,' I said.

'Of course you're not. The corporate world needs women like you and me to show the younger generation we can do it. You can be very successful and have children. Our daughters will thank us, not blame us.'

'You're so right. Thanks, Meredith, this chat's been really helpful.'

'You're welcome. Good luck with the baby. You'll have no problem – we career girls invented multitasking.'

I left her office on a high. It was going to be fine. In six weeks' time the baby would be born and a few weeks after that I'd be at work, back to my normal life and, hopefully, a normal vagina.

When I got back to my office, Jasmine said Julie was on the line.

'Hi, Julie.'

'Listen, I woke up in the middle of the night and realized you don't have a birthing partner, so I'd like to offer my services. I've had a C-section, so I know what to expect. I'm not squeamish, I'm good with doctors and I won't tell you what to do because I'm the only sister who didn't get the control-freak gene.'

'Thanks for the offer, but I don't need one.'

'Louise, I know you're Superwoman but everyone needs someone to hold their hand when a baby is born.'

'I don't. Honestly, I'd rather be on my own.'

'I'm coming to London whether you like it or not.'

'Fine, I'd like you to come, but not into the operating theatre. You can wait outside and come in when I've been stitched back up.'

'You know who else is coming over?' Julie giggled.

'Oh, God!'

'You can't stop her, Lou, she's your mother. She wants to be involved.'

'Well, you'll have to nail her shoes to the floor so she doesn't come into the theatre. I do not want Mum ordering me about.'

'OK. I'll pin her down while you're being sliced open, but then you'll have to let her in.'

'Fine, but she's not to hang around my hospital room all day telling me what to do. I've read all the books. I know what to do. I'm going to have this baby in a routine from week one.'

'*Hahahahahahahahahahaha.*'

'Gina Ford says it's –'

Julie interrupted, 'Louise, if you only take one piece of advice from me, please let it be this one – burn that book. You'll drive yourself insane trying to force your baby into a routine. I tried the Gina Ford routine with the triplets and I swear I almost lost my mind. Harry eventually threw it in the bin. Babies find their own rhythm. You can't and shouldn't force them into any routine.'

'Julie, I hate to state the obvious, but your boys still wake up at night.'

'That's because I'm too tired to discipline them.'

'Well, Gina Ford's routine works for millions of babies. And I love routine so I'm sure my child will too.'

'OK, but I really think it's a mistake.'

'Fine.'

'Are you worried about having to look after the baby on your own?'

'No.'

'A bit apprehensive?'

'Not at all. I can't wait, to be honest.'

'Oh, I know, it's so exciting.'

'No, I mean I can't wait for the baby to be out and for me to get my life back to normal.'

Julie started laughing hysterically again so I hung up.

12

Sophie

I was on my way home from dropping Jess to school when I got a call from Annabelle. I had phoned her after Victoria had told me about her husband, Frank, having to take a massive pay cut and left a message saying I was sorry to hear she was having a difficult time and if she wanted to meet for coffee and a chat to call me. I didn't want to become her confidante or to take on her troubles, but I felt it was important to say hi and not make her feel ostracized. I heard nothing back for ages and had almost forgotten about it when she rang. She seemed keen to meet up, so we arranged to have a coffee together. I was kind of dreading it. I didn't know her that well, and while I was glad I'd made the effort to call her, I was equally glad when she hadn't called back.

I decided it was better not to wear my new watch or my diamond S. I wanted to dress down a bit, so I wore my blue dVb jeans, my casual brown Miu Miu wedge boots, and a beige Jaeger polo-neck with my brown Donna Karan poncho.

I arrived to the coffee shop and looked around. I saw Annabelle sitting in the corner, hunched over a cup of coffee. I barely recognized her – she looked awful. She had always been very glamorous and I'd never seen her without her hair blow-dried, fully made up and wearing the latest fashion. Now her hair was thin and lank and she was wearing an old pair of jeans, runners and a sweatshirt. I was shocked.

'Hi, how are you?' I said, leaning in to give her a hug.

'Oh, God, you look gorgeous.' She sighed.

'You look good too,' I lied.

'I look wretched,' she said.

I ordered a coffee. 'How are things?' I asked.

'Nightmare. I can't sleep. I spend all day with a calculator going through every single thing we spend money on, trying to cut back so the boys can stay in private school. But it's impossible to come up with the fees. I asked the headmaster to give them a scholarship. James is fifteen, he only has three more years, and Freddie's only nine, so hopefully we'll be back on our feet by the time he gets to senior school.'

'What did the headmaster say?'

'He said that a third of the parents were defaulting on school fees, that the scholarships had already been allocated to people in dire straits and that he was willing to let the boys stay until the end of the year without paying the fees, but after that he couldn't help us. He said the school is barely surviving. So . . .' She began to cry.

I squirmed in my seat. 'I'm very sorry to hear that.'

'Can you imagine telling a fifteen-year-old that he can't finish school with the friends he's grown up with since he was six? He loves that school – he's on the debating team, the tennis team and the athletics team. His heart will be broken. But we have no choice. We tried to sell the house, but we can't. We bought it for two and a half million and it's now worth a million. One and a half million euros of negative equity. We'll never get out of this mess. The only room we heat is the kitchen. That's where we live now. We go to bed in jumpers and woolly socks. I took the boys' mobile phones away and I have a pay-as-you-go one now. The bills were huge. I do one bulk shop for a hundred euros a month – food, toiletries, cleaning products, clothes – and that has to last.'

One hundred euros a month for all your shopping! God, I spent that on a sparkly cushion for Jess's bedroom yesterday. Poor Annabelle, it must be hell having no money. I felt stressed just thinking about it.

'Obviously I had to let my cleaner go and the gardener,' she continued. 'We never go out for meals or drinks or even a sandwich any more. We gave up the golf club, the gym and the tennis club.

I don't see anyone and my phone isn't exactly ringing off the hook. Victoria and my other old school friends have dropped me.'

'They just wanted to give you space,' I mumbled.

'I don't need space, I need support. I'll tell you one thing, Sophie, you find out who your real friends are when something like this happens. You called me and we don't even know each other that well. It was nice of you to do that. I appreciate it. But, you know, in a way it's better that Victoria and the others have dumped me. I can't do any of the things they're doing. I can't go on holidays or to fancy restaurants or balls or on spa days. We live different lives now.'

'How's Frank doing?'

'He's OK. He was upset at first, but he's very practical. Frank came from nothing. He grew up in a home with very little money, so having to cut back, having to budget every single thing, doesn't frighten him like it does me. He keeps saying it'll be all right, it's just a phase and we'll get back on our feet soon. But I don't think we'll ever get out of this debt. And I'm just devastated about James and Freddie having to move schools.'

'Could your family help?'

'My parents are dead. My father left me a chunk of money in his will, but we used it to buy the house. Frank said the house we had was fine and I should keep the inheritance for a rainy day, but I wanted to move into a bigger, shinier house. I desperately wanted to live on Granary Road. I thought it would give me status. It's turned out to be a noose around my neck.'

'Would you be open to us girls putting a fund together so your boys can stay in school? I'm sure the others would be glad to help.'

She laughed bitterly. 'I don't think so, Sophie. I rang Victoria a few weeks ago and asked her for a loan. I was mortified, but I'd do anything for my boys. She said if it was her money she'd give it to me, but it was Gerry's and he never lent money to friends because it always ended badly.'

'Why don't I talk to Jack? He's very generous and I know he won't mind.' I was shocked that Victoria had been so cold to one of her best friends. Then again, it wasn't her money so in a way it was Gerry's decision to make. Still, Victoria could stop shopping for a week and the boys' school fees would be paid. Gerry wouldn't even notice. I knew he gave her a huge allowance – she could have used that.

Annabelle leant across and squeezed my hand. 'Thanks, Sophie, it's a really kind offer, but I can't accept. I need to figure this out myself. I will let you pay for my coffee, though.' She smiled weakly.

I paid for the coffee and said goodbye. She climbed into her battered old car and I got into my Range Rover. I felt awful for her. Her life was utter hell. I shuddered as I drove to my appointment with the beautician.

A few days later, Jack announced that he was going to New York on business and wanted me to come with him, go shopping, catch a show, have some fun. I jumped at the chance. I love New York – the shopping there is second to none. I'd need to bring an extra suitcase for my purchases. I set up three appointments with personal shoppers at Barney's, Bergdorf Goodman and Saks. The personal shoppers in America are so efficient and helpful – they treat you like a celebrity. I couldn't get enough of it.

'Where are we staying?' I asked.

'The Four Seasons.' He smiled when I whooped. 'It's all on expenses so get as many treatments as you want in the spa.'

'I can't wait. We're so lucky, Jack. Honestly, after seeing Annabelle I realized how lucky I am that your business is going well and that we have no money worries. She's so strung out. You should see her – it's awful.'

Jack put his coffee down on the kitchen counter. 'I actually called the principal at Mount Gladwell College yesterday. I couldn't stop thinking about Annabelle's kids having to leave the school because they couldn't pay the fees. I've given the school a hundred grand to cover those boys and a few other families who need help. But I said it had to be an anonymous donation.'

I hugged him. 'Oh, Jack, that's brilliant.'

'What's money for if you can't help people out?'

'You're so generous – it's one of the things I love most about you.'

He put his arm around me. 'What else?'

'You're a great dad, you're fun, you're gorgeous and you don't mind that your wife thought Dow Jones was a Welsh singer.'

Jack roared laughing. 'I forgot about that. What a classic. Of course I didn't mind. Look, Sophie, this may come as a shock to you, but I didn't marry you for your sharp financial brain. I love you because you're gorgeous, a brilliant mum and a fantastic wife. You never nag or moan when I'm working late or away and you're always up for going out and having fun. And I love the way you defended me on Christmas Day to my family. Marrying you was the smartest move I've ever made.'

I kissed him. 'Well, it was definitely the cleverest thing I've ever done.'

The only downside to our trip to New York was Jess. I was dreading telling her. In the last few months she'd suddenly begun to get upset when we went away. Until then she'd always been absolutely fine about it. She adored Mimi and she was used to Jack and me going away – we'd been doing it since she was born. Jack had insisted on having a break when she was just three months old. I remember finding it very hard to leave her when she was so small, but he really wanted to go, so we went to Capri for five days. But the last two times we'd left her she'd cried and asked us to take her with us. Mimi said that an hour after we were gone she was fine again, but I hated seeing her upset. I hoped she wouldn't cry this time.

I needed to pack carefully for the trip: New Yorkers were very stylish. I was going for an Elle Macpherson smart-casual style. She always looked amazing, even just in jeans and pumps, although I wasn't going to wear jeans. I wanted to look city-smart. Jack had planned a big night out with all his work colleagues, so I needed something really gorgeous for that night. I'd met a few of the people he worked with and they were nice but very over-confident.

I knew Jack wanted me to look my absolute best. He liked to show me off. I'd bring my Hervé Léger sequin-panelled black bandage cap-sleeve dress. Even Victoria, who rarely complimented anyone, had said it was fab.

I was trying it on with my new Yves St Laurent shoes when Mum rang. 'Hi, what are you up to?'

'I'm trying on clothes for the trip to New York.'

'I'm actually calling you about that.'

'What's up?' I asked, only half listening as I changed into my black Jimmy Choos, which were better with the dress.

'I want you to track down Louise's boyfriend and tell him about the baby.'

That got my attention. I sat on the end of my bed. 'Mum, Louise doesn't have a boyfriend. He's out of the picture, remember.'

'I know she said that and I understand that she doesn't want anything to do with him, but I can't sleep at night thinking about that poor baby with no father. Children need father figures.'

'Dad can be her father figure, with Gavin, Jack and Harry. She'll be fine.'

'Sophie, that man needs to stand up and take responsibility for his baby. Do you have any idea how damaging it is for a child to know her father rejected her?'

'I know it's not ideal, but the baby's better off with no father than a father who doesn't want her. Anyway, it's up to Louise to contact him if she wants to. I'm not getting involved.'

'Sometimes you have to get off the fence, Sophie.'

'I do get off the fence.'

'You don't really, pet. You always avoid confrontation. You just go off and do your own thing. And you're right most of the time not to get involved in your sisters' dilemmas, but this time you need to step in and help.'

I hated getting involved in any kind of drama. I didn't want to get dragged into arguments and heavy discussions. I just wanted to get on with my life and stay away from any hassle or unpleasantness. I felt very uncomfortable when people told me personal things. I didn't want to know because then they expected me to share secrets, too. I didn't do that. I didn't discuss personal things. I was a private person. I dealt with my own stuff my own way and never involved anyone else. I found that kind of intimacy uncomfortable.

I had lots of friends, but I never discussed my problems or innermost thoughts with them. They were friends I had fun with or shopped with or had kiddie play-dates with. I liked it that way. I had never been a girl who spent hours on the phone to her best friend agonizing over a guy. I didn't want someone calling me at three in the morning telling me their marriage was breaking up. I didn't want to know. I didn't want to get involved. I didn't want to listen to it. I didn't lean on people and I didn't want to be leant on. I knew how to fix myself. I'd done it after Jess was born. Private things should remain just that – private.

'Do you think you can get his address?' Mum asked.

'No, Mum. Louise hasn't told me anything about him and she's not going to.'

'I'll call Julie. She'll be able to get it out of her and then I'll call you back with it. If you turned up at his office and confronted him, it would shame him into stepping up to his responsibilities.'

'Fine.' I decided to let Julie deal with Mum. She was better at stonewalling her.

'I'll do that now. By the way, did I hear Gavin's staying in your house while you're away?'

'Yes, I said he could. It'll be nice for Jess and Mimi to have him around.'

'You know he has a new girlfriend?'

'I heard she's gorgeous.'

'Needless to say, he hasn't introduced her to us yet. Mind you, at least he's down from the tree. Thank God for that. Your father can play golf again and get out of my hair. It was driving me crazy having him in the house all the time. Honestly, when Jack retires, make sure he has plenty of hobbies. Men are hopeless at filling their time.'

'I hardly ever see Jack, he works so hard.'

'That's why I went to work in the business with your father. I knew it was the only way I'd see him. Doing the books for the company was a good way of spending time together and for me to get involved. I enjoyed it, actually. I liked being busy.'

'I don't think Jack would appreciate me coming in and trying to be a hedge-fund manager.' I laughed at the thought. 'I actually wouldn't have time to work between the house and my exercise classes and bringing Jess to all her after-school activities – I'm flat out.'

'Does she really need to do ballet, judo, swimming, tennis, music and drama?' Mum thought Jess did far too many things.

'It's what the other girls do and she seems to like it.'

'She's such a sweet little thing. Does she ever give out?'

'Not really, she's very good.'

'You were an easy child, too. You never complained, just got on with it, unlike your sisters. Well, I'd better go and get this number from Julie.'

'OK, 'bye.'

I decided to call Louise to warn her that Mum was trying to track down her invented New York boyfriend.

'Oh, God, she's like a dog with a bone.' Louise groaned.

'She's just thinking of the baby. You should have told her he was killed in a car crash – it would have been easier.'

'He might have to die soon. I can't handle the third degree again. I'm too busy to deal with Mum.'

'Go easy on her. She's worried the baby will feel abandoned.'

'There are millions of single-parent families and the kids grow up to be completely normal.'

'I know, but she's old-fashioned.'

'Well, I'll be able to dodge her for a while. I'm flying to Buenos Aires tonight so Julie can pretend she couldn't get in touch with me.'

'Should you be flying so late in your pregnancy?'

'It's fine. My obstetrician checked my blood pressure and said I'm OK to go.'

'How are you feeling?' I asked.

'Fat.'

'The last part is just awful – you feel like a whale.'

'I can't wait to have stomach muscles again.'

'You're so fit, they'll bounce back. Pilates is really good for that.'

'I've got a personal trainer lined up already. By the way, did you do the Gina Ford routine with Jess?'

'Totally.'

'And it worked?'

'She took a bit longer than Gina said, but she started sleeping through the night from when she was eleven weeks old.'

'I knew it worked. Julie told me to burn the book. She said it's crap.'

'Julie's kids don't sleep!'

'That's exactly what I said.'

'Follow Gina Ford's advice. Her feeding routine is really good too. Are you going to breast-feed?'

'Hardly. I'm going back to work after three weeks, and I've no intention of pumping my boobs like some kind of cow. She'll be on bottles from day one.'

'I did it for six weeks. It was nice, actually.'

'You weren't working twelve-hour days. It's just not a runner for me.'

It really annoyed me the way Louise dismissed my life. I took a deep breath and stayed calm.

'Which buggy should I get?' she asked.

'The Bugaboo Cameleon is streets ahead of the others.' It felt strange having Louise ask me for advice: she never usually asked anyone for their opinion. She always knew best.

'Yeah, that's what I thought.'

'I'm going to New York tomorrow if you want me to get you any baby stuff over there?'

'Thanks, but I've got everything. I just needed to make a final decision on the buggy. How long are you going for?'

'Four days.'

'You should definitely go and see Eugene O'Neill's *The Iceman Cometh*. Apparently the new production is incredible.'

'I think Jack's made plans already, but if not, we'll check it out,' I lied. There was no way I was going to some boring play. The last time we'd gone to New York, Louise had told us to go and see *Krapp's Last Tape*. Jack didn't want to but Louise had gone on and on about it so much I felt under pressure. I swear it was the worst thing I ever saw. Its only saving grace was that it was short.

A guy comes out on stage and eats a banana while playing a tape. Jack kept whispering loudly, '*Krapp's Last Tape* is crap,' and we couldn't stop laughing. The people around us were furious and kept glaring at us and shushing us. When Louise asked me if I'd enjoyed it, I'd just said it was interesting. There was no point in telling her I'd thought it was utter rubbish. She'd have gone on about how I'd missed the meaning of Beckett's exploration of expressing silence through sound, blah-di-blah. I really didn't care: it was just plain boring. Maybe he'd have been better off expressing sound through silence and giving us all a break.

When I was in New York, I wanted to shop, drink cocktails in fabulous bars and go to amazing restaurants. The last thing I was going to do was sit through another 'worthy' play.

We said goodbye and I continued with my packing.

The next morning, Gavin came over. I'd asked him to move in while we went to New York to help out with Jess while we were gone. He threw himself down on the couch and let out a contented sigh. 'God, I love this house. It's so comfortable.'

'It's also clean and I'd like it kept that way.' I pointed to his shoes, which he took off.

'You know I don't want your girlfriend sleeping over. I've never met her and neither have Jess and Mimi, so it's not fair to them. There's food in the fridge but you'll probably want to buy other stuff, so I've left you money for groceries and some new clothes.

You look like a down-and-out in those raggy combats.' I handed him an envelope.

He looked inside. 'Yowser! There's seven hundred quid here.'

'I also need you to help Mimi with Jess. She doesn't drive, so you'll need to bring Jess to swimming on Friday. I've organized for other mums to take her to and from her other extra-curricular activities. Remember to take your shoes off at the front door, and I'm locking our bedroom because I don't want you and your smelly socks in there.'

'Yes, ma'am.' Gavin saluted me. 'Any other orders?'

'If you want a drink, you can have any of the wines in the kitchen wine rack. Do not go near the cellar – that's got Jack's prize possessions in it. And – it goes without saying – don't get drunk in front of Jess.'

'Don't worry, Sophie. I won't throw any wild parties, I'll walk around shoeless and I'll take Jess swimming.'

Mimi came in carrying a basket of laundry. She smiled when she saw Gavin – she was very fond of him. He went over to hug her. 'Hey, Mimi, it's you and me, babe. We've got a free house for four days. Party time!'

'Don't spoil him, Mimi,' I warned her. Gavin had moved in a year ago when we went skiing and Mimi had spent a week cooking him banquets and doing all his laundry and ironing. 'He's perfectly capable of doing his own cooking and laundry.'

'I don't mind. Gavin is nice boy,' Mimi said.

'Right, well, I'd better go.'

'Your flight's in three hours!' Gavin said.

'Yes, but I hate being rushed. I want to have plenty of time to buy magazines and healthy snacks. The food they serve on flights is so fattening.'

I went in to get Jess, who was playing with her dolls. 'Come on, sweetie, we need to go to school now and then Mummy is going away for a few days.'

'Again?' she asked.

'It's only four days – which is actually only three sleepies.'

'Why can't I come?'

'Because it's a work trip for Daddy and Mummy is going to help him. You'd be bored.'

'No, I wouldn't. Please, Mummy, take me too.' Her sweet little chin began to wobble.

I held her shoulders. 'Jess, look at me. It's only three nights and Uncle Gavin and Mimi will be here to look after you. And if you're good I'll bring you back a big present. OK?'

'OK. I'll miss you, Mummy.'

I held her close. 'I'll miss you too, baby. I love you.'

Hours later I checked into our enormous room in the Four Seasons on 57th Street, freshened up and hit the shops.

Later that day I went to meet Jack in Whiskey Blue, the bar in the W Hotel on Times Square. He'd called to say he'd got stuck in work and wouldn't make it back to the hotel. I should hop in a cab and meet him there. When I arrived he was surrounded by three female colleagues, all flirting with him. I plastered a smile on my face, pulled my shoulders back, held my head high and strutted over to him. I was in my Hervé Léger dress and a new pair of Christian Louboutin shoes from Saks. I knew I looked good, but those women were so confident and ballsy they made me nervous.

When Jack saw me, he whistled. 'Babe, you look great.' He kissed me.

'Thanks. So do you.' I moved in beside him, nudging one of the girls out of the way.

'This is Jennie, Samantha and Holly.'

'Can you get me a drink, please?' I asked Jack, barely giving the girls the time of day. I'd seen it all before. Women were always coming on to Jack. He was good-looking, friendly, chatty and rich. Even in Dublin, where everyone knew everyone else, I'd seen women flirting with him at parties we went to. I was damned if any floozy was going to take my man. I worked far too hard at looking good and keeping him happy to let him go.

'Sure. Vodka and soda?' he checked.

'Yes, please.' I smiled.

'So what do you do, Sophie?' one of the girls asked me.

'I'm a full-time mum,' I said.

'You don't work at all?'

'No, I used to –'

Jack turned around to hand me my drink and said, 'Work! Sophie has a degree in shopping and a master's in shoes.'

They all roared laughing. I tried not to let it bother me, but it did. I felt belittled. I glared at Jack. I didn't like him in New York. He was all shouty and loud and brash. At home, he was attentive and affectionate when we were out and was always telling people what a great wife and mother I was. He made me feel loved and appreciated. But with his colleagues in New York he was different. I also felt out of place with his work people. At home I was in charge. I knew where I stood. I was second only to Victoria in looks and style. I had status. People knew who I was. I was comfortable, safe. I was Jack's wife, Jess's mother, Sophie the model-turned-yummy-mummy.

'Sophie, how are you, honey?' Jack's partner in the hedge fund, Brad Hooper, came over to greet me. 'You look sensational! What the hell are you taking? Youth pills? I'll tell you what, Jack, you've got a catch here.'

I leant over and kissed his cheek. 'Thanks, Brad, you look good too. How's Harriet?'

'We're getting divorced.'

'Oh, no. What happened?' Harriet was Brad's second wife. I'd only met her once, but she'd seemed very nice.

'She found out I was screwing my secretary. I know, I'm a walking cliché, but that girl had the best titties I'd ever seen.'

'Brad.' Jack put a hand on his shoulder. 'I don't think Sophie needs the details.'

'Are you still seeing this girl?' I asked.

'No. As soon as she found out Harriet had left me she started putting the squeeze on me to get engaged so I fired her. I don't need another wife or expensive divorce. I'm done with that. I just want someone to have sex with occasionally.'

'Gee, Brad, what a great offer. I'm sure the women will be queuing up to take advantage of it,' I said.

'Honey, this is New York. You can get anything you want.' Brad grinned. Then, throwing an arm around Jack, he added, 'You're very lucky with this boy here. He had women throwing themselves at him in the club last night, but he kept telling them he was happily married. It just made them want him even more. It was a riot. They were like bees to honey.'

I looked at Jack, who shook his head. 'Ignore Brad. He's talking through his arse as usual.'

Brad turned around to order a drink and I pulled Jack aside. 'What nightclub?' I asked.

'It's no big deal. We went for a few drinks after dinner in some new club in SoHo.'

'Who went?'

'Just the office gang.'

'Who was coming on to you?'

'Some random girls. It was nothing and, as Brad said, I told them all I was married.'

'I'd really prefer if you didn't go to nightclubs when I'm not around. It's just putting yourself in temptation's way. Why didn't you just go back to the hotel?'

'Brad wanted to go out and it was a bit of fun. Seriously, relax, it's no big deal. I wasn't tempted by anyone.'

We got interrupted again and the conversation turned to work and how much money they were making. There was a lot of back-slapping, then congratulatory drinks and numerous toasts about someone called Hartley. I watched Jack revelling in it all. What would I do if he was ever unfaithful? Would I forgive him? Would I take him to court and screw him for every penny he owned?

One of the models I used to work with, Daisy, married a very wealthy guy, a real catch, but after years of what seemed like a happy marriage, she found out he'd been having an affair and she left him. She got a big settlement in the divorce, but she was alone. Her life as she'd known it was over. People didn't invite her to parties and balls. She only ever got invited to women's lunches. I hadn't seen her in years until I'd met her at a cystic fibrosis lunch last May. She'd got drunk and was crying to me in the bathroom that she'd never meet another man. I'd tried to reassure her but she said, 'Look, Sophie, I'm forty-one. I can't go to bars on my own looking to meet someone. They'll think I'm a hooker. I never get invited to parties where I might meet a man because the wives don't want any single women around. I've gone from being one of the gang to being a threat. My social life was based around my husband, and now all of his friends' wives have stopped calling. I'm a social pariah. Sometimes I wish I'd forgiven him. And I wish I was still married because I was somebody, I had a place in life. Now I'm no one.'

I was really shaken by that conversation because she was right. The minute her marriage had broken up she was no longer part of the social scene. Single women made married women uncomfortable.

'Hey there, are we boring you with all our work talk?' Jack whispered in my ear.

'I was just thinking I'd like to go back to the hotel and show you my new lingerie.' I winked at him.

That got his attention. He told everyone I was jet-lagged and needed to lie down. We went back to our gorgeous hotel room and had sex in the bed, the bath and the shower. I was damned if any floozy was going to take my man. I'd do whatever I needed to do to keep him happy and satisfied.

The next morning Jack and I went to the gym to work out and then he went to the office. As he was leaving, he kissed me goodbye. 'Spend as much money as you like today, Sophie. Go mad, you deserve it.'

My stomach flipped. I had just been given *carte blanche* to buy anything I wanted. Yippeeeeeee!

I spent four hours in Bergdorf Goodman being worshipped by

the sales lady. I was shown to a huge dressing room, with a wall-to-wall mirror, a couch and a coffee table that had sparkling water and fresh flowers. I was offered champagne, which I accepted, and then Bernice, my new best friend, asked me what my style was and what I was looking to achieve today. I told her that I needed new smart-casual clothes for the daytime, a chic but not OTT look for school pick-ups and coffee mornings, and that I needed glamorous cocktail dresses and ballgowns for the evening events I'd be going to. I told her my favourite designers were Marc Jacobs, Hervé Léger, Dolce & Gabbana, Prada, Jason Wu, Moschino and Vera Wang.

'You must lead a fabulous life,' she gushed.

'I do, actually,' I admitted, sipping my champagne and enjoying every second of this indulgence.

'And you have such an awesome figure – you're so tiny. All the clothes are going to look beautiful on you. You're stunning.'

'Thank you.' I basked in her admiration.

While I put my feet up, Bernice left to go through the shop floor and came back twenty minutes later wheeling a large rail of clothes for me to try on. Everything was gorgeous. I could have bought the entire rack . . . I almost did.

I bought a charcoal grey Moschino coat, two Marc Jacobs jackets – one black, one midnight blue – three pairs of dVb jeans (blue, black and white), a sexy fitted black Dolce & Gabbana dress, two white and two black Prada shirts, an incredible silver Vera Wang evening gown from her Lavender collection, a pair of black Jimmy Choo boots, a pair of Donna Karan wedge sandals and a pair of silver Manolo Blahnik evening shoes to go with my Vera Wang dress. I also bought two Donna Karan casual daytime dresses and two Juicy tracksuits (one pink and one baby blue). The bill came to $11,087.

I winced a bit at the final cost. I'd never spent that much money in one go before. But Jack had told me to indulge myself and he'd said I deserved it, so what the hell? Besides, Victoria did this all the time and she never felt guilty, so why should I? No: I was going to enjoy it and not ruin the buzz with silly regrets. Jack liked me to look good and that cost money.

I handed over my credit card and waited on the couch while my clothes were wrapped and packaged. Bernice came in and said that as I had so many bags the store wanted to offer me their car to take me back to the hotel. I was accompanied downstairs to where a uniformed driver was waiting in front of a silver Bentley. As I climbed into the back seat, I felt like a movie star. People on the street were turning around to see who I was. It felt fantastic.

13
Julie

I picked up the triplets from Montessori and we were driving home when Luke asked, 'Mum, does God love everyone?'

'Yes, He does.'

'Even bad guys?' Leo asked.

'Yes.'

'Even robbers?' Liam wanted to know.

'Yes, He loves everyone.'

'Even when people are bold?'

'Yes. It's just like I love you guys even when you do naughty things.'

'Even when you put us in the bold room?' Leo asked.

'Yes.'

'Even when you shout at us?' Luke wasn't convinced.

'Yes.'

'Even when you say, "I'm sick of this shit"?' Liam reminded me of my bad language.

'I don't say that.'

'Yes, you do – you said it this morning when Luke took all his clothes off and ran into the garden.'

'Well, that was bold of me. I shouldn't say bad words.'

'Do you love us even when you say, "I hate my life"?' Leo sounded worried.

'Yes, I do. Listen, boys, sometimes Mummy says things she doesn't mean, so you mustn't take any notice. I don't hate my life. I love my life. And I love you very much.'

'Even when you say you want to go to Brazil by your own self?' Luke persisted.

Yikes, I really needed to watch my mouth from now on.

'Yes, pet. And you know I'd never go anywhere without you guys. I really, really love you and I know that I shout a lot and I know that I can be grumpy and I'm sorry about that. I'm just tired and sometimes when you're tired you can be snappy. So I'm going to try and be less grumpy and I want you to try and be really good and do what I say. OK?'

'Do you love us more than God?' Leo asked.

'I love you more than anyone.'

'But God's not a person. He's invisible,' he reminded me.

'Yes, that's true.'

'Where does God live?' Liam wanted to know.

'In Heaven.'

'Where is that?'

'In the sky.'

'In a cloud?' Luke was amazed.

'Kind of.'

'If we went in an aeroplane, would we see God?'

'No, you never see Him, but He can see you.'

'Does He have X-ray eyes?' Liam asked.

'Well, yes, in a way He does.'

'Cool,' they all said.

We pulled into the house before the interrogation could go on any longer. They were insatiable. Last year we had gone on a disastrous family holiday to Kerry where it had rained all day, every day. On the five-hour car journey there, the triplets had asked me and Harry endless questions about outer space. After two hours we had cracked, pulled into a garage and bought them piles of sweets to shut them up.

Now, as I was parking, I asked, 'Who do you love, boys?'

'Daddy!' they said in unison. I tried not to let it upset me, but it really did. I broke my back day in and day out for them, but they loved Harry more.

My father was waiting for me at the house. He never called in so this was very unusual.

'Is everything OK?' I asked, jumping out of the car.

'All fine. I just need to talk to you about Louise. Your mother is driving me round the bend. She wants us all to fly to New York and confront this ex-boyfriend of hers.'

'Oh, God! Come on in. You can help me make sandwiches for the boys and then we can chat.'

While Dad made ham sandwiches, I put Tom down for his nap. When I got back to the kitchen Liam was complaining that his crusts hadn't been cut off, Luke was shouting that he wanted his sandwich in triangles, not rectangles, and Leo was telling Dad he hated bread and wanted a cracker sandwich.

'Here's your mother now. She'll sort you out.' Dad looked relieved to see me. 'I don't know how you do it,' he said. 'I've only been here ten minutes and I'm worn out.'

'You get used to it,' I admitted, fixing the sandwiches and handing them to the boys just the way they liked them.

Dad removed a pile of laundry from one of the chairs and sat down. 'Right, about Louise and the baby. What do you know about the father?'

'Nothing,' I lied.

'There never was a boyfriend, was there?' Dad looked directly at me.

I could feel myself blushing. 'I don't really know,' I mumbled.

'I thought so. She was so casual about the break-up and doing it all on her own that I suspected there was no man. Is it one of those sperm banks she went to?'

'No!' I cringed. How did Dad even know about sperm banks? I really did not want to discuss sperm donors with him. I was going to kill Louise for putting me in this situation.

'A married man?' Dad asked.

'God, no, nothing like that.'

'What was it, then?'

'It was just kind of a brief fling.'

'A one-night stand, you mean?'

Now I was discussing casual shags with my father who had never said the word 'sex' in front of me in thirty-nine years. 'Something like that,' I muttered.

'How could someone as bright and sensible as Louise do something so stupid?'

'We all make mistakes,' I defended my sister.

'Louise has never put a foot wrong in her life.'

'Well, I guess there's a first time for everything. But it's worked out well. She seems pretty happy about the baby.'

'She has no idea what raising a child alone is like,' Dad said.

'Neither do you,' I pointed out. 'Maybe it won't be so bad. She's loads of help lined up and she's very organized and capable. If anyone can make it work, Louise can.'

'Where did I go wrong? One fella hugging trees, and my eldest having unprotected sex. What type of children did I raise?'

I needed to get him off the sex talk. 'Louise will be fine and so will Gavin. He's off to London soon anyway, so he'll be out of your hair.'

'Off to London to sit around on his arse doing more protesting.'

'Well, the expansion at Heathrow airport is a bad idea. You should go on to the Greenpeace site. It has a very convincing list of reasons to ban it. In a way you have to admire him for being so passionate about it.'

'Passionate?' Dad spluttered. 'The only reason he's going is because of that gobshite Forest's sister. His penis is controlling his brain.'

'Well, she is pretty gorgeous.'

'Stunning. If I were his age, I'd be tempted to go and live in a field with her, but the point is, he needs to cop on and stop being so easily influenced by other people. I did not spend thousands of pounds on his education for him to end up living in a tent, regardless of how good-looking his tent-mate is.'

'Gavin likes his creature comforts far too much. Don't worry, Dad, he'll be back home soon.'

Dad was on a roll now. He plonked his coffee cup down. 'I'd

144

understand if he wanted to get into politics and become a lobbyist. Or if he studied science or chemistry and worked on finding alternative energy sources. But sitting around in trees or fields protesting is a waste of time.'

'Give him a chance. He's only just out of college. Everyone needs to explore and experiment while they find out what they really want to do.'

'I set up my printing company when I was nineteen. I didn't have time to go around *finding* myself. Kids these days have far too much time on their hands. They're spoilt and indulged. They have no concept of reality, of hard times, of making ends meet. That's the problem with Gavin – he's been spoilt all his life. Your mother and I were too old and tired by the time he came along to discipline him. He got away with murder.'

'Well, that's true. You were definitely much stricter with us girls – he had it very easy. Look, I know he's a bit immature and has no concept of working and managing money or anything like that, but he's a good guy. He'll find his way. He just needs the space to do it.'

'Well, he'd better hurry up. I want him to get a proper job, start earning money and taking responsibility for himself.'

'I dunno, Dad. If I was him I'd stay as carefree as I could for as long as possible. Budgeting and paying bills and a mortgage aren't really a whole lot of fun.'

'He can't be a student all his life. You three girls were living away from home and being independent by the time you were Gavin's age.'

'Well, I bet you after a month he'll come screaming home to a bed, hot meals and clean clothes. He's not cut out for sleeping in mud and building camp fires to cook tofu on.'

Dad laughed. 'He'll die without his cooked breakfast every morning. Now, what am I going to tell your mother about Louise? I'm supposed to come back with the baby's father's details.'

'Couldn't you tell her I was out?'

'I was warned not to come home without the information.'

'Tell her to call Louise. I don't want to get stuck in the middle of this.'

'Louise won't return her calls.'

'Maybe you should just tell her the truth.'

'If I tell her that her eldest daughter, the Cambridge scholar, got pregnant on a one-night encounter, she'll go mad and I'll never hear the end of it.'

'Well, then, tell her that –'

Marian walked through the back door with her four kids in tow, interrupting my flow. Shoot! I'd forgotten we had arranged a play-date.

'Hey, Mr D, how's it going?'

'Hi, Marian, how are you? I see you've been busy since I last saw you.' He pointed at baby Ben.

'You'd think I'd have got my tubes tied in a fucking knot after Molly, but I stupidly didn't and now here I am, breast-feeding at forty-one, I'm too old for this.'

'Well, I'm glad to see the fourth child hasn't mellowed you.' Dad chuckled.

'The only time I'm mellow is when I've had six drinks. Listen, I can come back later if you guys want to chat.'

'No, it's fine – we're just talking about Louise's one-night stand.' I filled her in.

Dad looked a bit surprised that Marian knew all about my slutty sister.

'Don't sweat it, Mr D. I'm the soul of discretion. Julie and I tell each other everything. It gets us through the day. And, believe me, the days are bloody endless.'

Oscar came over and said he was thirsty. I got up to get him a drink.

'Sit down,' Marian ordered me. 'Oscar, you've just had lunch and drunk a litre of apple juice. Now go outside and play and don't come and annoy me until the first number on your digital watch says two.' Marian ushered the triplets, Molly, Brian and Oscar outside. 'Go on, go out and get some fresh air,' she said, as she pushed them through the door and closed it behind them.

'It's very cold out there,' Dad pointed out.

'Oi, come here.' Marian threw their coats outside after them and closed the door again. 'If they're cold they'll have to run around more to keep warm and they'll burn off more energy. So, what's going on with Louise?'

'Dad is trying to figure out how to tell Mum that her eldest daughter is a slapper. She's not going to react well to the truth.'

Marian sat back and thought about it for a minute. 'I know – why don't you tell her that she had a short relationship with this American guy in London and that he gave her his number and address, but when she tried to contact him after he'd gone back to New York, she realized he'd given her false information. That way, Louise wasn't a slut. She was just taken for a ride by a charming arsehole. With no number, no address and not even his real name, there's no way of tracking him down.'

'Impressive,' Dad said.

'I watch a lot of old police shows late at night when I'm up with the baby. You'd be amazed what you pick up.'

'It could work, Dad.' It was the best idea we'd come up with so far.

'I agree,' he said.

'If you want anything else sorted out, you know who to come to. If only I could sort out my own life.'

'What's up?' Dad asked.

'My mother-in-law is coming to stay for two weeks. She thinks Greg is the Messiah and I'm the devil incarnate. She thinks I should be down on my knees thanking God for giving Greg to me. She thinks a wife's place is in the kitchen with an apron on, baking apple pie with a smile on her face. The last time she came to stay I handed Greg a bowl of Crunchy Nut Corn Flakes for dinner and she nearly had a fucking seizure. All the kids had chickenpox and I hadn't been able to leave the house for days. She started telling me that poor Greg needed a decent meal after being out working all day. Why hadn't I gone to the shops and cooked him something nice? I pointed out that my kids looked

147

like they had the plague and the doctor had told me to keep them inside for a few days, and she started telling me that I should have batches of pre-cooked meals in the freezer for emergencies like this.'

'She's dead right.' Dad winked at me. 'A wife's duty is to look after her husband and children. No matter what kind of day my wife Anne had, she always produced a lovely meal for me when I got home.'

'People like her should be shot. She's making women like me look bad.'

Although Dad was winding Marian up, it was true: Mum had always managed to cook dinner for us every night, even with four kids and doing the books for Dad's company. I have no idea how she did it, but she also managed to look smart all the time.

'You modern women want it all – college, careers, husbands, babies and domestic harmony. It doesn't work like that,' Dad told us.

'Hang on there, Mr D, I gave up my job to have babies and look after them. When I worked, I managed a team of twenty-five people, no problem. Now I look after four kids and I can barely get dressed. It's a lot harder than it looks.'

'You also have your mum to look after,' I noted.

'Is she unwell?' Dad asked.

'She's been depressed since my dad left in 1979. She's very optimistic, though. She spends all day looking out the window thinking he's going to come home. Strangely, after nearly thirty-two years of no-show, I don't share her faith.'

'That must have been hard for you,' Dad said.

Marian shrugged. 'I was ten when it happened. I don't really remember him. I feel sorry for my mother. It's a waste of a life. When my kids were born all she said was "It's a pity your dad's not here to see them. He loved children." I just about managed to stop myself pointing out that he obviously wasn't too fucking crazy about them, seeing as he left me and my brother behind.'

'Does your brother have children?' Dad asked.

'No,' Marian said. 'He's gay. My mother thinks it's a phase. She still believes that Rock Hudson was straight and that he died of cancer, not Aids. She thinks Elizabeth Taylor spun the story to make herself look like Florence Nightingale, coming in to save her friend Rock.'

'Interesting theory.' Dad laughed.

'When's Dawn arriving up?' I asked. I knew Marian's mother-in-law was due some time this week.

'Forty-seven hours to go till the witch gets here. I'll be spending the next two days scrubbing. I don't want her commenting on my messy house. I've asked Natalia to come and help me do a big spring-clean tomorrow. I swear I wouldn't mind if Greg left me, but if Natalia left, I'd have a nervous breakdown.'

'Who's Natalia?' Dad enquired.

'My cleaning lady,' Marian explained.

There was a knock on the back door. We looked around to see six frozen faces peering in. Oscar tapped his watch. 'It says two, Mummy.'

I opened the door. 'Come on, I'll make you all a hot chocolate.'

'Right, I'm off,' Dad said. 'Good to see you, Marian, and thanks for the alibi for Louise. It'll make life easier for all of us. Good luck with your mother-in-law. You might consider going easy on the cursing while she's in the house. It's fairly full on.'

'I'm a fucking disgrace,' she agreed.

I walked Dad to the door. 'She's as mad as a hatter,' he said, shaking his head.

'True, but she's a really good friend. Very loyal, and generous to a fault.'

'I'll take your word for it.'

'Good luck with Mum. I'll call Louise later and fill her in on her sordid past!'

Later that evening, after the kids were finally asleep, Harry asked me to come and sit down.

'Oh, God, what's happened?' I asked. 'Have you lost your job?'

'No, but I've had to take another pay cut.'

My heart sank. 'How much?'

'Twelve and a half per cent.'

'But you already took a pay cut last summer.' I couldn't believe it. Harry had been cut by the same amount only six months earlier.

'I know. Look, it's across the board. Everyone has to take it. Believe me, I'm not happy about it. We're stretched as it is.'

'We'll just have to cut back.'

'I've been going through some figures today. If we cancel Sky Sports, Sky Movies and the cartoon channels, we can save over a hundred euros a month.'

'Hold on!' I stopped him. 'You cannot cancel the cartoon channels. They are the only thing I have to bribe the boys with. The hour they watch TV every day is the only time I get to actually do things like laundry, tidy up and read a few pages of my book.'

'They can play with their toys instead. They watch too much TV anyway. An hour a day is more than they need.'

'Harry,' I said firmly, 'you're not with them all day long. I need the cartoons. We can cut back on all the other channels, the heating, on groceries and we'll cancel my birthday trip to Paris, but we're not getting rid of the cartoon channels.' Over my dead body were we getting rid of the TV channels. Harry thought the boys only watched an hour of TV a day. In fact, on very rainy days when we were stuck indoors all afternoon, they sometimes watched considerably more.

'Julie, we're not cancelling the Paris trip.'

'Harry, come on, it's going to cost about two thousand euros for three days. It's too much now.'

'No. I promised you that trip. You deserve that trip. I want to treat you. I want the two of us to get away on our own. We are not cancelling the trip.' He looked upset.

I leant over and took his hand. 'It's OK – we can go next year when things settle down again and the economy perks up. It's just a trip. It's no big deal. We'll go for a nice meal here in Dublin.'

He sighed. 'I suppose it is a lot of money at the moment. I'm sorry, Julie. I know how much you were looking forward to it.'

'Hey, it's no big deal. Paris can wait.' I tried not to look disappointed, but I was utterly gutted. I'd been looking forward to it more than anything I could remember. The thought of three days away from the kids had been keeping me going for months.

'We'll need to cut back the heating bills. I was thinking we could just have it on from half six to half eight in the morning and then again from five till seven in the evening. I know the house is cold, but we'll just have to wear woolly jumpers.'

It was all right for him in his warm office, but we'd be freezing here all day. I'd have to stock up on thermal vests.

'Any way you can cut back on groceries?' he asked.

'I'll bulk buy in Lidl. That should help.'

Harry ran a hand through his hair. 'Julie, I'm really sorry about this. I can't believe we're bloody budgeting again.'

'It's fine, we'll manage. We have four healthy children, and that's all that really matters. And you still have a job. It could be a lot worse.'

'It feels pretty shit from here. I want to provide for my family.'

'You do. This is just a temporary blip that's out of your control. Salaries will come back up. Should we turn the heating off now?'

'No time like the present.'

'We could watch the last night of Sky Movies in our puffy jackets.' I grinned.

'I'll get the hats and gloves.'

'And hot-water bottles.'

'And a rug.'

'A flask of tea should help keep us warm.' I giggled.

He leant over and kissed me. 'I love you, Julie.'

'And well you might. Now go on, make me a cup of tea and bring in the Cadbury's chocolate fingers. It'll be the last time I taste them. They don't sell them in Lidl. It'll be Rich Tea multi-packs from now on. This could actually work out well – I might lose weight.'

While Harry went to make my tea, I sank back into the sofa and tried not to cry.

That night I couldn't sleep. I was really upset about the Paris trip and having to budget again. I was sick of counting pennies. I felt weighed down. I needed to distract myself so I logged on to the mumskeepingsane.com website. I checked to see if there had been any response to my comments. Oh, my God! There were more than sixty replies, all of them saying they felt exactly like I did and asking me to write again.

Threescompany:

Hi,

It's one in the morning and I can't sleep. I was thrilled to see so many responses to my posting. It's very comforting to know so many of you mums feel the same way I do.

My husband came home tonight and told me he has to take another pay cut. It's the second in the last year. We're now down 25 per cent. I cut back a lot the last time so it's going to be hard to cut back further. He wants to get rid of the cartoon channels. I'm sorry but I had to put my foot down. I'd rather live in a house with no heating than lose that hour (or two or, on a very bad day, three hours!) of TV. It's the only time the boys stop moving, shouting, thumping each other, wrestling, throwing things, pushing, diving, rolling and spinning. It's the only time I get to read, or talk to a friend on the phone, or just sit and listen to soothing music.

I need that time out. I need that little window of space. While the triplets are at school I barely have time to do the long list of things, like washing piles of laundry, tidying up after breakfast, grocery shopping . . . That hour when they're watching TV is the only reason I haven't gone off my rocker.

We had to cancel my fortieth-birthday trip to Paris. We'd been planning it for a year. It was going to be our first time away together alone since we had kids. I know it's only a trip and it's not as if someone is sick or dying or anything, but I'm devastated. That holiday was keeping me going. I'd been looking forward to it for months. I think it would have been so good for both of us to get away by ourselves and actually have a conversation about something besides the kids, money, paying bills and what needs to be fixed in the house. I wanted to go away and rekindle romance. Remember why we fell in love . . . Remember who we were before we disappeared under the weight of parenthood . . . Remember how much fun we used to have together . . . How we loved spending hours wandering around London, holding hands, talking about our hopes and dreams . . . lying in bed on Sunday mornings roaring laughing about the antics of the night before . . . having spontaneous sex everywhere . . . kissing for hours . . . telling each other how wonderful the other person was . . . how much we loved and admired them . . . how they were our soul-mate . . . how lucky we were to have found each other . . . how no one else had ever made us feel like this . . . how we wanted to spend the rest of our lives together and have children . . .

Anyway, we can't afford it now, so it's been cancelled. We'll go out for dinner, probably with my family, and it'll be fine.

I'm scared too. What if my husband loses his job? He's a civil servant so, as jobs go, it's very safe, but what if he does lose it? We'd be on the street within a month. We have no savings. We put everything into the house and the kids have been more expensive than we'd thought. I do have some money my dad gave me,

153

but I refuse to touch that. It's for the boys' education. I will not go near it unless we're really desperate. It's their future.

But what if my husband is made redundant? I haven't worked in six years. I had a job in recruitment in London. That's all I know how to do. But there aren't any jobs in recruitment, especially not for someone who's been at home for six years. I can just about use the Internet and email. I've no idea how to use Excel or PowerPoint or any of those computer programs. I can make a mean spaghetti Bolognese with hidden vegetables, and excellent flapjacks, but that's about it. If my husband does lose his job I can't go out and work and support us. Who wants to hire a mum? It's made me realize how dependent we are on him. It must be a lot of pressure for him. He knows that if he can't work, we'll be on the street. Obviously my family would help, but the bottom line is that we're really only a couple of pay cheques away from being homeless. It terrifies me. I think I need to learn a new skill. But where would I find the time? Even when the triplets are in school, I always have the baby with me.

You read about these women with fifteen kids and no husband, living in a shack somewhere, who go back to college, study medicine and become neurosurgeons. But realistically, by the time I've dropped the boys to school, driven into medical college, parked, got to the lecture hall with my little one in his buggy, I'd have to turn right around and leave to be back in time to pick the triplets up. How do these women do it? Are they real? Or are they just stories made up to make us real mortals feel even worse about our inability to achieve anything?

It is an achievement of sorts to stop your children choking, breaking limbs, drowning in the bath, running under a car, burning themselves, cutting off fingers with sharp knives, overdosing on tablets they find wherever you hide them, electrocuting themselves with sockets and TV plugs, drinking bleach,

getting bitten by dogs, knocked unconscious by swings or suffocated by plastic bags . . . I'd like to see a neurosurgeon who can
do all that!

Anyway, it's now almost two and I'll be up in four hours, so I'd
better sign off. Hang in there, Mums . . . Talk soon.

14

Louise

I dragged myself out of bed and waddled to the bathroom. I caught sight of myself in the mirror: I was disgusting. My boobs were stuck to my huge bump. It was gross. I hated the way I looked. How the hell could anyone think this was natural? What the hell was natural about your stomach muscles being stretched to breaking point? I had all these revolting stretchmarks all over my body. They'd better bloody go when the baby arrived.

I liked having small, pert boobs. I really disliked having large, saggy, fleshy lumps. I'd had to give in and buy some of those hideous maternity bras that looked like they could harness watermelons. And the clothes for pregnant women were a disgrace. It was very difficult to look smart and business-like in wrap dresses that didn't wrap fully or stretchy-waist trousers. I was finding the whole thing utterly unbearable – thank God I had only two weeks to go. I'd had enough.

Mum called to confirm the date of my C-section. I was tempted to lie, but I knew she would never forgive me so I didn't. She had been easier to deal with since she'd discovered the baby's father was a charming fraud who had made a fool of me – although she'd kept asking me if I'd given him any money. Maybe she thought he'd run off with my life-savings too. I'd assured her I wasn't that stupid.

'Well, you were foolish enough.' She sniffed.

'Romantically, perhaps,' I said, through clenched teeth, 'but not financially.'

'I'm glad to hear it. You'll need all the money you have to raise the baby alone. Children are not cheap.'

'I realize that.'

'Well, you were always good with money, much better than your sisters. I remember you asking me to put your Communion money in the post office because it had the best interest rate.'

'I've always wanted to be financially independent.'

'With all that hard work, you've certainly achieved it. And now you're about to become a mother. It'll be wonderful.' Mum's voice began to quiver. Oh, no, I couldn't handle her crying. 'Wait until you see how your life will change. I just wish you'd take some time off before the baby arrives. Going in to have a baby when you're exhausted is a sure way to get post-natal depression.'

'Mum, I've never been depressed in my life. I'm not going to start now. The only thing that would depress me is not being able to work. I think a lot of people's depression comes from having too much time on their hands to navel-gaze and feel sorry for themselves.'

'That's nonsense, Louise. Post-natal depression is very serious. Your poor auntie May had it very badly.'

'Well, I won't be getting it, so you don't need to worry. Now I really have to go.'

'OK. We'll all see you very soon. Now, mind yourself,' she said, as I hung up.

The birth was turning into a circus. Mum, Dad, Julie, Sophie and even Gavin were coming over. I sat down on my bed again and surveyed my clothes. It was Saturday so I didn't need to squeeze into a suit. I opted for a sweatshirt and baggy tracksuit bottoms I had bought. I hated badly fitting clothes but they were very comfortable. I stood up, went into the sitting room and sank into the couch. I put my feet in the air and turned on my laptop. There was an email from Zachary Gray, CEO of Higgins, Cooper & Gray, congratulating me on the Hollywell deal and saying what an asset I was to the company and how they wanted to show their appreciation with an early bonus. It looked like the hellish trip to Argentina had been worth it after all . . .

*

The Buenos Aires episode had been a nightmare. My back was killing me on the plane. I spent most of the thirteen-hour flight shuffling around, desperately trying to get comfortable so I could sleep. Usually on flights, I lie back and sleep for the entire journey. I've trained myself to do it, so that I arrive fresh and ready to go straight to meetings. But by the time I landed in Argentina, I was utterly exhausted. I looked and felt a mess.

I had just enough time to get to the hotel and have a quick shower before meeting Eduardo Rodriguez. But it was summer there and very hot. I had no idea that you could sweat so much when you were pregnant in a hot climate. I arrived at the meeting with two wet patches under my arms. My grey dress was stuck to my back and there were beads of perspiration running down my face. I tried to reapply my makeup in the taxi, but the minute I put it on, it began to melt.

Rodriguez, who had agreed in principle to the merger, had suddenly started to drag his heels, saying he didn't feel the offer was good enough. He had the ability to tip the balance so we really needed him to sign. Failure was not an option. I'd spoken to his solicitor the day before and he had said Rodriguez wanted to go through the details again before he agreed to sign anything. I had no problem with that. I'd been working on it since day one. I knew this deal inside out.

We had arranged to meet at Rodriguez's house, which turned out to be a mansion. The driveway was at least half a mile long and lined with an incredible array of purple, red and yellow flowers. I heaved myself out of the taxi. The front door was opened by a uniformed maid, who led me through a vast, tiled hall into the back garden, where her boss was sitting on the terrace drinking a gin and tonic by the swimming-pool. I held out a damp hand to greet him. He stood up, raised my hand to his lips and kissed it lightly. He was about seventy, tall with slim arms and legs but a protruding stomach that looked as if it had been fed too much red wine and steak. His face was very lined from the sun, but he had nice brown eyes. He had a full head of grey hair and was dressed in light cream linen trousers and a white shirt that was open almost to his navel – it did him no favours. I sat in the shade and tried to stop sweating.

He looked surprised when he saw my large bump. 'Señora Devlin, I had no idea you were with child.'

'Oh, yes.'

'When is the baby coming?'

'Five and a half weeks exactly. I'll be glad when it's over.'

'But it is the miracle of life. It is wonderful.'

'Uhm, yes, I suppose it is.'

'You don't seem very *entusiasmada. Cómo se dice en inglés?*'

'Enthusiastic?'

'*Sí*, yes, enthusiastic.'

'Oh, no, I am,' I pretended, and changed the subject. The last thing I wanted to talk about was my bloody pregnancy. I didn't want to be seen as a Mother Earth type, I wanted to be seen as a kick-ass lawyer.

In my research I had discovered that Rodriguez was a polo fanatic. He had even played professionally for ten years. 'I believe you are an excellent polo player,' I said.

'It is the passion of my life. First polo, then sex and then business.'

'That's a great list. Speaking of business –'

He held up his hand. 'Louisa, it's too early to talk about business. You've just arrived. Relax, have a drink and something to eat. Business can wait.'

I didn't want to relax and eat. I wanted to get on with the meeting so I could close the deal, go back to my hotel, take my clothes off and drift into a deep sleep in an air-conditioned room. I'd never been so tired in my life.

'If you are too hot, you are welcome to go for a swim to cool down.'

'Oh, thanks, but no. I'm fine.'

'But your face, it is very red. Go for a swim – it will be good for you and the baby. He is too hot in there, I think.'

'No, thanks, really. I'm not that hot,' I assured him, while dabbing beads of sweat from my forehead with my handkerchief.

'Just take your clothes off and jump in. We are not in London where everyone is so – *cómo se dice*? Full of reserve. In Argentina, we are more relaxed. Don't be nervous – take off your clothes and jump in. Be naked, be free. I'll find you a towel.' He stood up and went into the house to fetch one.

Did he really just ask me to swim naked in his pool? Even if I had a full wetsuit I wouldn't swim in his pool – pregnant or not. This was work, not a bloody nudist party. I took a deep breath and waddled after him into the house to stop him.

I met him coming back with a large towel. 'I won't be needing that. I'm not going swimming,' I said firmly. 'Now, if you don't mind, I'd really like to talk about the merger.'

He wagged a finger at me. 'Louisa, Louisa, did your mother not tell you that all working and no play is bad for you?'

'Yes, you're right, but I've travelled a long way to discuss the merger with you and I'd like to get to it as soon as we can. I believe you have some questions?'

He looked me up and down. 'I find pregnant women very sensual. The way your body changes to accept the baby. Your stomach growing like a melon and your breasts getting full of milk to feed the child. Your nipples growing to give the baby a perfect place to suck.'

If I was red before, I was purple now. The conversation was making me sweat twice as much. Was he crazy? Was he trying to wind me up? I knew Argentinian men were known to be flirty, but come on! The guy was ancient and I was about to give birth. How desperate was he? I was a bloody humpback whale! Did he really want to sleep with Moby Dick?

'Let's sit down and go through some of the details.' I was determined to remain professional.

'Louisa darling, love your body. Feel the beauty of what you are creating. Why don't we swim naked in my pool and go upstairs and make love?'

'What?'

'I would like to make love to you until you scream with the ecstasy. If you are not comfortable with my penis being close to the baby, I will make love to your behind.'

Anal sex! Was this guy for real?

'Eduardo, let's get something clear. There will be no sex, front or back.'

'Louisa, *querida*, you are like an angry cat. You need to let your emotions out. I can help you. I have made love to hundreds of women – white, black, Asian. They all had the best time. I love to satisfy women and God gave me a big penis to help me do that. Come to my bedroom and let me show you.'

I began to panic. Where was the maid? Was I alone? What if he lunged? I'd have to trip him up and roll on top of him to squash him. I looked around for something to hit him with.

He reached out to take my hand. I swatted him away. I stared him in the eyes. 'I am leaving now, Eduardo. When you are ready to discuss business, call my hotel.' I stormed out of the door and down the driveway, only realizing halfway that I had no idea where I was or how to get a taxi. I walked for twenty minutes before one finally came along.

I arrived back to the hotel, dripping with sweat, falling down with exhaustion and furious. How dare that pervert try to have sex with me? How dare he proposition me? I had a cold shower and crawled into bed. What a creep! How the hell was I going to deal with him? I'd have to get him to come to the hotel and have our meeting in a public place. I really didn't want to see him again, but I was not going back to London without his signature. As I was about to fall asleep, my phone rang. It was Alex and Dominic from the office.

'How's it going, Louise?' Alex asked.

'Um, OK.'

'Have you met him yet? Has he signed the Hollywell papers?'

'We had a brief meeting today but we didn't discuss details. We're meeting up again tomorrow,' I lied.

161

'Has he propositioned you yet?' Alex asked.

'What?'

'He's supposed to be a total pervert.' Dominic snickered.

'How do you know that?'

'Simon Hollywell mentioned it to me over lunch. Guys' talk,' Alex admitted.

'Why the hell did no one mention it to me?' I snapped.

'To be honest, I forgot. I presume he didn't try anything on with you in your current condition,' Alex said.

'Well, he did.'

'What? The pervert. Are you all right?' Alex was shocked.

'I'm fine.'

'You don't sound fine, you sound very shaken.' Dominic feigned concern. 'Maybe you should come home. I can fly over and deal with him, man to man.'

I had a choice: I could rant about what had happened and make a huge deal out of it, or I could play it down, get the papers signed as soon as possible and get the hell out of Argentina. I knew if I showed how angry and upset I was, they'd see it as a weakness: a woman who can't handle a bit of a flirt. So I bit my tongue.

'Don't be ridiculous, Dominic. I'm perfectly capable of handling Eduardo. You just concentrate on Singapore. When are you off?'

'First thing tomorrow,' he said.

'Well, don't mess up. I have to go. I've got work to do. Alex, I'll call you when the deal is done.' I snapped my phone shut and lay back on the bed. How dare Alex not warn me about Eduardo being a pervert? If I'd known, I would never have agreed to meet him alone at his house. I was furious. I'd be having stern words with him when I got back – in private, without that weasel Dominic listening in.

My phone rang again. It was Simon Hollywell. Simon was a self-made man from the East End of London. One of the reasons he had hired my firm was because I was Irish. His mother, to whom he was devoted, was Irish, and when I had approached Simon to represent his company in the merger, he'd felt we had a kinship of sorts.

'That Argentinian pervert just told me he tried to shag you. You all right, love?' he asked.

'I'm fine. I was taken by surprise, though. I wish you'd warned me.'

'I told Alex he was a randy bugger. But I have to be honest, I didn't think even Eduardo would try it on with a pregnant woman. These South Americans, they'd shag a donkey.'

'I look more like a hippo.'

Simon laughed. 'Glad to see you still have a sense of humour. Anyway, I gave him a right bollocking and I told him to stop arsing up the deal. He knows it's a good price, he's just trying to throw his weight around. He's going to meet you in the lobby tomorrow morning with his lawyer to sign the papers. Then you can get the hell out of there before someone else tries to shag you.'

I closed my eyes and exhaled deeply. 'That's great news. Thanks for helping out.'

'I owe you. My mother would kick my arse to Galway and back if she knew I'd put a nice Irish girl into a sticky situation with a randy old man. Now, get some kip and I'll talk to you tomorrow.'

'OK, thanks.'

'Sweet dreams. Think of beating him to death with his polo stick or something.'

'Sounds good to me.'

The next day a sheepish Eduardo signed the agreement and I got the first plane out of there.

15
Sophie

I packed everything I needed for the three days in London and left some room in the case for new purchases. I probably wouldn't have that much time to shop, but I was hoping to have a quick look in Selfridges the morning after Louise's baby was born.

Jess hadn't freaked out about me leaving because Jack was at home and had promised to look after her every day and have dinner with her on the two nights I was gone.

'OK, Mummy, I understand that you want to be with Louise for her baby because she has no husband.'

'Thanks, Jess. I know Daddy will take good care of you.'

Jack put his arm around Jess. 'We'll have a great time. I'll even watch *The Princess and the Frog* with you,' he promised.

'The whole way through? With no computer?' Jess looked thrilled. Jack always had his laptop with him.

'The whole thing – and I promise to leave my computer in my office.'

'Ooooh, great. Can we have popcorn?'

'Yes, angel, we can.'

'And jellies?'

'Yes.'

'OK, but only a few,' I warned.

'Of course.' Jack winked at Jess.

I put my coat on. 'It sounds to me like you're going to have great fun. I kind of wish I wasn't going now.'

'Come on, you can't miss Louise becoming a mum. I'm dying to hear how it goes. I just can't picture it. She's such a career woman. I don't see her turning into Mother Earth. I think she'd be terrifying to have as a mother.'

'That's a bit harsh. She has a softer side.' I fastened my buttons.

'Really? She hides it well.'

'She's just very independent.'

'Look, I admire what she's achieved. It's seriously impressive. I just think her talent lies in the law, not babies.'

'Louise is so capable, I'm sure she'll make it work. Although I do think three weeks' maternity leave is crazy.'

'I agree. Remember how difficult you found it in the beginning? You were all over the place.'

I bristled. 'It's very stressful at first, when you don't know what you're doing.'

'Well, as you say, Louise is very capable so she'll probably cope better than other women. Thank God you managed to get back to yourself so soon. Some of the guys I know said their wives went to pieces. They didn't get dressed for months, got fat and grumpy and nagged them every time they walked through the door.'

I turned around to pick up my bag. If only you knew, I thought.

I'd told the others I'd meet them in the airport. Mum and Dad were bringing Gavin and there was no way I was picking up Julie. She never arrived until the last minute. When we were younger we went on this one family holiday to Spain – it was a really big deal, a huge treat. Julie wandered off in the airport and we all got into a total panic looking for her. The airport security was calling her name over the intercom, but she was completely oblivious to it. She eventually strolled up to the boarding gate with ten seconds to spare. It took Dad the whole two-hour flight to calm down.

The other reason I didn't offer to pick up Julie was because I didn't want to sit beside her on the plane. I knew it was mean, but she was bringing Tom and I just did not want to be covered with yoghurt and dribble. Neither did I want to play peek-a-boo for an hour. I wanted to read the new catwalk special *Elle* magazine in peace.

I arrived at the airport early, bought some magazines and a low-fat soy-milk latte and sat down to wait. Twenty minutes later, Mum, Dad and Gavin arrived.

'Oh, my God! What did you do to your hair?' I asked my brother.

'I don't want to talk about it.' He pulled down his hat.

Tight curly ringlets were sprouting out from under it. 'Did you get a perm?' It looked ridiculous.

'I asked the dickhead hairdresser for dreadlocks.'

'And he gave you ringlets?' I tried not to laugh.

'It's so humiliating.' Gavin groaned. 'The dude was a total amateur.'

'I dunno – the Shirley Temple look suits you.' Dad snorted.

'Seriously, Dad, this is not funny. I do not want Acorn to see me like this.'

'Why did you go to a hairdresser who clearly has no idea what he's doing?' I asked.

'He was cheap.'

'There's a reason for that,' I noted.

'I know that *now*! I look like a total dork and I'm meeting Acorn this afternoon. What the hell am I going to do? She'll dump me when she sees the state of me.'

'Don't worry. I can straighten it with my GHD when we get to the hotel. We'll have you looking normal before you see her.'

'Really? That'll work? Oh, thank God! You're a life-saver, Sophie!'

'How long are you planning to stay in London?' I asked.

He shrugged. 'Dunno, really – until they stop the Heathrow expansion plan, I guess.'

'Or until I go over there and kick your arse back home,' Dad muttered.

'He's promised to come home in August and look for a real job,' Mum said.

'Thanks for the support. I'm actually trying to save the planet from pollution and meltdown for your grandchildren. Louise's kid will be sucking diesel if this airport expansion goes through.'

'You can donate half your salary to any cause you want when you get a decent job.' Dad glared at him.

'Did you not see *An Inconvenient Truth*?' Gavin asked.

'No. I watch films to be entertained, not depressed,' Dad retorted.

'You have to get on board, Dad. We're talking about the future of the planet. You can't ignore it. It's your generation's fault that we're in this mess. We have to get the governments to facilitate a low-carbon economy. The developed world has to lead the way in tackling these challenges and show the developing world how to do it.'

'Did you swallow a Greenpeace brochure?' I asked.

'You lot are always blaming my generation for everything,' Dad barked. 'Let me tell you something. The world is a lot better today than it used to be. I happen to think planes are fantastic. I like travelling. I have no intention of giving it up. And, in case you hadn't noticed, you're about to board a plane to get to your demonstration. If you feel that strongly about carbon footprint, why didn't you put your togs on and swim across the shagging Irish Sea?'

'There's no point talking to you – you're a lost cause.' Gavin crossed his arms in defiance.

'It would appear that the pot is calling the kettle black,' Dad replied.

'OK, guys. That's enough. Just agree to disagree.' I interrupted them before it got really heated.

Our flight was called. Still no sign of Julie. I rang her mobile. No answer.

'I hope she doesn't miss the flight,' Mum said. 'She's the only one who can get through to Louise. I want her to persuade Louise to let me be there for the birth.'

'Mum, Louise wants to be on her own. You have to let it go,' I said.

'You've had a child, Sophie. Would you have liked to be alone when Jessica was born?'

'No, but Louise is different from me. She likes doing things on her own.'

'Just talk to her.'

'She doesn't listen to me.'

'Try harder,' Mum said firmly.

They announced our flight would soon be boarding. Just as I was about to try Julie's mobile again, she came hurtling around the corner. Tom was in his buggy, wearing pyjamas covered with Weetabix. Julie's hair was wet. She was wearing jeans that were too tight for her, and an old sweatshirt that said 'Greece '98' on it. 'Thank God I didn't miss it. I was so scared I would.' She looked completely strung out.

'Sit down here and catch your breath,' Mum said. 'Why are you so late?'

Julie sat down. 'The triplets put my passport down the loo.'

'Little buggers,' Dad said.

'I was having a ten-second shower, and when I got out I saw it floating. So I had to fish it out and dry it with the hair-drier.'

'Why didn't you just bring your driving licence instead?' Dad asked.

'Because Luke coloured the entire thing in with black marker a month ago and I haven't had time to replace it.'

'It's a bloody zoo,' Dad mumbled.

'Then, while I was drying my passport,' Julie continued, 'Liam poured a smoothie into my suitcase, so I had to take the clothes out and repack.'

'Where was Harry?' I asked.

'He'd gone to the shops – we'd run out of milk and bread. I was terrified they wouldn't let me through security with my soggy passport.'

'Sit down there and drink this.' Mum handed Julie her tea, and picked Tom up from the floor where he was about to put a filthy lollipop he'd found into his mouth.

Julie took a sip of tea and sighed deeply. 'It would be really nice, just for once, to be able to leave the house without utter chaos. You had four kids, Mum. When does it get easier?'

'I spaced mine out, pet. You were unlucky to have three at the same time. It's hard for you. Maybe you should consider boarding school.'

'That's a great idea. It would make your life so much easier,' I agreed. With the triplets away all week, Julie would get her life back.

'Believe me, I've thought about it, but it costs a fortune and we're skint. Anyway, I'd probably miss the scallywags.'

Tom came over to me. He was about to put two sticky hands on my new dVb jeans. I jumped back, spun him around before he did any damage, then lifted him up and plonked him on Julie's knee. I didn't want him near me. Thank God I'd checked in early.

'Jesus, Gavin, what did you do to your hair?' Julie asked. 'You look less like Jason Donovan and more like Kylie.'

'For fuck's sake.' Gavin pulled his hat down further.

'He was trying to get dreadlocks,' I explained.

'Was the hairdresser blind?' Julie grinned.

'Do you think Acorn will dump me?' Gavin asked.

'I'd say she might,' Julie mused, 'considering that she looks like Angelina Jolie, only hotter, and you now look ridiculous.'

'Cheers, Julie, I feel so much better now.'

Julie put her arm around him. 'Come on, you know you'll always be gorgeous to me.'

When we boarded, I was at the front of the plane beside two clean, non-sticky, non-mush-covered businessmen. Perfect. I sat back and circled all the new fashions I liked in *Elle*. The hour flew by.

We shared a black cab to the hotel, which Louise had booked and paid for. It was around the corner from her apartment in Chelsea. I'd never stayed there before because Jack always booked the Dorchester when we were in London, but I knew

Louise would choose somewhere nice so I wasn't worried. The Draycott turned out to be very chic and close to some great shops.

'Wow.' Julie grinned as we walked through the stylish lobby.

'This must be costing her a fortune.' Gavin whistled.

'I wanted to stay with Louise in her apartment. I thought this hotel was a ridiculous expense, but she wouldn't have it.' Mum sniffed.

'It looks good to me,' Dad said, picking up a newspaper.

'I can't wait to see my room.' Julie clapped her hands. 'It's so exciting to be away with only one child.'

I checked in first. 'Hi, I'd like a double bed, not twins,' I told the receptionist. 'Also, I don't want to be near a busy street or close to the air-conditioning vents or the kitchens. I'm sensitive to noise.'

'You can put me anywhere. I can sleep in a tornado,' Julie said, over my shoulder.

'Can we just get on with it?' Dad huffed.

I went to my room. We had arranged to be downstairs at seven fifteen. We were meeting Louise for dinner at seven thirty and she hated anyone being late. I looked at my watch: it was twenty past five. I had time for a nap and would still have an hour to get ready.

There was a knock on the door. It was Gavin. 'Dude, you need to sort out my hair.'

'Sorry, I forgot. Come on in.'

He sauntered in and saw my outfits laid out on the bed. 'Did you need to pack everything you own? You're only here for a few days.'

'I like to have choices so I always pack extra.'

'You have enough choice there for three weeks.'

'You like trees, I like clothes. Sit down. Let's fix this mess.'

I ironed out the awful ringlets and made him presentable. 'There, she won't dump you now.'

'Thanks. I owe you big-time. I swear, Sophie, I am so into Acorn. She's my perfect woman.'

'Are you in love with her?'

'I dunno about love, but definitely in lust. She has a body to die for.'

'You must like her if you're willing to live in a tent with her. I wouldn't even do that for Jack.'

Gavin laughed. 'Come on, Sophie, you'd do anything for Jack.'

'Not anything.'

Gavin shrugged. 'Look, I think it's cool – you guys have a great thing going. He earns shedloads of cash, you live in an amazing house, drive cool cars, he gives you loads of money to spend and you never nag him or say no to him.'

'I do say no to Jack.'

'When?'

I frowned. When was the last time I had said no to Jack? I couldn't remember. I suppose I didn't say no to him, but he never said no to me either. Come to think of it, we never argued.

'Dude, you guys have the perfect relationship. Of all my sisters, I think you've got the best set-up by far. You won the lotto when you married Jack. I'd love to marry a millionairess – it'd be so cool never to have to worry about money. Look at poor Julie – she's always stressed about being broke.'

'You're right. I am lucky.'

'Well, thanks again for sorting my hair. I've got to fly. I'm meeting Acorn in twenty minutes.'

'Hey, Gavin?'

'Yeah?'

'Treat her to a few cocktails.' I handed him a fifty-pound note.

'You're the best.' He kissed my cheek.

'Have fun, but don't be late for dinner – you know what Louise is like about time.'

'I'll be there.' He strutted out, flicking back his straight hair.

I climbed into bed and listened. It was quiet. I'd been given a good room. I lay back on the pillows and closed my eyes.

'"E-I-E-I-O, and on that farm he had a *cat*, E-I-E-I-OOOOOO!"'

No! Julie was singing bloody 'Old MacDonald Had A Farm' to Tom. They must be in the room next door. I put a pillow over my head and groaned. I couldn't exactly call Reception and complain about my own sister's singing. Damn! I'd wanted to rest before dinner. I put in my ear-plugs but I could still hear her. How did she do it? She looked exhausted and there she was singing and clapping.

I tried to imagine Louise with a toddler. I couldn't see her sitting at play-groups singing 'Row, Row, Row Your Boat'. I couldn't picture her singing at all. I don't think I'd ever heard Louise sing. I used to love singing to Jess. When she was tiny and I was burping her after her feeds, I'd sing to her. She always smiled. She was such a sweet baby, so easy. But even so I'd found it hard, very hard . . .

At first I was ecstatic: a healthy baby girl. Jack was thrilled – he had wanted a boy, but the minute he set eyes on Jess he fell in love with her. However, when I got home from hospital three days after the birth, I realized that Jack wanted everything to be the same. He'd presumed the baby would just sleep in its own room and that Mimi would look after her in the evenings when he was home from work and we were having dinner and also at night if she woke up crying.

He didn't think Jess would be sleeping with us, or waking up five times a night screaming for milk. After a few nights of very little sleep he got annoyed. He said he needed his rest. He couldn't go to work exhausted. He said he'd made a mistake that day, due to lack of sleep, and it had cost the firm money. I suggested that I move into a different room with Jess until she settled. He didn't disagree.

I didn't mind – in fact, it was much easier. I could breast-feed her in peace and we bonded well. But when Jack came in from work on my third week home and found me still in my pyjamas, not showered, bleary-eyed, with leaking breasts, he didn't like it. He started to make comments, like 'Where's my beautiful wife?', 'Didn't you have time to get dressed?', 'Give the baby to Mimi, for God's sake. She's here to help you.'

But I didn't want to give Jess to Mimi. I was afraid that if I didn't look after her myself, she'd stop breathing, or choke on a burp, or pull her blanket over her head, or get too hot or too cold . . . I was afraid all the time. I was obsessed with the idea that Jess was going to die if I didn't watch her like a hawk. I couldn't sleep at night. I'd wake up every ten minutes and check she was breathing. It was completely irrational, but I couldn't control the fear and it got worse. I found myself crying a lot because I was so tired and worried. I didn't tell anyone how I was feeling. I pretended everything was fine and put people off from visiting, saying I had an infection and was laid low. I didn't want anyone to see me out of control . . . failing as a mother . . . falling apart.

When I tried to explain it to Jack, he didn't understand. 'Don't be ridiculous, she's not going to die. She's a healthy baby. You need to leave her with Mimi, get dressed and get out of the house. You've been locked up here for more than a month – no wonder you're getting paranoid. Call one of your girlfriends, go out for lunch, go for a run, buy some new clothes – do whatever you want but get on with your life. Try to get back to normal. You're letting it all get on top of you.'

Normal? I no longer knew what normal was. My vagina still stung every time I peed. My breasts ached and leaked. I was sweating all the time and my hair was falling out in clumps.

Jack continued dispensing advice: 'Come on, Sophie, perk up. We've got that ball for the children's hospital next Friday. It'll be good for you to get dressed up in that sexy red dress with the plunging back that I love, and have a few drinks. You need to relax, get yourself back. This neurotic person is not the Sophie I know and love.'

I tried on the red dress. It was too tight. I cried for three hours when I couldn't fit into it, but I didn't have the energy to go out and shop for a new one. So I just stopped eating. I survived on apples and pears for a week. I was even more exhausted and barely producing enough milk for Jess, which upset me even more. I had to start giving her formula so she wouldn't starve.

Mimi tried to talk to me, but I didn't want to talk. She made me lunches that I never ate and begged me to take naps that I never took. The only people who had visited were Mum and Julie. I'd tried to put them off, but they had insisted on coming to see me. They sensed I was struggling. But on the day they came, I forced myself into the shower, got dressed, put makeup on and pretended I was fine, just a bit tired. I was able to convince them because, for those few hours, I convinced myself that everything was fine. The minute they left I fell apart again.

After starving myself for a week I was able to fit into the red dress. I put on lots of makeup and added a small hairpiece to make my own hair look less limp. I stuck pads on my breasts to soak any leakage. When Jack got in from work that Friday, I was ready.

'There's my gorgeous wife. She's back. I missed you.' He kissed me.

Somehow I got through the night, and everyone kept saying how great I looked. All the women stared at my stomach to see if I'd lost the baby weight and then asked me how I'd done it. When we got home Jack wanted to have sex, but I said it was too soon. I told him we had to wait until after my six-week check-up. I told him I was still too sore. He sighed and rolled over. I went to the spare room and was up half the night with a hungry baby.

My days consisted of crying, feeding Jess, crying and then passing out whenever I couldn't stay awake any longer. But every day at five o'clock I handed Jess to Mimi, showered, got dressed, put on my makeup and was ready to greet Jack when he came home. I played with my dinner while he ate his and then at eleven, when

I couldn't keep my eyes open, I went to bed with my baby daughter, not my husband.

At my six-week check-up, I couldn't keep the façade in place any longer. I was hysterical with exhaustion and anxiety. I told my obstetrician everything and she was very understanding. She said lots of women struggled with newborn babies and I needed help to get me over the hump. She prescribed a mild dose of Prozac. I went to the chemist and got it, then sat in the car staring at the tablets. Prozac: anti-depressant, mood-enhancer, happy pill.

Was I weak? Was I pathetic? Why couldn't I cope with my baby? Why was I falling apart? What the hell was wrong with me? Although my doctor had been very sympathetic to my struggles, she had three children and worked full-time. She wasn't crying all day. She was able to get dressed and hold down a serious job. Even Julie, with triplets, was able to cope. I didn't see her popping pills. She was tired and worn out, but she was managing. She had three times the work I had. Three times less sleep. Three times more worry. Why was I such a basket case?

I'd always been able to control my emotions in the past. As a model I had faced rejection daily. I'd learnt not to take it personally. I'd just moved on to the next job. I'd never looked back, only looked forward. No matter what happened, no matter how much I wanted a job, or how hurt I was when I broke up with someone, I never got depressed. I just blocked it out and moved on. I'd never felt out of control before. I'd always had a game plan, a goal, a solution. But now . . . now I found myself drowning and I needed help. I had to get back on track or I'd lose Jack. I had to get myself together. I had to . . .

I started taking the tablets and hoped for the best. Initially there was no difference and I panicked even more. But slowly they began to take effect and after a couple of weeks the dark cloud started to lift. I began to stop panicking about Jess dying. I began to want to get up. I began to care about how I looked.

I began to exercise. I read Gina Ford's *The Contented Little Baby Book* and got Jess into a nice routine. I began to get my life back. I began to sleep with Jack again, have sex again, be a couple again. He was delighted, and so was I. But most of all I was relieved – and very grateful to have come back from the brink.

I continued to take Prozac for a year; no one ever knew. But I swore then that I would never have another baby. I knew in my heart that, if I did, the depression would come back and I might not be able to control it or hide it from everyone. The next time it might pull me under.

16

Julie

I lay in my bubble bath and closed my eyes. It felt wonderful. Tom was plonked in front of the TV in the bedroom watching *Peppa Pig*. All potentially dangerous objects – hair-drier, Bible, pen, notepad, lamp, hotel information booklet, telephone and TV remote control – had been unplugged, put out of his reach or removed from his sight, and I was able to relax and enjoy a bath for the first time in years. As I only ever had ten-second showers, this was a real luxury. I looked around the bathroom. It was so soothing – white, clean and uncluttered. The bubble bath smelt gorgeous and the towels and bathrobe were soft and fluffy. It was such a treat to be away for two days, almost alone.

The hotel was very swanky – it must have been costing Louise a fortune to put us all up there. I should have studied harder in school and had a successful career or married a millionaire like Sophie did. Would I always be the pauper sister? I felt as if I was doomed to a life of penny-pinching. I'd love to hire a personal trainer to come to my house and make me thin, I thought. He could tape my mouth shut, padlock the fridge and tie me to him while we did laps of the park. It would be wonderful to go shopping for clothes and not have to check the cost of everything, putting back ninety per cent of the items I liked because they were too expensive. I'd love to be able to go to a good hairdresser for regular cuts and blow-dries. Having to let my hair dry naturally meant my curls were wild and unruly, not soft and bouncy like they were supposed to be. It would be great to live in a house with a playroom, where all the boys' toys could be kept out of sight, instead of flung all over the kitchen, hall and TV room. I'd love to drive one of those fancy mummy cars, like an Audi or a BMW, instead of my battered people-carrier.

I looked at my toes. I'd love to have regular pedicures and manicures and facials and back massages, I thought. Deep massages to get all the knots out of my shoulders and back would be utter bliss. It would be fantastic to have a nanny who would come in and make the boys eat their vegetables, tidy up their toys, give them baths and put them in their pyjamas. I'd float through the door in my fabulous clothes and kiss their scrubbed faces goodnight, leaving the nanny to read them stories and persuade them to go to sleep without the Third World War erupting. It would be brilliant to go away for a weekend with Harry without having to plan and save for ten years.

I had the money Dad had given me, but that was sacred. I'd happily forgo holidays, nice clothes and a fancy car to make sure the boys went to a top-notch private school and got the best start possible. It was something I was absolutely adamant about. I reminded myself to check with Louise again about the investment – hopefully it was still making money. The last time I'd asked it was doing well, thank God.

Maybe we'd win the lotto. Maybe Harry was at this very moment choosing the winning numbers and tonight we'd be millionaires. Oh, that would be lovely . . . OK, Julie, stop fantasizing, I scolded myself. I was very lucky. I should count my blessings: four healthy children and a husband I loved. Harry and I had wanted babies, and I'd always said I wanted three children . . . but I hadn't expected them to come all at once. I'd known having kids would change my life and that it wouldn't be easy, but three at the same time was like being hit head-on by a steam train. And little Tom's birth had pushed me over the edge. Just when I was getting some kind of life back, just when I was feeling like the old Julie again, I'd found myself back in the haze of breast-feeding and sleepless nights. Before Tom was born I'd actually wanted to have sex with Harry instead of doing it because I'd realized that two months had passed since the last time. After Tom had arrived, I'd taken a big step back.

I'd always thought I'd be a good mum. I'd imagined painting with my children, making towers out of Lego, reading them stories, baking cakes with them, going for nature walks . . . I'd planned to raise fully rounded, kind, generous, caring, smart, responsible kids who were a credit to me. But when the triplets had arrived I'd done none of those things. There wasn't time to breathe, let alone spend hours baking cakes. It had turned out that I wasn't a good mother. I was grumpy and impatient and shouted a lot. I wasn't the Earth Mother I'd thought I'd be. The laid-back Julie had got lost somewhere along the way. I thought she was buried beneath mounting piles of laundry and bills.

Money wasn't the solution to everything, I knew, but a little bit more would have made things easier, nicer, less fraught . . . If I had help, like Sophie, I'd be less grumpy and kinder to the boys. If I had more time to myself I'd shout less . . . And if we had more money we wouldn't all be walking around our house in hats and scarves trying to keep warm while we saved on heating bills . . .

As I dried myself, I heard Tom shouting, 'Mama, Mama, Mama.'

Damn! *Peppa Pig* was over. It was the only thing he'd watch on TV.

'Yes, pet, come here.' I held out my arms to him.

Tom stumbled over to me, putting his wet, dribbly face up to mine. 'I dove you.'

I picked him up and hugged him. 'I dove you too, sweetheart, and I'm sorry for thinking you were a mistake when you're just a little angel.'

The hotel babysitter arrived at seven. I made sure she wasn't a psychopath, put Tom down to sleep in his little travel cot and skipped out of the door to dinner. As I was walking to the lift, my phone rang. It was Harry.

'Where's the bloody remote control?' he demanded.

I could hear pandemonium in the background. 'It should be on top of the bookshelf.'

'Well, it isn't.'

'I'M TELLING DADDY ON YOU. YOU'RE A MEANER. DAAAADDEEEE, LEO BITED MY ARM.'

'Did you try the shelf above the cooker?' I asked.

'Yes.'

'Down the side of the couch?'

'Yes.'

'DAAAADDEEEE, LIAM TRIED TO CHOKE ME.'

'Under the couch?'

'Yes.'

'DAAAADDEEEE, LEO IS A POOHEAD STINKY BUM. HE PULLED MY HAIR REALLY HARD.'

'In the fridge?'

'What?'

'I found it in the fridge one time. I must have been holding it and then gone to get something and left it on the shelf beside the yoghurts.'

'DAAAADDEEEE, WE WANT TV NOOOOOW,' they all screeched.

'Get off me! I'm trying to find the bloody remote control,' Harry snapped.

I could hear the fridge door opening.

'It's not here.'

'Well, the boys must have hidden it. Ask them.'

'I have already. They say they don't know where it is.'

'You have to sit them down and tell them to focus on where they put it.'

'They don't know!' he hissed.

'Put me on loudspeaker,' I ordered.

'Fine. Boys, Mummy wants to say something.'

'HI, MUMMY, WHERE ARE YOU?' Luke bellowed down the phone.

'I'm in London with Auntie Louise. She's having a baby – remember I told you I was going on an aeroplane?'

'Yeah, and they're going to cut it out of her tummy.' Leo loved that part.

'Charming,' Harry commented.

'Did the plane crash?' Luke asked. 'Did everyone die?'

'Yeah, was there blood everywhere?' Liam oohed.

'No, boys, the plane didn't crash. If it had, I'd be dead and that would be sad, wouldn't it?'

'No, it wouldn't because Daddy's super-nice and he let us eat pizza and jellies today,' Luke gushed.

I tried not to feel hurt. 'Now, boys, listen to me. Are you listening? I want you to close your eyes and think really hard about the TV remote control. Focus on it. Where did you last see it? Think about what it looks like. Think about what you did today and remember where you put it. Are you closing your eyes?'

'Yes, they are,' Harry said.

'Concentrate, boys, I know you can do it,' I encouraged them, even though they had just wished me dead.

'I REMEMBER!' Liam shouted. 'It's in the dishwasher. I put it in because it was dirty.'

'Well done, you clever cat,' I praised him.

I could hear Harry fishing it out. 'Thank God it hasn't been washed,' he said. He put on the TV and the boys simmered down.

'That was very impressive persuasion,' my husband said.

'Thank you. So, how's it going?'

'Oh, you know, the usual. Luke kicked me in the nuts during a *kung-fu* exhibition we had earlier this afternoon. I almost cried with the pain – I was bent double for twenty minutes.'

'No permanent damage, I hope?'

'I think they'll recover. Liam painted his name in your red nail varnish on our bedroom door.'

'Harry! You know you have to lock our bathroom door at all times. They always get my makeup and nail varnish out.'

'I was busy trying to get Leo out of the bloody bath, which he'd filled and climbed into fully clothed. It's a fucking circus here!'

'Tut tut! Mind your language, Harry.'

'MUMMY,' Luke shouted into the phone, 'Daddy said "fuck".'

'He's very bold. He won't do it again,' I assured my son.

'It's five past seven and I'm absolutely knackered,' Harry muttered. 'They never stop.'

'Welcome to my daily world,' I said, 'and you don't even have Tom to look after as well.'

'Any chance you fancy coming back from London early?'

'Hell will freeze over. This is the first time I've left the triplets in almost five years, and there is no way I'm coming home early. I'm going to cherish every moment of this trip because it'll be my last for probably another five years. Take them to the park tomorrow, and if it's raining, take them to the jungle gym. You need to tire them out more.'

'OK. How are you getting on? How's Louise?'

'I'm on my way to meet her now. We're all going for dinner.'

'Enjoy your nice relaxing dinner without children. I'll just stay here with the lunatics.'

'Can you hear the sympathy I feel for you over the phone?'

'Yes, it's deafening.'

'Right. Well, I'd better go. I don't want to be late for my pre-dinner drinks in the beautiful hotel bar.'

'You may come home to find the boys shackled to their beds.'

'Frankly, Harry, I really don't care what you do. For the next blissful forty-eight hours, it's not my problem. *Ciao*.' I hung up and smiled.

I was glad Harry was getting the full brunt of what it was like to look after the boys all day long. There was no harm in him being reminded of how hard it was. He'd appreciate my daily grind more now. I reapplied my lipstick and pressed the button for the lift.

I met my family in the hotel bar, which was very plush. I threw back a glass of white wine and ate almost a full bowl of peanuts before Mum pulled it away from me. Sophie drank a sparkling water and ate no peanuts. Mum drank a vodka and soda and kept saying it was a disgrace that her own daughter was refusing to let her see her grandchild being born, and Dad kept looking at his watch and saying we really should get a move on.

None of us wanted to be late for Louise, especially not on the day before she gave birth. At exactly seven thirty we walked into the French restaurant she had booked – it was called, aptly enough, Les Trois Soeurs. She was sitting at the table waiting for us.

'Mother of God, you're enormous,' Dad said.

'Thanks a lot. That's just what I needed to hear,' Louise snapped.

'You'll feel so much better when the baby's out,' Sophie reassured her.

'Bring it on. I couldn't feel more gross. I can't look at myself in the mirror.' Louise shuddered.

I felt like that most days. I couldn't remember the last time I'd thought I looked good.

'Louise Devlin!' Mum scolded. 'That's a terrible thing to say. A baby is a blessing. You're not gross, you look radiant. Pregnancy suits you.'

She actually didn't look radiant: she looked tired and very fed-up.

'Where's Gavin?' Louise flipped open her menu impatiently.

'He went to meet Acorn,' Sophie said.

'Well, I'm not waiting. I want to order and get back early to finish off some emails.'

'But you've been working all day,' Mum said. 'You need to rest, Louise – you're going to have a baby tomorrow.'

'I'm aware of that, Mum, but I have some last bits to finish off. I can rest while I'm typing.'

'You need mental as well as physical rest,' Mum remonstrated.

Dad took out his reading glasses. 'These prices are extortionate. Forty-two quid for a steak? Bloody ridiculous.'

'It's on me,' Louise announced.

'Don't be silly. I'm buying dinner,' Dad said.

'No, Dad, you've all come over to see me, so I'm paying.' Louise was firm.

'You're putting us up in a fancy hotel. I'll be getting the dinner,' Dad retorted.

'I've given them my credit card. It's fine.'

'*I* am paying for this meal, Louise.'

'No, *I* am.'

'This is non-negotiable.'

'Why don't you split the bill?' Sophie suggested.

They looked at each other and nodded. It was a compromise they were willing to accept. I could hear Dad muttering behind his menu: 'Twenty-seven quid for a crab salad is ludicrous.'

While they bickered, I tried to decide which delicious starter and main course to have. Everything sounded wonderful. The waiter came over and Dad obstinately ordered the cheapest starter, soup, and the cheapest main course, pumpkin risotto.

'But you don't like risotto,' Mum pointed out. 'Have the steak.'

'I refuse to pay that amount of money for a lump of meat,' he hissed.

'Suit yourself.' Mum turned her back on him and ordered the steak.

Louise ordered the walnut salad and the sea bass. Sophie opted for a side salad to start and the cod for her main course, but she made a big hullabaloo about wanting it steamed, not pan-fried, without any sauce – 'Also, can you steam some broccoli florets for me? No oil or butter, please.'

'For goodness' sake, Sophie,' Louise snarled, 'what's the point of going out for dinner if you're going to ask for steamed fish and vegetables all the time? Just eat the sauce and go to the gym tomorrow.'

'I can't. I'm allergic to a lot of sauces.'

'Allergic to what, precisely?' Louise quizzed her.

Sophie shrugged. 'I don't know, but they make me feel queasy.'

'All sauces?' Mum asked.

'More or less,' Sophie said.

Louise looked at me and rolled her eyes.

I ordered *foie gras* to start, followed by the steak with béarnaise sauce and dauphinoise potatoes.

'Would you like to see the wine list?' our sommelier asked.

Dad opened it and scanned it. 'You must be joking,' he said. 'It starts at forty quid a bottle.'

'I would recommend the Château Certan-Marzelle Pomerol 2005. It's a very nice –'

'Save your oxygen there, son. I have no intention of paying *eighty-seven* pounds for a bottle of wine. I don't care if the grapes were hand-picked by Napoleon Bonaparte himself. We'll be having the house wine, which at forty quid a pop is a total rip-off. And we'll have a jug of water – none of your fancy bottled nonsense. Tap water is just fine.'

The sommelier scurried off.

'Did you have to be so rude?' Louise glared at Dad.

'I wasn't rude, I was honest.'

Thankfully, Gavin's arrival stopped the argument before it esca-lated. Louise was in a foul mood and Dad seemed determined to moan about the cost of the dinner all night.

Gavin flung himself into a chair. 'Sorry I'm late. Before you blow a fuse, Louise, I was getting laid, and for any twenty-three-year-old man, that is his top priority.'

'Gavin! Do you have to be so crude?' Mum complained.

'Sorry, Mum.' He grinned at her. 'I'm starving. What's on offer?' He opened his menu.

'You can have a glass of tap water and a bread roll.' I giggled.

'Dude, I'm starving. I need red meat.'

'I thought you only ate nuts and berries,' Dad reminded him.

'I tried the vegan diet, but I was hungry all the time. Some humans just need meat, and I'm one of them.'

'Does Acorn know about your carnivorous ways?' I asked, taking a large gulp of the house wine, which was lovely.

'No, she does not, and I'd like to keep it that way. She's a dedi-cated vegan.'

'Maybe I should become a vegan,' Sophie mused. 'It's very healthy.'

'Newsflash, Sophie. Eating food is good for you. You should try it some time,' Louise said.

'I do eat,' Sophie flashed back. 'I'm just careful about what I put into my mouth.'

'A bit too careful by the look of it,' Dad commented.

'Leave her alone, she's always been very slim.' Mum defended her youngest daughter. 'Now, Louise, have you got your hospital bag ready?'

'Come on, Mum, this is Louise we're talking about. She's probably had it packed since January.' I grinned at my sister.

'February the sixth, actually.' Louise smirked back.

'Did you remember to put in breast pads and big cotton sanitary pads for your pants?' Mum asked, in a loud whisper.

'Jesus, please!' Dad muttered.

'Seriously, Mum,' Gavin said, 'that is way too much information. I do not want to know about this stuff. I see women as sexual beings and I'm far too young to be disillusioned.'

'I'm not sure how sexy you're going to find Acorn after sharing a wet, muddy tent with her,' I pointed out.

'Dude, she's a goddess. I'd live in a hammock with her.'

'Can we please focus on Louise?' Mum requested.

Louise put down her glass. 'Mum, I've packed everything I need. I haven't forgotten anything. You don't need to worry.'

'Louise,' Mum leant across the table, 'it's my job to worry and you are about to find out exactly what that feels like. From the moment that baby is brought into the world you will worry about her day and night. There is no time off, no break, no escape, no holidays from worry. Mothers exist in a constant state of low-level anxiety.'

'That's true,' Sophie and I agreed.

'Come on, how hard can it be? Feed, burp and sleep.' Louise threw her hands into the air.

We three mothers roared laughing.

I polished off my bread roll and raised my glass. 'A toast to my big sister Louise, who is about to discover that feed, burp and sleep also translates as fraught, brutal and strained.'

'Or fear, bewilderment and shock,' Sophie added.

'Or fortunate, blessed and starry-eyed,' Mum said, and our eyes welled – all except Louise's.

In the lift on the way up to our bedrooms, Sophie asked how I thought Louise would cope with motherhood.

'Knowing her, she'll probably breeze through it.'

'But you can't control babies. They cry when they cry and they feed when they feel like it,' Sophie said. 'It's not easy, even if you're organized and have help.'

'You're right. It'll be hilarious seeing her out of her comfort zone. She's always been in total control of her life. Can you imagine her saying, "Look here, kid, I've got an important meeting in the morning. Will you shut up and go to sleep?" or "Clara, I'm a senior partner at Higgins, Blah and Blah, I've got a big case to work on now, so knock that bottle back and roll over"?'

We fell about laughing.

'Hey, Sophie,' I said, as I put my key into my door, 'kids are great, aren't they? I mean we're lucky to be mums, aren't we?'

'Yes, we are.'

I went back to my room and stared at Tom, who was sleeping peacefully in his cot. The wine must have gone to my head because I decided to pick him up and cuddle him. His eyes snapped open.

Nooooooooooooooooooooooooooooooooooooooo . . .

17

Louise

When the dinner was finally over, Mum and Julie kept hugging me and telling me that tomorrow was going to be the best day of my life. Mum was emotional and Julie was drunk: she had knocked back the wine like a woman escaped from prison. Dad, meanwhile, was still muttering about the price of the meal. I couldn't wait to get home.

I eventually managed to peel Julie's arms off me as she was telling me how much she loved her children, even if sometimes she wanted to kill them, and waddled back to my apartment. Thank God, I thought, only one more day of feeling like a beached whale. I changed into my enormous pyjamas and sat up in bed to finish off some final emails. My phone beeped. It was Julie: Call me if u cant sleep. So exctd 4 u. Such big day. Kids so amazng, so much luv, so much happiness! I texted back: Going 2 sleep. C u 2mrw. I switched my phone off before she called for a chat, which I knew she would try to do.

An hour later I turned off my laptop and fell into a deep, dreamless sleep. I woke up when my alarm sounded at seven the next morning. I dragged myself out of bed and, avoiding all mirrors, pulled on my maternity togs, which I would be leaving in the bin at the pool today. I never wanted to see them or any of my other maternity clothes again.

I had to stop swimming after thirty minutes because I began to feel breathless and light-headed. I was annoyed. I always swam for an hour. Still, at least after today I could get back to running. I hauled myself up the steps at the side of the pool and went to the changing room where a woman asked when I was due. When I told her I was having a C-section that day, she looked at me as if

I was insane. I dropped my hideous togs into the bin, and headed home.

I checked one final time that I had everything I needed in my suitcase and got a taxi to the hospital. I was glad I'd chosen the Hartfield. It was expensive, but it was clean, modern, and had well-trained, helpful staff.

The family were all waiting for me in the lobby, except Gavin. Dad rushed over and took my bag from me. Mum led me over to a cream couch. 'Sit down. You look very peaky.'

'I'm fine, just hungry,' I admitted.

'Did you have to fast from midnight?' Julie asked.

I nodded. 'By the time this is over, I'll be ready for a large steak.'

'The hotel did a lovely breakfast,' Dad said. 'Crispy bacon and excellent scrambled eggs. I won't need lunch.'

My stomach grumbled.

'Look, Tom,' Julie said to her little boy, 'your auntie Louise has a baby in her tummy and it's coming out today. You're going to have a new cousin.'

'Baby, tummy,' Tom said, smiling.

As kids go, he was sweet and, thankfully, he didn't seem to be puking today, but I really didn't want him or any of my family here at the hospital. I wanted peace and quiet. I wanted to call the office, check in with Jasmine, then assure Alex one more time that I'd be back before he knew it.

'That's a beautiful blouse,' Mum said to Sophie, who was completely overdressed for ten o'clock in the morning. She was wearing tight black jeans held together with laces all down the sides, black patent boots with six-inch heels, and a black chiffon blouse with a black velvet military-style jacket over it.

'Thanks – I got it in New York. It's Prada. I thought I'd dress up – apparently lots of celebrities have their babies at Louise's hospital,' she admitted. 'It's always mentioned in the magazines as the top maternity hospital in London.'

'How was New York?' I asked. 'Did you get to see *The Iceman Cometh*?'

'Unfortunately we didn't have the chance. Too busy.'

'Shopping?' Julie grinned.

'You really should have made the effort. It's had incredible reviews,' I said. Sophie needed to get out of the shops and do some reading – *Grazia* and *Vogue* don't count – and go to the theatre before her brain stopped functioning.

'Maybe next time.' Sophie stood up and changed the subject. 'Does anyone want anything in the shop?'

'Can you get me some chocolate?' Julie asked.

'Why don't you have a nice banana instead?' Mum suggested.

'No binana.' Tom shook his head.

'Tom was up half the night. I'm tired and a bit hung-over, Mum. I need sugar,' Julie retorted.

'He'd be sleeping if she'd followed *The Contented Little Baby* routine,' Sophie whispered to me.

'Julie, I'm only trying to help you get your figure back,' Mum told her.

'Leave her alone – a man likes a few curves,' Dad piped up, from behind his newspaper.

'Why don't I get both? Tom can have the banana,' Sophie suggested.

'He won't eat it. Get him chocolate buttons,' Julie said.

'Yummy! Choco nuttons. Yummy!' Tom jumped up and down.

'Chocolate buttons?' Sophie looked shocked. 'Why don't I see if they have something healthy?'

Julie sighed. 'Sophie, I am aware that giving a toddler chocolate is not ideal parenting but it'll keep him quiet, so can you just get them, please?'

'Fine – no need to bite my head off. I was just trying to help. Sugar makes children hyper and causes behavioural difficulties. It's a false friend,' Sophie lectured Julie. 'You'll regret not giving your children a healthy diet.'

'Jesus, Sophie, just get the kid his buttons,' Dad snapped, 'and get yourself a doughnut while you're at it. You look like a toothpick.'

'Choco nuttons,' Tom shouted.

'I am extremely healthy,' Sophie retorted.

'You live on rice cakes and Evian,' I said.

'I didn't think watching what you eat was a sin.'

'Of course it isn't,' Mum jumped in. 'Don't mind them. Leave Sophie alone – you're always picking on her.'

'CHOCO NUTTONS!' Tom shrieked.

Dad threw down his paper. 'I'll get him a family pack of the shagging buttons.'

My head was starting to ache. Thankfully, a nurse came to show me to my room. I was very happy to disappear. I told my family to give me half an hour to settle in and then follow me up. I was desperate for some time to myself.

The room was small, but nice. It had a large window that overlooked Hyde Park and a single bed made up with good-quality cotton sheets. There were two comfortable brown leather lounge chairs for visitors, and a large print of Norman Rockwell's *Mother's Little Angels* hanging on the wall – it depicted a mother tucking up her two children in bed. I thought it was schmaltzy, but I'm sure it made other women teary-eyed in anticipation.

I changed into my hospital gown and climbed on to the bed. An attractive, cheerful midwife came in, took my blood pressure and strapped a big disc to my stomach to monitor the baby's heartbeat. 'Well, Louise, you must be very excited. The big day is finally here.'

'I can't wait for this to be over.'

She patted my arm. 'Don't be nervous, dear, it'll be fine. Jonathan Bakewell is the best obstetrician around.'

'Well, let's hope he does neat stitching. I do not want a big scar. I won't be having any more children and I want minimum damage.'

'Oh, that's what all the mummies say. "I'll never have another baby." A year or two later we see them coming back in for number two.'

'I can assure you that you will never be seeing me again.'

'Mark my words, once you become a mummy you'll feel differently.'

'No, I won't.'

'Will Daddy be coming in to hold your hand?'

'There is no daddy.'

'I see. Well, don't worry, we'll all be here to cheer you on.'

'I don't want to be cheered on. I want this to take place in silence. Please tell your colleagues not to cheer or whoop or make any noises at all.'

'All right, Mummy, whatever you say,' she said, bustling out of the door, muttering, 'Ice queen,' under her breath.

When my family descended on the room, Mum and Julie sat down, with Tom on Julie's lap, Dad hovered by the window and Sophie perched on the end of my bed. It felt claustrophobic. Dad was complaining about how hot it was and Tom kept trying to pull the monitor wire from my stomach. Mum was asking me how I felt while Sophie flicked noisily through her magazine, circling the clothes she liked.

Julie tried to stop Tom pulling the wire off my monitor by stuffing chocolate buttons down his throat, which actually worked.

When the midwife came back in to read the monitor printout she had to shuffle sideways to get to the bed. 'My goodness, you've a lot of support here today,' she commented.

'We've flown over from Dublin to be with her,' Mum explained.

'You're a lucky girl to have all these cheerleaders.' The midwife smirked at me. I didn't feel lucky, I felt stifled. 'But you do know that you can't all come into theatre with Louise?' she added.

'Of course,' Mum said. 'Just two of us will be going with her.'

My head snapped up. I glared at Julie.

She cleared her throat. 'Actually, Mum, I told you Louise just wants one person with her.'

'Nonsense, Julie. Louise needs all the support she can get. I'm her mother and it's my duty to be there, seeing as the father isn't showing up.'

'Mum, if Louise only wants Julie present, you have to respect her wishes.' For once, Sophie had got off the fence.

'If Jessica was having a baby on her own, would you abandon her in her hour of need?' Mum asked.

'You're not abandoning Louise,' Julie said. 'You're here, totally supporting her. She just doesn't want more than one person at the birth. She actually didn't want anyone, but I managed to persuade her to have one.'

'Well, it should be me,' Mum said, pursing her lips into a hard line.

'I think,' the midwife said, 'that the mum-to-be should have whatever she wants on this big day. We need to let her make the decision.' She nodded at me and left the room. Clearly she was feeling more sympathetic towards me now she had seen what a circus this birth was turning into.

'That woman is very opinionated,' Mum exclaimed.

'She's right, though,' Julie said. 'We need to listen to Louise.'

'Sometimes Louise doesn't know what's best for her,' Mum said tetchily.

'I'm here, in case you forgot or thought I'd gone deaf.' I waved my arm in the air.

'I'm coming in there with you to hold your hand and that's the end of it.' Mum crossed her arms.

'No, it isn't, Mum,' I said firmly.

'For goodness' sake, Louise, for once in your life stop trying to do everything alone. Let me help you.' Mum was exasperated.

'I am letting you get involved! You're here in the hospital with me. I just don't want a crowd in the operating theatre.'

'Having your mother with you is not a crowd!' Mum snapped.

'I can't listen to any more of this. I'm off to get a cup of coffee. Call me when the baby's born.' Dad disappeared out of the door.

'Mum, Louise isn't trying to hurt your feelings,' Sophie reasoned. 'She doesn't want me there either. She only wants one person and that's going to be Julie. We'll be right outside the door. You'll see the baby as soon as it's born. Come on, why don't we get a nice latte and see if we can spot any celebrities? We'll leave Louise to rest for a bit.'

'I'm only trying to help,' Mum said, beginning to get upset.

'I know you are,' I assured her, 'and I'm really grateful that you came over.'

Sophie led her expertly out of the room and away for coffee. As my youngest sister turned to close the door, I mouthed, 'Thank you,' to her. Then, to Julie, I cried, 'Mum's a nightmare. I should never have let her come over.'

'Go easy on Mum, Lou. She's emotional about the baby. She's worried about you not having any male support. Don't be so hard on her. Let her in a little.'

'I will. She can hold the baby as much as she wants when it's born. I just don't want her giving me instructions during the C-section. Is it too much to ask that at forty-one years of age I can give birth without my mother telling me what to do? I don't want her in there winding me up. I promise I'll let her be involved later.'

'Fair enough.'

Tom started pressing the buttons on the baby-heart monitor.

'Actually, Julie, I'm sorry to be a pain, but can you take Tom out? I'd really like to chill out for a while.'

'Sure, no problem. I'll give you all the space you need. I'll grab a coffee and come back at eleven – and I promise not to say a word to you during the birth.'

'Thanks. Tell Mum –'

'You're sorry for being a cold-hearted wench? OK, I will.' She grinned.

At eleven thirty I was wheeled out of my room and down to theatre. Mum cried as I left. Dad wished me luck and Sophie bent down to kiss my cheek. 'It's going to be great. Little girls rock,' she said.

Julie stayed outside and got into her scrubs while I was given the epidural. I laughed when I saw her coming in with her surgeon's outfit on. She looked hilarious.

'This is why I decided not to pursue a career in surgery – the uniform does nothing for me.' She twirled.

'Very wise decision,' I agreed.

'I find the stay-at-home-mum tracksuit is far more flattering.' She giggled.

'Sorry to interrupt, ladies, but we're ready to begin. Louise is about to become a mother,' Jonathan Bakewell, my obstetrician, announced. And he began to cut.

'Are you OK?' Julie asked, squeezing my hand.

'Fine.'

'Nervous?'

'No.'

Excited?'

'Um . . .'

'Emotional?'

'Julie!'

'OK, no more questions. I'll be nervous, excited and emotional for you.'

After a lot of rummaging about and pulling and heaving, I heard a cry. It was like a kitten mewing. Julie started bawling, drowning the sound.

'Congratulations, Louise, your beautiful baby girl has arrived.' Jonathan handed the baby to the midwife, who placed her on my chest. My baby was covered in bloody grey gunk. I looked at her and felt . . . nothing.

I didn't know what I was supposed to do. Was I supposed to kiss her through the gunk? I didn't move. The midwife came over and lifted the baby up. 'Why don't I clean her and get her all snug for you?'

'That would be great, thanks,' I said.

'Oh . . . my . . . God . . . Lou . . . she's . . . just . . . huh . . . huh . . . huh . . . beautiful,' Julie sobbed.

'Go and tell the others.' I wanted a moment alone. I needed to process what had just happened.

I closed my eyes, blocking out the noises around me. Was it normal to feel nothing? Did other new mothers want their babies taken away and washed? Was it terrible that I didn't want to kiss her little head through all the goo? But, then, wouldn't it have stuck to my mouth? Was I weird? Was I a freak? I felt completely numb. I waited for emotion to overwhelm me . . . Nothing.

The baby was handed back to me wrapped in a pink towel. She was clean and her eyes were open.

I looked down at her. 'Hello, Clara Rose Devlin. I'm your mum,' I introduced myself. She blinked. I held her face to mine and felt relief that she was healthy, pleased that she was safely out and that I was no longer pregnant, but no heart-stopping adoration, no rush of love, no breathless worship. Mostly I just felt tired and sore. Clara sighed and fell asleep on my shoulder.

I was wheeled out and my family descended on me again. Mum and Sophie were crying and even Dad had a tear in his eye. Julie was still bawling and trying to explain to a worried Tom that they were 'happy tears'. Gavin had arrived. He bent down to hug me. 'Well done, sis. It's official. You've gone over to the dark side now. You're a mum!'

Mum pulled him back. 'Now, let me see this little dote. Can I pick her up?' she asked me.

'Of course,' I said, as Julie gave me the thumbs-up.

Mum picked up Clara and held her close. She cooed at her, rocked her gently and kissed her cheeks. 'Oh, Louise, she's just perfect and she's the image of you.'

'How can you tell? She's all red and scrunched up.' Gavin snorted. 'Maybe she looks like her father.'

There was a deathly silence.

'Shit, sorry,' Gavin apologized.

'The baby looks like Louise and that's the end of it,' Dad hissed.

God, I hope she does look like me, I thought. If she looks like her father, it'll be the elephant in the room for the rest of her life.

'She's perfect, Lou,' Sophie said, patting her eyes with a tissue. 'I'm thrilled for you.'

I was wheeled off to Recovery, where I passed out for an hour. Then I was taken back to my room where my family were waiting. Mum was cradling Clara. I was given tea and toast. The food tasted great and I was enjoying every bite . . . until the midwife came in and asked if I was breast-feeding.

'No,' I said.

'Are you sure you wouldn't like to give it a go?' she asked.

'Yes.'

'It's very good for the babies.'

'Formula will be fine.'

'Breast is best,' she continued.

'Let me put it this way,' I explained. 'Hell will freeze over before I use my breasts to feed this child. For the past nine months I have put my body through things a body never should have to go through and I have no intention of having a child strapped to my nipples or milking myself with one of those God-awful expressing machines like some cow for another nine months. Clara will be having formula. OK?'

'Fair enough.' The midwife sniffed and rummaged around for a bottle. 'Would you like me to give the baby to you to feed?' she asked.

'No, thanks. Mum, would you mind feeding Clara for me?' I asked.

'I'd love to, Louise, but are you sure you don't want to do it yourself?' Mum looked shocked.

'No, I'd really like you to.' I took another large bite of my toast.

'Well, I'd be delighted.' She took the bottle and began to feed a hungry Clara.

'Nice one, Lou,' Julie whispered.

I'd like to say I was being generous to Mum, but I was happy to let her do it. I was exhausted and hungry and I didn't want to feed Clara. Not yet. I needed to get my energy back. Now that Clara was born, I was actually glad they were all there. I didn't want to be on my own with the baby. I'd read all the baby books out there, but now I wasn't sure what to do.

I watched Mum burping Clara. A stream of milk came back up and ran down Mum's shoulder. She patted Clara's back. 'Good girl – that's a wonderful burp.'

I winced. I didn't want puked-up milk all over my clothes. I'd have to put those muslin cloths over my shoulders at all times.

Gavin yawned. 'Sorry, late night. Look, it's been great seeing the baby and all, but I can probably skip the feeding. I think I'll head off. Well done, sis, she's a cutie.'

'When are you off to Heathrow to camp out on your protest?' I asked him.

'Tomorrow.'

'Do you have a decent tent?' I enquired.

'Yeah, I'm sorted. Sophie gave me the cash to buy a really good one. It's quite plush, actually.'

'Sophie,' Dad snapped, 'you have to stop giving him money. He needs to learn to stand on his own two feet.'

'Relax, Dad, it was just a few quid to get a tent that doesn't leak.'

'Sophie's always had a very generous nature,' Mum said.

'Well, good luck, and if it all gets too much or you decide to see sense, you can stay in my spare room. Temporarily,' I offered. 'But your hairy unhygienic friends are not welcome.'

'Get it out of your system, son. This nonsense is all going to end soon,' Dad warned him.

'Good luck cohabiting in a tent,' Julie said.

'It'll be cool. Acorn's pretty chilled out.'

'She's not chilled out about her veganism. You won't be able to cook sausages on your camp fire,' Julie reminded him.

'I know.' Gavin groaned. 'It's back to pretending I actually like tofu and lentils – but, hey, she's worth it.'

'What does this girl do when she's not hugging trees? What type of an education has she?' Mum asked.

'She's got a degree in chemistry. She's actually kind of a genius, like Louise,' Gavin said.

'It's hardly intelligent to live in a tent in a muddy field protesting against something that's inevitable,' Dad pointed out.

'That depends on your point of view – and the Heathrow expansion is not inevitable. People power can change the world. You should consider getting involved in climate change instead of criticizing it all the time. Your precious golf course could be six feet under water soon if we don't do something about global warming.' Gavin was on a roll.

'Don't lecture me on –'

'OK! Thanks, everyone, for coming,' I cut across Dad. 'It's been great having you here, but you can take the global-warming debate outside. I'm going to ingest some serious pain relief and hopefully get some sleep.' I suddenly felt as if I'd been run over by a bus. My eyelids felt like concrete. I was keen to sleep and, hopefully, to wake up tomorrow feeling less sore and more excited about my daughter.

'Come on, let her rest. The poor thing is exhausted.' Mum ushered Dad and Sophie out. She settled Clara back into her big plastic box beside the bed and kissed her head. 'What a beauty she is. Now, Louise, can I get you anything? Are you all right?'

'I'm fine, Mum, and thanks for feeding her. It was a great help.'

'I was delighted to do it. She's a gorgeous little baby. Try and get some sleep. I'd say she'll be up again in a few hours.'

'Do you want me to stay?' Julie asked.

I shook my head. 'Thanks, but I'm wrecked. I just want to sleep off the pain.'

'Ah, yes, I remember sleep – vaguely.' Julie chuckled. 'I'll pop in tomorrow on my way to the airport. And well done again. She's just gorgeous.'

They left. I swallowed my painkillers, rested my head back against my pillows and passed out. Twenty minutes later I heard a wailing in my sleep. It seemed far away but got progressively louder. I forced my eyes open. It was Clara. She was thrashing about in her bassinet, legs and arms flailing. I tried to reach over, but the pain in my stomach stopped me in my tracks. I rang the bell frantically, and a nurse came running in. 'Are you all right?' she asked.

'The baby's having some kind of a fit.' I was panicking.

The nurse calmly picked Clara up and patted her back firmly. My daughter let out an enormous burp and fell straight back to sleep. 'You see?' the nurse said. 'It was nothing to worry about, just a bit of trapped wind. You'll soon be used to it – they can get very uncomfortable with it.'

'Can you take her away, please?' I begged.

'Do you want her to spend the night in the nursery?'

'Yes, I do. I need sleep and I can't sleep if she's screaming like that. It's freaking me out.'

'OK, but you mustn't let her crying upset you. All babies cry. It sounds worse than it is.'

'Fine. Can you just take her?' I asked again. I didn't want a bloody lecture on babies' cries. I just wanted to sleep.

The nurse handed Clara to me. 'You can give her a goodnight cuddle.'

I didn't want to give her a cuddle. But the nurse plonked her on my chest. I held my daughter, kissed her head and handed her straight back.

'Call us in the morning when you wake up. I'm sure you'll be dying to see her,' she said.

I put in my ear-plugs and closed my eyes.

18

Sophie

I thought seeing Louise's baby might make me feel a little broody, maybe re-start my biological clock. But it didn't. It brought back all the bad memories of struggling to get through the day and panicking every time Jess cried. When I heard Clara crying, just before Mum fed her, my stomach had twisted. I'd felt physically ill. It reminded me of all the sleepless nights I'd spent thinking Jess was going to die every time she so much as whimpered. Jack was never going to have his son and heir. I was definitely not having any more children.

It was strange to see Louise with a baby. She was so capable in every aspect of her life, always in control, in charge, cool, calm and collected. But she looked unsure yesterday, awkward with Clara, nervous. I wondered if being a mother would be the one thing Louise struggled with. In a way I hoped she would find it hard, because then I wouldn't feel like such a loser – the pathetic sister who, despite having lots of help and a healthy child, had had to take drugs to cope, while the other sister with triplets and no help just got on with it. I didn't want my sisters to find out I'd had to take Prozac. I was embarrassed about it; I felt weak and pathetic for being unable to cope. Even though the doctor had said it wasn't my fault and there was nothing I could have done, that post-natal depression was very common and nothing to be ashamed of, I was ashamed of myself.

I wanted Jack never to know either. Whenever men talked about how much their wives changed when they had children, how they were tired and grumpy and snappy and put on weight and never wanted to have sex, Jack always put his arm around me and said proudly, 'Well, it didn't happen to my Sophie. She breezed through it. She was back in shape and raring to go after six weeks.'

The truth was that I hadn't enjoyed sex for a year after Jess. I pretended I did, but I had no desire for sex at all. One of the side-effects of Prozac was that it lowered my sex drive, but obviously I couldn't explain that to Jack because I didn't want him to know I was taking it. So I faked enjoyment and willingness until slowly I began to feel like myself again. Thankfully, after about a year, it became less of a chore. I finally got my mojo back and wanted to be with Jack physically again, which was a relief as I knew how important sex was to a happy marriage.

The morning after Clara's birth, Mum, Dad, Julie and Tom flew home, but I stayed on to do some shopping. I spent a blissful five hours in Selfridges and bought a fabulous Fendi clutch-bag, an Yves St Laurent draped jersey dress in a wine colour, an Etro kaftan for the summer in Marbella and a cute Day Birger et Mikkelsen cotton-voile ruffled tunic. I just had time for a soy-milk latte in the Starbucks on the fourth floor before I had to hail a taxi to the airport.

I was looking at makeup in Duty Free when I heard a voice from the past: 'Oh, my God! Sophie Devlin, is that you?'

I turned to see a small man in his fifties, with a shock of black hair, wearing blue-tinted sunglasses, a white dinner shirt and a navy velvet suit, waving at me.

'Quentin! How are you?' I rushed over to hug him. Quentin Gill was the owner of Beauty Spot, the model agency I'd worked for. I hadn't seen him in about five years.

'Darling, you look fabulous,' Quentin said, kissing me. 'I love the jacket – Marc Jacobs?'

'Yes, I got it in New York. Isn't it gorgeous?'

'To die for. But anything would look good on you. So, how's life? How are Jack and the baby?'

Quentin was not one of those gay men who loved children. He actually really disliked kids and hated it when any of the models had babies and brought them into the agency to see him. We used to laugh about it, so I'd never done it with Jess.

'They're great, thanks.'

'I can see the recession isn't affecting you.' He pointed to the huge Selfridges bag I was carrying.

'Jack's business is flying and he likes me to look good . . . so I oblige him.'

Quentin threw back his head and laughed. 'Sophie, I always knew you'd land on your feet. You were never just a pretty face. You were always focused on the end game.'

I grinned. 'I wasn't born a genius, but at least I was smart enough to know that my looks could get me what I wanted.'

'So many of the other girls were into drugs and sleeping around. I always admired you for keeping out of that. You never slipped up. You were always on time for your shoots, never hung-over, never a prima-donna. You were the most professional model I had on the books.'

'You old charmer.'

'I'm serious, darling. The young models today are a nightmare. They think the world owes them something. They're always complaining and asking for more money and thinking press calls are beneath them. I don't know, maybe I'm just too old for this.'

I laid my hand playfully on his arm. 'Stop that. You're as young as your surgeon makes you.'

We both laughed. Quentin was addicted to plastic surgery. He'd had a face-lift, hair implants, liposuction, laser hair removal and a tummy tuck.

As we walked to the boarding gate, he told me that Jill had left the agency.

'No way!' I was shocked. Jill had been with Beauty Spot since Quentin had founded it thirty years ago. She had done almost all of the bookings. She was Quentin's right arm. 'What happened?'

'She met a guy in Greece.'

'Jill!' I was shocked. Jill was at least sixty and had always been married to her job. I'd never heard of her even going on a date.

'She turned into Shirley shagging Valentine,' Quentin explained. 'She went to Greece, met the guy who owned the bar she drank in and never came back.'

'Wow! Good for her.'

'Not so good for me, though.'

'When did this happen?'

'Six weeks ago. I've got a new girl in, but she's not very good. I'm working sixteen-hour days trying to keep things running smoothly. I came to London to interview some experienced bookers. I think I've found someone.'

'That's a relief. You're supposed to be working less, not more.'

'Tell me about it.'

We stepped on to the plane. I found my row near the front and sat down. Quentin's seat was further back.

'Good to see you, Sophie.' He kissed me, and started to move away.

'You too, and I hope the new booker works out for you.'

'God, so do I.'

It had been really nice to see Quentin. He had always made me laugh. It was a pity we had lost touch. After I'd married Jack I'd stopped looking for modelling jobs, happy to give it all up – it had been a struggle to get work in my early thirties. Quentin had always been really good to me and we had got on very well over the fourteen years I'd been with him. At first, after I left, we met up for the odd coffee, but what we had in common – work – was gone, so things just kind of fizzled out.

When we landed in Dublin, I waited for him and offered him a lift home.

'Oh, you sweet thing, I'd love one.'

'Do you still live upstairs from the agency?' I asked.

'I certainly do, although I've changed the décor. I've gone from the Moulin Rouge vibe you'll remember to a completely minimalist look. Honestly, Sophie, you wouldn't recognize the place. It's fabulous.'

'Good for you. I hate clutter.'

'Darling, it overwhelms the senses.'

'Has the agency been affected by the recession?'

'Last year was a nightmare – we were barely breaking even – but things have picked up in the last six months. We're busy again, thank God.'

'Great.'

'Here we are – home, sweet home.' Quentin leant over to kiss me. 'Call me some time. Let's do lunch and gossip about all the people we used to work with. Here's my card – all my new numbers are on it.'

'Thanks. I'd love that.'

When I got home there was a message from Jack saying he had had to go to New York suddenly, but would hopefully only be gone a few days. I tried calling his mobile but it was switched off. He must be in the air. I left him a message saying I missed him and not to forget that we were going to a drinks party in Victoria and Gerry's that weekend. Then I admitted I'd done some damage on the credit card in London, but that when he saw my new Yves St Laurent dress he'd agree that it was worth the money.

Jess was thrilled to see me. I hugged her tight, my baby, my one and only baby. I brought her up to my room and gave her her present – a beautiful princess dress I'd bought in the Disney Store. She was thrilled. We both put on our new dresses and twirled around the bedroom. Then we put our pyjamas on, snuggled up in bed with some air-popped popcorn and watched *The Princess and the Frog* for the zillionth time.

A few days later I went out for lunch to celebrate Victoria's birthday. Saskia had booked a table in the Harvey Nichols restaurant for four of us. Daniella was away, so it was just Victoria, Saskia, me and Paula.

I'd decided to wear my new dress. I knew the others would be all dressed up and I wanted to show it off. When I arrived, Saskia admired it: 'Oh, Sophie, what an amazing dress! You look fantastic.'

I beamed. 'Thanks – it's new. I got it in London.'

'It's so stylish,' Paula gushed.

Victoria said nothing. She didn't like other people getting compliments when she was around.

'Hi, Victoria, happy birthday.' I bent to kiss her. 'You look great. Red is a good colour on you.' She was wearing a very fitted red suede dress and strappy red Jimmy Choo sandals.

'Thanks.' She smiled, clearly happy that the attention was back on her.

'Every colour suits Victoria,' Saskia said.

'Well, actually lime green doesn't.' Victoria flicked her long caramel hair back.

We ordered our food. We all had a side salad to start, except Saskia, who ordered a goat's cheese salad that she'd throw up later. And for our main course we had the steamed fish while Saskia went for steak and chips.

'Did you hear about Georgina and Trevor?' Victoria asked us. Georgina and Trevor were well known around town. He was a businessman and she owned a very successful PR agency. They were a nice couple, fun, good company and not full of their own importance.

'No – what?' Paula asked.

'He's left her for a twenty-five-year-old Russian nightclub hostess he met in London.'

'No way!' Saskia put her fork down.

'And the girl is pregnant.'

'Oh, God, poor Georgina! What a nightmare!' I exclaimed.

'It's a mess,' Victoria agreed, 'but, you know, she spent far too much time in work. When he went to London on business, she hardly ever went with him. If you let your man out of your sight for too long, he'll stray.'

'But she has a business to run. There's no way she could go with him on all his trips,' I pointed out.

'Sophie,' Victoria placed her jewelled hand on mine, 'we are married to successful, handsome men. Most women would kill to be in our shoes, and we have to be very careful to keep our husbands happy. As Jerry Hall said, a woman needs to be a maid in the living room, a cook in the kitchen, and a whore in the bedroom.'

We all laughed.

'But she broke up with Mick Jagger,' I said lightly.

'For goodness' sake, it's just a quote.' Victoria sighed. 'All I'm saying is that we need to keep a close eye on our husbands. I rarely let Gerry out of my sight. I go on all his business trips with him and never refuse him sex.'

'Never?' Paula looked sheepish.

'Never.' Victoria was firm. 'If you refuse them sex, they'll look elsewhere.' In fairness, she knew all about that because she was Gerry's second wife. He'd left his first for her.

'But what if you're exhausted and want to go to sleep?' Saskia put a large piece of steak into her mouth.

'It doesn't matter, it's part of the deal – they provide us with a great lifestyle and credit cards and we keep their stomachs and libido satisfied.' Victoria took a small sip of her wine.

'Gosh! I turned Kevin down twice last week. I'd better hop on him when he gets home tonight. I don't want him running off with some nightclub hostess.' Paula giggled. 'I love my life – I enjoy my comforts.'

'Do you know what I like about this recession?' Victoria said. 'People are willing to work harder for less money. You know Valda left me to go back to Russia and I was devastated? She was by far the best cleaning lady I'd ever had. Anyway, she recommended her cousin, who was a disaster. I mean, she didn't even dust the light shades so I had to let her go. But I've found another girl – she's from one of those countries, Ukraine or Lithuania or something – and she's willing to do four hours a day, six days a week for nine euros an hour. Valda was eleven euros an hour, so I'm actually saving money. It's fantastic.'

I prayed no one at the next table had heard that comment.

'Good staff are hard to come by. I had to send four cleaning ladies back to the agency before they found me a really good one,' Paula said.

'Your girl seems good, Sophie,' Saskia commented.

'Honestly, I'd die without Mimi. She's great with Jess and keeps the house so tidy.'

'Look! There's Kate Richardson,' Paula murmured.

Kate Richardson had been in school with the girls and was now a successful actress, starring in a long-running BBC drama about lawyers.

'She looks amazing,' I said, admiring her beautifully tailored cream dress.

'I think she looks old,' Victoria said.

'Kate!' Saskia waved her over.

Kate came to the table. 'Hi, Saskia, long time no see.'

'I know, it's been years. You remember Paula and Victoria from school, and this is our friend Sophie.'

'Victoria Murphy?' Kate looked shocked.

'Yes, she's Victoria Ward now,' Saskia said.

'My God, you've changed.' Kate roared laughing. 'You used to have frizzy brown hair and buck teeth.'

'Did you?' I tried not to laugh. Victoria's face was like thunder.

'Yes, she did.' Paula giggled.

'Well, I don't any more.' Victoria glared at Kate.

Kate grinned, ignoring Victoria's hostility. 'So, what are you all up to, these days?'

'We're all boring stay-at-home mums,' Saskia told her.

'Speak for yourself,' Victoria snapped. 'My life isn't boring at all.'

I decided to jump in. 'I love your show,' I told Kate. 'You're absolutely brilliant in it.'

'Thanks. It's really nice of you to say. I recognize you – are you an actress too?'

'No, nothing as glamorous.' I blushed. 'I used to be a model.'

'That's it – I remember you from the Special K ad. You look great.'

'Thanks.' I was thrilled. Kate Richardson had recognized me! She was a big star. It was a buzz just meeting her.

'Well, I'd better get back to my friends. See you around.' She turned to Victoria. 'You should buy your dentist a big present. He performed a miracle with those teeth.' With that, Kate walked back to her table.

'Bitch,' Victoria muttered. 'She was always a cow.'

'I thought she was lovely,' I said.

'You don't know her. She was always full of herself.'

'I liked her,' Saskia said.

'Well, you're not a very good judge of character,' Victoria snarled. 'Now, can we please talk about something else?'

After lunch, by which time Victoria had calmed down and was back to herself, the two of us decided to go downstairs to the Harvey Nichols department store. I had spotted a gorgeous Missoni scarf that I knew would look great with my Miu Miu coat.

'It's lovely,' she agreed. 'You should definitely buy it.'

As I went to pay for it, Victoria came over to me. She was wearing two different shoes – both Jimmy Choo. One was a black sling-back and one was a black open-toe high heel; they were quite similar. 'Which one?' she asked.

'They're both lovely, but I think I like the sling-back better.'

'Mmm.' She looked into the mirror. 'Oh, I can't decide . . . I'll take them both.'

Nora, the woman at the counter, swiped my credit card. 'It's a really beautiful scarf,' she said.

'Yes, I love it.' I smiled.

'You can't go wrong with Missoni,' Victoria said, drumming her nails on the counter as she waited for the other shop assistant to box up her shoes.

'There seems to be a problem with your card, madam,' Nora said. 'It's probably this machine, though – it acts up sometimes. Would you mind coming over to the other till?'

'No problem.' I glanced at my watch. I needed to go to pick up Jess.

She tried the card on the second machine. 'Um, I'm so sorry about this, madam, but the card seems to be blocked.'

209

'OK – use this one.' I handed her another. Victoria was hovering behind me, talking loudly to someone on her phone.

'I'm terribly sorry, but this one won't go through either.' Nora looked flustered. 'I'll give them a quick call for you.'

I tapped my foot impatiently as she muttered down the phone to the Visa people. She hung up and handed me back my card.

'Is it sorted out? What did they say?' I was getting annoyed.

'Um, well, they're saying that you have insufficient funds,' she whispered.

'What? That's ridiculous. Try the other again.' I handed it to her.

The same thing happened.

Victoria hung up and sighed impatiently. 'What's taking so long?'

'The machine won't take my Visa card for some reason – it's really annoying.' I was embarrassed. I knew there were ten thousand euros in the account. I'd spent about four thousand in London, so there was no way I had insufficient funds, unless Jack had been using the same card in New York instead of his business card.

'Here, let me. You can pay me back.' Victoria handed over her American Express black card.

'No, it's fine – I'll come back tomorrow.'

'Don't be silly, Sophie, it might be gone by then. It's no problem.'

'OK, thanks.'

Victoria's card was accepted straight away.

19

Julie

I don't know what the hell is wrong with Harry. He came home from work in a foul mood. I thought at first it was because he'd seen the car. I'd reversed it into a wall and dented the boot. Leo and Luke were fighting over a book in the back of the people-carrier while I was reversing out of the school car park. Eventually Leo grabbed it and flung it away. It hit the side of my face and I got such a shock that I stepped on the accelerator instead of the brake. It wasn't the first time the car had been dented, but this was a big one.

He came in and barely said hello.

'How was work?' I asked.

'Daddy Daddy Daddy Daddy!' The boys ran over to him.

He pushed them away. 'I'm tired. I'm not in the mood to play.' I was taken aback. Harry could be grumpy coming in from work, but once he saw the kids he always cheered up. He never took it out on them.

'You're a meanie, Daddy,' the triplets said, and slunk back to their game.

'What's wrong? Is it the car?' I asked.

'What?' He looked at me blankly.

'Nothing.' He obviously hadn't seen the damage and I didn't want to tell him . . . yet.

Tom followed him around with his arms in the air, saying, 'Dada up up up.'

'Pick him up, Harry,' I said.

Harry looked through his toddler son.

'DADA, UP!' Tom pleaded.

'Go on – look at the poor little thing. Just pick him up and give him a cuddle.'

'Julie, I've had a shit day and I want some peace.' Harry took a beer from the fridge and went into the TV room with his laptop. He must have had the worst day ever. Even when his salary had been reduced for the second time, he hadn't ignored the kids. He'd hugged them even tighter. They'd been a comfort to him.

I followed him in. He snapped the computer shut when I opened the door. 'What's going on?'

'Nothing. I just need some space.'

'What happened in work? Did they cut your salary again?'

'No, Julie, they didn't. Can you just drop it and leave me alone?'

'Listen, Harry, you may have had a rotten day, but it's not the kids' fault, so don't take it out on them. It's not fair. They love when you come home and so do I because I get a brief break while you play with them. So whatever's wrong, you just have to park it and come back in and see your children. You can come back to your computer and your bad mood later.'

'Jesus, Julie, I just want ten minutes to myself. Ten lousy minutes. Is it too much to ask?'

'Yes, actually, it is. I'd like ten minutes to myself too, but I don't get it – ever. You can have peace in the office whenever you want it – you can go for a coffee or lunch. I don't get that. You drive home on your own. That's half an hour of peace and quiet. I'm never in the car on my own.'

'I'm working on a very important project and I need to send an email. Can you please take Tom out and close the bloody door?'

'What project?'

'It's a new thing that's just come up.'

'Will you get paid more for it?' Maybe the project would be a good thing. I'd take his grumpiness if it meant more money and less scrimping.

'No, Julie, I won't. Now, give me some space.'

'Why can't you do it later when the kids are in bed?'

'Jesus Christ, I just can't. I need to send this off now.'

'Fine.' I picked Tom up. 'But I have to give the boys a bath tonight and I'd appreciate it if you'd help out. So when you've finished your incredibly important email you might get off your arse and give me a hand.'

'Fine.'

I slammed the door.

I went in and gave the boys macaroni and cheese for dinner. Leo only ate the pasta. Luke only ate the cheese. Tom liked to chew it and then spit it out. Liam ate it all, like a normal person.

After dinner I told them they had to have a bath. I only subjected myself to it once a week. That's not very hygienic, but it was an ordeal I couldn't face any more frequently. Every week was the same: the minute they heard the word 'bath' they'd all run in different directions. I had to chase them and yank their clothes off. Then they'd run off naked and hide. Eventually I'd lift them one by one into the bath and they'd all proceed to pee. They thought this was hilarious. I thought it was disgusting. It was the reason Tom didn't have a bath with them – I figured he was a bit too young for golden showers.

Once they were in the bath they had great fun. They threw water over each other, splashed, kicked and wrestled. A good third of the bathwater ended up on the floor and all over me. I sometimes thought I should wear a raincoat on bath nights because I always ended up soaked. Hair-washing was another ordeal. They hated it. They roared and screamed, and if a tiny bit of shampoo got into their eyes, all hell would break loose. They'd jump up and down, screeching and flailing their arms as if they'd been stabbed. I never had enough time to rinse the shampoo out because they wouldn't sit still. So their hair, like mine, was limp.

Then they'd refuse to get out of the bath they'd refused to get into. I'd have to drag one out and quickly dry him, but as I grabbed the next, the first would jump back in. This could go on for ages until I'd explode and threaten them with no TV, no sweets, no toys, no Santa and no Easter bunny. While they ran around naked, I mopped the floor and rinsed out the bath.

Then the pyjamas race would begin, lots of chasing and putting them on only to take them off again, until I lost my temper. Finally they would sit down in front of the TV, I'd put Tom to bed and collapse into a chair. How I wasn't thin was beyond me. I never stopped. I ran around all day. I should have been a stick insect.

Just as I was psyching myself up to chase them around for the bath, Harry came in to help me. He looked very pale and stressed. I felt bad about giving out to him. 'You look shattered,' I said.

'I'm fine. Sorry about earlier.'

'Maybe you're coming down with something – you're very pale.'

'No, it's just . . . this project. I need to sort it out.'

'Can I help?'

'No. Just forget about it. Come on, let's get these rascals clean.'

Harry did the chasing and I did the washing. It was so much easier when he was home to help. We had them washed, dried and in their pyjamas within twenty minutes.

Later, when Tom was asleep and the triplets were watching cartoons, Harry disappeared to the bedroom with his laptop. I decided to call Louise to see how she was getting on with Clara. 'Hi, Lou, how's it all going?'

'Fine, thanks. I'm back to work tomorrow and I can't wait, to be honest.'

'Aren't you tired?'

'No. I put her in the nursery every night in hospital and slept for ten hours, and I've had a night nurse since I came home, so I feel fine.'

Oh, the luxury of a night nurse – it sounded like heaven. 'What time does she come in?'

'She arrives at seven in the evening and leaves at seven in the morning.'

'Wow, it sounds great.'

'It is. By seven I'm ready to hand Clara over. My cleaning lady babysits for three hours during the day, from eleven to two, so I can exercise and do some work. But I find after five hours of just changing nappies and giving bottles, I'm ready to hand the baby over. It's pretty boring and she cries after her bottles and vomits up a lot. I've actually started putting a bath towel over myself when I'm feeding her. My clothes were getting ruined.'

'I don't remember the triplets as babies at all. It's a complete blur. And when I had Tom they still needed to be looked after, so I was never bored – overcome, overworked, overtired, yes, but never bored. You sound like you have it sussed.'

'Well, I need to be clear-headed, going back to work. The night nurse is going to stay for six weeks to get Clara sleeping through the night and then I'll just keep her routine exactly as it is and that's it.'

I smiled. No baby, not even Louise's, would stick to a routine. She'd get colds and coughs and teeth and earache: there would be many nights when routine went out of the window. 'When does she start in the crèche?'

'Tomorrow.'

I winced. It just didn't seem right to put a tiny baby into a crèche, no matter how posh it was. 'Couldn't your cleaning lady look after her for a few more weeks until she's a bit stronger?' I suggested.

'Julie, it's not a big depressing room stuffed with babies. They only have six under three months in the nursery room. They have three properly qualified maternity nurses looking after them. It's a lovely room, white and pristine. Everything is washed and disinfected daily and there's a GP who specializes in kids next door, should they need him. She'll have better care there than with any childminder. To be honest, I feel much happier leaving her with professionals than with my cleaning lady. Agnes is great, but if Clara got sick or anything happened, I'd prefer her to have nurses and a doctor close by.'

'I suppose you're right. How's your scar? Is it sore?'

'It hurts a bit today. I went for a run and probably did too much.'

'You have to be careful, Lou. You don't want it to open up.'

'I know, I know. I'll take it easy tomorrow. I'm just dying to get fit again, although I'm already back in my jeans, which is great.'

Typical. The skinny cow was back in her jeans after three weeks and I hadn't got mine over my thighs since the triplets were born almost five years ago.

'You lucky thing! Have you been starving yourself?'

'No, I've just been following a high-protein/low-carb diet that my trainer gave me. I'm only doing it for a month and then I'm going to start reintroducing carbohydrates and eat the way I always do. When I'm running for an hour a day I can eat what I want – and I never liked junk food anyway. It's not hard to maintain.'

'Can you fax me the diet?'

'Julie, I gave you the perfect regime to follow in January.'

'I know, but I was hungry all the time. Maybe this one will suit me better.'

'OK, but what you need is more willpower.'

'Well, I guess you got all the self-discipline genes when you were born and there were none left for me.'

Louise laughed. 'I'd better go. I want to get ten hours' sleep so I'm fresh for tomorrow.'

'Do you have any idea what a luxury that is for a new mum – or any mum for that matter?'

'Maybe you should try The Contented Little Baby routine on the boys again. I'm sure it works on all ages.'

'Louise, the triplets are almost five. How am I supposed to do controlled crying on kids that can walk, run and jump? If they don't want to stay in bed, they just get up. Even Tom can climb out of his cot. I'm way beyond routines.'

'Well, Clara is doing the routine, no matter what. I need my sleep.'

'Won't you miss her all day?' I asked.

'I doubt it. I'll be too busy. I barely have time to grab a sandwich in work. Besides, I'll see her in the evening and the morning, so it'll be fine.'

'Well, good luck in work.'

'Thanks. I need to show those vultures that I'm still at the top of my game and haven't become a leaky, bleary-eyed mess.'

Louise had just described me and millions of other new mothers.

I went in to talk to Harry. He jumped when he realized I was there and closed his laptop. 'Louise has Clara in a routine that the SAS would find difficult to follow.'

Harry half smiled. I could see he wasn't listening. I sat down beside him. 'Harry, what's wrong? You're not yourself. Talk to me.'

He put his hand out and took mine. 'I'm just stressed with work and tired. I'll feel better after a decent night's sleep. I'm going to crash out now.'

'If you're not feeling better tomorrow, you should go to the doctor. And if that project is going to make you this strung out, maybe you should pass it on to someone else.'

'It's fine, Julie, seriously. Forget about it.'

I left him and went to clean up the mess in the kitchen. Then I logged on to see if I'd had any replies to my last posting on mumskeepingsane.com. Wow! There were more than two hundred. They had come from women whose husbands had taken salary cuts, like Harry, and from women whose husbands had lost their jobs and were now trying to survive on the dole. Harry's request for us to cut back on all TV channels, including cartoons, was a hot topic.

MiniMum responded: Under no circumstance are you to let that husband of yours take away the cartoon channels. They are our lifeline. We will DIE without them.

Hazel5 said she thought TV was bad for kids and made them hyper. She said I'd be better off letting them play and reading them books and doing arts and crafts with them.

MiniMum ranted at Hazel5: Who the hell wants to do arts and bloody crafts at seven o'clock in the evening? You've just tidied up the kitchen. The last thing you want is cotton balls, glue and paint all over the table. Clearly, Hazel5, you don't have sons. Arts and crafts my arse.

Hazel5 was quick to respond: Actually, MiniMum, I do have a son and he loves to paint and doesn't make a mess. He goes to bed calmly and without any fuss because he hasn't been driven into a frenzy by noisy and violent cartoons.

MiniMum: Well, he's obviously weird.

Hazel5: He's perfectly normal. In fact he's extremely clever.

MiniMum: I knew it. He's one of those nerdy kids with intellectual snobs for parents. I bet all he wants to do is play and be a normal kid but you and your husband insist that he reads books and paints and listens to classical music and learns Japanese in his spare time.

Hazel5: It's Mandarin, actually – which is Chinese to a Philistine like you.

MiniMum: **%&&*%£$'* – which is a line of expletives to a knob-head like you.

There was a lot of sympathy for my cancelled fortieth-birthday trip to Paris. Lots of women made suggestions of alternatives and one kind mum offered to lend me her apartment in Paris if I wanted it. Imagine a stranger offering to lend you their apartment! Obviously I couldn't accept, but it was still a really nice offer.

The biggest response by far was to the part about having lost the romance in our relationship. Almost all the respondents said they felt the same way – too swamped to give time to their husbands and their relationships, but desperate to rekindle romance.

One woman disagreed. JayneyB wrote: Seriously, ladies, get a grip. Do you think your husbands go to the pub with their mates and sit around talking about how they wish they could fall in love with their wives again? That they want to hold hands and kiss? No, they don't. They're talking about sport and cars. We should be out drinking wine and having fun, not sitting around moaning about lost romance. It's pathetic.

Needless to say, there was a big reaction to that too.

I started a new posting:

Threescompany:

Hi, Mums,
I was delighted to see the response to my last message. There were some lively debates, which is always healthy!

I've just been on the phone to my sister. She lives in London. She's forty-one, had a baby three weeks ago and is going back to work tomorrow. Can you believe it? I think she's mad, she thinks I'm mad. My life to her is hell, her life to me is hell. She works twelve-hour days in an incredibly stressful job. She said if she didn't go back to work after three weeks, they would presume she'd lost her edge. She'd be considered a lost cause, a mother, a woman no longer married to her job, distracted, unreliable, unfocused, unworthy of being a partner in the law firm.

So, after three weeks, she's going back. She thinks it's going to be fine. She thinks the baby will just slot into her life. But anyone who's had a child, no matter how sweet and angelic they are, knows that babies march to their own drum. You might get them into a routine, but one ear infection, one cold, one night of teething and it's back to square one .

I'm worried about her and the baby. I'm worried that she won't have time to bond with the baby and the baby won't know who her mother is. The child is going to a crèche, starting tomorrow – she's only three weeks old! It's a super-posh one with loads of maternity nurses and all that, but can you imagine putting a newborn into a crèche for ten hours a day? It just seems cruel. I suggested she should get a childminder into the apartment, but she shot me down. The crèche is open all year round – it only closes on Christmas Day and Easter Monday. My sister always works during the holidays, so I guess it'll suit her to be flexible. Did I mention the dad isn't involved? She got pregnant on a one-night stand. So she's on her own, which is so tough. Although if anyone can do it on her own, it's my sister. She's so capable.

And now for a little moan. Both of my sisters were back in their jeans three weeks after giving birth. It makes me sick. How come I didn't get those genes (pun intended)? They are so disciplined and focused. Then again, they do only have one child each. I often wonder if the triplets had been just one baby would my life be completely different? Would I have got my figure back and enjoyed the early days? I honestly can't remember anything about the first year but the searing pain behind my eyes caused by exhaustion. I wonder if I would have enjoyed the happy-clappy playgroups with one baby, instead of dreading them because my three kids were the noisiest and the most boisterous, and all the other mums avoided me like the plague. I stopped going after a while because I knew that the boys and I weren't welcome. Even the playgroup leader used to roll her eyes when I staggered in, three babies in tow.

I'm always beating myself up for not being as together as my sisters but, actually, I'd like to see how they would have coped with triplets. I'd like to see how slim and toned and well dressed they would be after giving birth to three feisty little boys, who were always hungry and rarely slept. Maybe I should give myself a break – maybe I didn't do so badly. I can say this now because the really hard drudge is almost over. The triplets will be going to proper school next year from 9 a.m. until 1.30 p.m. with the option of after-school care. I am determined to start getting my life back then. I swore I'd drop two dress sizes before my forti-eth. I wanted to look well in Paris, but when the trip was cancelled I ate because I was depressed. Now I've probably gone up a size. I know I need to be more disciplined. I know I need to stop making excuses and just get fit, but it's hard. Isn't it? Don't you think? Or is it just me? Am I just lazy and pathetic?

I don't know why my husband even wants to have sex with me. I'm all flabby in the wrong places. But he still seems very keen. If I look at him sideways, he jumps on top of me. Maybe if I was thinner and fitter I'd feel sexier and be more up for it too. Maybe if I had more sex I'd be thinner and fitter. I don't know. Maybe I just need to stop pontificating and get off my arse and do something about it. If my sisters can do it, why can't I?

I also have one brother – an afterthought. He's sixteen years younger than me and is currently living in a tent near Heathrow, with a girl who looks like Angelina Jolie. He has no responsibilities, no dependants, no bills (well, he has Visa bills, which my mother pays for him), no mortgage, no car, no baggage. He just packed a small knapsack and took off to London. I envy him his freedom. He can go anywhere and do anything. He is not permanently stalked by four children. He can shower and go to the loo in peace. On the other hand, he doesn't have a clue what he's doing with his life. He's currently going through an eco-warrior phase, which I know won't last.

He's at that stage where he's just left college and still has no idea what to do. I was the same. I drifted to London and ended up in recruitment because I was offered a job and it seemed easy. I think if I could turn the clock back, I'd focus more on finding a career I really enjoyed. Something I could pick up again after the boys are in school. I'd hate to see my little brother drift through life. It's harder for men because they are traditionally the bread-winners, hunter-gatherers, protectors. I see it with my husband – he feels so guilty every time he gets a pay cut. Even though it's not his fault, he feels responsible. He feels he's let the family down. But he hasn't and I don't feel that way at all about it. But if I'm being totally honest, sometimes I do fantasize about being married to a millionaire . . .

Anyway, I hope my brother figures out what he wants to do with his life while he's in the tent – in between shagging the stunning girl and trying to save the planet! It's important that he likes his career: he'll be working in it for forty years. I look at my older sister and I see how much she loves her job and what satisfaction and fulfilment it brings to her life. I want that for my little brother too.

I thought being a mother would bring me that – and sometimes I do feel fulfilled and content, but if I'm being totally honest, a lot of the time I don't . . .

20

Louise

It felt great to be back in work. I had set my alarm for six, gone for a short run before the night nurse left, then taken my time getting ready. I wanted to look good. I wanted to look unchanged. I wanted to look in charge. I put on a new black Jaeger trouser suit and high heels.

Walking into the office I felt a huge surge of adrenalin. I could see everyone checking me out. The women were looking at my stomach to see if I'd lost the baby weight and the men were impressed that I was back so soon.

My secretary, Jasmine, jumped up and hugged me. It was awkward: we'd never hugged before, it wasn't that kind of a relationship – she was my secretary, not my friend. I just patted her shoulder and stepped back.

'How are you? How is little Clara? Can I see a picture?' she enthused.

'I'm fine, she's fine, and I don't have any photos.'

She stared at me, open-mouthed. 'Didn't you take any at all?'

'Um, no, I just forgot. I think my mother took a few but . . .' I trailed off. Jasmine was looking at me as if I was a freak. I'd never thought about photos: I'd been too busy trying to look after Clara and get myself ready for work. I'd take some at the weekend.

'Well, congratulations,' she said, and handed me a present.

'Oh, God, you shouldn't have.' I felt rotten. I'd never bought any presents for her kids. I always gave her a very generous voucher for Selfridges at Christmas, but that was it.

'It'll come in useful. My babies loved being in it.' Jasmine pointed at the present.

She was clearly waiting for me to open it, so I did. It was a – ?

'It's a sling,' she said, coming over to show me how to put it on. 'If Clara gets fussy and you want to calm her down but still need to do things, you put her in the sling and you still have two free arms. It's great for doing things around the house or going shopping or going on the tube, all those kinds of things.'

'Very useful. Thanks, Jasmine, it was really thoughtful of you.'

'No problem. It must have been hard leaving her today,' she said, her voice full of sympathy.

'Oh, yes – yes, it was,' I lied. I hadn't found it hard at all. The difficult part was trying to get out of the house without forgetting something – soothers, change of clothes, bibs . . . I'd been determined to get to the office for seven fifteen. The crèche opened at seven, and I was standing outside at five to. I had literally handed her to the nurse with a list of instructions about adhering strictly to her routine and then I had rushed into work.

Just as I was trying to get the baby-sling off, Alex arrived. He looked at it and frowned. 'Welcome back. How is the little fellow?'

'Fine, thanks,' I said, not bothering to correct him. Alex wouldn't care if I'd had sextuplets: he just wanted to know that I could function. I showed him into my office, ripped the sling off and threw the stupid thing under my desk.

'Where are we with the Gordon Hanks acquisition?' he enquired.

Gordon Hanks was an American client, who also just happened to be married to Alex's sister. Alex had his brother-in-law on a bit of a pedestal. I could see why – Gordon was a charismatic man. He was also a hugely successful entrepreneur, a multi-millionaire and a philanthropist. He was a personal friend of Bill Clinton. He played golf with Jack Nicklaus, tennis with Jimmy Connors and had dined at the White House with three different presidents.

I turned to face my boss. 'I spoke to Gordon yesterday and he seems very keen to forge ahead with the purchase of Lifechange TV. He wants us to negotiate on his behalf.'

Alex looked relieved. 'Excellent. You know how important it is to me that we do a good job on this. That's why I chose you to be in charge. It's good to have you back, Louise. I was worried you'd come in sleep deprived and longing to be at home with the baby. I can see I was wrong. Let's do lunch and discuss the finer details of the purchase. I've got meetings all morning so I'll meet you in Goff's at one.'

'Perfect. See you then.'

As Alex left, Dominic slunk in. 'Hell of a round on Saturday, Alex,' he smarmed.

'Ah, yes, I was on form.' Alex beamed.

'You were on fire – three birdies in a row on the back nine is very rare.'

God, Dominic was sickening. Could he crawl any further up Alex's arse?

'It was a very enjoyable day. Your father was excellent company, as always,' Alex said.

'He said the same thing about you. We must have a rematch soon.'

'Absolutely, excellent idea. I might ask Zachary to join us.'

Bloody hell! Alex had just offered to get Zachary Gray, CEO of the firm, to play golf with Dominic. Damn, damn, damn! Why hadn't I taken up golf in college? It was the one area I fell down on. I couldn't play, and every time I had tried to get lessons and practice, work had got in the way.

'That would be wonderful,' Dominic purred. 'I know my father and Zachary would get on famously. They have a passion for classic cars in common.'

'Ah, yes, of course. Well, let's set it up in the next week or so.'

'I look forward to it,' Dominic said, smirking at me.

'I'll see you for lunch at one, Alex,' I reminded him, determined to show Dominic that he wasn't the only one spending time with our boss.

Alex waved over his shoulder and hurried off to his meeting.

Dominic looked me up and down, his green eyes boring into me. 'Well well well, look who's back,' he said, and plonked himself down in one of the club chairs in my office. 'So it's true, you are Superwoman. I'm impressed. Three weeks and here you are.'

'Are you disappointed that I didn't decide to stay at home singing nursery rhymes and pumping breast milk? I know you've had your eye on my office, but I'm afraid you're just going to have to wait.'

'*Au contraire*, Louise, I'm glad to see you back. We lose far too many good women to motherhood. It would have been a travesty to see you go. I just hope you can sustain the pace. Babies can be very demanding.'

'Don't worry your pretty little head, Dominic. I'll manage just fine.'

'So how is little Tara?'

'Clara is thriving, thanks for asking.'

'Who's looking after her?'

'She's in a crèche.' I didn't like talking to him about my daughter. I hated discussing anything personal in work.

'Crèche? Isn't she only a few weeks old?'

'Yes. Now, tell me how the meeting went yesterday with Gordon Hanks.'

'I emailed you the details last night. You must have been too busy changing nappies to read them.'

I'd never wanted to thump someone so badly. He must have sent it after eleven, because I had checked my emails just before I'd fallen asleep. 'Well, I'll have a look at them now. I hope you've kept the notes clear and concise. Gordon is a very important client and a valued one. I don't want any slip-ups.'

'I'm aware of that. I just hope you can find the time to read my notes. If it all gets too much, don't hesitate to ask for help. I'm always available to oblige a colleague in need.'

'That's very reassuring to know. I could use some help right now, actually. I need a coffee, black, no sugar. Thanks, Dominic.'

He glared at me and flounced out. I sank into my chair. I needed to watch my back: he was ruthlessly ambitious. Still, I'd met his type before and had dealt with them the only way I knew how – I'd worked twice as hard, was more prepared, more thorough, more professional, more conscientious and more skilful. In this world of male domination, we women had to be even better than our male counterparts to get the respect we deserved.

There was a knock. 'Just leave it with Jasmine,' I shouted.

Someone peered round the door. It wasn't Dominic, it was Meredith Baker. She was wearing a grey trouser suit with killer heels. Her hair and makeup were perfect. 'Is this a bad time?' she asked.

'No, not at all, I'm delighted to see you. Sorry, I thought you were someone else – a weasel.'

'There's a lot of them around.' She grinned. 'How are you doing?'

'Good, thanks. I'm relieved to be at work again. I was worried I might have squatters in my office.'

'Believe me, there was a lot of talk about who was going to get your job if you couldn't cope with the baby. I heard some chubby guy with marbles in his mouth – Dominic something or other – spouting on in the canteen about how he was going to get your job because no woman could juggle the hours you have to put in as a senior partner with a baby.'

'The little shit.'

'Don't worry. I dealt with him.'

'Fantastic. What did you say?'

'I tapped him on the shoulder and introduced myself. "I'm Meredith Baker, senior partner and mother to a nine-month-old."'

'How did he react?' I was loving this.

'He came over all sickly sweet. He said of course he knew who I was. I was a legend in the office. He had meant no disrespect, but I was the exception rather than the rule.'

'Arsehole,' I muttered.

'My sentiments exactly. I told him he'd better get used to having mothers around him, because women were managing to juggle high-powered careers with having children. I said that men needed to raise the bar. We mothers were coming after their jobs.'

We roared laughing.

'I'd say that shut him up,' I said.

'Temporarily, but I'd watch him. He's a snake.'

'God, don't I know it.'

'Anyway, it's good to see you back and looking fantastic. How's the baby sleeping?'

'So far, she's great. I have a night nurse for another few weeks, so she'll be in a routine by then.'

'Well, good luck, and don't let that Dominic creep get to you.'

'Thanks, I won't.'

I spent the rest of the morning going through memos and emails. I had kept on top of the urgent ones at home, but now I wanted to deal with all of my correspondence and clear my desk and in-box. It felt wonderful to be back in my role as a lawyer. This was me; this was who I was; this was my identity. I was an expert in my field; I was in my comfort zone. I was in control, in charge, in the driving seat. At home with Clara I was still learning and making mistakes. I didn't like it. I wasn't used to being at sea: it was a new experience and not one that I was enjoying much. I still felt no great love for my baby. I liked her, she was sweet, but she didn't feel like part of me. I didn't feel like a mother. She didn't feel like a daughter. I felt protective and responsible for her well-being, but not particularly attached. She was just a baby.

I turned back to my computer. I didn't have time for navel-gazing: I was too busy. Besides, I was sure Clara would grow on me as she became more interesting, when she started walking and talking. Right now she was just a blob who drank milk, slept and pooped.

21

Sophie

Jack is due back today, thank God. I don't know what on earth is going on with my bank account – I haven't been able to get any money out for three days. I had to borrow from Mimi this morning to pay for my coffee.

I'd left several frantic messages for Jack, but his phone was permanently switched to voicemail. Eventually, after the sixth, when I asked him to please have the courtesy of letting me know if he was still alive, he sent a brief text saying he was up to his eyes but he'd be back home today at about eleven.

I'd put a sundress and a clutch-bag on hold in Harvey Nicks and I wanted to pick them up and pay for them this afternoon; I also wanted to pay back Victoria for the Missoni scarf. I didn't like owing people money: it made me uncomfortable. I'd never borrowed money from anyone. I'd been working since I was eighteen, so I'd always had my own money, and then I'd married Jack. Since then I'd never had to think about it.

As I drove home after the coffee, my phone rang. It was Victoria.

'Hi, Sophie. Listen, Gerry's been trying to get in touch with Jack for days. He needs the cheque for our weekend in Venice. Everyone else has paid, so we're just waiting on you guys.'

'Sorry about that. He's been in New York and completely swamped with work. I've barely heard from him myself.'

'We really need the money by tomorrow.'

'He's due in this morning. In fact, I expect he'll be home when I get back to the house. I'll drop the cheque in to you this afternoon and the money I owe you for the scarf.'

'Great, thanks.'

'I can't wait for Venice. The Cipriani is supposed to be incredible,' I said.

'It's lovely. We've been there a few times. Gerry's booked a suite for us.'

'Oh, wow. Is the shopping good?'

'You have to know where you're going. I'll show you around – I know Venice pretty well.'

'Great! It'll be nice to get away.'

'I know – it's been a month since I was in Paris and I badly need a change of scenery. It's so dreary here, nothing but doom and gloom and recession talk.'

'I agree. I'll call you later. I've just arrived home and Jack's car is here, so I'll sort out the payment for you.'

'I'll see you later. 'Bye.'

I opened the door and walked into the kitchen. 'Jack?' I called.

The kitchen was empty, but his suitcase was lying on the floor.

'Jack?' I shouted.

Nothing. He must be in the shower. I began to go upstairs to find him when I heard a strange noise coming from his office. It sounded like . . . hiccuping. I opened the door and found my husband sitting at his desk, with his face in his hands . . . sobbing.

I froze. In all the years we had been together, I had never seen Jack cry. His whole body was shaking. I pulled myself together and ran over to him. 'Jack! What's wrong?'

He was too upset to speak.

'Jack?' I turned his chair to face me and knelt in front of him. 'You have to calm down and talk to me. What is it? Oh, my God, is it Jess?'

He shook his head.

'Well, then, what?'

'I'm so sorry . . . I'm – uh – uh . . . sorry.'

'Sorry for what?' My heart was pounding – I was beginning to panic.

'I've let you down . . . terrible mistake.' His chest heaved up and down.

What had he done? He was having an affair. With whom? It must be one of those American girls. 'Are you sleeping with one of those cheap tarts in work?' I shouted.

He shook his head again. 'No – I'm such a fuck-up . . . uh – uh . . . sorry, Sophie.'

'Jesus, Jack, talk to me, I don't understand. What did you do that's so terrible? Did you have sex with another woman?'

'No.'

'Are you sick? Is it cancer? We can get over cancer – lots of people live long happy lives after cancer. I love you. I'll nurse you back to health.'

'I'm not sick.'

'Is it your parents? Has someone died?'

'No.'

'Roger? Fiona? Grace?'

'No one's dead,' he bawled.

I stood up and racked my brains. 'Did you hurt someone? Oh, God – did you run someone over in your car? Did you kill someone?'

He shook his head a third time.

I grabbed his arm. 'Well, what is it? Tell me. You're really scaring me. Whatever it is, we can work it out. I promise. Talk to me, Jack.'

'It's – uh – uh – all – uh – uh – gone.'

'What is?'

'Everything.'

'What are you talking about?'

'I've lost everything, Sophie,' he said, staring down at his hands.

I put my hands gently on his shoulders. 'Take a deep breath and tell me what the hell is going on.'

He looked at me for the first time. His eyes were completely bloodshot and his face was ashen. He had aged ten years. He took a long breath and said, 'All of our money is gone.'

'What do you mean?'

'The company invested in a Ponzi scheme.'

'What the hell is that?'

'It's an investment fraud.'

'So go to the police.'

'It's not that simple.'

'Why not? If someone stole your money, report it and get it back.'

'The guy has no money. There's nothing to recoup. The whole thing was a scam.'

I frowned. 'What guy? Who is he? Why did you trust him? Why did you give him the company money?'

'It wasn't just us.' Jack defended GreenGem. 'Half the hedge funds in New York were involved. It was a no-brainer, a sure thing.'

'So what went wrong?'

'We made a mistake. A huge one.'

'Well, fix it.'

'I can't.'

'Why not?'

Jack sat back in his chair, wiped his eyes and tried to explain. 'The guy's name is Terence Hartley.'

'I know that name. He's the guy you and Brad were toasting that night in New York.'

'Yes, we were. He had made us a lot of money, or so we thought. I met him four years ago at a party in New York. I'd heard about him through one of the other hedge-fund guys, Larry Holm. He said Hartley was a sure thing. Larry's no idiot. He runs a well-established hedge fund and has years more experience than I do. I asked around about Hartley, and a couple of the other guys I know from the business vouched for him too. Hartley was one of the founders of the NASDAQ stock exchange, for Christ's sake. So, one night at a party I managed to get introduced to him and we got chatting. I said I'd heard about his consistent returns and was interested in investing some money with him. He said he wasn't taking on anyone else and made this big song and dance

232

about not needing any more investors because he wanted to look after the ones he had.'

'Why didn't you walk away?' I asked.

'Because the guys who had invested with him were getting seven per cent returns every year without fail, despite the down-turn. Hartley seemed to have the Midas touch. So I kept at him. Eventually he said he'd think about it and let me know. A week later he called and said I could come on board, but the minimum investment was a hundred million. I spoke to Brad about it, then introduced him to Hartley. He was impressed too. We decided that the GreenGem hedge fund would put up the money. We piled everything we had into it – we managed to come up with twenty million ourselves and borrowed eighty million from the bank. We were borrowing at three per cent and making returns of seven per cent for the first two years. It was a sure thing, a fail-safe.'

'But what do you mean you put everything in? How could you put all the company's money into one investment? I know nothing about this, but Dad always said you never put all your eggs in one basket.'

Why was Jack being such an idiot? Why did he keep saying we had lost everything? I didn't understand what the hell was going on. We still had all his salary and bonuses in the bank. Didn't we?

'The investments were spread across lots of different financial streams. We were flying. Brad and I couldn't believe our luck. Hartley was a genius.'

'Well, why are you in here crying?'

'Because the whole thing was a house of cards, and it started crashing a few weeks ago. We found out the full extent this week.'

'How did it all crash?'

'Hartley was using the money from new investors to pay old investors the returns he had promised. There were never any invest-ments. He was just taking from new clients to pretend to old clients that their investments were going well.'

'Why did he bother? What did he get out of it?'

'He was taking a slice of every investment and living like a king.'

'So why did it all crash?'

'Because he ran out of new investors to cover his arse. The whole thing blew up in everyone's faces. All of GreenGem's previous good investments have been swallowed up by this Ponzi scheme.'

'Jesus Christ, Jack, how could you trust this guy?'

'Because everyone thought he was a genius and for the first two years he proved he was.'

'Until you found out he was a cheat and a fraud?'

'Yes.'

'What about your bonuses? You still have those, don't you? They were personal money, not company money?'

'No, they were in there too.'

'What do you mean? How? Why would you do that?'

'Because Brad's company policy for all the partners in Green-Gem was that our bonuses had to be reinvested in the company for five years.'

'What about your salary?'

'Sophie, the GreenGem fund has shut down, the company has folded. It's over.'

I took a step back. I felt as if I'd been shot. 'So what is our situation? How much do we have left in the bank? What do we have to live on until this blows over?'

'Sophie, you're not listening to me. We have nothing left.'

I stared at him. I needed to try to stay calm. I needed to process this information. I needed to understand what was going on. I coughed to suppress the panic rising in my throat and bit my lip.

Jack held his arms out. I pushed him away. I didn't want him near me. I felt suffocated. I had to think.

'What about the house? It's worth a lot,' I said.

He looked at his shoes. 'We bought it for three million, it's now worth one. We're mortgaged to the hilt. I borrowed two and half million to buy the house, which was fine because I had a big salary that we spent every month, but we didn't save anything because I looked at the company fund as our savings.'

'What are you saying? That we don't own our house?'

'Yes.'

'But . . . how can we not own it? It's ours – you bought it.'

'Because we owe two million on it and it's worth one.'

I began to shake. 'So you're telling me we're one million in debt?'

His eyes welled up again. 'Yes.'

'What about my dad's money? My rainy-day money? We can live on that until you get sorted.'

'It's gone too,' he whispered.

'*What?*' I shouted. 'Are you insane? You invested my money in some crazy scheme with a gangster you met at a party? That was *my* money. You had no right to do that.'

'You told me to invest it. You said you wanted me to look after it for you.'

'Yes, I did, but looking after it doesn't mean throwing it away. What have you done, Jack? What's going to happen to us now? There must be some money somewhere.'

'I'm so sorry, Sophie.'

'There has to be some money left. You can't have given this guy every penny. Come on, Jack, think. You must have money in some account somewhere.'

'My other investments were in Irish bank shares, which are worth nothing now either. I lost a fortune on them as well.'

I screamed at him, 'Jesus Christ, what is wrong with you? Why didn't you just leave it in a bank account where it was safe? Why did you have to invest in all these things that just lose money? I thought you were smart. I thought you knew what you were doing. How can we be rich one minute and have nothing the next?' We couldn't be poor. We couldn't have no money at all. That was just not possible. I wouldn't accept it. There had to be some tucked away somewhere – there just had to be.

'Look, it's not just me. Brad lost everything as well. So have hundreds of other people who invested with Hartley – smart guys, experienced guys, Ivy League guys. He fooled us all.'

'There must be some way to get it back. We can't live on air!'

Jack began to lose his temper. 'I've spent the last week trying everything to get some of it back. I haven't slept in days. Brad and I went over every single bit of paperwork, but it's all gone. There is nothing left. I wish I could tell you different, Sophie, but I can't. We looked into suing Terence Hartley for the money he lost us, but the case would take years and lots of legal fees and it's pointless because he's broke. The GreenGem fund has blown up. It's over. I tried to protect you. I tried to fix it – I did everything I could.'

'Protect me?' I roared. 'My credit card got refused in Harvey Nichols and you ignored all my calls. Now you come home and tell me we have nothing. How the hell can we live on nothing? What about Jess? What about our life?'

'I don't know. I need to try to figure it out.'

'There's nothing to figure out! We can't live without money. What's going to happen to us? Are we going to lose the house?'

'I'm trying not to let that happen, but we may be forced out.'

I felt physically ill. I couldn't process it all. How could we suddenly have nothing? This was my life, my house, my car, my clothes, my lifestyle. It was a happy life. I was happy, Jack was happy, Jess was happy. How could it all be snatched away? Where would we go? What was going to become of us?

Jack came over and wrapped his arms around me. 'Come on, Sophie, we'll be OK.'

I shoved him away forcefully. 'What happens if we have to leave the house? Where will we live? Do you expect your daughter to sleep on the *street*?'

'We might have to move in with your family for a little while,' he said quietly.

'Move in with my parents?'

'I can't afford rent.'

'But what about my life? What about Venice and Marbella in the summer and –'

'Jesus, Sophie,' he snapped, 'what part of *we have no money* are you not getting? There will be no more holidays or shopping or beauticians. We're *broke*.'

'What about Jess's school?'

'I can't pay the fees so she'll have to stay at home for a while.'

'*You bastard!*' I screamed. 'You promised to look after us and now you're ruining our life. What am I going to tell her? How am I going to explain that she can't go to school or ballet or drama or swimming any more because her dad's an idiot? She loves that school – she loves her friends.'

'You don't need to stick the knife in,' Jack barked. 'I feel shit enough as it is. Do you think I like having to take my daughter out of school or tell my wife that I've lost all our money? Do you think this is *easy* for me? I'm having a nervous breakdown here trying to think of ways around it. I'm devastated about what's happened.'

'*What about me?* You've ruined my life.' What was I going to do now? My friends would dump me. I'd have no life. I'd seen the way you got dropped when you couldn't keep up. Look at what had happened to Annabelle. God, I'd be the new Annabelle but worse – at least her husband still had a job, even if his salary was very low. My heart was thumping and I was sweating profusely. I just couldn't process what was happening. I'd married Jack for love, but also for security. He was supposed to look after me and Jess. This was not part of the deal.

'Look, Sophie, I know it's a lot to take in, but we'll be OK. We have each other and our health, and I'll find another job.'

'Who the hell is going to hire someone who lost all his company's money by investing in a stupid fraud? They're not going to be queuing up to get you, Jack.'

'I'll find something, I promise.'

'Your promise means nothing to me. You promised to take care of me and now you're telling me we could be on the street soon. You've broken your promise. I don't believe you any more. How could you do this? How could you be so stupid?' I began to sob . . . and once I'd started, I couldn't stop. I was shocked, terrified and devastated. We would be outcasts, rejects, pariahs.

Jack came over to comfort me, but I pushed him away and ran upstairs. I locked myself in the bathroom, lay on the floor and wailed.

22

Julie

I was sitting in Marian's garden, watching the kids fight each other.

'More wine?' she asked.

'Lovely.' I held out my glass. It was four in the afternoon, a bit early to be drinking wine, but not social-services-will-take-your-kids-away early.

'Do you ever hit the boys?' Marian asked.

'I've smacked them on the bum once or twice, but I always feel sick after, so I really try not to.'

'I walloped Brian yesterday.' She took a gulp of wine. 'He was being a nightmare, writing on the wall with my mascara when I'd asked him ten times to stop, so I smacked him on the back of the head. I feel awful. I've been awake all night. I had to bribe him not to tell his dad. Greg would divorce me if he knew. I just lost it. I swear, Julie, for the five seconds between deciding to hit him and hitting him, everything went blurry. I was so angry that I literally couldn't see straight. It gave me a fright. I was out of control.'

'Everyone has those moments. Obviously we have to try to control ourselves, but sometimes kids push your buttons until you explode. The best thing to do is walk away from them when they're like that.'

'Yeah, but how can I walk away when he's painting my fucking bedroom walls with mascara?'

'I dunno. Grab the mascara and run into the kitchen or something. I just know that if I didn't walk away from the triplets at times I would probably hit them.'

'You should have seen the way he looked at me. It was pure hate. I don't blame him – it's shocking to hit someone on the back of the head. It'll be one of those things he remembers for the rest of his life. I guarantee he'll be dragging it up in therapy in twenty years' time.'

'Don't beat yourself up too much. All mothers have days when they lose control. It's just a matter of learning from mistakes and trying to avoid them.'

Marian looked down at her glass. 'I'm thinking of going on anti-depressants.'

'What?' I was surprised. Marian always seemed well able to cope. Yes, she cursed like a drunken sailor, yes, she drank a little bit too much, but underneath all that she was a brilliant mum. She took her kids to exhibitions, art galleries, concerts, puppet shows, outdoor theatre, adventure parks, petting farms . . . she never stopped. She was constantly doing creative and fun things with them. And although I knew she was tired, like all mums, and sometimes overwhelmed, I hadn't thought she was depressed.

'I'm struggling, Julie. Every day is like a fucking eternity. I have to drag myself out of bed in the morning and I spend all day looking at the clock, praying for bedtime. By the time they're asleep it's nine, and I haven't the energy to do anything but tidy up, put on another bloody wash and collapse into bed. I have no life. It's really getting me down. It's like being a hamster on one of those wheels.'

'You need a break. Why don't I take your kids while you and Greg go off for a night somewhere? It'll do you good.'

She shook her head. 'Thanks, Julie, but the last person Greg wants to go away with is me. I've been biting his head off lately. All we seem to do is fight. We used to have such fun together. I used to make him laugh – he thought I was a riot. Now he thinks I'm a fucking nightmare. I dunno, I just feel crap all the time.'

I reached over to squeeze her hand. 'You've got too much on your plate. Four small kids and your mum – it's a lot to deal with.'

'My mother's getting worse. She can't really look after herself any more. I need to put her into a home, but every time I bring it up, she freaks. She starts telling me that if she leaves the window, she'll miss Dad when he comes home. She's wasted her whole life waiting for that prick.'

'Can your brother help?'

'He just got dumped by his boyfriend and has buggered off to Australia to shag his way through his broken heart. He said he was sorry to leave me to deal with Mum on my own, but he needed some time out.'

'No wonder you're feeling down. Everything's falling on your shoulders. It's a huge amount of responsibility for one person.'

She exhaled deeply. 'I can tell you it feels very heavy at the moment. I think if I go on anti-depressants I'll stop drinking so much. Let's be honest here, Julie, I have my first glass of wine or brandy-coffee at lunchtime. I need to stop before it gets out of hand. And I refuse to end up like my mother, a miserable, depressed mess. I need to deal with my shit and get myself sorted.'

'Maybe you need some counselling. It'd be good for you to talk about your dad leaving and how you feel overwhelmed by everything you're dealing with.'

'Jesus, they'd never get me out of the place. I'd be in there moaning for months. If I can just lift this black cloud hanging over me, I'll be fine. If I don't do something, Greg will leave me and then I'd be totally screwed. He might drive me around the bend at times, but he's a good dad and occasionally when we're not roaring at each other I remember why I married him.'

'You should talk to your GP. Maybe he could put you on a mild anti-depressant to help you through the next few months. I'm sorry you're feeling like this. I didn't realize you were so down.'

'How the hell could you? You haven't got time to think. You're as swamped as I am. You just deal with it better. You don't hit your kids and you're not a bitch to your husband.'

'Sometimes I'm a total cow to Harry, especially if the kids have been acting up all day, or if he comes in from work in a bad mood. He's been really grumpy lately and we've been snapping at each other constantly. He's working on some new project and he's really uptight about it. The sooner it's finished, the better. I wouldn't mind if he was getting paid more for it, but he isn't.'

'Husbands are not allowed to come home in a foul mood. We've spent all day dealing with tantrums and mood swings. The last thing we need is a long face walking in the door at six o'clock. I want to see a smile. I want to get a hug. I want to be told I'm a fucking legend for having got through the day without killing one of the kids, and I want to sit down and put my feet up while he persuades Molly that green beans are not the devil's food.'

'Amen to that.'

Marian pointed to her wine. 'I'm going to give this up for a while and try to sort out my mother and my head.'

'Good for you. Let me know if I can do anything to help. I'm always here for you.'

'Thank God you moved in next door and not some fucking Stepford Wife who would make me feel really shit about myself.'

'Are you implying I'm not the perfect wife and mother?' I pretended to be offended.

'Yes, I am, and thank God for that too.'

We chuckled.

'Marian, does Brian take his willy out much?'

'Jesus, where did that come from? What do you mean?'

'The triplets are going through a phase of exposing themselves. We were in Tesco earlier and when I turned back from getting ice-cream out of the freezer, they were all standing there with their willies hanging out, giggling. There was an old man staring at them in shock.'

'No, Brian doesn't take it out in public, but he came in the other day and said, "Mummy, my willy's all excited." I didn't know where to look. Greg thought it was hilarious.'

'What are we going to do when they have wet dreams and all that stuff?'

'Steady on there.'

'Well, it's going to happen and I'll have three at the same time.'

'You'll have a lot of laundry.' Marian roared laughing.

That evening Harry came home in a better mood. He sat down and helped me feed the kids and was his old patient self. After dinner, when I was clearing up, I told him about the boys exposing themselves in Tesco. Harry, of course, thought it was very amusing.

'It's not funny, Harry. They could attract paedophiles and all kinds of weirdos with their willies out.'

'Come on, it's just a bit of fun. Sometimes a willy just needs a bit of fresh air.'

'It needs to stay in their pants. I don't see you slapping yours out in supermarkets.'

'I'd get arrested.'

'Seriously, talk to them. It's dangerous. They'll catch the wrong people's attention.'

Harry called the triplets in. 'Boys, your mum said you took your willies out in the supermarket today.'

They giggled.

'You must always keep your willies in your pants,' Harry continued.

'What about when you have to pee?' Leo asked.

'Obviously you can take them out when you need to go to the toilet,' I told them.

'But sometimes my willy gets really hot and sticks to my nut balls,' Luke complained.

'I know – Daddy gets that too,' Harry sympathized, 'but when it happens you need to go to the toilet, take your pants down and give it some air.'

'But there is no toilet in the shop,' Liam said.

'In that case you have to wait until you get home,' Harry explained.

'But it was itchy,' Luke said.

'Mine was scratchy,' Leo said.

'Mine was so hot it was on fire,' Liam added.

I leant down. 'The thing is, boys, there are some bad men in the world who like to look at little boys' willies and touch them, and if you go around taking your willies out, the bad men might see you and come over to you.'

'Would they try to touch us?' Leo's eyes were round.

'They might,' I said.

'Why?' Liam asked.

'Because some men are mean and nasty and like to touch boys and girls in their private parts. If anyone ever tries to touch you or asks you to touch them, you must say, "No way," and tell Mummy immediately.'

'Should we shout, "NO WAY"?' Luke roared.

'Yes,' I said.

'Really loud, like – NO WAY?' Leo screeched.

'Yes, as loud as you can. No one is allowed touch your willy, ever.'

'Not even you, Mummy?' Liam was confused.

'Mummy and Daddy can when we're washing you in the bath, but no one else.'

'Not even my brothers?' Luke wondered.

'Well, no, not really. You should just keep your willy to yourself.' They were exasperating.

'What do the bad men look like?' Leo wanted to know.

Harry sighed. 'Why did you start this?' he whispered.

'Because I want them to be aware,' I replied. 'Leo, the bad men look like Daddy or Greg next door – they just look like normal guys.'

'Does Greg want to touch our willies?' Liam asked.

'No!' I said.

'Does a bad guy have scary teeth like a vampire?' Leo was peering at me from behind his fringe.

'Not necessarily. He could have normal teeth,' I answered, brushing his hair out of his eyes.

'Why does he want to touch our willies?' Luke asked.

'Because some men are very naughty and like to touch little kids.'

'But why?' Luke insisted.

'Because they're just weird.'

'Mummy, are you allowed touch Tom's willy, too?'

'Yes.'

'And Daddy's?'

'Any time she wants.' Harry grinned.

'And Greg-next-door's?'

'No!' Harry jumped in. 'Mummy most certainly is not allowed touch Greg-next-door's willy.'

'Look, boys,' I said firmly, 'just remember that no one is allowed touch your willies except Mummy and Daddy. OK?'

'Do the bad men go to the supermarkets looking for willies to touch?' Leo was relentless.

I looked at Harry. 'Help me out here.'

'I told you not to start.'

'There can be bad men anywhere. You just need to be careful.' I tried to reassure them.

'OK, boys, that's enough about willies. Who wants to watch cartoons?' Harry asked.

They all cheered and ran into the TV room. Harry came back in, smiling. 'Well, that was an interesting conversation.'

I shrugged. 'I had to try to explain it to them. But nothing is ever easy with the boys.'

'Would you like a daughter?' Harry asked, suddenly very serious. Was he suggesting we have another baby? Had he lost his mind?

'Harry, I'm nearly forty and we have four kids that we're struggling to manage, not to mention afford. There will be no more babies in this house.'

'I know – but would you have liked a girl?'

'Well, yes, I suppose I would. I mean, if all my kids were as good and saintly as Jess, life would be a lot easier, but I wouldn't change the boys for anything. I love every hair on their little heads. They're my guys, my boys, my lads.'

Harry came over and hugged me. I waited. No, it was just a hug. Not a hug and a pull towards the bedroom, not a hug and a suggestive pinch on the bum, just a hug. A big bear hug. Wow! I hadn't had one of those in years. I hugged him back.

'I love this family,' he mumbled into my hair, sounding a bit choked up. I pulled back and looked at him.

'Harry, have you lost your job?' I asked.

'No, no, my job is fine. It's totally safe.'

'So why are you all emotional?' I was suspicious now: something was up.

'I just looked at you and the kids tonight and I felt lucky and I wanted to tell you. That's all. Sometimes you forget what you have and how lucky you are.'

'OK, but why are you feeling this now, tonight?'

'Jesus, Julie, you're always telling me I don't say anything nice to you and now that I tell you I love you you're quizzing me. I can't win.'

'Well, it's just –' The phone rang. Harry picked it up.

'Hello? . . . Who is it? . . . What? . . . Oh, Louise, sorry, I couldn't hear you.'

He handed me the phone. 'It's Louise, there's an awful racket in the background.'

23

Louise

Jesus Christ, I think I'm having a nervous breakdown. Clara has gone crazy. She's getting worse by the minute. She's ten weeks old now and she's been screaming blue murder after every feed for the past five weeks, but she's hungry all the time and screams just as loudly if I don't feed her. The nurses at the crèche keep telling me it's just colic and at twelve weeks it'll stop. The GP beside the crèche said it was reflux and that she'll settle in the next few weeks or months. Months!

My bloody night nurse handed in her notice last week. She said she was very sorry but she's never had to look after a baby who screamed all the time and she was exhausted. What about me? I'm exhausted and I'm trying to close Gordon Hanks's purchase of Lifechange TV. The agency is trying to find me a new night nurse, but they said most of them are booked up months in advance. I'm going mad here. The only time Clara stops crying is when she's in the sling.

I can't handle the shrieking: it cuts right through me. I've tried all the things the GP told me to do – I've raised the end of the Moses basket where her head is, put Gaviscon in all her bottles, given her Infacol before every feed, kept her upright for an hour after her milk to help her digest, but she only ever sleeps for two hours and then wakes up and screams for two hours.

I don't have time for this. I don't have time to pace the bloody floors every night. I need to focus on work. Today I'd been stuck in meetings until ten p.m. When I got home, Agnes – my cleaning lady – was sitting on the couch and Clara was asleep on her chest.

'Sorry I'm so late,' I said.

'It's OK. She crying a lot but she OK now. She like to sleep like this. Poor baby is very uncomfortable.'

'Tell me about it. All she does is cry.'

'She very sweet, she just have sore tummy.'

'Well, I'm trying everything the doctor said and it's not making any difference.' I sat down on the couch, exhausted. I'd been up for the last five nights in a row with Clara and she was relentless.

'I see this with my cousin. When he four months it stop. Sometimes babies have sore in their stomach when they drinking.'

'I hope it stops soon – it's not easy to listen to.'

Agnes patted my arm. 'You works too hard. You needs spend more time with baby. Then you understands how to keeping her calm.'

Agnes very gently lifted Clara from her chest to mine. She rustled briefly and then resettled herself on me.

'Can you pick her up from the crèche tomorrow? I've got meetings until eight.'

Agnes nodded. 'OK, but you needs tell your boss that you have baby now and you needs come home and see her. You needs to be with baby more. Childrens is growing up very fast. Only babies for little while. Baby needs Mummy.'

'Yes, fine.' I wasn't going to get into a debate about working too hard with Agnes. I just wanted to get into my pyjamas and sleep. My eyes felt like lead.

Agnes left and I gingerly stood up, being careful not to make any sudden movements that might wake Clara. But as soon as I took a step, her eyes snapped open and she began to cry. I sat down again and patted her back. She whimpered and closed her eyes. I was too afraid to move, so I closed my eyes and passed out on the couch. Clara woke up screaming at eleven. I settled her at one. She woke up again at three, and finally, after lots of walking in the sling, fell asleep at four thirty. We were both out cold when the alarm went off at six. I hit what I thought was the snooze button, but I actually turned it off and we both slept right through until seven thirty.

I woke with a start. Shit!

I leapt out of bed and started throwing Clara's things into her bag. I was still in my work clothes, somehow I'd never managed to get undressed. I smoothed the shirt down and decided to stay as I was. A shower would hold me up. My skirt was a bit crumpled, but it would pass. I changed Clara's nappy, threw a pair of dungarees over her Babygro and rushed to the crèche, then on to work.

It was the first time in my twenty-year career that I had overslept and been late for work. I was mortified and furious with myself. And, of course, sod's bloody law, Alex was standing outside my office when I came panting around the corner. I hadn't had time to do my makeup. I'd been planning on locking my office door and pulling myself together before our ten o'clock meeting, but there he was, waiting to ask me something about the Hanks case. I could see him looking at my appearance unfavourably.

'Is everything all right, Louise?' he asked.

'Absolutely great, thanks.' I beamed at him.

'You look a little . . . um, dishevelled.'

'Do I?' I feigned surprise.

He took his glasses off and fiddled with them. 'You know how important it is that we stay on top of the Hanks case, don't you?'

'Of course, Alex. I know you want everything to go smoothly for your brother-in-law. I'm on top of it.'

'What was the final purchase figure agreed on last night?'

'Thirty million plus their significant debts,' I said. 'I was about to email you the final details. Everything went according to plan. Lifechange TV finally agreed to the price Hanks wanted.'

'Excellent. He will be pleased.'

'We just need to finalize the paperwork and we'll have it all wrapped up.'

'Was Dominic with you at the meeting?'

'Yes.'

'Good. I want to keep him in the loop. He's a very sharp young man.'

'He certainly is.' I attempted a smile.

'Right, I'll leave you to it. Keep me posted on any further developments.'

'Of course.'

Alex left. I sank into my chair and took out my makeup bag. Christ, I looked awful. I had black rings under my eyes from sleep deprivation. Jasmine came in with a coffee. 'Thanks.' I took a big drink.

'Rough night?' she asked.

'Um, yes, she's been a bit unsettled lately.' I didn't want to get into a big baby chat with Jasmine. I wanted to keep our relationship a working one. I did not want to swap baby pictures and cute stories about our kids. Besides, I didn't have any cute stories about Clara. I wanted to give her back, and I didn't think that qualified as a sweet tale.

'The first few months are the hardest,' Jasmine said. 'Hang in there.'

'Right – thanks. Can you get me Gordon Hanks on the phone?' I asked her.

'Sure.' She turned on her heels and I continued to try to make myself look presentable. It took a lot more makeup than usual. As I was trowelling on the blusher to get some colour into my cheeks, Jasmine buzzed. 'It's Julie. She's calling to see if Clara is sleeping,' she said.

I grabbed my phone. 'Julie, I've told you before that I do *not* want you discussing anything personal with my secretary.'

'Keep your hair on. I just said I was calling about Clara.'

'I know, but I don't discuss her in work. And I don't want people knowing I'm getting no bloody sleep.'

'I take it from your sunny disposition that things have not improved?'

'She's worse. I nearly killed her last night.'

'Did you try the Infacol?'

'Yes, I bloody did.'

'Are you feeding her little and often?'

'Yes.'

'And you've raised the mattress?'

'Yes.'

'Keeping her upright after feeding?'

'Yes.'

'Is she getting sick after her bottles?'

'No. She just goes rigid and screams.'

'It does sound like reflux. I Googled it and they're the symptoms. But they say it almost always goes by six or nine months.'

'Six months! I thought it would be gone by four.'

'It probably will. The Internet always gives the worst-case scenarios.'

'It has to stop soon, Julie – I'm going insane. I didn't realize how much I need sleep. I often worked until eleven, but I was still getting six or seven hours' uninterrupted sleep. I can't handle this. I almost fell asleep in a really important meeting last night. I had to keep digging my nails into my arm to keep myself awake. I haven't been for a jog in four days. It's a mess. I wish I'd never bloody had her.'

'Louise!'

'I'm just being honest.'

'You can't say that.'

'Why not? It's true. I can't cope with her and her screeching. She's been bad for the last five weeks, but at least I had some help at night. I'm on my own now and it's hell. I'm sick of it. I dread going home and the bloody weekends seem never-ending.'

'OK. Now listen to me. The first few months are the hardest for any new mum, especially one with a difficult baby. It will get easier, I promise. You'll start really enjoying her when she's settled down a bit. Has she smiled yet?'

'Smile? She's too busy wailing.'

'Did you try sleeping with her on your chest?'

'Yes. It works for about two hours and then she's off again.'

'You sound really fed-up, but I promise it'll get better. This is temporary. Why don't you take a couple of days off work, get some rest and spend some more time with her? It'll help you bond with her.'

Spend more time with her? Julie wasn't getting it. The last thing I wanted to do was spend more time with Clara. I hated going home. My clean, minimalist apartment was a mess. The hall was stuffed with buggies and baby bags. There were clothes and toys, playmats and rattles, nappies and wipes, bottles and muslin cloths all over the place. I hated the chaos. I hated the clutter. I hated the untidiness.

'Julie, I can't take any more time off. Look, I'll be fine. I just need to get her into a routine. I'm going to try the *Contented Little Baby* one again this week.'

'Do yourself and Clara a favour and forget that stupid routine. Just go with her. Let her find her own routine.'

'Clara's current routine is to sleep for an hour, eat for an hour and scream for an hour or two. It's not exactly ideal. I need to work. I want to work. I like to work. And, by hook or by bloody crook, I'm going to get her sleeping.'

'Go easy on her, Lou. She's a tiny baby, not a soldier.'

'I know, I know.'

'By the way, you need to call Mum. She said she's left six messages and you still haven't phoned her back. She's getting worried. I told her everything was OK, that you were swamped in work and that Clara was a bit lively at night, but that all was well. You need to ring her, though.'

'I haven't had a second to myself. I'll get around to it soon, but it's not high on my list of priorities.'

'She's your mother, Louise. She's just worried about you – give her a break.'

'Look, I have to go. I've got a meeting that I need to try not to fall asleep in.'

'Good luck, and go easy on Clara.'

I hung up and typed a summary of last night's meeting with Gordon Hanks and Co and sent it to Alex. I wanted to prove to him that I was still on top of it, still in control.

Later, in the canteen, Dominic sidled over to me. 'I heard you were late in this morning, and that you looked – I think "dishevelled" was the word Alex used to describe you.'

I tried not to show him how much it bothered me that Alex was criticizing me. Granted, Dominic was climbing the corporate ladder faster than anyone I'd ever seen, but he was still a junior partner and I objected strongly to being discussed in this way.

'I think he used the word "drunk" to describe you at the partners' dinner last year,' I retorted.

'Ah, yes, but that was before Alex got into Harrington House and got to know me properly over rounds of golf. Now we play every other week. It's a pity you don't play, Louise. We had a tremendous day out last Saturday with my father, Alex and Zachary Gray. It was nice to spend so much quality time with the CEO. But I'm sure you were having the time of your life bonding with your baby.'

I tried to think of a good put-down, but my brain was too fuzzy.

'Be careful you don't crawl too far up Alex's arse. You may suffocate,' a voice behind me said to a stunned Dominic.

I turned to see Meredith holding her lunch tray. I beamed at her.

Dominic sputtered, 'There's no need to be so –'

'Crass? What's wrong, Dominic? Can't you take a joke? You're pretty good at dishing them out.'

'I'm perfectly capable of –'

Meredith put her hand up to stop him. 'I don't have time to waste talking to you. I need to speak to Louise about a client.' Meredith beckoned me over to a table in the corner of the canteen.

'Thank you!' I squeezed her hand.

'He's a little upstart. You look like death. Is the baby not sleeping?'

'She's a nightmare.'

'Damn – it's hard when they don't sleep. Where's your night nurse?'

'She did a runner, said she was too tired. The agency is trying to find another. How the hell did you do it, Meredith? I'm really struggling.'

'My husband did the nights from Monday to Thursday. I did the weekends.'

'I think she has reflux. Her father obviously had shitty digestive genes that he passed on to her.'

'You need to find some kind of night nurse or babysitter to do a few week nights. You can't survive on no sleep. Your work will suffer and that little prick is dying for you to mess up. He's just waiting for his opportunity to pounce.'

'Tell me about it. I can feel him breathing down my neck.'

'I'll ring around and see if any of my friends know of any good night nurses or someone who can help you out.'

'Thanks – you're a life-saver.'

'Don't let the bastards get you down – and remember, Louise, it's up to us to shatter the glass ceiling!'

I ate a slice of chocolate cake for dessert for the first time since the canteen had opened eight years ago. I needed the sugar to keep me going. I tried calling Sophie again. I'd left three messages for her. I wanted to know if she had any advice on how to deal with Clara. She spent all her time drinking coffee with other mothers. Maybe one of them had had a baby with reflux. But Sophie hadn't returned my calls, which wasn't like her. She always phoned back, and it wasn't as if she was busy.

'Look, Sophie, this is the fourth message I've left in the last three days. Can you just call me back, please. I need to ask you something about Clara. I know you're busy with your trainer and your Pilates, but I really need to talk to you so just call me.'

I drank my seventh coffee of the day and willed myself to stay awake.

24

Sophie

When Jack had first admitted to the mess we were in I'd cried for three days solid. He had kept trying to explain, to apologize, to excuse his mistakes, but none of it mattered. We were broke. We were nothing. We were nobody. It was all just words. None of it meant anything. None of it made any difference. He had lost everything we had, including my dad's rainy-day fund.

I was catatonic with shock. All I did was lie in bed, with the door locked, to cry. I didn't want to see or talk to Jack. I needed to be alone. It was Jack who took Jess to Montessori and picked her up. I told him to tell her and everyone else that I was sick – that I had a really bad contagious flu and he was helping out for a week or two.

On the third day the home phone rang. I let the answering machine pick up. It was Jess's school. In a polite and roundabout way the secretary informed me that the cheque for Jess's last term had bounced and they were just wondering if we could arrange payment as soon as possible.

Days passed, and I tried to pull myself together before Jess got home from school. I washed my face and put some cream on my eyes to make them look less puffy. I sat up in bed with a magazine on my lap, trying to look sick as opposed to suicidal. I heard her coming in, chatting happily to Jack. She had no idea our world had fallen apart, and I wanted to protect her from it for as long as I could.

Jess always came straight up to see me, to check on how I was feeling. She climbed into my bed to cuddle and asked me why my eyes were still all red and sad. I told her it was part of the flu. 'It's a nasty flu that makes your eyes water all the time,' I explained.

'But you look so sad, Mummy.'

'Well, I am a bit sad because I'm stuck in bed and I want to be well so I can take you to school and hang out with you.'

'It's funny having Daddy collect me.'

'Is it?'

'Yes, he never did before so it feels weird, but nice weird.'

'You really like school, don't you, Jess?'

'Oh, yes, Mummy, I love it. Mrs Garner is so nice and I love all my friends, especially Bella. Do you know what we did today?'

'What?'

'We planted teeny-tiny seeds in little pots of mud and Mrs Garner said they'll grow into beautiful flowers soon. And tomorrow we're having a tea party and we all have to bring in our favourite toy. So I'm going to bring my doll Sisi in, because she's so pretty in her Spanish-dancer dress.'

'That's a good idea,' I said, tucking her silky hair behind her ears. Then, fighting back tears I asked her, 'Jess, do you think it would be fun to stay at home with Mummy instead of going to school?'

'For one day?'

'Well, how about for a lot of days? How about staying with me every day?'

Jess's sweet little face crinkled up. 'Can't I do both? Can't I go to school and then be with you after school, like we do now?'

'Or maybe you could stay at home and I could be your teacher in the morning and your mummy in the afternoon. We can have school here in the house.'

'But what about my friends? What about Bella?' Jess's lip began to quiver. She didn't understand what was going on, but whatever it was she didn't like it.

'You'd still see her. She could still come for play-dates,' I lied. How could you have a play-date if you didn't have a house?

'No, Mummy, I want to go to school.'

'OK, sweetie, don't cry. You can stay at school. Mummy will sort it out.' I hugged her close and forced myself not to cry.

'I hope you feel better soon, Mummy. Would you like me to bring you some soy milk?' she asked.

'No, thank you, pet, I'm fine. Why don't you go and play for a while?'

Jess ran off to her toys and I lay back on the pillow. I hadn't showered in days. I felt disgusting – I *was* disgusting. Who cared what I looked like? My life was over. I couldn't even give my baby girl the one thing she wanted – school. What was the point in getting out of bed?

One day my personal trainer rang my mobile phone. I didn't answer. I had messages from everyone telling me my cheques had bounced and they were owed money. Victoria had left five messages about the money for the holiday. Eventually I texted her to say I was too sick to talk, but we had changed our minds about Venice: we were backing out. I'd pay her for the scarf as soon as I was well. She sent me a frosty text telling me that it was very late notice about the holiday and she was extremely disappointed that I had waited so long to tell her.

There were several messages from Louise, demanding I call her back. She sounded incredibly stressed and I could hear Clara crying in the background, but I couldn't face anyone right now. Julie had called to ask me to take her shopping for an outfit for her fortieth. Mum had called a few times too. Jack had told her I was sick, so she was checking up on me. Gavin had called looking to 'borrow' some money. Apparently his tent had a rip and needed to be repaired. Saskia had called to remind me about the charity lunch next week and to ask what I was wearing. Daniella called to say that Harvey Nicks were giving her a preview of the new Marc Jacobs collection, did I want to come? Paula left a message reminding me that we were due to go for lunch in the new Michelin-starred restaurant in town on Friday.

One night, when Jess was asleep, Jack came in to talk to me.

'Go away. I've nothing to say to you.'

'You can't stay in bed for ever. You need to get up.' He shuffled about at the end of the bed, hands in his pockets.

'What for? To face all the people I owe money to? To be made a public mockery of – "Oh, look, it's Sophie Wells. She used to have a life, but now she's in the gutter"?'

'We'll get over this. We'll move on – we're a team. We need to be strong and stick together. I know I fucked up, but I'm doing everything I can to fix it.'

'Oh, really? Like what? Are you going to get our money back? Because that's the only way to fix this mess. And you've told me a hundred times that it's all gone, that there is no money and no way of recouping it – so what exactly are you going to do, Jack? Magic it out of thin air?'

He ran his hand through his hair. Grey strands had appeared, literally overnight. 'Come on, Sophie, I'm doing my best.'

'Well, your best is rubbish. Not only have you managed to throw all of your company's money down the toilet, but you did it with my personal money and even our house too. We're going to have to take Jess out of school – do you have any idea what that will do to her, how upset she's going to be? You're a real genius, Jack.'

He glared at me. 'I may not be a genius, but I'm the one who has been funding your five-star lifestyle for the past six years while you've swanned about dripping with jewels and designer clothes. You haven't had to lift a bloody finger because I was working my arse off making millions. And I was happy to do it. I liked being able to spoil you. I loved being able to give you and Jess everything you wanted. Don't throw that back in my face.'

I lashed out: 'I spent six years working my arse off to look good for you because Jack Wells likes a hot wife. Jack Wells doesn't want his wife putting on weight or looking older. When Jess was born Jack Wells didn't like his wife being tired. He didn't like his wife being hormonal. He wanted his life exactly the way it was. He expected his wife to be the same, unchanged even though she'd given birth. So, yes, Jack, I *have* spent tons of money – on injecting rat poison into my face so I don't age, working out every day and starving myself so I don't put on weight, buying expensive clothes so I always look groomed, because that's what you wanted. You wanted a trophy wife and I was one. I held up my part of the bargain. You have failed miserably at yours.'

'Give me a break! You loved every minute of it. You loved the money and the clothes and the ladies-who-lunch crap. You loved the flashy jewellery and the cars and your new rich friends and your ten holidays a year. Don't try and pretend you were doing it for me. You spent it as fast as I could make it.'

'I trusted you to keep us safe and secure. That was your job. I did everything to make your life easy. You never had to do anything but work. I looked after Jess. I made sure the house ran smoothly. I made sure your suits were dry-cleaned, your shirts freshly ironed, your shoes polished, your dinner cooked, your favourite TV shows recorded, your holidays organized, your –'

Jack threw his arms into the air. 'You had staff to do all of it. You barely lifted a finger in this house. I gave you a life of bloody luxury.'

'So where is it *now*?' I shouted.

'I made a bad business decision! I didn't kill anyone!' he bellowed back.

'You might as well have. Our life is over.'

'Stop being so melodramatic. It isn't over. It's just going to be different for a while. Until I get back on my feet.'

'Different? Our house is probably going to be repossessed – we're going to be on the street.'

He looked away. 'I've got Anthony trying to stop that happening. He's the best lawyer I know, and he's helping me as a favour, but we may have to sell it.'

'Aargh,' I cried. 'We'll never be the same. You've ruined everything. How could you put our house, our family home, into a dodgy business deal? Your home is your haven! You don't risk it like that! You do not risk making your family homeless. Is nothing sacred to you?'

'You don't understand – I used it as collateral against borrowings.'

'I may not know anything about the corporate world, Jack, but

I do understand that you've ruined us with your greed. It wasn't enough for you to be making money for the company, you had to pump all of our money and savings and even our home into this deal too.'

'My so-called greed provided you with the luxurious lifestyle you love. I don't remember you ever saying, "Take it easy, Jack, don't work so hard, Jack, you don't have to make more money, Jack." You loved it when I got big bonuses. You loved it when I bought you expensive jewellery and cars. Every time one of your friends got something bigger or shinier than you, I'd be the first to hear about it. So I worked harder and provided more money to fund your lifestyle.'

'MY LIFESTYLE!' I shouted. 'What about you, Jack? I'm not the one who spent two hundred grand on an Aston Martin or thirty thousand on a Rolex watch. And you spend as much on your custom-made suits as I do on my clothes, so don't you dare try to make out that I spent all your money. You enjoyed the lifestyle as much as I did.'

Jack shook his finger in my face. 'You were always going on and on about Victoria having nicer clothes and a bigger car than you. How whenever they went on holidays, Gerry booked the presidential suite in whatever hotel they stayed in. When Saskia got a diamond S from Tiffany's, you described it to me in excruciating detail. I got the message loud and clear, and I bought you a bigger one for Christmas. You were always pushing for more.'

'I was not. I was happy with what I had. I loved my life. I didn't always want more. Sometimes I was embarrassed in front of my family because I had so much and Julie had so little.'

'Maybe in front of your own family, but with your friends you always wanted more. You had that idiot Victoria on a pedestal. For God's sake, Sophie, you worshipped her. You wanted to be her. Well, newsflash: I'm not Gerry Ward.'

'You can say that again. He wouldn't piss his whole fortune down the drain on one stupid lousy deal.'

Jack narrowed his eyes. 'Maybe not, but he's riding half of Dublin.'

'What?' There was no way Gerry was unfaithful to Victoria. He adored her. She was always telling me how romantic he was. Besides, she was beautiful and glamorous and stylish. She was the perfect wife.

Jack laughed bitterly. 'Yes, Sophie, the amazing Gerry is screwing around and has been for years. Victoria may have great clothes, but she can't keep her husband's trousers on.'

'That's bullshit – he adores her. I've seen the way he looks at her. He'd never cheat on her. She's stunning.'

'Believe me, Sophie, he's having affairs left, right and centre.'

'How do you know?'

'Because he told me.'

'When?'

'Last year, when we were skiing. We went for a few beers while you girls were getting a massage. He told me very openly that he played around. His exact words were "I don't do monogamy."'

'What did you say?'

'Nothing. I just listened.'

'Why didn't you tell me?'

'Because Victoria's your friend and I didn't want to put you in the awkward position of knowing that her husband was having sex with other women.'

'Why are you telling me this now? Have you been unfaithful to me too?'

'No, I have not,' Jack snapped, looking furious. 'Unlike Gerry I do believe in monogamy. I also believe in marriages where the spouses support each other and stand by each other through thick and thin.'

'And I believe in marriages where the husband doesn't make irresponsible decisions that leave his wife and child homeless. And I wouldn't worry about me telling you what amazing things Victoria has any more because I won't be seeing her. She doesn't hang around with VAGRANTS!' I shouted in his face.

'There's nothing you can say to make me feel worse than I already do. I messed up. I get it. You hate me. You think I'm a worthless piece of shit. Kick me while I'm down. Go on, tell me again what a loser I am,' Jack yelled back.

'STOP!'

Jack and I spun around. Jess was standing at the door in her Minnie Mouse pyjamas. She had her hands over her ears and was sobbing her little heart out. 'Stop being mean to each other.'

I leapt off the bed and scooped her up in my arms. 'Oh, baby, I'm so sorry. It's OK – Mummy and Daddy are just being cross. We're sorry for waking you.'

'Daddy said you hate him. Do you, Mummy? Do you really hate Daddy?'

I hugged her. 'Of course not.'

Jack crouched beside me and wiped a tear from his daughter's face. 'Hey, Jess, we were being really silly. But it was just a little fight, nothing serious. It's OK, honey, don't cry.'

'Family hug,' Jess said, putting her little arms around both of us. Jack put his arm around me. My arm hung limply beside him.

25
Julie

Harry had been even more secretive and jumpy lately, but now I knew why. My birthday was only a week away and I thought he must be organizing a surprise dinner. Seeing as we couldn't afford to go to Paris, he'd had to arrange something local. I hoped he'd booked Pico's – it was my favourite restaurant, a little family-run Italian bistro on the sea front and the food was simple but gorgeous. It wasn't glamorous enough for Sophie and Jack, but I loved it and it was my birthday so I got to choose.

I hadn't heard from Sophie in nearly two weeks. I'd rung her to ask her to help me find a dress for my birthday night, but she'd never called back, which was unlike her. She always returned calls and, besides, she *loved* shopping and I knew she'd find me something perfect to wear – she had a really good eye. Mum said she'd spoken to her a few days ago and she'd sounded awful, really snuffly and miserable. Apparently she had some horrible flu that was highly infectious so she was staying away from everyone. I hoped she'd better by Friday for my surprise party.

I didn't think Louise would make it back from London. Clara seemed to be getting worse. I could barely hear my sister on the phone the other day because the baby was howling so loudly. I felt sorry for Louise. It was the first time in my life that I'd heard her sound overwhelmed. To be honest she'd sounded like I do most of the time. I'd tried to give her advice but she'd kept shouting, 'I've tried that and it doesn't work,' every time I suggested something. She was hoping Clara would grow out of it soon. So was I – Louise had sounded really strung out.

Gavin wouldn't be coming home for my birthday because he

had no money and was still living in his tented community with his hairy smelly friends and was still madly in love with Acorn.

I had actually been dreading my birthday. What was so great about turning forty when you were fatter than you wanted to be, poorer than you wanted to be, wrinklier than you wanted to be and a stay-at-home mum who never achieved anything despite running around in circles all day every day? But now that the day was so close, I was excited about it. I'd decided to embrace it. I loved parties and it would be nice to dress up and go out and drink lots of wine and get presents.

I'd hinted to my family that I wanted a voucher for the House of Fraser, which was where I ended up buying my dress for Friday night. I'd asked Mum to come shopping with me as Sophie was sick and I knew that at least she'd be honest . . .

'No, Julie, it makes you look huge,' she said, as I squeezed myself into a plunging red dress. 'Besides, you're forty, not twenty, and it's far too revealing.'

I peeled it off and tried on the seventh dress. It was pink. 'Off,' she said waving her arm at me. 'Why in God's name would you think a pink satin dress would be flattering? You look like a big flamingo.'

'Less of the "big", thank you.' I wrenched the dress over my head.

'Try this on.' Mum handed me a plain black dress that looked really dull and old-fashioned.

'I'm not seventy,' I reminded her.

'Just put it on,' she said. 'It's very chic.'

I zipped it up and turned to look at myself in the mirror.

'I told you. It's lovely.' Mum smiled.

It was fine. It was black, it was respectable – it was boring.

'It's too conservative.' I craned my neck to look at my back in the mirror.

'Conservative is a good thing. You're not a young one going to a disco, Julie. You're a forty-year-old mother of four who needs a well-tailored dress to flatter your shape. It makes you look much slimmer than you are.'

'I want something fun and sexy. This is frumpy.'

'No, it isn't. It's stylish and simple.'

'Mum, I want Harry to look at me and say, "Wow." He's going to look at me in this and ask me if I'm off to a nuns' convention.'

Mum shook her head. 'I don't know why I bother. You never listen to me anyway. You and Louise always ignore my advice and Gavin just switches off as men do when women talk to them. Sophie is the only one who ever listens to me.'

'I do listen to you. You're the one who isn't listening. I'm going to be forty. I'm not thrilled about it. I feel a hundred and ninety so I want a dress that gives me a lift, makes me feel younger than I am, thinner than I am and sexier than I am.'

'Julie, I'll be sixty-five next year. Forty is young. Enjoy it. Look, why don't we ask the shop assistant for help?' Mum suggested. 'She knows all the dresses in here and should be able to find a nice one.'

'Great idea.'

It turned out to be a brilliant idea. The girl brought in three dresses, all of which were exactly what I was looking for. They covered up my lumpy bits (which was most of my body) and flattered my good bits – which were my legs from the knee down and my cleavage. Even Mum said they were nice.

'But I think orange is a common colour for anyone over twenty-five,' she commented. 'The green dress is too strong – it's draining. You should go for the navy one.'

She was right: the green *was* too strong. Although I loved the brightness of the colour, it made me look washed out. The navy was lovely and not too conservative. It had a nice low – but not plunging – neckline and the hem fell just to my knees. It had a big sparkly waistband made up of tiny silver beads that made me seem much slimmer than I was and gave the dress a bit of an edge.

'You're right. This is the one.' I twirled happily in it. 'I can't wait for Friday now.'

'What are you planning?' Mum asked.

I smiled at her. 'I don't know yet.'

'Well, I'm sure Harry will take you somewhere nice,' she said, not letting on about the surprise dinner.

Mum bought me the dress as a present, which was really kind as it was more expensive than I could afford.

'Thanks, Mum, that's really generous.'

'I'm only delighted to treat you, pet. I know you and Harry have had a difficult year financially. I remember in the eighties when your father's business suffered with the recession and we had to tighten our belts – it's not easy with four children to educate and feed and look after.'

'I didn't mind the first salary cut so much – I was kind of expecting it – but the second one has been difficult. We've cut back on just about everything. Harry's very uptight about it. I hope things improve next year,' I confided.

'Well, he's lucky to have his job. Lots of people have been made redundant,' Mum pointed out.

'I know. I see a lot more dads collecting their kids from school now.'

'It's tough out there. It amazes me how Jack has continued to make so much money during the recession. He certainly has the Midas touch. They've a fantastic life.'

'They sure do. It'd be great not to have to worry about money at all. Sophie never looks at the price tag on anything. She just chooses what she likes and, regardless of how expensive it is, she buys it.'

'Well, she always looks a million dollars, so it's money well spent. You know, successful men like Jack want their wives to look their best. He's very handsome so he'd have a lot of women eyeing him up. Sophie needs to maintain her looks and keep Jack close to her. Being married to a wealthy man has its own challenges.'

'I suppose you're right. I never thought of it that way,' I admitted. 'At least I don't have to worry about women trying to run off with Harry. He wouldn't be able to afford to buy them a glass of wine, never mind pay for a hotel room.'

We roared laughing.

'Harry's a good man and a great father. You did very well,' Mum assured me. 'Have you spoken to Sophie recently? She still sounds awful, very sick altogether. I wanted to call over to her, but she refused to see me. She said the type of flu she has is highly contagious. Jack seems to be at home helping out, which is nice.'

'I've just been on text to her and she did seem down. Hopefully she'll feel better this week.'

'And wait till I tell you about Louise!' Mum said. 'She rang me the other day and asked for my *advice*. I nearly fell off my chair. Louise asking *me* for advice! She asked if any of you had had reflux or colic as babies and did I know how to cure it. She sounded very fed-up.'

'Poor Clara seems to have a bad dose.'

'Well, I told her she'd had it herself when she was a baby.'

'Did she?' I was surprised.

'She certainly did. Louise used to roar after every bottle until she was three or four months old – it was horrendous. But one day it just stopped. I think she was relieved when I told her that.'

'Have you heard from Gavin?' I asked.

'He called the other day, reversing the charges from a phone box – his mobile had run out of credit. He was looking for money to fix his tent or something. So your father said he'd give him two hundred euros and that was it. Not a penny more. The only thing he'll give him now is a return ticket home.'

'I think he's getting tired of it,' I said. 'He called me a week ago. It had been raining non-stop and his tent had flooded. He's still pretending to be a vegan and said he was absolutely starving, not to mention cold, wet and miserable. I think the novelty of trying to save the world is definitely wearing off.'

'Good. The sooner the better.'

I glanced at my watch. 'Oh, shoot, I have to go and pick the boys up. I'll see you on Friday,' I said, and kissed my mother goodbye.

'No, you won't. I've a bridge competition,' she answered.

267

'Oh, right, yes, of course.' I winked at her and headed off with my new party dress under my arm.

I wondered if Harry would invite anyone apart from my family to the surprise dinner – maybe Marian and Greg? It'd be nice to have them there, but then again Sophie and Marian didn't get on so it might be awkward. Even if it was only Mum and Dad and Sophie and Jack, I'd have a great time. I planned to drink too much, eat a huge portion of pasta followed by tiramisu and have fun. It'd be nice to have some attention for once. I felt like a non-person most of the time – the triplets' mother, Tom's mother, Harry's wife, Sophie and Louise's sister . . . On Friday night I'd be Julie Devlin, birthday girl, in a sparkly dress. Hurrah!

The triplets were a bit confused. I was twenty-one last year and now I'm going to be forty. Thankfully, maths isn't a strong point so they've just accepted it. They know it's a big birthday, though, because when Harry turned forty last year I spent the whole day decorating the house with banners and balloons and cards, and the boys helped me make a big cake and we had a party in the house that night for twenty of Harry's friends and the kids were allowed to stay up late and eat chocolate and watch whatever they wanted on TV. They loved it. They think it's going to be the same on Friday night – to be honest, I don't care what they do. I've booked Gloria – my cleaning lady who does no cleaning – to babysit. She's the only person who the kids are scared of and I know I can rely on her not to let them burn the house down.

I woke up on my birthday with butterflies in my stomach. I was excited. I couldn't wait for tonight and my surprise party. Harry was already up and dressed.

'Morning.' I beamed at him.

'I'm late – I have to dash. I'll see you later.' He rushed out of the door, looking hassled.

'I've booked Gloria for seven thirty,' I shouted after him.

'Great,' he replied, closing the door.

I looked around the bed and under my pillow for a card or a hidden present, but there was nothing. He must be saving it all until later. My phone rang and I grabbed it: the first of my birthday calls.

'Will you accept a reversed charge call from London?' the operator's voice asked.

'Yes.'

'Hi, sis.'

'Hi, Gavin.'

'Happy birthday.'

'Thanks – look, I can't stay on the phone long. Reversed charge calls are too expensive, we're broke and I'm hoping Harry's going to spend the few euros we have left on my present.'

'Tell me about it. I'm skint too and Sophie's refusing to call me. I think she's fed-up bailing me out and Louise just shouted at me to get a life when I called her last week. She sounded like she was totally losing it. What's going on?'

'Baby trouble.'

'OK – that explains the background noise. I thought she had the TV on at full volume. So, what are you doing for the big day?'

'Not sure yet. Harry's being all secretive and weird so I think he's organized a dinner for me. Probably just Mum and Dad and Sophie and Jack, but it'll still be nice. I wish you and Lou were coming too, though.'

'Dude, if you could fly me home, I'd be there. I'm in need of a good meal.'

'If I had the money, you know I would. So, the whole vegan thing isn't such fun any more?'

'It was never exactly a riot, but I don't know how Forest does it – a man cannot live on nuts and berries and frigging tofu. I'm dying here, Julie. I've lost about a stone.'

'How's your tent?'

'Dad gave me some money to fix it, so at least I'm not waking up damp every day.'

'Are you and Acorn still loved up?'

'She's a total fox, but to be honest, living in a tent with someone isn't very romantic. It kind of sucks. We're cold and wet and I'm hungry all the time and there's mud everywhere. I'd kill for a long, hot bath. That's what I wanted to ask Louise for, a decent bath and maybe a night's kip in her spare room, but she was so busy snapping my head off that I just left it.'

'She's having a tough time, but she'll come round. So, are you going to give it up and come home and get a "real" job, as Dad would say?'

'There's no point in coming home now. No one hires in the summer. I'll wait until the autumn.'

'How are you going to survive on no money?'

'I've actually written an article about the struggle to ban the new Heathrow runway and it looks like the *Irish Times* are going to use it, so hopefully that'll bring in a few quid.'

'Good for you. Let me know if it gets printed. I don't read the newspapers – too depressing. I can only cope with fiction. I want to escape from my life, not read about other people in worse situations.'

'I'll let you know.'

'OK. Look, I have to go – Harry'll kill me when he sees the phone bill.'

'Enjoy your party, and have a big steak for me!'

As I hung up, the triplets came in, with Tom toddling behind them.

'Is it today?' they asked.

They had been asking me every day for the past week if that day was my birthday.

'YES!' I exclaimed.

'HURRAH!' They jumped up and down on my bed and on me.

'Ouch, be careful, don't break Mummy's leg,' I warned them.

'Can we have sweeties on your birthday?' Leo asked.

'Yes, you can, after school.'

'*Coooool*,' Luke squealed.

'Can we watch TV all day and all night?' Liam asked.

'No, but you can watch *Ben 10* with Gloria when she comes to babysit.'

'Is she coming now?' they asked.

'No, after school Gloria will come and Mummy will go to her party.'

'Are you going to have a princess cake?' Luke asked.

'I hope so.'

'Yuck! Princess cakes are for stinky girls.' Leo made vomiting noises.

'CAKE! CAKE!' Tom's eyes were wide at the prospect of cake. He was a sugar addict, which was my fault as I shovelled whatever was nearest to me into his mouth.

'Well, I'm a girl and I'm not stinky,' I objected.

'Mummy! You're not a girl, you're a woman,' Luke reminded me.

'Do I look like a young woman or an old woman?' I fished.

'*Old!*' they said in unison.

Charming.

'How old?' I was determined to dig my own grave. 'Old like a witch or old like, uhm, Auntie Sophie?'

They thought about it for a minute and then Liam said, 'Not like a witch, but not like Auntie Sophie. She looks like a princess, you look old like Mrs Walsh.'

Mrs Walsh, their teacher, was looking down the barrel of sixty.

After dropping the boys to school I went home to tidy up the breakfast dishes. Tom was pottering around, playing with his toys, being his sweet self. I was feeling a bit hard done by. I didn't think I should have to clean up on my birthday, but no one else was going to so I grumbled my way through it.

'Put that down,' a voice ordered. It was Marian at the back door. She had Ben with her, asleep in his buggy. She pushed him into the utility room and closed the door. Then she took the dishes out of my hand and told me to sit down.

She finished loading the dishwasher, then produced a small chocolate fudge cake, a carton of orange juice and a bottle of *cava* from her bag.

'Ta-da! Happy birthday, Julie.'

I was thrilled. 'Oh, wow! Thanks!'

I went to get some glasses and plates while Marian opened the *cava* and mixed in the orange juice. 'It's never too early for Buck's Fizz.' She grinned.

'Bring it on!' I held my glass out.

'Mmm, that tastes good,' she said. 'I haven't had a drink in weeks. So, what did Harry get you?'

'Nothing so far. I'm presuming he'll produce it later. I was a bit cheesed off he didn't even leave me a card under my pillow or anything.'

'He's probably picking it up today or something,' Marian said. Since going on anti-depressants she was much more positive. Maybe I should take them too.

I raised my glass. 'Here's to forty. May the next ten years bring me sleep, a thin body, a husband who gets a salary rise for a change, children who don't trash my house daily and something for myself.'

'Like what?'

'I don't know . . . some kind of outlet for me. Being a mum isn't quite enough. I want to do something else. Even if it's gardening or helping out with a charity. I want my own little thing just for me.'

'Amen to that. When Ben finally stops sucking the life out of my tits and goes to play-school in eighteen months' time, I'm going to go back to work part-time.'

'Really?'

'Yeah. I've decided that all this black-cloud shit and depression is partly because I feel so out of control. I don't have my own money. I have to ask Greg for cash to dye my fucking hair and I know that sooner or later he's going to figure out that Soul is a shoe shop and not a fishmonger. He asked me the other day how the hell I could have spent a hundred and ten euros on fish. I told him I'd stocked the freezer up because the guy told me that cod was an endangered species.'

I roared laughing. You had to hand it to her: she was ingenious.

'Are you really thinking about going back to work?' I asked.

'Yeah – I like having my independence. It works better for me and Greg. I hate being dependent on him and I know he doesn't like having to fork out for my waxing and hair colouring and stuff. He doesn't get that it's important. He thinks it's extravagant. I told him if I don't get waxed it'll be gorillas in the mist down there.'

'The Black Forest.' I giggled.

'The Australian bush.' She grinned.

'That reminds me. I need to shave my legs for tonight – Harry might get carpet burns later if I don't.'

'You shouldn't shave.'

'It's cheaper and quicker than waxing.'

'True, but the hairs grow back like spikes.'

'I'm actually not that hairy, so it's OK.'

'You lucky cow – I'm a fucking chimpanzee. Seriously, I have thick black hair all over my body. I've been waxing since I was fourteen.'

'Yikes.'

'Anyway, for all those reasons I've decided I want to earn my own money. Greg and I fight about money a lot, so it'll be good for our marriage too.'

'How are you feeling these days?' I asked.

'Very fucking Pollyannaish, actually. I should have taken anti-depressants years ago. I haven't hit the kids or screamed at them in almost three weeks. I'm not saying I haven't wanted to but I'm able to control it better. I'm less on edge all the time. I don't feel like everything that happens is a mountain to climb.'

'God, it sounds great. Maybe I should get some too.'

'I highly recommend it. But I'm hoping to be on them just for six months. I don't want to get addicted to them. I'd prefer not to have to take anything. I feel like a bit of a loser having to take drugs to get me through the day.'

'Don't be ridiculous! You have four small kids and a mother who needs constant care. Your father abandoned you and your brother is living on another continent. Of course you feel weighed down. You're doing the best you can. We're all just struggling along. Don't beat yourself up. There's nothing wrong with needing a little help.' The Buck's Fizz was kicking in. I reached over and hugged her, my eyes welling up. 'You're a brilliant person and a great friend to me.'

'Stop! You'll set me off.'

'You are, though. I know I have my sisters and they're brilliant, but you really get it. You totally understand what my day-to-day life is like. You know the daily grind of having four small kids. You appreciate how hard it is and how sometimes you think you're going to go insane doing the same things over and over. I'm more honest with you than with anyone else.'

'Well, you're really going to love me when you hear what your present is.'

'You've already given me cake and bubbles.'

'I'm going to take your kids for the afternoon while you're having a facial. It's booked for three o'clock at Le Spa salon.'

'No way! That place is supposed to be amazing. But I can't let you take eight kids for the afternoon – it's not fair.'

'Don't worry, my friend Carla's calling over. She only has one boy. She can help me out. I want you to go and relax.'

'Are you sure?'

'Positive.'

'Thanks.' I hugged her again. 'This is the best present ever.'

At seven o'clock the boys were plonked in front of the TV while I got ready. Tom was in the bathroom with me, watching me put on my makeup. My mobile beeped: it was a message from Harry to say he was running late in work. He'd be home as soon as possible.

It was obviously a ruse so that I wouldn't be able to quiz him when he came home. He must have been planning to come in at seven thirty and whisk me off to the restaurant before I started asking questions and ruined the surprise.

I knew I hadn't heard from my sisters or parents as they were going to see me tonight too. Louise must have been flying in as she hadn't called. I was thrilled as I really wanted her to be there.

I applied my makeup carefully. My skin felt wonderful after the facial and when I'd finished I smiled at my reflection. I looked good, better than I had in ages. I wrestled my body into my Spanx – sweating as I peeled them up – then slipped on my new party dress. It looked fantastic. The Spanx had all my flabby bits tucked in and under control and the dress fitted perfectly. I felt a chill of excitement run down my spine. I was pretty and attractive, sexy and glowy. I hadn't looked this good in years.

The doorbell rang. It was Gloria. 'Bloody hell!' she exclaimed, when she saw me.

'I know I look a lot better than normal.' I twirled for her.

'You look like a different person, love,' Gloria assured me. 'You should make an effort more often. I didn't know you had so much potential. Harry'll be chuffed when he sees you – you're gorgeous.'

'Thanks.'

'Now, go and sit down in the kitchen away from the boys. You don't want any mucky paws on that dress. Where are the little horrors?'

'Watching TV.'

'Right. I'll go in and sort them out. You have a great night and don't worry about coming home late. I've brought my knitting.'

I went and sat down in the kitchen. It was seven forty-five. Harry would be here any minute. I poured myself a glass of wine and waited . . .

By nine thirty I had called Harry's phone fifty-six times. I had called Louise seven times, Sophie eight times, Mum ten times and

Dad six times. I had consumed four glasses of wine on an empty stomach. I was drunk and furious.

Harry came in the door, pulling his tie off. He stopped when he saw me. 'You look nice! Where are you off to?'

'Ha-ha. This better be a really good surprise, Harry.'

'What are you talking about?' He looked around suspiciously.

'Come on, what's going on? What's the plan?'

'What plan?'

'Seriously, Harry, I'm not finding this funny. I've been sitting here looking out the window, waiting for you to come home for two hours. Gloria keeps coming in and patting me on the back and saying, "Don't worry, love, I'm sure he's on his way." So what is it? What's my surprise? Come on, Harry, I'm sick of waiting – where is everyone? Are they outside? You should have warned me the dinner was going to be late and I wouldn't have drunk so much.'

Harry scratched his cheek. 'Julie, what dinner?'

'Stop it. I'm getting really pissed off now. What's the surprise? Just tell me, come on.'

'I don't know – Oh, Jesus.' Harry's hand flew to his mouth. 'Your birthday.' I stared at him and then, finally, the penny dropped. Harry hadn't been planning anything. He had forgotten my birthday. This was the first time in all the years we'd been together that he had forgotten. There was no surprise party, no treats, no presents, no dinner . . . nothing.

I FREAKED. I called him every name under the sun. I cursed, swore, threw wine in his face, kicked him in the shin, cried, bawled, howled, and eventually locked myself in the bathroom.

Harry knocked gently on the door. 'Julie, I'm so sorry. I swear I'll make this up to you. I can't believe I forgot. You're right – I am an arsehole. But we can go out now. I'll call Pico's and see if we can get a late sitting. Come on, we can drink champagne. We can salvage the night.'

'GO TO HELL! I do everything for everyone in this family and no one gives a shit about me. I don't count. I made a huge fuss for your birthday – I spent weeks organizing it and cleaning and cooking and baking for it, and you didn't have the decency to remember one of the most important days of my life. I hate you, Harry.'

'Julie, I know I messed up. I've been distracted lately and I just totally forgot. I promise you I'll fix this. I'll make it right. Hold on while I go and call Pico's.'

I opened the door, pointed to my puffy, blotchy, mascara-streaked face. 'I can't go out like this. Tonight is ruined. I was so excited. I thought you were being cold and distracted because you were so busy organizing my party when in fact you were just busy with your stupid project. Well, I hope it's worth it because it's going to take me a long time to forgive you for this.'

'I'll book a table for tomorrow night. I'll look after the kids all day so you can go and pamper yourself in the beauty salon.'

'I DID THAT TODAY – I HAD A BLOODY FACIAL, WHICH IS NOW RUINED FROM CRYING SO MUCH.' I slammed the door and continued to cry. Then I called my sisters and my mother and left messages telling them all that they were selfish wenches. I reminded them that I never forgot any of their birthdays and that I would never forgive them for forgetting my fortieth.

Ten minutes later my phone rang. 'Julie! Have you been drinking?' Mum asked. 'I came out of bridge and switched my phone on to see ten missed calls and an irate message saying you disowned me. What on earth is the matter? Of course I didn't forget your birthday. I sent you flowers today but the delivery man said no one was home, so I told him to leave them with that vulgar girl next door who curses all the time in number six.'

'Marian doesn't live in number six, she's number eight.'

'Well, number six has your flowers. I'm sorry for you that Harry forgot your birthday, but that's between you and him. Please refrain from leaving abusive messages on my phone.'

'But no one else remembered, except Gavin, and his call probably cost me thirty euros. My two self-centred sisters forgot.'

'You'll have to take that up with them. I think Sophie's still sick, the poor thing, and Louise is very uptight about the baby. It's not all about you, Julie.'

'It's never about me,' I sobbed, and hung up.

I stayed locked in the bathroom for two hours. Gloria tapped on the door to say goodbye. 'I'm off now, Julie. The lads are in bed, asleep. I'm sorry your birthday was a disaster – it's a terrible waste of a lovely dress. Harry's an awful eejit for forgetting, but he's very upset about it. I can see he really feels bad. I think you should let him sweat it out for a bit, but forgive him tomorrow.'

Harry continued to apologize and grovel through the bathroom door, but eventually he gave up and went to bed. When the house was quiet I tiptoed out and went to log on to the mumskeeping-sane.com website. I needed to offload.

There were tons of responses to my last posting, but I didn't want to read them yet. I needed to write and get my hurt and anger off my chest.

Threescompany:

It was my fortieth birthday today and my husband forgot. So did both my sisters. I am so upset I can barely type. My eyes are swollen from crying. Is it too much to ask for my family – the people I love most – to remember my fortieth birthday? I NEVER forget their birthdays. I always call and make a fuss. But the worst thing is, I thought they were all ignoring me because they were organizing a big surprise. Well, I can assure you there is no bigger surprise than no one remembering.

I feel like such a fool. I was so excited. I thought, finally, a day for me. A day about me. A day where I become visible again – albeit briefly. A day where I get spoilt, pampered, focused on. How stupid of me to think it would actually happen. I am insignificant. I don't count. No one remembered. No one cared. No one bothered. I know I sound like a whingey teenager, but it was a big deal to me. It mattered to me. My day-to-day life is drudgery. I never get a break, and now that we have even less money, I can't treat myself to a nice mascara or body cream every now and then to give me a lift.

We were supposed to go to Paris for my birthday, but I cancelled it because we couldn't afford it and that was fine. But the fact that I didn't even get a card from anyone in my family makes me furious. My younger sister has the flu. You can still pick up the phone and call someone when you have the flu. Or she could have asked one of her many members of staff to go out and buy a card and post it for her. And my older sister, who I have been counselling on the phone almost daily about her new baby, didn't even bother to call either. They are so wrapped up in their own lives that I don't register. They only have one child each and they're too busy to call me. I have FOUR kids, and even when the triplets were just born and I couldn't see straight from exhaustion, I remembered my sisters' birthdays.

As for my husband, he's been so grumpy lately and distracted with work – I'm sick of it. And the worst part is that he's normally really good about birthdays. He never forgets and always gets me a really funny card and writes a lovely note to me on the inside. I never would have thought he'd forget. I know we're all busy and I know that birthdays aren't that important in the bigger scheme of things, but when your days are spent cleaning up after others and cooking and driving your kids around, a day where the focus is on you is a big treat. It's nice for your family to notice you, remember you exist, remember you matter, remember that you too like cakes and candles and cards . . . Remember that you're not invisible.

26

Louise

Julie left me a message telling me what a selfish cow I was. I feel really bad about forgetting her birthday, but I honestly don't know what day it is. Clara is a nightmare. I shouted at her last night. I just lost it. It was four o'clock in the morning. I had been up since midnight, feeding her, burping her and pacing the floor with her in the sling. I was beyond tired, beyond worn out. But every time I laid her down in her Moses basket she started screeching.

I can't go on like this. A new night nurse came last week but left after three nights, saying she was too tired to do any more. I tried bribing her – I offered to double her rate – but she said she had two kids of her own to look after during the day and she couldn't function without sleep. Well, neither can I!

The agency can't find me anyone else at the moment. So I've been up all night every night for the last six nights. I had to go for a nap in work yesterday. I told Jasmine I was not to be disturbed and I put my head down on my desk and passed out for an hour. I woke up with a horrible crick in my neck and dribble all over my arm. I'm turning into a mess. I'm turning into one of those bleary-eyed mothers who look at you vacantly when you talk to them. I always thought it was because they had given up work and their brains had turned to mush, but now I know, now I understand – it's sleep deprivation.

But I can't have this. I can't work at my level without sleep. I have to be alert, sharp, on the ball. I can't read long, complex, intricate documents with my eyes swimming from exhaustion. I can't make decisions when my brain is three steps behind everyone else's in a meeting.

I haven't been for a run in three weeks. I haven't got the energy. I'm eating things I would never normally eat. I had banoffi pie for dessert yesterday. It's full of fat and cream and sugar. I don't eat sugary things – but I needed the energy rush it gave me. I'm also drinking at least ten cups of coffee a day. I feel awful physically. I hate eating badly and not exercising. I've lost control of my life. I need to get it back, but I don't know how.

I took Clara to a different GP last week. I recorded her screaming and played it to him so he would understand how bad it was and not fob me off like the other doctor. But he just said the same bloody thing . . .

'She's thriving. Don't worry, she'll grow out of it.'

'When? I need a date.'

'It's impossible to say, but almost all children grow out of it by nine months.'

I burst into tears. I couldn't believe he had just potentially sentenced me to six more months of this torture. 'There must be something you can give her? This can't be normal,' I pleaded.

'Lots of babies are unsettled in the first few months,' he said soothingly.

'If all babies were like this, the population would be extinct. Do not tell me that this is what all babies are like because I don't believe you.'

'You seem very stressed, Louise. Maybe you should consider getting some help.'

'HELP! No one will look after her for me at night. She's OK during the day in crèche. It's at night she goes ballistic.'

'A lot of women get blue after their babies are born. It's not easy. Perhaps you should consider taking something to help you with this stage of motherhood. Post-natal depression is very common.'

'I'm not depressed, I'm demented. I don't need drugs, I need sleep,' I snapped. Clearly he wasn't getting it either. I picked Clara up and took her home.

She'd turned twelve weeks and nothing had changed. If anything she was even worse. I called Mum.

'Remember you said I stopped roaring at twelve weeks? Was it exactly twelve weeks? Or was it thirteen?'

'It was forty-one years ago, Louise. I can't remember. It was around three months.'

'How can you not remember? The day this child stops screaming will be etched in my memory for ever because it will be the best day of my bloody life.'

'Have you tried gripe water?'

'Yes, Mum, I've tried everything.'

'And you've had her checked for ear and urine infections and tonsillitis?'

'Yes yes yes. Everything's been checked. She's fine.'

'Well, I'm afraid you'll just have to sit it out. She'll wake up one day and her little tummy will have settled.'

'Did I cry all night long?'

'Yes, Louise, you did.'

'How did you cope?'

'On bad days I reminded myself how lucky I was to have a healthy baby. And, to be fair, your father helped me out some nights. It's hard for you on your own. I warned you, having a baby with no father is very difficult.'

'I'd marry someone now just for the help.'

'Louise, you are not to go and do anything foolish. Your life is complicated enough.'

'Tell me about it. I'm sorry, Mum, I have to go. I've got another bloody meeting.'

'Why don't you come home for the weekend and I'll mind Clara at night for you and give you a break?'

'Really? Would you?'

'Of course I would. I'd love to see her. Come home and get some rest.'

'That would be great, Mum. Thanks.'

'By the way, your brother's article got printed in the *Irish Times.*'

'What article?'

'He wrote a piece about the Heathrow expansion being a disgrace and they printed it. It was a full page. I must say it was very well written. Your father was pleased. He said he was glad his money wasn't entirely wasted on Gavin's education. At least he was literate.'

'That's good news. He left a message on my phone, but I've been too busy to call him back.'

'I hope you called Julie. She's very upset.'

'I've left messages for her, but she hasn't called back. I think I'm getting the cold shoulder.'

'Well, try her again. She felt very let down.'

'OK, I will, but I just don't have time right now. I'll try her later.'

'I'll let you go. Call me when you've decided which weekend to come home and I'll make up your old cot for little Clara.'

'I will. Thanks, Mum.'

I dug my nails into my thigh, forcing my eyes open as Lifechange TV's lawyers went over the finer points of the contract. Gordon Hanks's purchase offer of £30 million plus the TV station's debt had been accepted and we were now finalizing the contract details. The meeting had been running for two hours and I was struggling.

'Are you all right?' Dominic whispered.

'Fine – why?'

'You look like you're about to nod off.'

'I do not.'

'Is the baby not sleeping?'

'She's fine.'

'You're exhausted. Why don't you go home? I can finish up here.'

'This is my deal. I'm going nowhere.' I poured myself another cup of coffee, added three sugar lumps and forced my eyes wide open. I didn't hear a word of the remaining forty minutes of the meeting: my brain literally shut down. This was a disaster. I was scared now. I had to make sure Gordon's purchase of Lifechange went smoothly. I had to stay on my toes. Alex was counting on me.

When the meeting finally ended, I rushed back to my office and called the night-nurse agency again. 'You have to find me someone! I can't function in work. I'll pay double – I'll even pay triple. I need sleep!'

'I'm sorry, Louise,' Gwen, the owner of the agency, said. 'We have no one this week. I might have someone for two nights next week. Did you try the other numbers I gave you?'

'Yes. There's no one available this week.'

'I'll do my best to get you help next week,' Gwen reassured me.

I was facing at least five more nights of no sleep. I hung up, put my head in my hands and sobbed. How was I going to get through the next week?

There was a gentle knock on the door. 'I'm busy,' I croaked. I didn't want anyone in the office to see me crying. It would be a nail in my career coffin. They'd all be talking about how I wasn't able to juggle the baby and work. No way was I letting that happen. Alex had to think I was still at the top of my game.

Jasmine's head popped around the door. I swung my chair away from her, so she wouldn't see me crying. 'I'm off now, Louise. Do you need anything before I go?'

'No, thanks.'

'Louise?'

'What is it?' I wanted her to get out and leave me to gather myself.

'Here.' A tissue appeared in front of me. 'I knew you'd crack soon,' she said, leaning against my desk as I wiped my eyes and blew my nose. 'You look utterly worn out.'

'I'm fine. I just had a bad night.'

'Louise, you don't have to put on a front with me. I have three

284

kids. My second daughter didn't sleep for eighteen months. I almost had a nervous breakdown.'

'How did you cope?'

'I spent a lot of time in the ladies' bathroom here crying.'

'Why didn't you say anything?'

Jasmine threw her head back and roared laughing. 'Say anything – to you? Come on, Louise, you made it crystal clear from the day I started that you never wanted to hear about my personal life.'

She was right. I had always changed the subject when she brought up her kids. I'd wanted to keep the relationship purely professional. I'd wanted a really efficient secretary, not a buddy.

'I'm sorry if I was rude.'

'You were just trying to keep up with the men. It's dog-eat-dog in here. But I can tell you now, Louise, you cannot raise a baby alone and keep working the way you do. You'll burn out.'

'It would be fine if Clara would just bloody sleep. She's up all night, every night. If she slept like a normal baby, I could manage. I have everything set up for the daytime so that I can work freely. But I can't function on no sleep.'

'Why is she up?' Jasmine asked.

'I don't really know. She screams after every bottle and seems to find it really hard to digest. The doctors keep saying it's just a bit of colic or reflux and tell me to give her Infacol and Gaviscon and raise her bed and she'll be fine, she'll grow out of it . . . but she's getting worse.'

'Does her body go rigid after her bottles?'

'Yes.'

'Does she do really loud burps that sound as if they come from way down in her stomach?'

'Yes.'

'Is she happy when she's upright?'

'Yes.'

'Does she vomit her bottles back up?'

'No.'

285

'She has reflux. Not mild over-in-three-months reflux. She has the bad reflux that my Jane had.'

'Oh, Jesus, you said she didn't sleep for eighteen months.' I began to cry again.

'That's because I kept getting fobbed off by doctors telling me it was colic, a little reflux, she'll grow out of it, et cetera, et cetera. But she didn't and it was only when I found Dr Jacobs that I finally got her sorted. What Clara needs is Losec. It's a miracle cure for reflux.'

'*What?* There's a cure? Where is this doctor? I'll take her now.'

'Calm down. I'll make you an appointment. The Losec takes about three to five days to kick in and then your life and, most importantly, Clara's will change. The acidic burning will stop after every feed and she'll be able to sleep without pain. The poor little thing is in agony, but the Losec will sort her out.'

'Oh, God, thank you, Jasmine, thank you so much. You've just saved my life.' I got up and spontaneously hugged her.

'Steady on there, Louise, you're invading my personal space.'

'Sorry.' I stepped back.

Jasmine grinned. 'Relax, I'm joking. Come on, let's call the doctor and get poor Clara sorted out.'

I was on a high after seeing Dr Jacobs, who did not dismiss me as a fussy mother, or tell me that Clara would miraculously stop crying one day. She was kind and patient and thorough and gave me the magic prescription that would make her better.

'Most children's reflux clears up within a year. In some rare cases it can go on longer. But don't worry, we'll monitor her closely and see how she goes,' Dr Jacobs assured me.

I went home, gave Clara her medicine, put her down to sleep and called Julie to tell her the good news.

'Yes?' she snapped.

'I've finally got Clara sorted,' I gushed.

'Great.'

'I'm so relieved – I was going crazy. I was so worried about work.'

'Right.'

'Come on, Julie. I've left you five messages apologizing profusely for forgetting your birthday and I'm going to buy you an amazing present to make up for it.'

'Do you have any idea what it's like to be completely forgotten and overlooked?'

'I'm sorry – we're all sorry.'

'Sophie still hasn't bothered calling me. She just sent me a text. I'm seriously pissed off with her.'

'Well, Mum said she's still sick. She must have caught something awful. I haven't heard from her in weeks either.'

'She's going to have to do a lot of grovelling.'

'Speaking of grovelling, how's Harry getting on?'

'He keeps saying he's sorry and he took me out for dinner on the Saturday night, but it didn't work. It was just the two of us and I was still furious and he's just not himself at the moment. He's very distracted. STOP STICKING YOUR FINGER IN THE SOCKET. YOU'LL ELECTROCUTE YOURSELF.'

'Is he still working on that project?'

'Yes, unfortunately.'

'When will it be finished?'

'He says he has another month or so to go. The sooner the better. I want the old Harry back. He always seems miles away and he's working late, which he never used to do. The only good thing about being a civil servant – because it certainly isn't the big salary – is that you never work late. I SAID, NO JUMPING OFF THE KITCHEN TABLE. YOU'LL HURT YOURSELF.'

'What's the project?'

'He says it's some kind of new programming thing and that it's too technical to explain.'

'Will he get a bonus or a promotion out of it?'

'I don't think so.'

'Well, what's the point, then? Why be stressed and working harder for no gain?'

'He said it'll look good on his CV.'

'Fair enough. I suppose in this climate you have to try to impress your bosses.'

'I TOLD YOU THAT WOULD HAPPEN. Sorry, I have to go. Luke's just fallen off the table and cut his lip open.'

'OK, 'bye.'

Four days later Clara slept for six hours in a row – I was in heaven.

27

Sophie

After seeing how upset Jess was by the tension in the house, I'd realized I had to try to keep her life as normal as possible, protect her as much as I could. Every morning I forced myself out of bed, had a cold shower – our heating had been turned off – got dressed and tried to be normal under very abnormal circumstances.

But I still couldn't face taking Jess to school. I didn't want to see anyone – I wasn't ready yet. I was still too shaken, too emotional and too ashamed. I couldn't even speak to Julie or Louise. I knew they'd be sympathetic, I knew they'd want to help, but I didn't want to admit it. I didn't want to tell my sisters what a mess my life was. Besides, what could they do? Julie had no money, and Louise needed to save hers because she was raising Clara alone. Anyway, I always sorted out my own problems. I didn't like burdening people. There was no way I was telling Mum and Dad. They'd be so upset for me and they had enough on their plate worrying about Gavin and his lack of direction. I didn't want to worry them. I was thirty-eight years old: I'd have to figure this out on my own. Somehow.

Jack continued to bring Jess to and from school. We had given Mimi a few weeks off while we tried to work out what to do. We seemed to spend most of our time going around in circles, blaming, shouting, cursing, crying . . .

A few weeks after Jack's revelation, I woke up one morning and decided I had to take action. I had to get some kind of a handle on our situation. I sat alone in my vast kitchen, overlooking my manicured garden, and willed myself to be strong. I picked up the phone and cancelled the appointment I had made with my doctor. I had called yesterday to see him and get a prescription for Prozac. I wanted to numb the pain of this. I wanted help in getting through the day. I wanted something to make me not feel so crushed, devastated, bereft. But deep down I knew this wasn't depression: this was shock, anger, confusion and turmoil, not a chemical or hormonal imbalance, not something that could be treated with drugs. I had to find another way to cope with this. I had to find a way to make money, a way to keep a roof over my daughter's head.

I looked down at my nails. I had started biting them again. They were a mess. I went over and opened the fridge. I wasn't hungry, but I knew I had to eat something. I couldn't afford to get sick. I had to stay focused and be clear-headed.

I forced myself to eat two slices of pumpkin bread with sugar-free jam and drink a cup of organic green tea. When Jack came back from dropping Jess to school, I offered him a cup of coffee. It was the first time I'd done that since he'd told me about the Ponzi scheme.

'I'd love one.' He looked pleased. 'You seem brighter today. Do you feel better?'

'Not really, but I can't avoid reality for the rest of my life.' I told him to sit down. I took out a pen and paper and began to make a list of all the people we owed money to. 'The cheque for Jess's school fees bounced and they've left six messages about it. I also have tons of other irate messages on my phone. The gardener is waiting to get paid, my personal trainer's cheque bounced, Jess's ballet teacher called, her swimming teacher called, her drama teacher called and her music teacher called. None of them have been paid.'

Jack rubbed his hand across his eyes. He looked like hell. 'I tried to postpone telling you for as long as possible so any cheques written since early May have bounced.'

I bit my lip to stop myself crying. 'Mimi has to be told. She'll need to find another job. I'll write her a reference and see if I can think of anyone who needs help. We need to get rid of our expensive cars and get a small one to share. Now, what's happening with the house?'

'It looks like it's going to be repossessed by the bank, but Anthony is trying to stall it to buy us some time.'

I swallowed the bile rising in my throat. The thought of being homeless was terrifying. 'I'm going to stop putting it off and call Jess's school, explain our situation and ask them to let Jess stay for the final few weeks of this term. I can't imagine they'll kick her out now. But she can't go back next year.'

'She loves that school. I'll find the money somehow.'

'Where, Jack? Where are you planning to come up with nine thousand euros for Jess's fees next year? Did you suddenly remember stashing some under the mattress? It would have been a lot wiser than giving it to a gangster.'

He glared at me. 'There's no need to be so cold. I didn't do this on purpose. I'm a bloody good trader. I made millions for the fund over the years. I made one bad decision. Which, by the way, was an investment that Brad and all the other partners in GreenGem agreed on. The same investment that ten of the other top hedge funds in New York went in on too. It was just one bad decision.'

'Well, it was a bloody big one.'

'I do have some good news. I forgot to tell you we still have a pension.'

My head snapped up. 'Where is it? How much is in it?'

'It's worth three hundred thousand euros, but I can't touch it until I reach retirement age, fifty-five at the earliest.'

'What do you mean *can't touch it*? Did you tell them we're homeless?'

He shook his head. 'It's locked in. There's no way of getting any of it out. No way at all.'

I slammed my cup on the counter. 'Well, that's fantastic, Jack. Jess can go back to school when she's twenty.'

'There's no point talking to you.' Jack stormed out. That was the way most of our conversations ended, these days.

'Go on, walk away. Leave me to clean up your mess and try to explain to everyone why they won't be getting paid and that their jobs are gone,' I shouted after him.

The front door slammed. I took a deep breath and continued to make a list of all the people I had to call to explain why we couldn't pay them.

I had always found writing lists calmed me down. When you wrote down everything you had to do, it became clearer, less daunting, and once you began to cross things off you felt in control again. But this list was endless, awful, humiliating and heartbreaking. Why hadn't I gone to college and studied something proper? If I was a lawyer like Louise I could go back to work, earn good money, keep Jess in school and pay our mortgage.

Who the hell would hire a thirty-eight-year-old ex-model who hadn't worked in six years? What was I good at? Posing and smiling at the camera. I hadn't scored enough points to study law, but why hadn't I become a nurse or a teacher or a beautician, something I could go back to, something that would bring in money? I was useless to Jess. My baby would have to leave the school she loved because her parents were a pair of losers.

My phone rang. It was Mum again. I ignored it. I'd been hiding from everyone for weeks. I think my flu story was beginning to sound fake, but I just couldn't face people: I knew that once I started telling everyone it would become a complete reality. It would be out there in the public domain – our private business, our personal affairs – out there for people to gossip about and judge and exaggerate and speculate on. I felt sick every time I thought about it.

What would people say? What would they think? I knew that Victoria and her gang would probably turn their backs on me. Look at how they had shunned poor Annabelle when her husband still had a job and they still had a house. What was to become of us? Where were we going to live? I knew my parents would put us up if we were stuck, but for how long? Would Jack ever get another job? Would anyone hire someone who had lost money in a Ponzi scheme? What kind of a life were we going to have? I felt panic rising in my chest and tried to breathe deeply. I had to stay calm. I had to find a way to make some money.

I racked my brains – what could I do, what did I have, who would hire me . . .? I looked down at my Jimmy Choo boots and then it came to me: eBay! I could sell my clothes and jewellery on eBay and make some money. I had accumulated lots of things over the years – they must be worth a few quid. I felt a tiny wave of relief. Maybe all my shopping would actually help us now. I ran upstairs and switched on my laptop.

The eBay site gave a simple step-by-step guide to becoming a seller online. It told me exactly what I needed to do to sell my things. I decided to put them up for international sale. I wanted as many people as possible to see them. I also decided to put half of the things on at auction and half at a fixed price to see which did better. If two people wanted my Dolce & Gabbana coat badly, they might bid up to a good price. Then again, I needed cash quickly, so I wanted to put a lot of things on at a fixed price to get some money coming in.

I trawled through the eBay site to get an idea of pricing. The things selling quickly seemed to be marked at about a third or less of the original price. I was going to be selling my clothes, shoes, bags and jewellery at knock-down prices, but it was better than nothing.

I knew that taking photos and describing my belongings would be easy enough for me. I was good on detail. I could describe the materials and fabrics of my clothes and shoes with my eyes closed. I knew the carat and clarity of my diamonds. I went through my wardrobe, pulling out everything. I found clothes that still had price tags on them. Things I had completely forgotten buying. I discovered shoes that had never been worn, bags that had never been used. Sitting there, surrounded by mountains of stuff, made me realize how much I had. Far too much. It was kind of obscene. I had twenty pairs of black boots alone; one hundred and fifty-six pairs of shoes in total, most of which I never wore.

The best find was an old mannequin I had stuffed at the back of one of the wardrobes in my dressing room. I had it from my modelling days – a designer had given it to me after a shoot I'd done. He didn't want to keep it because its left foot had fallen off. So I'd taken it home and used it to pin my clothes when I wanted to take them in or alter them. That was before I'd had the money to have a seamstress do it for me. The mannequin would showcase my stuff perfectly.

I hung a white sheet on the door-frame of the dressing room, pinning it tightly so no creases would show up in the photos. I dressed the mannequin and began to take photos. It took a while to get the lighting right so that the clothes were shown at their best. I had learnt the importance of lighting from modelling. I wanted everything to look gorgeous so people would flock to buy my clothes. For the shoes, I covered my dressing table with a white sheet and photographed them above and from the side. I took pictures of my jewellery, mostly in the boxes it had come in, but for some of the bigger pieces I used a black background. I had a black velvet cushion, which I laid my diamond necklaces on. I adjusted the lighting so that you could see the diamonds sparkling in the photos.

Hours went by and I had gone through only a quarter of my wardrobe. I decided to put what I had up on the eBay site and finish the rest of my things over the next few days. I was anxious to see if I'd have any luck selling. I loaded up the photos I had taken and painstakingly described each item. Then I waited nervously for bids and purchases.

By doing a quick calculation of all of the articles in my wardrobe, I figured that if I could get around a third of the price for most things, I'd make about sixty thousand euros. I prayed that people would want to buy my things. The photos looked good, more professional than most of the others on the site, and my descriptions were very detailed. I began to feel calmer. Doing something was making me feel better, less useless, less pathetic.

Jess came running into my room after school. She stopped when she saw the chaos in my normally pristine bedroom. 'What are you doing, Mummy?'

'Well, I decided I have too many clothes and I'm going to try and sell some and make some money.'

'But, Mummy, you always said that a girl can never have too many clothes or diamonds.' Jess put one of my diamond bangles on her tiny wrist and twirled it.

'I was wrong, honey. You can have too much. Look at all these things. I could never wear everything that I have. I even found things I'd forgotten I bought. So it's time to clear out my wardrobe and just keep the things I'll wear all the time.'

'What about your jewels?'

'I have too many of those too.'

'But you told me diamonds are a girl's best friend.' Jess was looking worried again. She didn't like the changes going on.

'Yes, I did, but I only have two hands, two wrists, two ears and one neck. I can't fit all of these jewels on, so I'm just going to sell some. Look, I have five diamond necklaces but I can only wear one, so I'm going to sell four.'

'Are you going to keep this?' Jess picked up the diamond Tiffany S Jack had bought me the Christmas before last.

'No, sweetie, I'm going to keep this one.' I held up a small diamond cross that Jack had bought me on my birthday six months after we had started dating.

'But it's so small. This one is so much bigger and shinier.'

'I know, but small can be good too.'

'Mummy, you always said the bigger the diamond the better,' Jess reminded me.

I cursed my stupidity. I had said all those things to her in a joking way, but now I understood that they were really silly things to say to a four-year-old. I had been far too flippant. I had filled her sweet little head with idiotic notions. I had become so wrapped up in my luxurious lifestyle that I had unintentionally instilled ridiculous beliefs in Jess.

I sat down on the floor beside her. 'Listen to me, Jess. When Mummy said all those things about diamonds she was just joking. Diamonds are fine, but they don't make you happy.'

'You always looked really happy when Daddy gave you diamonds.'

'Yes, but only for a little while,' I said, deeply ashamed of the heavy emphasis I had placed on material things. 'What makes a person really happy, Jess, is having people they love close to them.'

'I know that, Mummy. When you go away I'm always sad and then when you come back I'm always happy.'

A lump had formed in my throat. What kind of a mother was I, leaving my baby with Mimi all the time to travel around with Jack, always putting him and his needs before hers? What kind of mother tells her daughter that material goods matter so much?

I lifted her on to my lap and kissed her cheek. 'Well, the good news is that Mummy won't be going away for a long time.'

'Really? Why?'

'Because Mummy has realized that she'd much rather stay at home with you.'

'Hurrah. Is Daddy going to be at home lots like he is now too?'

'I think so, yes.'

She threw her arms around my neck. 'Oh, Mummy, that's the best news ever.'

I hid my face in her hair so she wouldn't see me crying.

28

Julie

Not long after my birthday fiasco, I was driving the boys to school.

'Is Daddy still in enormous trouble for forgetting it was your big birthday?' Luke asked.

'Yes, he is.'

'But he said sorry loads of times,' Leo reminded me. 'When we say sorry we're not in trouble any more.'

'Well, Daddy was very bold and I'm still cross.'

'But, Mummy, you've been cross for ages,' Liam said.

'And he brought you a cake and candles and a present,' Luke pointed out.

'I know, but I was very sad because everyone forgot and I had my party dress on and no party to go to. If everyone forgot your birthday you'd be annoyed too.'

'Are you going to be cross for lots more time?' Leo wondered.

'Probably.'

'For infinity time?' Luke asked.

'Not quite.'

'For infinity four hundred and fifty times?' Liam wanted to know.

I knew this would go on for hours until we got up to infinity trillion zillion, so I decided to change tack. 'Would you like me to stop being cross with Daddy? Is that a good idea?'

'YES!' they cried.

'OK, then, I'll try.'

When I got home, I decided to vacuum the previous three days' crumbs off the kitchen floor. I had been on a post-birthday house-keeping strike – but all it had done was allow the mess, which I'd eventually have to clean, to build up. I was making good headway when the phone rang. I picked my mobile up and realized it wasn't ringing. I looked around and found Harry's hidden under the newspaper on the kitchen table.

'Hello?'

'Is that Julie?'

'Yes.'

'It's Dick Fogarty here.' Dick was Harry's boss.

'Hi, Dick, I'm afraid Harry's left his phone at home.'

'Did he leave on time this morning, Julie? He's late for a meeting and I just wanted to make sure he was on the way.'

'He left forty minutes ago. He should be there by now. Is it a meeting about the big project?'

'What project?'

'The new programming your department's been working so hard on.'

'Um . . . I'm, eh, not sure what you mean – Oh, speak of the devil, Harry's just arrived.' I could hear my husband's voice, apologizing for being late, saying that the traffic had been awful due to the rain.

'I'll let you go, Julie,' Dick said. 'Sorry to bother you. Oh, hold on, Harry wants a word.'

Harry sounded very hassled. 'I can't believe I left my phone at home. I'm so stupid. Please turn it off the minute you hang up. Switch it off and leave it somewhere where the kids can't get it. No one is to touch it – no one, not you or the kids.'

'OK, chill out. Hey, Harry, how come Dick doesn't –'

'Julie, I have to go. I'm late.'

I hung up and felt something shift inside me. I had wanted to ask Harry how it was possible that Dick didn't know anything about his big project when Harry had told me it was a department thing. How could his boss be totally unaware of it?

I looked at Harry's phone. He had been very stressed and distracted lately. Maybe there was no project. Maybe he was in trouble in work. Maybe he was sick. Dying? Or . . . maybe he was having – NO! I must not jump to conclusions. But what if he was

298

– STOP! Don't think bad thoughts. Harry wouldn't, couldn't, daren't . . . would he?

I needed to think about this. I grabbed Tom and plonked him down in front of the TV. With wobbly legs I went back into the kitchen and stared at the phone. This was Harry. My Harry – reliable, loving, caring, family-man Harry. How could I be suspicious of him? Harry was my rock, my soul-mate, my husband, my best friend. Harry would never do anything to hurt me. He protected me, looked after me, made me feel safe. How could I doubt him? I would turn the phone off and put it away.

I picked it up. My hands were trembling. Don't do it, I told myself. I stared at the phone. It was no good. I had to look. I had to see for myself that nothing was going on.

With shaking fingers I opened his text messages. Most of them were from me, telling him how selfish he was for forgetting my birthday. But then I found one sent on the day of my birthday from a foreign number: U have 2 cum & c me in Paris. U cant put off telling ur wife any more. Christelle.

I screamed and dropped the phone.

Tom came waddling in from the TV room. He picked up the phone and handed it to me. 'Tank uuuu,' he gurgled. 'Mama, tank uuuuu,' he said.

'Thank you,' I whispered.

He looked at me quizzically, then padded back to his cartoons.

Who the bloody hell was Christelle? An affair? Harry? How could this happen? How could this be possible? I could feel my chest tightening – Jesus Christ, I was having a heart attack. I took a deep breath, tried to calm down. I mustn't jump to conclusions. I needed more evidence. I opened the sent menu on the phone. Harry had replied to her message at eight thirty on the night of my birthday: I really do want to see you. I promise I will come asap. I just need to find the right time to tell my wife.

I stuffed my fist into my mouth to stifle the wail. I didn't want to scare Tom. There was no project. Harry, my Harry, was having an affair with some slut called Christelle who lived in Paris. How the hell did he meet her? Who was she? How long had it been going on?

I scrolled down through his other messages, but he had deleted everything up to a few days ago. I covered my face with my hands and tried to gather my thoughts. How long had Harry been behaving strangely? Three months? Four? What had happened around that time? Oh, my God, it had started around the time I went to London for Clara's birth. He must have met Christelle that weekend. But how? Where? He'd told me he hadn't gone out, that he'd stayed at home with the kids. But he was obviously out and about chatting up slappers called Christelle. Had he slept with her? Was he in love with her? Was he going to leave me? Oh, my God, he was going to leave me destitute with four kids.

NO! There was no way he was leaving the kids with me. If Christelle wanted him, she was getting the triplets too. I wondered how long the romance would last once she realized Harry was bringing three hyper boys with him. The *bastard*. How could he do this to me? I was his wife! I had given him four beautiful sons. I had been with him through thick and thin. If anyone should be planning on leaving, it should be me. I'd put up with salary cuts and raising four boys on my own with no help . . . making ten euros stretch a mile . . . never complaining, well, not all the time . . . constantly telling him money didn't matter, I loved him anyway . . . that he was a great dad and husband . . . that we'd ride out the storms . . . things would pick up. And he'd had the audacity to go out and meet some French whore while I was helping my sister give birth.

I was shaking with rage and shock. I needed a drink. I opened the fridge and took a glug of wine. I should have known she'd be French. Harry always went on about how Juliette Binoche was so good-looking, but then he used to say I looked like her with curly hair. I used to say, 'Yeah, with curly hair and two extra stone,' and we'd laugh. Bastard!

There was a knock on the door. I jumped. It was Marian. I closed the fridge and composed myself. I wasn't going to tell anyone. I was going to keep this to myself until I had sorted it out in my head. No one was going to find out.

She came in. 'Sorry, did I give you a fright? You look like you've seen a ghost.'

'Harry's having an affair with a French tart called Christelle.'

'What the fuck?'

'There is no project. The two-faced bastard has been lying to me.'

'I think I'm having a stroke.'

'How do you think *I* feel?' I sobbed.

Marian came over and hugged me. 'Tell me everything.'

Through hysterical tears I told her about the phone call with Dick and showed her the texts.

'I never would have thought it of Harry,' she said. 'He's mad about you. He's always going on about how great you are. He thinks you rock.'

'Well, apparently he doesn't any more,' I bawled. 'He's off chasing French women. How could he do this to me? We're happy – OK, we fight a lot about the kids and sleep deprivation, but we do love each other. At least, I thought we did. Was I wrong? Have I been fooling myself? Oh God, oh God, oh God . . . what am I going to do?' I began to hyperventilate.

Marian handed me a paper bag. 'Blow into it, slowly, it'll help your breathing. Now, listen to me. That man loves you. I've seen you guys together, I've seen the way he looks at you. He definitely loves you. Maybe it was just a one-night stand and she's stalking him.'

'But he says he really wants to see her and he promises he'll come to Paris. It doesn't sound like he's being stalked. It sounds like he's mad keen. How did this happen? How could I be happily married one minute and not the next? He obviously can't stop thinking about her, he was texting her on the night he forgot my bloody birthday.'

'Breathe.' Marian put the bag up to my face as I began to panic again. 'We need a stiff drink.'

While I paced up and down, breathing into the bag, Marian proceeded to make extra-strong brandy-coffees.

'Where did he meet this whore?' she asked.

'I don't know, but I think it must have been the weekend I went to London, because he started acting weirdly shortly after that.'

Marian took a sip of her coffee. 'I just don't see it. Harry isn't the type. He's a real family man – he loves you guys. He never looks at other women. He never comments on other women. He thinks you're the best thing since liposuction.'

I sniffed into my mug. 'Maybe it's because we haven't been having much sex. I often brush him off when he wants it, but it's only because I'm so tired all the bloody time. Is it my fault? Did I make him go looking for sex elsewhere?'

'Sex,' Tom gurgled. He had come back in to see what all the shouting and crying was about.

'Fuck that. Harry has no right or reason to go dipping it where it doesn't belong. I don't care how little he was getting at home. Listen, Julie, after I had Ben, Greg got no action for five months. Eventually he said he thought it was going to fall off from lack of use, so I gave him one. They think it's about them, about us not wanting to have sex with them – they don't get it. It's not about them at all. It's about us being too exhausted to brush our teeth, never mind have sex. The other night Greg was all about the fore-play – forget about it, I told him, just get on with it and let me go to sleep.'

'But maybe if I had made more of an effort to keep him satis-fied, he wouldn't have gone looking elsewhere. All the books say you shouldn't neglect your sex life.'

'You're not neglecting it. It's just slowed down a bit. I told Greg that when I get one week of uninterrupted sleep I'll give him a blow-job. I haven't had three consecutive nights in five years.'

'I feel the same way – but look at what's happened. Harry's sleeping with someone else – some sexy French girl with lacy underwear and pert boobs and cellulite-free thighs who isn't tired all the time.'

'That does not make you responsible. It just makes him a prick.'

'Pick.' Tom bustled over to me. I picked him up and cuddled him.

'You need to find out more,' Marian said.

'I could ask the triplets what happened that weekend, if Harry went out,' I suggested.

'Great idea. Milk them for information. Kids only learn to lie when they're six.'

I suspected I was over the alcohol limit and shouldn't have picked up the triplets that day – the brandy-coffees had been very potent. When the boys had climbed in and put their seatbelts on I began my interrogation.

'Boys, you remember the weekend Mummy went to London to help Louise when she was having the baby?'

'No,' Leo said.

'What baby?' Luke asked.

'Who's Louise?' Liam looked confused.

'Your auntie Louise, Mummy's sister.'

'The one we only see at Christmas, who gives us the crap presents?' Luke wondered.

'Don't say "crap",' I scolded. 'Yes, that's Louise. Anyway, do you remember when I went away with Tom for two sleepies and Daddy was looking after you?'

'No,' Leo said.

'Did Daddy buy us sweeties?' Luke asked.

'I thought Sophie was your sister.' Liam was finding it hard to work out the family tree.

'Sophie is my sister and Gavin is my brother and Louise is my other sister.'

'Who's your mummy?' Liam asked.

'Granny is Mummy's mummy,' Luke told him.

'Who's Granny's mummy?' Liam wanted full disclosure.

'My great-granny.'

'Why was she so great? Did she buy you lots of sweeties?' Luke's obsession with sweets continued.

'No – look, can we just forget about sisters and grannies for a minute? Do you remember when Daddy was on his own with you for a weekend and he let you watch lots of TV and eat pizza?'

'Oh, yeah, I remember the pizza.' Leo's brain finally caught up.

'Did we get sweeties after the pizza?' Luke asked.

'Jesus, Luke, I don't know. But I want to ask you if you can remember if Daddy went out and left you alone that weekend. Did a babysitter come and put you to bed?'

'I dunno.' Leo shrugged.

'What babysitter?' Liam asked. 'Gloria? I like Gloria. She sometimes gives us sweeties.'

I tried to remain calm. 'OK, listen to me carefully. When Daddy was taking care of you when Mummy went away, did he go out and leave you with a babysitter or did he stay in and put you to bed himself?'

'Where did you go?' Leo asked.

'Mummy, why do you ask so many questions? I've got a headache,' Liam grumbled.

'Me too,' Luke said. 'Sweeties are good for headaches.'

I thumped the steering-wheel in frustration. Sherlock Holmes could rest easy: my triplets were not going to be taking his place any time soon.

29

Louise

Clara was a different child. She had stopped screaming after all her bottles. She still woke up sometimes at night, but settled back quickly. I felt so much better. I'd even started running again. I was back in control, back in charge.

I decided to go to Dublin to see my family. I wasn't afraid to travel with Clara now that she was settled. I wanted to take her back and let her get to know her grandparents. I also wanted to hand-deliver Julie's present and apologize in person for forgetting her fortieth birthday. Mum seemed worried about Sophie, so I'd look in on her too. Before leaving I called Gavin. I had bought him fifty pounds' worth of credit for his mobile so he'd stop calling everyone and reversing the charges.

He answered his phone on the first ring.

'How's it going?' I asked, looking out of my office window at the teeming summer rain.

'Pretty crap. The tent leaked again last night. I thought the whole camping thing would be OK over here because you sometimes get good summers in England. But all it's done is bloody rain. I'm sick of being wet and I can't handle another week of berries and tofu. I need meat.'

'Why don't you pack it in?'

'Because you have to fight for –'

I cut across him: 'I know you have to fight for what you believe in. I get it. But you can do it from a dry office. You can do it via different and more effective routes, like the article you wrote. It was pretty impressive. It was well thought out and convincing.

Stop living like a homeless person and start campaigning with your brain. Write more articles, do interviews on TV, film documentaries, work for Greenpeace or Amnesty or whoever you want, just get out of that bloody tent and do it properly.'

'What about Acorn?'

'She must be fed-up too. And if she isn't, then the whole tree-hugging road is hers to follow. But you've tried it and you know it's not for you. You don't like it and you could be much more effective on dry land.'

'Actually, Acorn is fed-up.'

'So she's not hard-core, after all.'

'No – her brother Forest is, but she's more like me. She likes the idea of it, she believes in the cause, but she doesn't want to fight it from a leaky tent in a muddy field.'

'Good for her. At least she sees sense.'

'So what should I do?

'Pack up and go home. It's time to get your shit together.'

'The thing is, we don't have any cash.'

'So what else is new? Look, I'll book you both on my flight to Dublin. I'm taking Clara back on Friday. You can come and stay on Thursday night to shower and wash your clothes so Mum doesn't have a heart attack when she sees you.'

'Thanks, sis, I owe you one.'

'Gavin, you owe me hundreds. Just go home and save the world with a salary.'

'By the way, what's up with Sophie? I've left loads of messages for her and I told her I wasn't looking for cash, just calling to say hi because I had credit on my phone. Have you heard from her?'

'No, I haven't. Mum's really worried about her. I'm going to call into her when I'm home. Why don't you come with me?'

'Cool. Has Julie forgiven you witches for forgetting her birthday?'

'You know Julie – she can't hold a grudge for long. She's too nice. But she was really annoyed with me. I've never heard her so angry.'

'Well, it was a big deal for her and her life is pretty stressful.

Seriously, those little dudes are hard-core to look after. I'm always totally wiped out after an hour with them.'

'Now that I have a child, I think she's Superwoman to cope with four.'

'Jeez, Louise, did you actually admit to a weakness?' He laughed.

'No, Gavin. I just said it was a challenge.'

'A big one?'

'Bloody huge! See you on Thursday.'

Now that I was getting sleep, work was fun again. The Gordon Hanks purchase of the Lifechange TV station was almost complete. We were just finalizing some late changes. Their head lawyer, Hamilton Goodge, had played hardball, but so had I. Gordon said I was doing a great job and that he was glad to have a ball-breaker representing him. Alex was very pleased and I was both delighted and relieved.

It was fantastic to feel like myself again. I had my life, my energy and my focus back. The deal was closing tomorrow at five and then Gordon was taking me – and Dominic, unfortunately – for celebration drinks at the Blue Bar in the Berkeley Hotel. While they would be celebrating the close, I'd secretly be celebrating the fact that my baby was finally sleeping.

That evening, as I was packing up to leave, Alex's head popped around my door. 'All on schedule for tomorrow?' he asked.

'Yes, Alex, everything is on track. We'll close at five. I'm waiting for Lifechange's lawyers to email me their final changes in the morning, but there won't be any surprises. It's all down to marginal changes of wording at this point.'

'Excellent. You've done a wonderful job. It was important to me personally that this acquisition went smoothly. I would only have allowed my brother-in-law to be represented by the best. I must confess, Louise, I was becoming a little concerned that you were no longer at the top of your game. You looked very tired and you seemed somewhat below par. But I'm delighted you've ironed out whatever problems you had.'

'Don't worry, Alex, everything's back to normal. I had a minor adjustment period, but it's all under control now.'

'I'm very glad to hear it. Senior partners need to be committed and dedicated. It's part of the job description. I'm afraid it doesn't leave a lot of time for family. I was concerned when the child was born that you would find it difficult to juggle everything, particularly as you're the sole parent. But I can see that you've found a solution and I must say it's good to have you back, firing on all cylinders.'

'Thank you, Alex. You know how dedicated I am to my job and this firm. I would never let anything come in the way of my work.'

'Excellent, glad to hear it. Well, carry on the good work. Gordon is really pleased with your handling of this case. You may be getting more business from him in the future.'

'That's very good to hear.' I was thrilled. Alex was not someone who gave compliments lightly. I had been so worried that he was going to start sidelining me because I was a walking zombie. It was also fantastic to know Gordon was thinking of sending business my way. He only did big deals.

'Well, goodnight, Louise,' Alex said. 'I look forward to a celebratory drink tomorrow.'

'Me too.' I beamed at him.

When I got home, Agnes had collected Clara from the crèche and was giving her a bottle of water. The apartment smelt of vomit.

'Clara sick,' she said, as I took my coat off.

'What's wrong?'

'I collects from crèche and when I brings her home, she vomit three times. She have temperature of thirty-eight point four.'

I went over to pick Clara up. She was very pale and miserable. I touched her forehead: it was hot. I took her temperature – 38.6.

'It's gone up. Damn. Do you think it's just a tummy bug?' I kissed my daughter's hot little cheek.

'Yes. The lady at the crèche say that three of babies have sick tummy.'

'What do I do?'

'You must keep giving drinks, water and milk, and for temperature give Nurofen and Calpol and check her every one or two hours.' Agnes picked up her bag. 'If temperature is not going down, give her a cold bath.'

'Is there any way you could stay and help? I've got a really important day tomorrow.'

'Louise,' she said, looking me in the eye, 'you always having very important day.'

'But this really is a big one.'

'I sorry. I needs go home now.' She kissed Clara's forehead. 'I will looks after baby tomorrow. She must not go crèche. I be here at seven.'

As the front door closed, Clara vomited all over me . . .

The alarm went off. It couldn't be six. It just couldn't be. I peeled my eyes open. Christ, it was six. Clara was lying across my chest, breathing deeply. During the night she had vomited four more times and her temperature had spiked up and down. I had ended up giving her a cool bath at two a.m., which had brought her temperature down considerably. We had both finally fallen asleep at three.

I carefully slid from underneath my baby, who remained fast asleep, and stood in the shower. I felt like death. As I got out, I felt my stomach rumble and threw up. Shit! Clara had given me her bug. The combination of no sleep and the bug made me feel dizzy. I grabbed hold of the sink to steady myself. Damn – of all the bloody days.

Skipping work was not an option. I slowly got dressed. Put some makeup on to hide my grey face and threw up again. When I looked up, Agnes was standing by the door watching me. 'You have bad tummy like Clara.'

'Yes.' I wiped my mouth.

'You no go to work. I minding baby, you go to bed.'

'I can't. I have to go in. It's a really –'

'Important day.' Agnes shook her head. 'Louise, you needs to have energy to minds Clara tonight. If you going to work, you being too tired. The baby needs Mummy. Work is not number one. Baby is number one.'

'I know, but today work has to be number one or I won't have a job and you won't have a job and Clara won't have a home.'

I left before she could lecture me any further. I felt wretched. I hailed a cab, feeling too weak to walk, but then I had to get out because I thought I was going to throw up. Typical. Just when I'd thought I had everything under control, it all went pear-shaped again. I took a deep breath and prayed to get through the day.

Dominic was waiting for me when I arrived. 'You look ill,' he said.

'Good morning.' I ignored him, walked into my office and sat down. He followed me in, chomping a bacon sandwich. The smell made me want to vomit.

'I've checked the email from the Lifechange lawyers,' he said. 'They've made a few final changes to clauses seven and eleven – they're a bit cheeky so we'll need to go back to them on those.'

'I'd like to go through the document now myself. I'll call you when I'm finished.' I dismissed Dominic and his pungent sandwich.

I opened my email, went into the amended document and scrolled down through the two clauses. Their changes were red-lined. They had altered the wording relating to the warrantee provisions and the indemnity clause. I was going to print out the documents and go through them by hand, but I was too tired and I knew that these two clauses were the only sticking points we'd had left.

This had been going on for days now: we needed to find a compromise. I decided to tackle it head-on. I called Hamilton Goodge directly and thrashed it out with him on the phone. After hours of toing and froing with draft after draft – and me retching into my wastepaper bin – we finally agreed on the exact wording of clauses seven and eleven. They sent over the amended copy. I checked it, called Hamilton to say it was all fine, and he said he'd draw up the execution versions for signing.

I sank back into my chair and gingerly sipped some water. I felt awful. Tiredness washed over me, but I felt too ill to drink coffee or eat anything to give me energy. I was utterly worn out. I looked at my watch. It was four o'clock. Thank God today was nearly over. Once the execution versions had been checked, we'd go over to Hamilton's office where the Lifechange team and Gordon Hanks would sign, shake hands and I could go home and die.

Dominic came in for the tenth time that day. 'Is it done yet? Gordon's on his way. He'll be here in twenty minutes. I've ordered a car to take us to Hamilton's at four thirty.'

'The execution copies are being printed out as we speak. We're good to go.'

'Do you want me to look over the final draft – second pair of eyes?'

'No, Dominic, I don't need a babysitter. I've been doing this for twenty years.'

'OK, Louise, no need to bite. You look dreadful. Are you ill?'

'No, it's just been a stressful day. Excuse me a minute.' I got up and went to the bathroom to put on some makeup. I didn't want to scare Gordon Hanks. The reflection in the mirror was that of a ghost. I looked horrendous. I piled on makeup, blusher and bright red lipstick to try to distract from my green hue.

When I got back from the bathroom, Dominic was telling Gordon and Alex about some golf competition he had played in. Gordon looked genuinely interested. I was going to have to take up golf. Even if I had to strap Clara to my back while I did it. I needed to get into it. The older I got, the more important a networking tool it seemed.

We piled into the car and headed over to Hamilton's office. Gordon was in a very good mood. He praised me and Dominic for our hard work and the speed with which we had finalized the paperwork. Alex smiled at both of us. I was annoyed that Dominic was basking in my limelight. I had, after all, done most of the work on the deal. He had only done a small amount, but he soaked up the credit.

'We'll be drinking brandy and smoking cigars tonight.' Gordon beamed at us as I tried not to retch.

In the company boardroom, Hamilton laid the twenty documents in front of Gordon. I double-checked clauses seven and eleven and then told Gordon he was OK to sign. He went straight to the execution pages and scrawled his name across each, as did the Lifechange representatives.

We all shook hands. Hamilton then opened a bottle of champagne and we toasted the deal, wishing Gordon luck in his future with the TV station. I pretended to drink, but the smell made me nauseous.

Then we headed to the Berkeley to celebrate. I had to go along for a while as it would look really bad if I went home now, although I was almost fainting with tiredness and weak with lack of food. I was planning on staying for an hour and then slipping away. I was furious that I was feeling so awful. This was a great opportunity to stay and talk to Gordon. I could have done some schmoozing and tried to confirm future business deals. But I knew I couldn't last much longer and bloody Dominic would be there all night, drinking and smoking and talking about golf and crawling up Gordon's arse. Damn. Damn. Damn.

Alex had insisted on personally bringing the signed documents back to our office for safekeeping. He said he'd join us in half an hour. Gordon, Dominic and I got a nice table in the Blue Bar and Gordon ordered a bottle of Richard Hennessy cognac and some cigars, which thankfully they would have to smoke outside. I silently cheered the non-smoking ban. My stomach could not have taken cigar-smoke fumes. While they knocked back their brandies, I pretended to sip mine.

'Come on, Louise, drink up, girl. It'll put hairs on your chest.'

'This may come as a surprise to you, Gordon, but women don't actually aspire to have hairy chests.' I smiled as he roared laughing.

'I gotta say, I like you, Louise. You're a sassy broad. Alex told me you were the best around and he was right. Cheers.'

We clinked glasses and Gordon continued to praise me while Dominic sat back and simmered.

My phone rang. It was Alex.

'Hi, are you on your way?' I asked.

'Louise, I need you to come back to the office right away. Do not let on to Gordon that anything is wrong. Make an excuse and get back here now.' He hung up.

Shit, what the hell was going on? He'd sounded furious.

'What's wrong, Louise? Do you have nanny problems? Do you need to go home to the baby?' Dominic smirked.

'No, Dominic, one of the other cases I'm working on needs me. I'm so sorry, Gordon, I have to leave you. Work calls. You know how it is. I never let my clients down.' I milked it.

'Always on. I admire that. I'll be in touch, Louise. Thanks for everything.'

'It's been a real pleasure. Maybe we could do lunch the next time you're in town.'

'I'd like that,' he said.

As I was leaving I turned to Dominic. 'Don't stay up too late, Dominic. I need you clear-headed tomorrow. You have work to do.'

'I'm usually in before you, these days,' he drawled.

I didn't have time to retort. I had to get out of there. My legs were shaking. Why did Alex need me back? What had gone wrong?

Alex was standing outside my office when I rushed in. He shook the signed documents in my face. 'I thought we agreed on a purchase price of thirty million,' he said, trying to keep his voice calm.

'We did.'

'Well, then, please explain to me why on all these signed versions it says *fifty* million.'

'You must be mistaken.' I took the copies from his hand and went to the purchase price, which I knew from memory was on page nineteen of the document. This time I retched out of shock. It clearly stated fifty million. SHIT!

'Look, Alex, this is a typo. It's a mistake. We agreed thirty million. It never changed. I'll sort it out, don't worry. This is not going to be a problem. I will have it changed immediately.'

'Louise, I want the revised documents on my desk first thing in the morning. You'll have to explain to Gordon why he has to sign new versions. It's a very serious oversight. You know how important this was to me personally. I'm extremely disappointed. The old Louise would never have made this mistake. Fix it.'

After he left, I opened my laptop and went through the final draft – version thirteen that Hamilton had sent me. I scrolled down to the red-lined parts in clauses seven and eleven and then went to the purchase price page – there it was, underlined in red, fifty million.

I went back and checked draft twelve of the documents – the purchase price was thirty million as agreed. The bloody computer had picked up the change in draft thirteen and underlined it, but I hadn't seen it. If I'd printed out the pages of the thirteenth draft, as I usually did, I would have seen the red line – but I'd done it onscreen. I had only checked clauses seven and eleven. I had missed this because I was tired and sick. I had completely messed up. I wanted to bawl, but I didn't have time. I could fall apart later. Right now I had to fix this. I called Hamilton. I decided to go on the offensive.

'We have a problem,' I snapped. 'Your execution documents have the purchase price at fifty million when you know we agreed on thirty million as stated and documented in previous correspondence.'

'Calm down. I have no idea what you're talking about.'

'The purchase price on the documents you produced for Gordon to sign state the purchase price as fifty million. We need to sort this out now, tonight, or it will look very bad for all of us.'

'Hold on a minute, it was up to you to check the execution draft and note any changes to it or typos in it.'

'I checked the two clauses we had changed. I presumed that you wouldn't have altered the purchase price. I have emails that state very clearly that we agreed a price of thirty million, never fifty. Twenty million pounds is a large discrepancy.'

'I'll have to speak to my client. He may not agree to amend it. You know as well as I do, Louise, that if this went to court, you'd lose.'

'Are you threatening me?' I was shaking with fear, rage and exhaustion.

'No. I'm merely reminding you that the contract your client signed, the contract you agreed on, would stand up in court. The change in purchase price is your oversight, Louise, not mine.'

'Don't mess me around, Hamilton. You know this was your error. In draft twelve it states thirty million, in draft thirteen it's fifty. Just draw up amended execution documents and have them ready for signature tomorrow.'

'I'll talk to my client and see what I can do. Tomorrow may not be possible.'

'Tomorrow, Hamilton, no later.'

'I don't think you're in a position to order me about, Louise. I'll call you when I've had a chance to review the situation.'

I swallowed my pride. 'Hamilton, help me out here, please. I need this sorted by tomorrow. My arse is on the line.'

'Are my ears deceiving me? Is Louise Devlin, the tigress of Higgins, Cooper & Gray, begging?'

'Don't be an arsehole.'

'I'll see what I can do.'

I knew that Hamilton would amend the price and come back to me. Lawyers didn't screw each other around like that. It was a typo, a mistake, and we both knew it, but it had been up to me to catch it. I was now going to have to explain to Gordon that I had messed up. He wouldn't have such a high opinion of me tomorrow and, worst of all, I had let Alex down. And Dominic was going to gloat all over me. He'd also make sure everyone in the office knew. The snake would hang me out to dry. But I had no one to blame except myself.

I picked up my laptop and headed home. I thought I'd cry in the taxi, but I was too tired, too stressed, too overwrought. I had never, ever made a mistake like that. I knew lots of people who had – but not me, never me. I always printed out the final draft and looked over it, scanning each page for any changes or amendments. This time I hadn't. I had cut corners. I had been too exhausted to do my job properly – and look what had happened. Disaster.

I wearily entered the apartment to find Agnes and Clara asleep on the couch. Clara was lying across Agnes's considerable chest, breathing deeply. I had an urge to hug my baby, to smell her, to hold her cheek to mine. I gently picked her up. She stirred, opened her blue eyes, gave me a sleepy smile and snuggled her head into my neck. That was when I began to cry.

Agnes woke up to find me sitting on the couch beside her, holding a sleeping Clara, crying my eyes out.

'What happening? Did you lose job?' she asked.

'No,' I whispered. 'But I'm in very big trouble. And when I came in I was so depressed and then I saw Clara – my baby, my beautiful baby who I wanted to give back, the baby I didn't want, who drove me crazy, who I shouted at, who I yearned to give away and I just . . . I just . . . wanted to hold her so badly and when I picked her up she smiled and I . . . I uh – I – uh . . .' I sobbed.

Agnes patted my arm. 'Baby makes bad day go away. You take baby into your bed tonight and you sleeping well.'

'Yes, I think I'll do that.'

Agnes left, and soon I was curled up in bed, holding my angel baby close. I cried myself to sleep.

30

Sophie

Selling on eBay became an addiction. I spent all the time Jess was in school online, checking how my items were doing. Some of the sales were very slow, so I had to slash the prices. But I'd already made ten thousand euros, which was brilliant. I hadn't told Jack yet. I was keeping the money in an account I'd opened with the Post Office. I was hoping to make at least four times that with the rest of my sales.

My favourite Chloé coat went for 370 euros; I'd paid 1,400 for it. Whoever bought it was getting a real bargain. Still, it was a relief to have money coming in. It made me feel less useless.

Jack was spending all day every day in his office on the phone. I could often hear shouting and lots of cursing. We barely spoke any more. He was wrapped up in trying to get us out of the mess we were in and I was busy trying to make some money and keep Jess occupied now that all her after-school activities had ceased.

In the meantime a lot of people were leaving increasingly abusive messages on my phone because we still owed them money. Our gardener had threatened to come back and dig up all our plants, my personal trainer had threatened to sue me, and Jess's drama teacher said we were nothing but common thieves who had stolen a term of teaching from her. It had been a horrendous few days telling people they weren't going to get paid and dealing with their anger.

The only people who were nice about it were the management at Jess's school, who said we were by no means the only parents who hadn't been able to pay the last term's fees and that Jess was welcome to finish up, but that they would need payment up front if she was coming back next year.

Mimi had been wonderful. She was so kind. I couldn't stop crying when I told her we had to let her go and *she* had ended up comforting me. 'Don't worry, Sophie. I find another job.'

'I'm so sorry, Mimi. I'm so ashamed that we can't pay you for the last six weeks. Please take this instead.' I handed her a pair of diamond stud earrings.

'Sophie, I not taking these. You are nice family. You very good to Mimi. You have hard times now. It OK. I have save money. I be fine.'

'Oh, Mimi, I wish I'd been smarter and saved money too. I've been so stupid.'

'You just young and having good time. This is lesson for you. Next time you not shopping so much and you putting money in bank.'

'I think we're going to lose the house,' I said, blowing my nose.

'House is just bricks. I grow up in tiny house. But I happy. Clothes and jewels not making you happy. You needs be happy in here.' She tapped her heart. 'We have saying in Philippines, *Ang kaginhawaan ay nasa kasiyahan, at wala sa kasaganaan.*'

'What does it mean?'

'Well-being found in happiness, not in prosperity.'

'You're very wise, Mimi. I'm really beginning to see how true that is now. I just don't want Jess to be homeless. Where will we live? How will we pay our rent? Who is going to give Jack a job?'

'Jack is good man. He love you and Jess. He work very hard so you have nice things. He making a mistake. Everybody making mistake in life. Jack intelligent, he be OK.'

'I hope so, Mimi.'

When I told Jess that Mimi was leaving, she was inconsolable. She cried for hours and kept asking, 'But *why*, Mummy, why does Mimi have to go?'

I tried to explain that Daddy's job was different now and for the moment we had to stop spending money. But her poor little mind didn't understand why her life was being turned upside-down.

Jess spent Mimi's last day curled in her lap, crying. Mimi was like a second mother to her or, if I'm being honest, Mimi was like a first mother to her. Jess spent more time with her than she did with me. I was too busy being at Jack's beck and call, making sure that his needs were my top priority. Well, that was going to change. From now on, Jess came first in my life.

'Now, now, my big girl.' Mimi wiped Jess's tears away. 'No more crying. You need be a good girl for your mummy and daddy.'

'I love you, Mimi, please stay.' Jess threw her arms around Mimi's neck.

'I have to go, Jessie, but you know you always be in here.' Mimi put Jess's little hand up to her heart. 'You are my special girl. I will always think of you and send you big kisses in the sky.'

'But, Mimi, who's going to do my hair in French plaits?'

'You mummy will.'

'But she doesn't know how to do it the way you do.'

Mimi held Jess's face in her hands. 'Jessie, listen to me, baby girl. You very lucky. You have a mummy and a daddy who love you very much. You are wonderful girl. You sweet and kind and gentle, but the world not so gentle, so you need be a bit stronger, OK? Remember what Mimi say?'

'Be nice to everyone, but if someone hits you, hit them back.' Jess sniffled.

'Good girl. Now, Mimi has to go. Give me one last big hug.'

Jess clung to her like a drowning man. I eventually had to peel her away so Mimi could leave. We both sobbed as she drove away in her friend's car, waving all the way down the drive.

I was still avoiding everyone and had been receiving concerned messages from Victoria and others saying that if I was still ill after all this time I clearly needed to go to hospital and have tests.

I knew I had to come clean. I decided to tell my family over the weekend. Louise had left a message saying she was coming home

319

and, if I could be bothered to get back to her, she'd like to see me. She sounded stressed and fed-up. I could relate to that. Julie hadn't called in a week, but Mum was stalking me. She knew something was up and I couldn't fob her off any longer. She was having a big lunch on Sunday for the whole family to welcome Clara home, and she said if I didn't come, she'd drive over and drag me out.

As it happened, I ended up having to tell them on Friday night . . .

Shortly after I had put Jess to bed, Jack came home. He stumbled into the kitchen. He was shaking and sweating.

'Jesus, Jack, what is it?'

'I did everything, Sophie. I've just spent all day in court trying to fight it, but the bank's repossessing the house. They're coming for the keys tomorrow . . . at one.'

I stared at him. 'What did you say?'

He began to cry. 'I begged them, I pleaded with them – I offered them ten different alternatives – but with so many people default-ing on their mortgages, they're not letting anyone off the hook. They're clamping down on all arrears.'

I gripped the kitchen counter. 'Are you telling me we're going to be homeless *tomorrow*?' I whispered. I was having difficulty breathing.

Jack came over to me. 'I'll call my father. I'll ask him for a loan. We'll rent somewhere small until we get back on our feet.'

'NO! You are not calling that smug, arrogant bastard. All he ever does is put you down. You're not going to give him the satisfaction of asking him for money. I'd rather live on the street. I'll call my family. We can move in with my parents for a few weeks.'

Jack looked relieved. 'If you're sure, that would be brilliant. I really didn't want to call my father, but I thought I'd have to.'

'How are we going to get all our things out in time? Is there a removal truck coming?'

Jack looked down at his hands. 'The bank wants the furniture, too.'

I looked at him, my husband, the man I loved, the man I

admired, the man I trusted. I knew that if I opened my mouth I'd say something terrible . . . vicious . . . unspeakable. So I turned and ran upstairs.

I screamed into my pillow for ten minutes. It was happening. My worst nightmare was coming true. We were losing our home. How was I going to explain to Jess when she woke up that she'd never see her bedroom again? Oh, God, how had we ended up here? What had I done to deserve this? Why was this happening to me? Should I use the money from the eBay sales to rent somewhere? No, I needed time to think, time to figure out what to do. We'd stay with Mum and Dad and get our heads together. Come up with a plan. But what plan? How would we ever get out from under this debt? I screamed into the pillow again.

When I came up for air, I logged on to eBay, praying for something to lift my spirits. There was some good news: the diamond Cartier watch Jack had bought me for Christmas was in a bidding war, and they were up to 900 euros. It was worth so much more than that, but it didn't matter: every penny counted now.

I braced myself, picked up the phone and dialled my parents. Dad picked up. The minute I heard his voice I began to cry.

'Who is this? Is this one of those prank calls? Are you one of those perverts preying on innocent people?'

'Daaaad, it's – uh . . . uh – me . . . Sophie.'

'Jesus, what's wrong?'

'Uuuh, we lost our . . . uh – uh . . . house.'

'What? I can't understand you. What do you mean you lost it? ANNE,' he roared at Mum. 'GET IN HERE! SOPHIE'S ON THE PHONE AND SHE'S HYSTERICAL. I CAN'T UNDERSTAND HER.'

'What's wrong, pet?' Mum sounded worried.

'It's all gone,' I sobbed.

'What is?'

'Everything. There's nothing left.'

'Sophie, love, what are you talking about?'

'THE MONEY!' I shouted, my anger rising to the surface. 'We

have nothing left. It's gone – every penny. Jack's company lost everything. And the bank is coming tomorrow to take our house. I'm homeless, Mum. I have nothing. Nothing. They even want our furniture.' I broke down again.

'Mother of God.'

'Can we come and stay for a little while?' I asked.

'Of course you can, pet. You can stay for as long as you like.' I heard Mum talking to Dad, filling him in on my destitution.

Dad came back on the phone. 'What happened to all the money?'

'Jack's company invested in a Ponzi scheme.'

'Jesus. Is there any way of getting it back?'

'None. Jack said they've tried everything. He's in a state. The bank's taking the house and the furniture tomorrow.'

'What type of gobshites go into a Ponzi scheme?' Dad fumed.

'Apparently the guy was well known, reputable. Loads of the hedge funds invested with him and lost. It wasn't just Jack's company.' I'd defended my husband for the first time.

'What about his salary and bonuses and other investments?'

'The bonuses were all tied up in the fund and his other investments in bank shares are worth nothing. Look, Dad, can you stop asking questions and help me?'

'Sorry, pet. Of course I'll be right over.'

'I don't need you to come now. I need you to come first thing tomorrow with a van. Can you borrow one, Dad? I can't pay for one. I want to take some of our stuff – I'm not letting the bank have everything. I want to take my baby's toys and uh – uh . . . photos and . . . china and . . .'

'Anne, talk to Sophie – she's hysterical again,' I heard Dad say, as Mum came back on the line.

'Oh, my poor Sophie,' she soothed, as I continued to bawl. 'I'm on my way over. We'll help you, love. We'll all rally together.'

'Don't come now, Mum. Jess is asleep and I don't want her worried. But I do need you here first thing tomorrow – and can you ask Julie and Harry to help too and bring their big car?'

'Of course I will. But can I not come over and see you now?'

'No, Mum, thanks. I need to talk to Jack and sort out what we're taking with us. I'd better go. I'll see you tomorrow.'

'Good luck, pet. Try and get some sleep.'

When I hung up, I realized Jack was standing in the doorway. 'What did they say?'

'They're coming tomorrow to help us take our things. I presume the bastard of a bank will at least allow me to keep family photos and my wedding china.'

'That's a good idea. What did your dad say?'

'He said we can stay as long as we want.'

'I mean about my investment.'

'You don't want to know.'

'I bet he said I was a gobshite.'

'Got it in one.'

'Did you defend me?'

'I tried, but it's hard.'

'Not if you believed me. Not if you listened to what actually happened. Not if you understood anything about trading. Not if you lived in my world.'

'Well, I may not be a genius, but at least I didn't get my family into deep shit.'

'I'll get us out of this.'

'I hope you do it soon because I don't fancy living with my parents long term.'

'Can you stop being a bitch for ten minutes and think about how I feel?'

I rounded on him: 'I don't have time for your *feelings*. I'm fighting to keep people we owe money to from beating down our door. I'm trying to keep Jess's life as normal as possible and protect her from this, but every time I turn around you have even worse news for me. I am now trying to keep us from living on the street, so can you stop looking for sympathy and help me pack our personal belongings before we're thrown out of our home?'

He stormed back down to his office and I began to pack. Photos, china, clothes, cutlery, Jess's favourite toys, anything that would fit in a suitcase. I packed until dawn broke.

Mum, Dad, Julie, Louise and Gavin were on our doorstep at eight the next morning. I opened the door and Mum hugged me tightly, followed by Dad, Julie, Louise and Gavin.

Jack was inside with Jess. We'd told her we were going on a little holiday to Granny and Granddad's and she was to pack her favourite cuddly toys and dolls.

'I'm so sorry, Sophie.' Julie's eyes welled up. 'Life's a bitch, isn't it? Men are bloody useless.'

'You should have called me,' Louise said.

'Dude, if I had any money, you know I'd give it to you,' Gavin assured me. 'You and Jack have always been so generous to me. When I get a job, my first pay cheque is yours.'

'Thanks.' I tried not to cry.

'Where's Clara?' Julie asked Louise.

'Acorn's minding her.'

'Where's Jack?' Dad asked.

'In the kitchen,' I said. 'Come on in. By the way, Jess doesn't understand. She thinks we're going to stay with you for fun. So we need to be careful around her. She knows something's up, but I don't want her traumatized.'

They all made a fuss of Jess, and Dad took Jack aside for a quick chat. All I could hear was '. . . seemed like a sure thing . . .'; '. . . very risky . . . shouldn't have piled in . . .'; '. . . checked his background, very solid . . .'

'Is it really all gone?' Mum whispered, as Gavin swung Jess around in circles. 'All of it?'

'Yes.'

'There must be a way of salvaging some of it. I'll go through the legal work for you,' Louise said. She looked as exhausted as I felt.

'I've been poor for ages,' Julie said. 'I can show you how to live on very little.' She looked awful, too. They must have all been up worrying about me last night.

'How long have you known?' Mum asked.

'Ages. I just couldn't face telling anyone. It's all so real now.'

'There, there, we're all here to help.' Mum rubbed my back. 'You look worn out. Sit down now and I'll make you a nice cup of tea and we'll get those cars loaded.'

'We don't have any cups, Mum, they're all packed. Come on, let's just get it over with.'

The van Dad had borrowed and Julie's car held most of our things. The rest went into the boot of the beaten-up Ford Fiesta that Jack had brought back from the garage when he'd traded in the Aston Martin and my Range Rover.

Jess sensed the tension and began to get upset. She kept asking why we were bringing so much stuff if we were just going on holiday.

I bent down. 'Jess, sweetheart, we won't be coming back to this house. We'll be going to a different one after our stay with Granny. This house is too big for just the three of us. We're going to find somewhere more cosy.'

'But I like this house.'

'We'll find another nice one, I promise.'

'But what about my *Princess and the Frog* duvet?'

'I'm bringing that.'

'What about my princess bed?'

For Jess's fourth birthday I had ordered a custom-made bed that looked like a huge throne and was hand-painted with scenes from her favourite movie – *The Princess and the Frog*. It was a work of art. She absolutely loved it.

'I'm sorry, pet, we can't fit it into the car. But we'll get you a nice new one soon.'

'*Nooo*,' she sobbed. 'I want my bed. Everything is yucky now. I hate it. You and Daddy are mean to each other and Mimi's gone and you have sad eyes all the time. I don't go to ballet or drama or swimming or anything any more and I don't go on play-dates. I don't want a new house, I want *this* house. I don't want a new bed, I want my princess bed.' I put my arms round her and she sobbed into my shoulder.

325

Dad knelt down beside her. 'Jessica, listen to your granddad. If you want that bed, then I'll get it for you. I'm going upstairs now to bring it down and we'll set it up in your mum's old bedroom in our house.'

Dad stormed up the stairs, followed by Gavin and Jack. They came down carrying the bed and, with a lot of shouting, cursing and manoeuvring, somehow managed to tie it to the roof of the van.

While they did that, Julie fed Jess chocolate buttons and sang her funny songs to make her laugh. She cheered up in no time.

Louise pulled me aside. 'What happened to the money Dad gave you?' she asked. 'That should tide you over for a while.'

I winced. 'It went down in the Ponzi scheme – and please don't say I should have given it to you to invest. I'm all too aware of the stupid mistakes I've made and the ridiculous amount of money I wasted on material things. I've been a total idiot.'

'Don't be so hard on yourself.' Louise sighed. 'We all make mistakes. Let me go through Jack's contracts. Maybe I can salvage something.' She patted my arm.

We walked outside and I went over to Jess and Julie. Jess had chocolate all over her face and looked happy. 'I ate some chocolate, Mummy, but I'll brush my teeth when we get to Granny's.'

I kissed her. 'You can have any treat you want today, baby. Are you OK now?'

'Yes. Julie told me funny songs and then she said that all men are very silly billies and that us girls need to stick together. She said when I grow up I should study hard like Louise and never get married.'

'She's right.'

'But princesses always get married to princes.'

'Sometimes princes aren't what they seem,' Julie said.

'Why don't we live in a castle together? Just us girls,' I suggested. 'What about Daddy?'

'He could live in the dungeon with Uncle Harry,' Julie said.

'Bloody good idea,' I agreed.

'But it's dark and cold down there,' Jess reminded us.

'Yes, I know.' Julie sighed.

'Right, then, we're all packed up,' Dad said.

Jack came over to us. 'Do you want to go in and say goodbye to the house, Jess?' he asked.

'No, thank you, Daddy. I did it already.'

'Sophie?'

I shook my head. 'No point looking back.'

He shut the front door and slid the key under the mat.

As we were driving away, Jess piped up, 'Daddy, Auntie Julie wants to put you and Harry in the dungeon.'

'What?'

'Yes, and Mummy said it was a bloody good idea.'

I couldn't believe it: Sophie and Jack were homeless . . . It was shocking. They'd been so wealthy, had had so much – how could they suddenly have nothing? Everyone kept muttering about a Ponzi scheme and shaking their heads. I felt sorry for Jack: he'd lost loads of weight, his eyes were all red and bloodshot and his hair was suddenly speckled with grey.

But I'd got a real fright when I saw Sophie. She was skin and bone and she had aged ten years. Her normally thick, shiny hair was limp and greasy. She looked completely drained and had huge black circles under her eyes. And poor little Jess didn't know what was going on.

The whole situation was just awful. When we'd finished packing the cars, I drove back to Mum and Dad's house with Louise. I desperately wanted to tell her about Harry's affair, but I just couldn't get the words out. How would I start? 'Hey, Lou, how's Clara? By the way, Harry's screwing a French bird.' It wasn't easy admitting your husband was a cheat.

'What a bloody mess.' Louise peeled off her jumper. 'How could they have been so stupid, investing in a Ponzi scheme?' She had put on weight, which was unlike her. She'd been a size ten since she was sixteen. She looked exhausted, too. Clara must still be up at night.

I stopped at the traffic lights. 'Sophie said lots of the top hedge funds in New York jumped into the scheme. It's not as if Jack's company was the only one.'

'I know, Julie, but to leverage yourselves so high that you lose everything? It's just crazy. You have to spread your investments wide.'

'A lot of people have lost their shirts in the last year or two, even really smart people with lots of experience,' I reminded her.

'I suppose you're right, but they seem to have absolutely nothing left. Jack even put Sophie's rainy-day money into it.'

'Oh, shit – really? I thought she gave it to you.'

'She said she trusted Jack to invest it.'

'Yikes. By the way, how is my money doing?' I asked. Now that my husband was screwing a French slut, I'd need it to raise my family.

'Very well. It's worth a hundred and two thousand now.'

I turned to smile at her. 'Wow, that's brilliant. Thank God I let you look after it.'

'I wish Sophie had done the same thing.'

'I'm sure she does too. How did you get Gavin home by the way? Mum's thrilled.'

'It wasn't hard. He was broke and his usual bank-roller, Sophie, wouldn't answer his calls. He was also damp and cold and miserable. The novelty had worn off. I just told him I'd fly him and Acorn home and he could save the world from an office.'

'That was it?'

'Pretty much.'

'He's no martyr to the cause, is he?'

We laughed. It felt good. I hadn't laughed in weeks.

'How's Clara?' I asked.

'Well, the reflux is much better, thank God, but she had a tummy bug this week, so I was up all night minding her and then I got the bloody bug. I've actually had the week from hell. Just when I thought everything was sorted and I had my life back, it all went pear-shaped again.' Louise tugged at her fringe. Her normally perfectly blow-dried black bob was pulled back in a ponytail.

'Sorry to burst your bubble, but you never get your life back. You get a different life. One that never goes according to plan. One that you have to be flexible, patient and adaptable to get through. On all really important days they'll get sick, or fall over and break their arm or set the house on fire or something.'

'Gee, thanks, Julie, you really know how to make someone feel better.'

I shrugged. 'Life's a bitch.'

Louise leant her head back against the car seat. 'I messed up badly in work.'

'What? You've never messed up in your life.' I was genuinely shocked: Louise was the most meticulous person I knew, which was what made her such a brilliant lawyer.

'I was so busy vomiting and trying to keep my eyes open that I missed a mistake in a very important acquisition. It's all been sorted now, but it could have been catastrophic. The reason I missed it was because I took a short cut. Something I'd never done before in twenty years. I can't believe it – I can't believe I did that. It's just not me. I don't cut corners. I'm not that person, which is why I'm successful.'

'Give yourself a break. You had no sleep and you had a vomiting bug. Ninety-nine per cent of the population wouldn't have got out of bed in the first place.'

'It's no excuse. If I'd printed out the documents instead of check-ing them on the screen, I would have spotted the error.'

'Did Alex find out?'

'Yes, and he's furious. I managed to fix the problem, but it reflected really badly on me. Since Clara came along I've been averaging three hours' sleep a night. Alex thinks I'm losing my edge. And the awful thing is, Julie, he's right. I am. I can't work at my level without sleep.'

I reached over and squeezed her hand. 'It's only temporary, Lou, I promise. She'll start sleeping through the night regularly soon enough and you'll feel more like yourself. Come on, she's only four months old. Most normal women don't go back to work for at least six months.'

'Meredith did it, and she managed fine.'

'Yes, but you said she has a husband who helps her out. You're on your own, which is much harder.'

'I don't know what to do. I can't afford to mess up. I'm just praying that Clara doesn't get sick again. I need to prove myself. I need to get back to my best.'

'I don't know how you do it. I can barely get through the day and all I have to do is housework. The idea of negotiating multi-million-pound deals would freak me out.'

'Well, I don't know how you do it with four kids. I honestly had no idea it was this hard. I know it's a cliché, but until I had Clara I really didn't get it. It's a parallel universe. It's so consuming and tiring and relentless. I know you're going to think I'm a rotten human being for admitting this, but some nights when Clara cries for hours and hours, I feel like walking out the door and never coming back.'

I threw my head back and whooped. 'Louise, I feel like that every single day!'

Louise's head snapped around. 'Do you? I thought you loved being a mum.'

'I hate it. It's pure drudgery.'

'But you always seem so happy with the kids.'

'All I do is roar at them day and night.'

'I know you shout a bit, but only to stop them doing mad things or hurting themselves. I always thought you found motherhood really fulfilling. You have a lovely relationship with the boys. I see a really strong bond between you.'

'Bond!' I snorted. 'Most of the time they hate me. And as for fulfilling, it's not – not for me anyway. Sure there are days when the triplets are good and we're playing a game and laughing and I think, Wow, this is it, this is family life, happiness, fulfilment, but it only ever lasts about five minutes. One of them will smack another, all hell will break loose and I'll start shouting again. There's nothing about the daily grind that I like – cleaning, cooking, shopping, laundry . . . I'm not saying I don't love every hair on their heads. I'm not saying there aren't moments when I love them so much I can't breathe. But most of the time I find parenthood a pain in the arse, to be honest.'

Louise stared at me, open-mouthed. 'I'd no idea you felt that strongly about it.'

331

'Maybe if I had money and was able to pay someone to mind them one afternoon a week it'd be easier. I do think that a big part of the problem is that I never get a second to myself. If it's not Tom, it's the triplets. It's relentless.'

'What about Harry? Why don't you get him to look after them on Saturday mornings for a few hours and let you have some time out?'

'Because Harry is a selfish prick.' I smacked the steering-wheel for emphasis.

'Harry?' Louise looked startled.

'Yes,' I said, through gritted teeth.

'But he always seems so hands-on.'

'He can't handle the four boys at the same time. He panics. Besides, he's too busy with work and other stuff at the moment to give us the time of day.'

'Are you still annoyed with him for forgetting your birthday?'

'Yes, but, Louise, something terrib–'

'You know,' she interrupted me, 'I think you're lucky with Harry. He's a good guy – solid, reliable, into his kids. Look at Jack! Millionaire one day, destitute the next. Who wants that? Harry may never earn big bucks, but he'll always bring home a regular salary and you won't ever have to worry about being homeless. There is a lot to be said for that.'

'Yes, but –'

'Look, Julie, I understand that you're angry about your birthday, but as husbands go, Harry's pretty great. Since I had Clara I've been looking at men in a whole new light. I used to think that if I ever ended up with someone he'd be career-focused, driven, ambitious and hard-working. Now I'd like to meet a domestic god. I'd love him to stay at home with Clara while I go out to work and bring home the bacon. I want to meet someone reliable, trustworthy, calm, considerate, mellow, laid-back.'

It was my turn to be shocked. 'Laid-back?'

'I know. Would you ever have imagined I'd say that? But it's true. I need to meet the polar opposite of me. I need a Mr Mum.'

'Be careful what you wish for. Men are not what they seem. They can surprise you even when you think you know them really well,' I muttered darkly.

'You have a point there, all right. Jack certainly gave Sophie the surprise of her life, didn't he? Poor Sophie . . . She really loved her lifestyle.'

'Who wouldn't? She lived like a queen. It must have been fantastic. They both seemed so happy all the time, never stressed, never tired or grumpy . . . They seemed so carefree.' I sighed.

'Yes, but Sophie's life lacked purpose. She must have been bored.'

'I'd never be bored with time to myself,' I said, parking the car in my parents' driveway.

'Me neither. Come on, we'd better get this stuff unloaded. Clara's due a bottle soon,' Louise said, jumping out of my people-carrier, which was now parked beside Sophie and Jack's Fiesta.

Within half an hour the boxes and cases had been unloaded and stored in our old bedrooms. Dad and Gavin had just about managed, with a lot of cursing and roaring from Dad, to get Jess's princess bed up the narrow staircase.

When we had finished, Mum sat us down to a big fry-up. Everyone tucked in, even Sophie, but I played with my food. Since I'd found out about Harry's affair, I had lost my appetite. Typical: now that I was losing the weight I'd always wanted to, my husband was staring at someone else's bum. I tried not to cry.

'Dude, what are you doing?' Acorn said, as Gavin took a huge bite of a bacon sandwich.

'Newsflash: Gavin is not vegan. He loves meat,' Louise said, giving Clara her bottle.

'Is she serious?' Acorn glared at him.

He nodded. 'I'm sorry. I tried, I really did, but I can't live on couscous and falafel. I'm starving all the time.'

'You're very thin,' Mum noted.

'But you seemed so into it,' Acorn said.

'I was trying to impress you.' Gavin put down his bacon sandwich guiltily.

'Let the poor lad eat meat. What difference does it make to the trees, anyway?' Dad asked.

'Vegans see life as a phenomenon to be treasured, revered and respected. We don't see animals as the enemy, to be subdued, or as the materials for food or fabric, put on Earth for human use.' Acorn sounded a bit like one of those religious zealots.

'This pig was respected. These rashers come from a free-range pig farm in Wexford.' Mum was offended.

'He was slaughtered for this meal,' Acorn countered.

'Gavin looks malnourished. Clearly the vegan diet doesn't suit him,' Louise pointed out.

'I thought you lot were all into love and compassion,' Dad said.

'We are,' Acorn replied.

'Well, have some compassion for Gavin's empty stomach and let him eat what he wants.'

'I'm sorry, babe, I didn't mean to let you down, but I just can't do it.' Gavin reached over and took her hand.

Acorn shook him away and stood up. 'I can't be with someone who doesn't have the same ethical commitment and moral convictions as I do. Someone who doesn't see that there is no moral justification for using non-humans for our purposes.'

'He hasn't killed anyone. It's only a few rashers,' Mum riposted.

'I've been a vegan all my life. I can't change who I am.'

'So just accept him for who he is,' Sophie said.

'But I don't know who he is because he lied to me. I'm sorry, but I can't stay.' She turned to Gavin. 'Willow, don't call me unless you're willing to commit yourself fully and honestly to veganism.' With that, Acorn picked up her grubby rucksack and flounced out of the door.

We all turned to Gavin. 'Are you OK?' I asked.

He took a large bite of his bacon sandwich, chewed and swallowed. 'Even girls who look that good can do your head in after a while.'

334

'Yet another of Gavin's obsessions bites the dust.' Louise grinned.

'Why was the pretty girl so cross, Auntie Julie?' Jess asked me.

'Because Uncle Gavin lied to her. And men who lie are very, very naughty.'

After lunch, during which Jack didn't open his mouth and ate even less than I did, Louise and Dad took him aside to discuss his financial and legal affairs. Clara was having a nap. Gavin was playing with Jess in the garden. Sophie was curled up on the couch and Mum and I were clearing up.

My phone rang: Harry. I stepped into the hall.

'Hi, Julie, are you coming back soon?'

'No.'

'Oh. I thought you might be finishing up.'

'Well, I'm not.'

'Jesus, Julie, can you please stop snapping at me? I've apologized ten million times about forgetting your birthday. Can we not move on now?'

I still hadn't confronted Harry. I'd thought about doing it a million times, but I couldn't. I was terrified of saying it to him and him telling me that he was leaving because he was in love with a slim, sexy French girl. Once we'd had the conversation it would be over. I'd be on my own. Broke and alone at forty, with four kids. I was petrified of facing reality. I convinced myself that I was putting it off so I could gather more evidence before confronting him, but what more did I need? He was grumpy, distracted, forgetful, absent . . . He didn't love me any more and I didn't have the courage to face it. So instead I was being horrible to him, pushing him even further away.

'I'm busy looking after my sister right now. She's homeless and she needs me. I'll be home when I'm ready.' I hung up.

'You don't need to stay, Julie,' Sophie called out to me. 'Honestly, you've been brilliant, but go home to the boys.'

'No. Harry can look after them for once.' I went in and sat down beside my emaciated sister. 'So, how bad is it?' I asked her.

335

'On a scale of one to ten? Fifty.'

'Had you no idea?'

'None. Even when my credit card got refused in Harvey Nicks I just thought it was a bank error. It never crossed my mind.'

'Can you get any of it back?'

Sophie bit a nail. 'According to Jack, no. He says he's going to try to get another job, but who'll hire him?'

'All those traders and hedge-fund guys seem to make and lose millions all the time. They always seem to bounce back. He did well for a long time, so I'm sure he's good at what he does.'

'That's what he keeps saying, that it was just one bad decision.'

I looked down at my hands. I knew all about bad decisions. Harry had made a huge one. I tried to concentrate on Sophie: it was better for me to be distracted from worrying about Harry's affair. 'Unfortunately for Jack and you, it was a big one.'

'Monumental,' Sophie said. 'You know, Julie, I actually kind of hate him right now. I know it's not really his fault and I know he gave me an amazing life for years, but every time I look at him, all I can think of is Jess having to leave the school she loves, give up all the activities she loves, her bedroom, our home. Everything is gone. We're homeless nobodies. What will become of us? Who am I now?'

I pushed her hair out of her face. 'Come on, Sophie, you're still you.'

'No, I'm not. Me is Mrs Jack Wells, a woman who has a fabulous jet-set lifestyle. Now that's all been stripped away, who am I really?' Tears ran down her cheeks.

'You listen to me, young lady.' Mum rushed into the room and crouched down in front of Sophie. She took my sister's raw, bitten hands in hers. 'You are Sophie Devlin, youngest daughter of Anne and George Devlin, a beautiful, kind and generous person. A wonderful mother to Jessica. A sister. A daughter. A friend. A modern woman, who will find that, at this very difficult time, she has a lot more courage than she believes. I want you to hold your head up high, Sophie. You have done nothing wrong, you've just fallen on hard times. This will pass. You'll find your feet again. The most important thing is that you don't let yourself get depressed. You must stay strong for Jessica and Jack. They need you right now.'

'What about me?' Sophie began to cry.

'You've got us,' Mum said, and hugged her.

I handed my sister a tissue.

She wiped her face. 'Thanks, Julie. God, I wish I was you.'

I stared at her. 'Why in God's name would you want to be me?'

'You've always been so content and happy with your life, never looking for more, never dissatisfied, never insecure about who you are. Your life is steady. It's not up and down like a bloody roller-coaster. No huge highs and terrible lows. Harry's so safe. He has a steady job with a monthly salary. He doesn't gamble for a living. You won't come home one day and find out that your entire life has been turned upside-down.'

I was unable to speak. If only she knew . . .

32

Louise

Jack's situation was disastrous. Dad and I talked to him for three hours and looked through his contracts and finance agreements. I called a lawyer I knew in a top New York firm and she said there was carnage on Wall Street due to the Hartley Ponzi scheme. She said it hadn't hit the media yet, but it would all come out over the next few weeks and that really big names had been duped. She told me to forget about getting the money back: Terence Hartley had nothing; suing him was a waste of time.

The rest of Jack's savings had been invested in bank shares, which were now worth nothing. His pension was lock-tight, so he couldn't get any money out until he was fifty-five.

'It's not looking too good,' Dad said, blunt as always.

'Not right now, but I'll get back on my feet. I'll find a new job. I'll fix this,' Jack assured him.

'With this Ponzi fiasco reaching far and wide, there are going to be a lot of out-of-work hedge-fund managers looking for jobs. It could take a while,' I said, wanting him to be realistic.

'I'll find one,' he insisted.

'Well, in the meantime, you can't stay here indefinitely,' I said. 'I have an apartment in town. It's rented at the moment, but I only have to give the tenants two weeks' notice. I'll call them today. You can move in as soon as they're gone. It's nothing fancy, just a regular two-bedroom flat, but it's yours for as long as you need it, rent-free.'

Jack looked relieved. 'Thanks, Louise. That's very generous of you. I'll pay you as soon as I get back on my feet. I wouldn't dream of sponging off you.'

'It's not charity, Jack, it's just family helping each other out. You and Sophie would do the same for me.' And I meant it. They had always been really generous with their money. In recent years they had gone over the top with the gifts they had bought, but it was a nice quality.

'Well, it's really decent of you.' Jack stood up and paced the room nervously. 'Look, I know you both think I messed up. One minute I'm driving an Aston Martin, buying extravagant Christmas presents, the next my family's homeless. The Hartley deal brought in seven per cent returns for two years. Everyone on Wall Street was bailing in. I just can't believe it turned out to be such a disaster.'

'Lookit, Jack, I ran my own business for forty years,' Dad said. 'I survived through two recessions. Everyone makes mistakes. It's how you handle them, how you learn from them and how you move on from them that's important. Mistakes are part of life. You'll survive this.'

'George, that means a lot to me. I feel I've let you down badly. I promised to look after your daughter and now she's back living in your house. I got too cocky and too greedy. I won't make that mistake again, I can promise you.'

'I know some traders and fund managers in London,' I told him. 'Email me your CV and I'll pass it around – you never know who might be looking to hire someone.'

'Thanks again, Louise. That would be great.'

'In the meantime, here's a few quid to tide you over.' Dad handed Jack a bulging envelope.

Jack blushed. 'I can't take it.'

'Jack, this is so you can take your family to the cinema and dinner and for petrol and whatever else you need. You can't be staying in every night while you're here.'

'I'll pay you back as soon as I'm working.'

'I know you will.' Dad patted his son-in-law's arm.

When Jack went to take a call, Dad sighed. 'What a mess.'

'Total disaster,' I agreed. 'But I see these guys in the City all the time. They make millions and then they lose millions, but if they're any good they never seem to be out of work. They just bounce around from firm to firm and fund to fund. Jack made a lot of money for years. He's only had one bad investment so he should be OK. He'll find something.'

'I hope you're right. I don't fancy having him living here long term. Thank God you offered him the apartment. I know he means well, but he'd drive me mad. I'll pay you for the rent.'

'Don't be silly. It's fine. I'll cover them for six months and then see where they are.'

'Can you afford that now you have a baby to look after?'

I smiled up at him. 'It's fine, Dad. Thankfully, I spread my investments wide like you always told me to.'

'I'm glad you listened to some of my advice at least. If only Sophie had been as sensible with the money I gave her. It's all gone now. Every penny.'

'Well, Julie's and Gavin's is safe and doing well.'

'How did you get to be so smart?' Dad asked fondly.

'Good DNA.' I winked at him.

When Jack came back, Dad left us alone. Jack sat down and fidgeted in the chair. 'I'll bounce back from this, you know.'

'I'm sure you will. You've been successful before. There's no reason you won't be again.'

'I'll make it all back, every penny.'

'Well, just be a bit more cautious the next time a deal comes up that seems to be too good to be true.'

He eyeballed me. 'Louise, traders gamble for a living. It's what we do. We don't always go for the safe option and that's how we make big bucks. Yes, it's also how we lose big too. But if you don't gamble, if you're not willing to take a chance, you can't be a trader. You're in the wrong job. What I do for a living is high risk. I can guarantee you that I will never again put so much of a fund's money into one deal, like I did on the Hartley scheme, but as I said, for two years it worked fantastically. Everyone in the company thought I was a genius. We were making huge returns while everyone else was dying out there.'

I leant forward across Dad's desk. 'Yes, Jack, but the whole point is that it was false success. I understand that you need to take chances, but you're going to have to be more careful in future.'

'I will, believe me. I've been bitten badly this time. My wife can't stand to be in the same room as me and my daughter keeps asking me why I don't work like the other daddies any more.'

I felt sorry for him. He was worn out, emotionally and physically. 'Jess will be fine. She's too young to be badly affected and she'll have a great time being lavished with attention living here with Mum and Dad. And Sophie will come around. She's still in shock.'

Jack twisted his wedding ring around his finger. 'I thought she'd be more supportive. I know she's furious, and ashamed of cheques bouncing, Jess having to move school and all that, but after a few weeks I thought she'd be on my side. I need her. What happened to the through-thick-and-thin part of the marriage vow?'

Thick and thin didn't mean total wipe-out, I thought. 'People react differently to things and she was keeping it all bottled up. Now that she's told us and she knows we're here for you guys, I'm sure she'll feel less overwhelmed and be able to see things more calmly and clearly.'

'I hope so, Louise, because it's been a horrendous few weeks for me and I don't have a supportive family like yours to lean on. I only have Sophie.'

'Have you not told your family yet?' I was surprised. I knew from Sophie that Jack's parents were intellectual snobs, but I'd presumed he would have called them. He hadn't fallen out with them, as far as I knew.

'No. I can't bring myself to talk to them. I'm the family dud, the black sheep who didn't study medicine. I've been a disappointment to them all my life. I was hopeless at music while my brother Roger was playing Chopin on the violin aged six. I never got the hang of chess and Roger was a junior champion. You get the picture. I know that my father would consider this as just another of my failures as a son, and I can do without that right now.'

'Well, this family is here to help you,' I said, getting up to go and rescue Clara, who was wailing in the kitchen.

Later on, I took Sophie into my old bedroom for a chat. I told her I was letting her and Jack have my apartment for as long as they needed it. She spent the next ten minutes bawling her eyes out. 'Thanks so much . . . such a disaster . . . I'm such a fool . . . should have given money to you . . . so reliable . . . not a risk-taker . . . life is over . . . destitute . . .'

'OK, Sophie. I need you to stop crying and listen to me.'

She wiped her eyes and looked up.

'It might take Jack a while to get another job. In the meantime you need to find work, even if it's just for a few months, until Jack gets sorted. You need an income to live on – and it'll keep you sane. You can't both be sitting around the apartment all day. You'll end up killing each other.'

'But what can I do? I've been racking my brains for weeks, but I'm useless. I'm a thirty-eight-year-old ex-model. Who the hell is going to hire me?'

'What kind of contacts do you have?'

'From modelling?'

'Yes.'

'None. I mean, I met lots of people, but when I married Jack and had Jess I just hung around with other mums.'

'So you kept in touch with no one?'

'No.' She was crying again. 'I'm such an idiot. I dropped everyone and threw myself into my role as Jack's wife. I know you think I'm pathetic, that my life was empty and vacuous with my shopping and my yoga and my holidays – and you were right, it was. But I was so immersed in it that I got sucked in. I never had a plan B. I never thought I'd need one. I just presumed Jack would keep earning big money and look after me and Jess.'

'Well, your life looked great to me,' Julie said, coming in and plonking herself on the bed. She looked even more exhausted than usual, but thinner. The weight loss made her face look older. 'You can't blame yourself for enjoying a nice lifestyle,' she said to Sophie.

'Can't I?'

'No. If I'd had your money, I probably would have done the same,' Julie told her.

'No, you wouldn't. You would have read every book ever written, you would have put money away for the boys' education and you would have found the talk at all the mums' coffee mornings boring and stupid.'

'Not necessarily. I only found your friends dull because I'd never been to Dubai and knew I'd never get there. I'd never owned a Range Rover and knew I'd never own one. My kids weren't in private school because we couldn't afford it. I just felt like the odd one out. I was the only chubby one, the only badly dressed one, the only one driving a shitty car and the only one who ate.'

Sophie was chewing her nails – they were bitten down to the quick. 'Well, that life is over now. Oh, God, guys, what am I going to do? I'm useless.'

'You have to think, Sophie,' I told her. 'There must be some contact who might be useful, or some area you could work in. Could you train models, or do makeup or styling? Did you ever keep in touch with the guy who owned the model agency? Maybe he needs someone to help keep the models in check.'

'Quentin Gill?' Sophie's head shot up. 'Yes, I did, actually, and I bumped into him a few months back –' She jumped up. 'He said Jill had left the agency and he really needed someone with experience as a booker to take over from her. I could do that. I could be a booker. I know how it works. I know the ropes.'

'There you go. Call him up,' I said, handing her the phone.

Sophie hesitated. 'But it was months ago – he's probably got someone now.'

'If he has, he might know someone else who's hiring. Call him, Sophie. Do it now. You need a job.'

'What'll I say? Should I tell him about being homeless?'

'No,' I said firmly. Sophie wouldn't be very good in an interview: the last thing your future boss wants to know is that you're homeless and desperate. 'Just say that now Jess is in school, you've decided to go back to work and you were wondering if he still needed a booker.'

Sophie dialled the number, then hung up. 'I can't – I can't do it.'

'Sophie,' I snapped, 'you're broke. You need to do something to get out of this hole. You need to support Jess. You have to step up to the plate. Pick up that phone and call Quentin now.'

'OK, OK! Don't shout at me.' Sophie picked the phone up.

'She's not shouting at you, she's trying to help,' Julie said.

'I know, but I'm having a really shit time, so go easy on me.'

'We all have shit to deal with,' Julie muttered.

Sophie took a deep breath and dialled the number again. She got Quentin's answering machine. She left a message asking him to call her as soon as possible.

When she hung up she shut the bedroom door and beckoned us closer. 'I've actually made some money, but don't tell Jack,' she whispered.

'How?' I asked.

'I'm selling all my clothes, shoes and jewellery on eBay. I've made twelve thousand three hundred euros as of this morning and only a quarter of the stuff is sold.'

'Good for you,' Julie said. 'You see? You're not useless. Far from it.'

'Great idea. Well done. Now, what are you doing with the money?' I asked.

'I'm putting it in the Post Office. I want to leave it there for Jess's education. I want to save, like Julie has been for the boys. I don't want Jack touching it.'

'Leave it there for the moment. I'll have a look around and see which bank is offering the best interest rates and get back to you.' I was really impressed with Sophie. Selling her designer clothes on eBay was a great idea.

'How are you and Jack getting on? Do you feel like killing him every time you look at him?' Julie clenched her fists.

'Yes, I do – I hate him and I blame him.'

'Hang on a minute.' I jumped in to defend Jack. Now that I

knew what it felt like to make a big mistake in a work situation, I had more sympathy with the underdog. 'I agree that Jack made a bad business decision, but as Julie pointed out earlier, so did lots of really experienced high-end traders and investment funds.'

'I know all that,' Sophie said. 'When I'm thinking rationally – which is hardly ever at the moment – I can see it's not his fault. I know he feels terrible and is beating himself up. But on a raw emotional level, I want to kill him for putting us in this situation. I trusted him, I admired him – I was dazzled by him. Now I can't bear to look at him. We haven't slept in the same bed since he told me. I can't even stand to be near him physically. He keeps looking for reassuring hugs and I keep pushing him away. I need space. I need to work it all out in my head.'

Gavin poked his head around the door. 'What are you three witches plotting up here? Jack's burning at the stake?'

'Not a bad idea.' Sophie half smiled.

'Don't be too hard on him. He looks like a man going through hell. So, I guess we're going to be housemates again.' Gavin sat down beside Sophie and put his arm around her.

She leant her head on his shoulder. 'Looks like it. It's going to be very cosy for the next few weeks.'

'It'll be like old times.' Gavin grinned. 'Remember when Louise and Julie were in college and we lived here on our own with Mum and Dad? It was fun not being bossed around all the time.'

'I never bossed you,' Julie objected.

'True. It was Louise – but you were hardly ever here, and when you were, you had your head permanently stuck in a book so you weren't much fun,' Gavin explained.

'I didn't boss you that much, did I?'

Gavin and Sophie laughed. 'Come on, Louise, you can't help it – it's in your nature to try to sort other people's lives out,' Sophie said. Then, holding her hand up, she added, 'And before you get huffy, I'm glad you do because you've been brilliant today at helping me.'

'I'm glad you'll be around, Sophie,' Gavin told her. 'You can keep Dad off my back. He's on a rampage. I just got a twenty-minute lecture on getting my life together and finding a proper job . . . not wasting money . . . saving for a rainy day . . . look at Jack, nothing left . . . have to be careful with investments . . . be responsible . . . On and on he went.'

'He's right,' Sophie said. 'I'm sorry, Gavin, but it is time you got yourself together. Look at me. I'm a thirty-eight-year-old woman who can't support her child. Do not end up like me. You've had twenty-three years of fun and no responsibilities, but it's time to get a job, stop sponging off the family and pay your own way. Jack and I can't help you out any more. Louise is now using her spare cash to bail me out and Julie doesn't have any. Mum and Dad need what they have for their retirement. You have to stand on your own two feet.'

'I agree,' I said. 'By the time we were all twenty-three we'd moved out of home, found jobs and were supporting ourselves.'

Gavin groaned. 'I came up here to get away from Dad but you're worse. OK, I get it, I need to grow up and be responsible. That's why I moved back – to look for a job.'

'Bullshit,' I said. 'You moved back because your tent leaked, you were starving and the novelty of shagging an Angelina Jolie looka-like in the mud had worn off. And because none of us would give you any more money to fund your "save the world" baloney.'

'It's not baloney,' he said angrily.

'It is when you're living in a tent and not achieving anything. Get out and lobby the UK government, research alternative ener-gies, become an environmental consultant, a climate-change strategist, a climate-policy analysis consultant. There are tons of interesting, relevant jobs that actually pay salaries.' I had been researching the job market to give him alternative career options when the tent phase wore off, as we had all known it would.

'Wow – I didn't know there were so many choices.'

'You obviously haven't looked very hard. All you have to do is Google "climate-change jobs",' I told him.

'How come there were none of those interesting kinds of jobs when we left school?' Julie asked. 'I would definitely have become a climate-policy analysis consultant. It sounds a lot more exciting than recruitment.'

'I'll tell you one thing,' Sophie said. 'Jess is going to study hard and get a good job in a steady profession. There's no way she's going to end up being a model. She needs something solid and safe, like the law. Look at you, Louise, you're completely independent. You're not relying on any man to pay your mortgage or your bills. I really admire you for it, and I want that for Jess. I don't want her depending on her husband for everything like I do.'

'Be careful what you wish for,' I warned her. 'My life used to be great, totally under control, until I had Clara. But as I found out all too recently, it's bloody difficult juggling motherhood and work. For the first time in my life, I'm really struggling with something. I want Clara to have a career but I would never, ever want her to bring up a baby alone. You need two parents to share the load. Nannies don't pace the floor with them at three in the morning when they're screaming or throwing up, but a dad would. It's lonely doing it all on your own – and, to be honest, it's scary too. You guys are really lucky to have nice husbands to help you look after and raise your kids.'

Julie burst into tears.

'What's wrong?' I asked. 'What did I say?'

'Nothing, you're just so right. Kids do need their dads. They really do.'

My phone beeped. It was an email from Alex: Gordon has gone back to New York. He was not happy with the purchase price error, despite it being resolved. He has asked Dominic to represent him on a large merger he is involved in. Dominic leaves for New York on Tuesday. He will be gone for at least three weeks, so I need you to cover his files. We're meeting at seven thirty on Monday morning to discuss the hand-over.

'Bastard.' I threw my phone on to the bed.

'What happened?' Sophie asked.

'I messed up at work and now Dominic, the junior partner, is

347

getting a huge contract that should have been mine. Christ, it's so bloody frustrating. How can I compete with someone ten years younger than me who gets eight hours' sleep a night and plays golf like a bloody pro? He can stay out drinking and smoking cigars until three in the morning while I have to go home to Clara. I can't compete. It's no longer a level playing field. Before Clara, I could keep up with the best of them. I never drank much, but I stayed out and talked and schmoozed and won business. I can't do it any more. I'm tied down. I'm shackled. I'm screwed. God, I hate men!'

'I couldn't agree more,' Sophie said.

'Me too.' Julie sniffled.

'Hey, we're not all arseholes,' Gavin reminded us. 'And you women are no picnic either, let me tell you.'

'I don't go around stabbing my colleagues in the back,' I snapped.

'I don't lose millions,' Sophie said.

'I don't screw –'

Mum came into the room, interrupting Julie. She handed me Clara. 'Louise, your daughter has a smelly nappy. I've fed her and burped her but you can change her.'

The others left the room. Sighing, I changed my baby's nappy and pictured Dominic's transatlantic flight crashing into the sea.

33

Sophie

It was actually a relief to come clean. It was out in the open now. I didn't have to hide any more, pretend I was sick, act as if nothing was wrong and lie to everyone. They all knew we were broke.

Louise had been amazing – it had been brilliant to move into her apartment. Mum and Dad were great to take us in, but it had been cramped and tense. Jack couldn't relax and spent most of his time in the bedroom on his laptop.

Jess was still on her summer holidays, so I had to keep her occupied during the day. When we went out as a family, it was always a disaster – Jack and I either fought or didn't speak to each other. I spent a lot of time with Gavin and Jess, hanging out in the park. On rainy days, Jess and I would curl up on the couch and watch movies.

It was hard not having any money to spend. I kept forgetting I was penniless and going to buy things. Before when I got petrol I would always have bought at least three magazines in the shop. Now I couldn't. When I was out walking, I looked in the window of every boutique I passed, but could no longer go in and buy anything I wanted. I had to think about and justify every euro I spent. It was a difficult adjustment.

Quentin called me back, and instead of the story Louise told me to tell him, I blurted out the truth. I said I was desperate, that I'd take any job he had going. I even offered to be his driver. He was very kind and sympathetic and we arranged to meet when he got back from his business trip to London.

I dressed up for the interview in one of the few outfits I hadn't put up for sale on eBay. It was a light grey Armani trouser suit that was businesslike but flattering. I spent ages applying my makeup. My skin was dry, patchy and lined from stress. I couldn't afford expensive creams or Botox any more, so my wrinkles were back with a vengeance. For the first time in my life, I looked my age. I used lots of concealer and the end result wasn't too bad. I didn't look like me. I looked like an older, more stressed, worried and tired version.

'You look nice, Mummy,' Jess said.

'Thank you, angel.' I kissed her, careful not to get lipstick on her face.

'Where are we going?'

'Actually, you're going to stay here with Daddy. I'm going to an interview to get a new job.'

'Why?'

I decided to be honest. 'Because we need money.'

'Does Daddy not have any left now his job is gone away?'

'At the moment, no. But hopefully he'll find a new job soon.'

Her lip began to wobble. 'But if you and Daddy are working, who will mind me? I'll be all by my own.'

I hugged her. 'You will never be on your own. Lots of children have mummies and daddies who work and they have minders, like Mimi, who look after them.'

'Is Mimi coming back?' She looked thrilled.

'No, Jess. At the moment Daddy has no job so he's going to look after you. If he gets a new job, we'll sort something out.'

'If Daddy gets a new job, you can stop working. You always said it was better for mummies to be at home to look after their little girls.'

'Well, that was before I realized that sometimes it's better for mummies to work too.'

'Why?' She frowned. She did that a lot these days.

'Because then if the daddy loses his job, the mummy can still pay for things.'

'But you said that happy mummies didn't have to work because the daddies made lots of money and the mummies could spend it

350

on treats. And you said that I should marry a man like Daddy who makes lots and lots of money so I could have lots of beautiful things and look like a princess and never have to work.'

Had I really said that to my child? What kind of ideals was I teaching her?

'OK, Jess, I need you to listen to me. Mummy was wrong when she said that. It is very, very, very important that you work hard in school and get a job when you're older.'

'But I'm going to be a model like you, Mummy.'

I pulled her on to my knee. 'No, pet. I want you to be a doctor or a lawyer or an accountant. Modelling is not a very good job.'

'But you said you loved it and Daddy said he married you because you were the most beautiful model in Ireland.'

'Modelling is a job you do when you're young. I'm too old for it now. You need to have a job you can do for a long time, like Auntie Louise.'

'But she's cross all the time and she's always shouting into her phone.'

'Louise is a very good person. She gave us her lovely apartment to live in, so we have to be extra nice to her because she helped us out a lot.'

Jess curled my hair around her index finger. 'She's good at sharing.'

'Yes, she is. And Louise was able to help us because she worked hard in school and has a good job. I don't want you ever to be stuck with no money, pet. It's scary. So that's why I want you to work even when you get married and even when you have children. It will keep you and your family safe.'

'But, Mummy, if you're too old to be a model now, what job are you going to do?'

'I'm going to look after young models and help them get jobs. I'm going to be like a mummy to them.'

Jess's eyes filled. 'But you're not their mummy, you're my mummy. I need you to look after me.'

I held her face in my hands. 'Jess, I will always be your mummy and you will always be the most important person in my life. I love you more than anything in this world and I'm always going to look after you, I promise. Now I have to go.' I kissed her and walked out of the door before I burst into tears and ruined my makeup.

I paused outside the front door of Beauty Spot. This was the agency that had launched my career, the agency that had represented me for fourteen years. It felt very strange walking in, although the décor hadn't changed much. The office was on the first floor of an old Georgian building in the centre of Dublin. It was actually only a five-minute walk from Louise's apartment.

The carpet had been updated from a dark blue to a dark green, but that was all. The reception area was still bright, with two comfy couches and a coffee-table laden with fashion magazines. Photos of the agency's better-known models covered the walls. My picture was still up there – a black-and-white photo taken when I was twenty. I was wearing a bikini and a big straw hat. I looked gorgeous – young, happy, carefree, wrinkle-free, stress-free, debt-free . . .

The receptionist was new. She asked me to have a seat while I waited for Quentin. I flicked through the magazines on the coffee-table. Usually I would have stopped every time I saw something I liked and noted it on a piece of paper. Now I just kept flicking, looking but not seeing.

Quentin came out, wearing red trousers, a blue-and-red striped shirt and a lemon jacket – somehow he got away with it. He hugged me. 'Darling Sophie, you look wonderful. Come on in.'

He led me into his office, which was completely minimalist except for a large colour photo of his current pug. Quentin was obsessed with pugs – whenever one died, he immediately replaced it.

'New dog?' I asked.

'Yes. I called her Stella.'

'What happened to Coco?'

'Oh, honey, she died a million years ago. Since then I've had Dior, who choked on a chicken bone – very traumatic, I didn't get out of bed for three weeks after it – and Galliano, who got run over.'

'Sorry for your loss,' I said, sitting down.

'Not as sorry as I am for yours. Is it all gone, darling? Everything?'

I nodded. 'Every last penny.'

'It's a travesty, and you were so well suited to the good life. When you met Jack, I knew he was perfect. Handsome, confident, successful, and he adored you. It's a nightmare for you, but you'll bounce back. I always said you were one of the hardest-working girls I ever had on my books.'

I willed myself not to break down. 'Thanks, Quentin, it's been a shitty few months, but I need to start looking forward, not back.'

'How right you are. That's what my therapist kept saying after Dior passed away. Now, as I told you on the phone, I've already hired a booker to replace Jill. She's not amazing, but she's a lot better than the first two I found. I think what we'll do is get you to work with her. You can be like an assistant to her and then when you get up to speed you can start booking the girls directly.'

'That would be brilliant. When can I start?'

He clapped his hands, like a little child. 'Eager! That's the way I like it. You can start on Monday. We'll say ten till four for the first two months, until you're trained up, and then you can go nine to five. But, Sophie, I have to warn you, I can't pay you much starting out. Our bookings are still down twenty per cent. After tax you'll only be taking home sixteen hundred a month. But as soon as you start booking the girls yourself, you'll be on commission so it'll go up considerably.'

I stood up and grasped his hands. 'That's fine. I'll take it. Thank you, Quentin. I promise I'll do my very best for you.'

He kissed my cheek. 'I know you will. It's good to have you back.'

I left the agency on a high. I had a job! I had managed to get myself employed after six years out of the workplace. I was thrilled. I went for a celebratory cup of tea – coffee was too expensive – in a café around the corner and dug out a pen and paper. I began to break down my earnings. We'd been living rent free in Louise's flat but I was determined to give her something as soon as I got paid. She had admitted that nine hundred a month would cover her mortgage. That left seven hundred for petrol, insurance, tax, phone bills, electricity, heating and food. Last month all of our bills and sundries had come to almost six hundred euros. That left a hundred for extras.

I shook my head. Two months ago I would have spent a hundred euros on a T-shirt that I would have put into my wardrobe and probably never worn.

When I got home there was a note from Jack saying he had taken Jess to the park. I called his mobile. 'I got the job!'

'Brilliant. Well done. How much are you on?'

'Sixteen hundred.'

'Oh.'

'It's all he can afford right now.'

'Did you ask for more? Did you try to negotiate?'

'No, I bloody didn't. He's doing me a huge favour, Jack. No one else would hire me. I haven't worked for six years. I'm an ex-model, not a neurosurgeon.'

'OK, OK. I just thought it would be more, that's all.'

'Well, at least one of us will be earning and I'll be on commission soon so it'll go up. I start on Monday, so you're going to be looking after Jess full-time from then.'

'I can't! I need time to look for jobs.'

'You can do that while she's playing with her dolls or colouring.'

'I'm not going to call people while my daughter is singing beside me or asking me questions. It doesn't look very professional.'

'So put a movie on for her and call them from the bedroom.'

'It's not a solution, Sophie. I need a couple of free days a week to focus on finding a job.'

'I'm going to be working full-time and there isn't any money for childcare so you're just going to have to multitask. Women do it all the time.'

'Don't start with that feminist crap.'

'It's not crap, it's true.'

'Daddy!' Jess called.

'Hold on,' Jack said to her. 'I'm talking to Mummy.'

'Mummy,' my daughter came on the phone, 'did you get the job?'

'Yes, sweetie, I did.'

Jess burst into tears.

'It's OK – I'll still see you all the time and Daddy's going to look after you while I'm working.'

'Everything's different and I hate it. I want it to be the same again. I want to go back to our house and see my friends.'

'I'm sorry, pet. I know it's been hard for you, but sometimes change can be good. It's all going to be OK. No more crying. I'm going to make chocolate Rice Krispies cakes to celebrate my new job.'

'Really? Will you? I thought I wasn't allowed to eat them because they're bad for my teeth and my skin.'

'Well, today you can. You can help me make them and you can lick the chocolate off the spoon.'

'Oh, Mummy, I can't wait.' She squealed with delight.

Later that night, when Jess was asleep and Jack had gone out to meet some old colleagues for a drink to talk about possible jobs, Julie called.

'Hi! Sorry I didn't ring earlier. How did you get on today?'

'I got the job. I start on Monday,' I said, feeling proud of myself. It was a strange sensation, one I hadn't felt in a long time. I had been happy with my life and the way I looked, but I hadn't felt real pride in myself for achieving something in ages. It felt good.

'Well done! That's bloody brilliant. Good for you.'

'I can't believe it, really, me going back to work.'

'I hope you're celebrating with a glass of wine.'

'Unfortunately not. Jack took our last twenty quid to go and meet some guy about a job, so I'm sitting here with a cup of tea.'

'Sod that. I'll call around with a bottle.'

'Brilliant.'

Julie arrived twenty minutes later with two bottles of wine. We opened one and toasted my new job. Before I had taken my first sip, Julie had downed her whole glass.

'Thirsty?'

'Long day.'

'Triplets acting up?'

'Um, yeah,' she said, pouring herself another glass.

I suddenly noticed how thin she looked. 'Julie, have you lost weight?'

'Yeah, a stone.'

'Wow, that's great – well done. You must be pleased.'

'I should be – I should be over the moon. I should be thrilled. I've wanted to shift a stone for years, but now that I have, I feel nothing. I hadn't even noticed until I realized that my clothes were suddenly really baggy on me.'

Julie knocked back her second glass of wine. I looked at her properly – I'd been so wrapped up in my own situation that I'd barely registered other people. She was thinner and also very tired, really black around the eyes, much more so than normal. 'Julie, is everything OK?'

She began to cry.

'Julie, what is it? Is it the kids?'

'No,' she wailed.

'Is it Harry? Did he lose his job? Oh, no – here's me banging on about Jack's job and everyone running to help me and Harry's lost his too. I'm so sorry, Julie. I've been so selfish, going on about my situation and there's you in a similar predicament. Look, we'll all pitch in. We'll work something out.'

'It's not his bloody job. I wish it was. I really, really wish he was unemployed. It's not that.'

'Well, what else could – NO!'

'Yes.'

'No way – not Harry.'

'Yes, Harry.'

356

'Who?'

'French bitch.'

'When?'

'Started when we went over to London for Clara's birth,' she sobbed.

'How did you –'

'Text.'

'Harry?'

'Yes.'

'But he's not the type. He loves you and the kids.'

'Apparently he loves *Christelle* more!'

'Are you absolutely sure?'

'Positive.'

'Hold on, start from the beginning. Tell me everything . . .'

34

Julie

I shouldn't have drunk the bloody wine. It was like a truth serum. The words tumbled out of my mouth like a waterfall. I hadn't planned on telling Sophie. I had genuinely called over to celebrate her job. I was really impressed that she had got one so soon. Maybe there was hope for me. Maybe I could get a job and support my family when Harry left us for that French whore.

When Sophie asked me how I was, I wanted to say, 'Fine,' but I just couldn't. The word refused to come out of my mouth. How could I say that when I was living in hell?

The last few weeks had been a nightmare. You'd think when you find out your husband is cheating on you that you'd confront him immediately. But I hadn't. When he'd come home that night, I'd opened my mouth and nothing had come out. I'd panicked and ended up acting as if nothing had happened. And the really weird part was that it hadn't been that difficult to hide my devastation. Harry and I never talked any more. We never looked at each other. We muttered to one another about the kids, the bills, and that was pretty much it. He hid in the TV room with his phone and his laptop, pretending to work on his project, and I stayed in the kitchen reading.

Except that I couldn't read because I couldn't concentrate. I kept thinking, How? Why? When? Where? But I didn't want to confront him because I knew that when I did he'd admit it and leave me. And I didn't want that. I couldn't bear that. I'd rather live a lie. I couldn't believe that I, Julie Devlin, would rather live with a husband who I knew was cheating on me than kick him out. I was pathetic . . . and terrified.

If we broke up I'd be on my own. I'd have four boys, no money, no husband – nothing. How would I cope? I'd been struggling when I thought I was happily married and had some money to live on. How the hell would Harry be able to support two houses on his crappy salary? He couldn't afford a mistress. We were barely managing to get by as it was.

What kind of life would I have if he left me? I'd have no one to talk to, no one to call when the boys did something funny. No one to cry to when the boys were being bold. No one to share my hopes and dreams with. No one to tell that my kids were the best in the world, that Luke could read perfectly, and that Tom could sing along to the whole of 'Mamma Mia'. No one to cuddle up to, no one to reassure me that I wasn't damaging my kids or turning them into monsters by shouting at them daily, no one to laugh with, no one to have sex with, no one to watch movies with, no one to go to parties with, no one to come home from parties with, no one to assemble Christmas presents with, no one to giggle over the boys' letters to Santa with, no one to give out to about my family, no one to go on rainy holidays with four hyper boys to a caravan in Wexford with, no one to tell me that I was beautiful in their eyes, no one to tell me that I was sexy in my own way, no one to tell me they loved me.

No one.

So, I avoided Harry and he avoided me. We talked, but said nothing. We existed side by side, but didn't live together. We went to bed together, but didn't sleep. We continued as normal when nothing was the same.

I told Sophie everything. She was gobsmacked.

She took a large drink of wine. 'OK, let's not panic. One text, although it sounds very bad, isn't proof of a full-blown affair. We need more evidence. You have to get hold of his laptop and phone to check his messages.'

'He never leaves them out of his sight.'

'What about when he's asleep?'

'He has them on his bedside locker and he isn't sleeping well. He tosses and turns all night. It's the guilt – it's eating him up, the bastard.' I sobbed.

'Well, what about when he's in the shower?' Sophie suggested.

'I got another chance to look at his phone a few days ago, but he had deleted everything.'

'We need the laptop. Do you have his password? You could log on to his email from Jack's computer.'

'I tried that, I used Marian's computer, but he's changed his password. It used to be uh – uh – uh – Julie.' I buried my face in a tissue.

Sophie rubbed my back. 'Look, Julie, I'm sorry to be blunt, but did you try "Christelle" as a password?'

'Yes, I bloody did, and our kids' names and dates of birth. None of them worked.'

Sophie took out a pen and paper. 'Come on, we have to figure the password out. Think of any pets he had as a kid or favourite football players or sportsmen, his dream car, favourite movie or drink – anything.'

I sat up and tried to concentrate. 'He had a dog called Snoopy, he supports Liverpool, he loves Steven Gerrard and Fernando Torres, he likes Jack Daniel's and Coke. If he won the lotto he always said he'd buy a Maserati. He pretends his favourite movie is *The Shawshank Redemption* but actually it's *Armageddon* – he always cries when the colonel guy says to Liv Tyler, "Permission to shake the hand of the daughter of the bravest man I've ever met." I used to slag him about it all the time.'

Sophie noted this, while I cried over happy memories. She put her pen down and gave me a hug. 'I know this is a nightmare for you, but you have a family who love you and will support you no matter what happens.' She began to get emotional. 'Honestly, I never knew how important you guys were to me until I was in trouble. You were amazing to me, all of you. I don't know what I would have done without your support and encouragement. I promise you, we'll help you through this.'

'I wish I wasn't so useless. I have no job, no money, no independence.'

'Neither did I. I know how scary it is to wake up one day and realize you can't support your children. But you'll find a way.

I've made over thirty thousand on eBay, which I've put away for Jess, and today I got a job. Who the hell would have thought I could get a job? The only degree I ever had was in shopping. I swear when Jack told me we had nothing, I thought I was going to lose my mind, but then I looked at Jess and knew I had to keep going.'

'I'm afraid of being on my own, Sophie. I know it's weak and sad, but I don't want Harry to leave me. I'd rather pretend I don't know about Christelle and have him stay and help me raise the boys. I don't want them to come from a broken home and I'm too scared to be alone. No one is ever going to want to be with me. I'm forty with four kids and no career. I'm a loser with tons of baggage. I could live until I'm ninety. I don't want to be on my own for fifty years –' I started bawling again.

'It's not weak or sad to be scared. I totally understand. I used to feel that way about Jack. I thought if I wasn't the perfect wife, with the perfect figure and clothes, he might leave me for one of the younger women who were always throwing themselves at him and then I'd be alone with Jess. My phone would stop ringing. No one would call or invite me anywhere. I'd be a pariah, the divorcee no one wants around. Married women hate single women – they're a threat. I saw ex-wives being cast aside and it wasn't pretty. But, as it turned out, no one wants me *or* Jack around. We're both an embarrassment. A reminder of what could happen. A living example of how hard you can fall.'

'Haven't any of those Victoria ones called you?'

'No. They sent texts saying they were sorry to hear that we were having "financial challenges". Victoria phoned into my voicemail and left a message saying she was busy travelling but she'd try to give me a buzz between trips.'

'Bitches.'

Sophie shrugged. 'If I'm honest, all we had in common was that our kids went to the same school and our husbands made lots of money. There wasn't much depth to the friendships. Thank God I have sisters.'

'And a husband. You still have Jack. You have someone to share the burden with. I'm on my own here.'

Sophie squeezed my hand. 'No, you're not. I'm here for you and so is Louise. So are Mum and Dad and even Gavin. He's been great with Jess.'

I stood up. 'I have to go. I'm pissed and I'll be up with Tom in about two hours – he's teething again. How many bloody teeth do they get? I'm sick of it. I'm sick of getting no sleep. I'm sick of my crappy, shitty life. How the hell did I end up here?'

Sophie held me by the shoulders. 'Hang in there. Let's take this one step at a time. Take this list of possible passwords and try to get into Harry's computer. When we know more we can call Louise and come up with a plan. She's very good in a crisis.'

'You're not too bad yourself.' I hugged my little sister and stumbled home.

It took three days, but eventually I got hold of Harry's laptop. He had left it behind when he took the triplets to football. I plonked Tom in front of the TV and tried the passwords Sophie had written out in her neat loopy writing.

The fifth one worked – Armageddon. I went into his hotmail address and did a search for 'Christelle'. I held my breath.

Only one message came up. He must have deleted the others. It had been sent this morning, at eight twenty-five. My God, the bastard had been emailing her while I was giving the boys their breakfast.

> Dear Christelle, I promise I won't let you down. I'll be in Paris on 20 August. I'll tell Julie it's a work trip. After we've talked I'll break the news to her and the boys.

I logged out, turned the laptop off and put it back under the bed, where Harry had hidden it. I walked calmly back into the kitchen, patted Tom's head as he laughed at a *Tom and Jerry* cartoon. I climbed up on to a chair and took the large scissors down from their hiding place. I stood in front of my reflection in the window and proceeded to cut off my hair.

'What the hell are you doing?' Marian shouted, as she barged through the back door, grabbing the scissors from me. 'Have you lost your mind?' She plonked Ben and Molly in front of the TV with Tom and closed the door. 'Julie, talk to me. What's happened?'

'He's going to Paris to see her.'

'When?'

'August the twentieth. He said in the email that he's going to tell me it's a work trip.' I sounded very far away. I could hear my voice, but I didn't feel as if it was coming from my body.

Marian fished around in her bag. 'Here, take these.' She handed me two small tablets.

'What are they?'

'Valium. I keep them for very bad days. Take those now.'

Normally I would never have dreamt of taking Valium, but today I swallowed them.

'Good girl. Now, you need to breathe and promise me you won't do anything stupid like cut your hair off. Seriously, Julie, it's your crowning glory. You've taken a big chunk out of the right side and now it looks ridiculous. I'm going to have to even it out. Don't worry, I used to be quite good at hair – I did my mother's for years because she wouldn't leave the fucking house in case Dad showed up.'

While Marian cut my hair, I cried big, salty, silent tears.

'Stop it, you'll set me off,' she said, sniffing as she snipped. Brown curls surrounded me on the floor. 'Now, let me look at you.' She stood in front of me and examined her work. 'It really suits you. It's like a cool wavy bob. Take a look.' She handed me a mirror from her bag.

My hair had been down past my shoulders but now it stopped just past my ears. The curls looked nicer short, less straggly, less unkempt.

'Thanks,' I croaked.

'No problem. But from now on stay away from the scissors, OK? Any shorter and you'd have looked like Pete Sampras.'

'It doesn't matter what I look like. Harry's leaving me,' I sobbed.

'Well, why don't you put the scissors to good use and stab the fucker? No court in the land would convict you. A husband cheating on a wife with triplets and a toddler – are you kidding me? They'd stand up and applaud you for taking him down.'

'I'm not going to maim him.'

'I'll do it for you. I have a lifetime of pent-up rage. I can pretend Harry's my useless father.'

'Marian, seriously, you're not going to hurt Harry.' The Valium was kicking in. I felt calmer, less panicky.

Marian waved the scissors at me. 'You're far too nice. That's always been your problem. You're nice to everyone. You need to toughen up. Your sisters are tough bitches. You need to grow some balls, Julie. You can't let people walk all over you. Harry needs to be punished. He's screwing someone else. You can't ignore it.'

I put my hands up to my head. 'I need time to think. My head feels like it's going to explode.'

'Hardly surprising, with everything you're dealing with. I'm telling you, if I ever find out Greg's cheating I'll nail him to the fucking cross. Jesus's death will look like a picnic compared to what I'd do to him.'

'That's the strangest part. You think you're going to react one way, but when it actually happens, you don't. I can't explain it. I just can't face confronting him. I'm not ready. Not yet.'

'Fine. But when you are, let me know and I'll stand outside with a big chef's knife in case it gets ugly and you need back-up.'

That night I texted Sophie about Harry's planned trip to Paris. She told me to call over immediately. Jack was watching a football match and Jess was asleep so we went into Sophie's bedroom and rang Louise.

I was crying too much to speak, so Sophie filled Louise in on the situation and put her on loudspeaker.

'Jesus Christ, Julie, I've never been so shocked,' Louise said. 'If Harry can be unfaithful, anyone can. He worships you and the kids.'

'Everyone keeps saying that, but it makes no bloody difference. He's still screwing some tart called Christelle.'

'What kind of a name is that? She sounds like a hooker,' Louise said.

'She's a home-wrecker. She's destroying my marriage and my boys' lives.' I started crying again.

'OK, we need to get organized. The only thing to do here is catch him in the act. You need hard proof. I'm going to book the three of us tickets to Paris and we'll confront them in person. Let's see him try and explain his way out of that.'

'That's a brilliant idea,' Sophie said.

I hugged a pillow to my chest. 'I don't know, Lou. I'm not sure I want to see her and him and make it all real.'

'Julie, you can't hide for ever. Pretending it's not happening won't make it go away. You have to deal with this. You won't be alone. We'll be with you every step of the way.'

'Now you just need to find out where he's staying and we'll give him the surprise of his life,' Sophie said.

So, I was finally going to Paris, but instead of a romantic trip with my husband for my fortieth birthday, I was going to catch him and his mistress together and prove to myself beyond doubt that my marriage was over.

When I got home, Harry was in bed. I logged on to my computer and went into mumskeepingsane.com. There had been a huge response to my last posting, when Harry had forgotten my birthday and I'd said I felt invisible. At least three hundred women had written about it. Most of them said they felt invisible too, that since they'd had children they'd been relegated to second place. Their husbands were more interested in the kids or their work or even the football on TV than their wives. One woman wrote that her husband hadn't asked her how she was in five years. They were all shocked that my sisters had forgotten my birthday too. They said they were selfish witches and that I was unlucky to have such rotten

365

siblings. They all wanted to know what had happened after the birthday fiasco and how my life was, these days.

Threescompany:

Hi, everyone,

Sorry it's been so long since my last message. Things have actually, believe it or not, got worse. Yes, I'd thought spending my fortieth birthday locked in the bathroom crying my eyes out was an all-time low, but it turns out that it wasn't such a bad day after all . . . I now know that my husband forgot my birthday because he is having an affair with a French woman called Christelle.

The so-called company project he was working on, that was making him so grumpy and distracted, is actually a French whore and he is planning to leave me for her. I found out today that he is going to Paris to meet her, and after that he's planning to break the news to me. He's going to leave me with our four sons and run off to Paris to this slut.

My sisters can't believe it. By the way, they were horrible to forget my birthday but I have to say they have been brilliant about this crisis. And they have both had awful things happen to them. Their perfect lives have been turned upside-down lately. They are dealing with a lot of problems and yet they are being very supportive of me. We've actually got really close, helping each other out. My older sister thinks we should go to Paris to confront my husband and his mistress. But I'm scared. I know it's weak and pathetic but I don't want him to leave me. I can't raise the boys alone. It's too hard. It's too much for one person. I'm barely managing to get through the day with a husband to help me. I'll definitely go off the deep end on my own.

Mind you, I think I've gone a bit mad already. I cut my hair off this morning. Thankfully my neighbour arrived in before I had chopped it all off and she managed to make a short bob out of it. I never used to understand people who self-harmed. Why on earth would you want to cut yourself? But I get it now. Honestly, I want to cut my arm and feel physical pain, so the mental anguish will go away for a while. I want to numb myself. I want to be someone else. I want to be living someone else's life. This wasn't my plan. Being a single mother of four boys was not my childhood dream. I'm not high-maintenance. I'm not looking for Ferraris and mansions. All I want is for things to go back to the way they were. I don't mind having to budget, I don't mind not having childcare, but I do mind not having a husband. I do mind my kids not seeing their dad because he's shacked up with some French floozy.

I keep thinking, Is it my fault? Did I push him away? If I'm being honest I don't make much of an effort any more about how I look. I just wear jeans and sweatshirts because I'm with the boys all day and I always end up covered with yoghurt or banana or mud. I don't bother wearing makeup unless we're going out at night – what's the point? My underwear is old and shapeless and I've put on weight. Although I've lost over a stone since this all happened.

So maybe it is my fault. If I looked better, dressed better, put on some makeup and some decent underwear maybe my husband wouldn't have looked elsewhere. I also have to be honest and admit that I often swat him away when he wants sex. Most of the time I'm just too tired. And, besides, I don't feel sexy, I don't feel attractive. I know I don't look good, I know I've lost my mojo. I used to be curvy and sexy and cute-looking – shiny curly hair and big brown eyes – but since the triplets I've let myself go. It wasn't intentional. I didn't decide to do it. It kind of crept up on me. If you keep wearing nice tops that get ruined with carrot stains and snot, you realize there's no point. If you wear thongs that ride up your bum when you're pushing swings and making sandcastles, you stop wearing them and opt for comfy pants. What's the point in putting on makeup when your face inevitably ends up with dribble all over it?

And, yes, I know there are mothers out there who look immaculate in the park. Women who do that daytime glamour thing so well. I admire them and envy them . . . but do they have triplets? Do they have four hyper sons? Maybe they do and they're just smarter than me because they know how to keep their husbands happy. My mother is constantly telling me to lose weight and smarten myself up. I used to think it was so old-fashioned – put on some lipstick before your husband comes home – but maybe she's right.

I just keep thinking that, despite me looking like crap, we were happy. You know, we laughed a lot. We may not have been having hot sex every week, but we held hands and hugged. We were tactile. We had fun together in the middle of the chaos. We were in it together. A team, a partnership, a couple, parents, husband and wife, best friends, soul-mates . . .

How can he walk away from that? How can he leave it all behind? How can he abandon us? We're his family! Don't we count any more? Doesn't he love us any more? What happened? Where did it all go wrong? What did I do? What should I do? What can I do? Help!

35

Louise

Harry – a cheat? I didn't think he had it in him. He just wasn't the type. From the day he met Julie he'd been besotted with her. They used to come around to my apartment when they first started dating in London and he would just stare at her adoringly and laugh loudly every time she said anything remotely funny. He still looked at her that way. If Harry could cheat on Julie, there was no hope for anyone.

Then again, at the moment everyone was behaving out of character. Look at Sophie getting a job and managing to live on 1,600 euros a month. I was really impressed with her. I told her not to pay me rent until she started working on commission and could afford it, but she insisted. She said it made her feel better, less like a leech and a failure. She hadn't fallen apart, as I would have imagined, she had been resourceful and tenacious. I was proud of her.

She had called me to discuss Julie. 'It's terrible, Louise – she's in such a state. The poor thing is terrified. I don't blame her – imagine having to raise those boys alone. I know you're doing it with Clara, but four boys is a lot to deal with for a single mum.'

'She sounded devastated. I just keep thinking – Harry?'

'The least likely person.'

'He's so solid and reliable.'

'Well, they say it's often the quiet ones.' Sophie sighed.

'But I can't even see him chatting up a Frenchwoman.'

'Me neither. But the evidence is there. I mean, she's not imagining it.'

'Maybe he just needed a blow-out because he was feeling weighed down with responsibility.'

'To hell with him. He has four healthy kids and a great wife. He doesn't have any excuse to be poking it elsewhere,' Sophie barked. Clearly the topic of husbands letting their wives down was a touchy one.

'You're right, he is lucky. Julie's great.'

'She's a saint. She's with those kids twenty-four seven with no help, no time out and no cash. Her house is trashed, her car is falling apart and she never complains. When his salary was cut she just got on with it. The only thing I think she did do wrong was she let herself go a bit after the kids were born and her self-esteem plummeted.'

'I agree with you, actually. Her self-confidence was down because she didn't look good. Although, in fairness to her, she tried. She started a diet every year, but it never lasted more than four days.'

'She was never very disciplined,' Sophie laughed, 'but I envy her relaxed attitude to food. I've spent my whole life starving myself. I've been hungry since I was eighteen. First of all I did it for modelling and then for Jack. It's miserable to be hungry all the time.'

'Well, I've been overly disciplined about work. For the last twenty years my career has defined who I am. Now I'm a mother I've discovered there is more to life and that you can really enjoy simple things, like giving Clara a bath. I still run into work every morning, but now sometimes I actually want to leave early to spend time with her.'

'My God, Louise, you almost sound maternal.' Sophie giggled.

'Don't tell anyone. Now, back to Julie. I'm going to book the tickets for Paris. She can't live in denial. She needs to face the truth and deal with it. If he's going to leave her, she has to accept it and screw him for every penny he has, which won't be a lot, but we'll all be here to look out for her and support her.'

'Poor Julie – it's such a shock when your husband lets you down. I feel so sorry for her.'

'Look how well you've coped,' I reminded her. 'You've been so strong.'

'Believe me, I still have my bad days, but it was an incredible help having you guys there for me. And Gavin's been great, too. He's really helped out with Jess. I think he's finally growing up.'

'About bloody time. OK, I've got to go. Clara needs her bottle.'

'Careful, Louise, someone might mistake you for a mother some day.'

I laughed and hung up.

Work was a nightmare at the moment. Dominic was unbearably smug now that he was Gordon Hanks's 'chosen one'. While he swanned off to New York to represent Gordon's new acquisition, I was left to look after all of his files as well as my own. Alex had been cool with me since the oversight with the purchase price, so I had been working twice as hard to prove myself yet again. I was sick of always having to prove myself. I was fed-up competing with men who had wives to make their lives seamless while I had to juggle everything alone. I'd had enough of everyone watching me to see if having a baby would make me trip up, mess up, be unable to cope. And the worst of it was, I'd made that bloody mistake and given them a reason to question my commitment and ability to do my job properly.

After twenty years of giving a hundred per cent at all times, of being totally loyal to the firm, I had finally messed up and it felt awful. I was furious and disappointed with myself. Dominic called daily from New York to check up on his files. It was his way of rubbing salt into my wound and it succeeded: he was really getting to me. The phone rang at exactly one o'clock every day, which was eight o'clock in New York.

I looked at my watch. Here we go . . .

'Hi, Louise, it's Dominic.'

'Hello.'

'So, how are things going? Are you still managing to cope with all the work Alex has landed you with?'

'Believe it or not, Dominic, your files aren't really that complex. I'm coping just fine.'

'I don't know – you sound very tired. Is the baby up again?'

'I'm not tired at all. It must be the phone line.'

'Did you call the lawyers about clause eight of the Hilton-Paltery merger?'

'Yes, Dominic. It's been sorted out.'

'Did you check the amendments on screen or did you actually print them out this time?'

I gripped my desk and forced myself not to get angry. 'The papers have been thoroughly checked.'

'Yes, well, I'd like to see for myself. We don't want another potentially disastrous oversight on our hands, now, do we?'

I knew if I didn't hang up, I'd blow a fuse. 'I'll forward them to you now. Look, I have to go, I'm busy.'

'Me too. I need to finish up early today. Gordon is taking me for dinner with his family to celebrate his daughter's eighteenth birthday. We're going to Per Se, the three-star Michelin restaurant in Columbus Circle. He's booked the private dining room. I believe we're having the tasting menu.'

I had been to Per Se. It was a fantastic restaurant. I couldn't believe Dominic had been invited to a family celebration. The weasel had obviously really wound his way into Gordon's affections. 'Well, as I said, I have to go.'

'I'll send Gordon your best.'

I slammed down the phone and resisted the urge to throw it across my office.

The next day I ate lunch at my desk. I was waiting for my daily call from Dominic, but it never came. He was obviously sleeping off a hangover from all the fine wine he'd been drinking with the Hanks family last night, I thought glumly.

My office door opened and Meredith's head popped around. She was wearing a perfectly tailored red suit and looked fantastic. I was glad I'd worn my grey wool dress with the cap sleeves: it was really smart and I knew I looked good in it. I didn't want Meredith thinking I was letting the side down.

'You got a sec?' she asked.

'Sure, come in.' I hadn't seen her since my screw-up. She'd been away in Edinburgh, working, but had heard about it – everyone in the office was talking about it – and had sent me a supportive email saying, Don't let the bastards get you down. It was a mistake. We all make them. You fixed it. Move on.

She sat down opposite me, crossed her legs and grinned. 'I thought you might be interested in some news I have regarding your colleague, Dominic.'

That got my attention. 'What is it?'

'You know that my secretary, Shirley, and Alex's are cousins?'

'Yes.'

'Well, Shirley just came in and told me that the shit has hit the fan in New York.'

'Go on.' I sat up straight in my chair. This sounded good.

'Our friend Dominic, a.k.a. the Rat, was out with Gordon Hanks and his family last night.'

'He told me it was the daughter's eighteenth birthday and he was the guest of honour.'

Meredith snorted. 'According to my sources, it seems that old Dominic had a little too much red wine. After dinner Hanks and his wife went home, while the birthday girl – Abbey – went to meet up with some friends in a nightclub. Dominic, ever the gentleman, said he'd escort her and make sure she was OK. Hanks woke up this morning to find his daughter missing. She never made it home. He freaked and started calling her friends only to discover that she had gone back to Dominic's hotel for a "nightcap".'

'No!'

'Yes! Dominic shagged Hanks's only child, his pride and glory.'

I whooped with glee. This was fantastic. 'What did Hanks do?'

'He went to the hotel, shouted and beat on the door until Dominic opened up and then he punched him right in the nose. You'll be very sorry to hear it's broken.'

'No!' I was loving every second of this.

Meredith laughed. 'Yes! And when Alex found out an hour ago, he called Dominic and shouted at him for twenty minutes, calling him every name in the book. His secretary said she'd never seen him so angry.'

'Is it terrible that I'm absolutely thrilled to hear this?'

'Hell, no. I barely know Dominic, but I can see he's a back-stabbing snake. I'm delighted he's got his comeuppance.'

'What an idiot.'

'These cocky, over-confident guys with their blue-blood back-ground and sense of entitlement always mess up in the end,' Meredith assured me.

'And, boy, did he do it in style!' I laughed. 'I almost feel sorry for him.'

'But not quite.' She grinned. 'Anyway, how are you getting on – apart from Dominic, who will no longer be a problem?'

'Better, thanks. At least Clara's sleeping now and being much easier. But the mistake I made with the purchase price really threw me. What if it had been something I hadn't been able to resolve? I pride myself on never missing anything, never taking short cuts, being thorough. But Clara was sick and I was running on empty.'

'Louise, you have to cut yourself some slack. You're doing fantastically well. No man would be able to juggle being a single dad, getting no sleep and working as a senior partner. We women are too hard on ourselves. If there's one thing I've learnt since having Hermione, it's that I can't control everything. I'm a control freak by nature – I've had to be to get where I am – so that has been a very difficult thing to accept. There are nights when she's up crying for hours. The next day I'm exhausted and have to be extra careful with whatever I'm doing. You have to learn to work around it, not fight against it. And I have a husband who shares getting up at night. It's so much harder for you. I think you're doing a marvellous job, so pat yourself on the back and be proud of your achievements.'

'Thanks, Meredith. That really does mean a lot. I've been feeling very unsure of myself lately, which is a completely alien emotion for me. I've always known exactly where I was going and what I was going to achieve next. I had yearly goals that I never failed to meet, and now sometimes it's just about all I can do to get through the day. I'm finding it hard to let go of my old life and embrace this new one. Having Clara has brought unpredictability and change into my life and it frightens me at times. I keep trying to get a handle on it and failing. I feel as if I'm being a bad mother because I spend very little time with her during the week, and I'm not doing my job as well as I'd like to.'

Meredith uncrossed her legs and stood up. 'I'm months ahead of you on the baby front and my best advice to you is not to let yourself feel guilty. It'll eat you up. Remind yourself every day that you're doing the best you can. I firmly believe that our daughters will appreciate the fact that we didn't give up careers we loved to stay at home. They're going to admire us, not blame us. So no more guilt, OK?'

'OK. Thanks for the advice, and the glorious gossip – it's made my day, week and year!'

'Any time.' She grinned and left my office.

I sat down and spent a wonderful ten minutes picturing Dominic with a broken nose.

Just before I went home that night, Alex came to see me. He looked tired, distracted and cross. 'Dominic will be coming home early from New York. There has been a bit of a set-to, which I'd like to keep under wraps as it is of a personal nature. Suffice it to say that Dominic behaved appallingly and let me down very badly. You can hand his files back to him tomorrow. Thank you for keeping an eye on them. You've been very magnanimous about it. Goodnight.'

'Goodnight, Alex,' I said, forcing myself not to cheer.

I got home at seven that night, which was the earliest I'd been in weeks. Clara was in her Babygro, sitting on Agnes's knee. When she saw me, she smiled. I rushed over to pick her up. She nuzzled her head into my neck and I inhaled her scent – talcum powder and milk. I closed my eyes. All of the day's stresses left me. There was just Clara. I held her tight.

'Baby loves Mummy. Mummy loves baby,' Agnes said, walking towards the door, smiling. 'This very good. You looking at baby now. You seeing baby now.'

'I always looked at her – don't be silly.'

'But you not seeing her.' Agnes wagged a finger at me. 'Now you understanding what baby means. Now you understanding. I see in your face. I go now.'

I sat down and held Clara on my knee, facing me. I stared into her clear blue eyes. She was beautiful. She was perfect. I smiled at her and she waved her little hands about and grinned. A small flash of white caught my eye. I looked more closely. It was a tooth! An actual tooth! I turned to tell Agnes, but she was gone. I went to call Julie, but realized that my baby's tooth wouldn't be very important to her right now. I considered calling Sophie, then decided not to: she was dealing with a lot of stress. A tooth was not a big deal . . . but it was to me. I called Mum instead.

'Well, that's wonderful,' she enthused. 'Sure she's a little dote. It was so nice to have a good go of her when she was home. She's so placid. You've got a gem there.'

'She's been so easy since the reflux medicine kicked in. She's so much more alert and her sweet nature is really coming through. She smiles all the time.'

'You can see she's a happy baby. Long may it last. Children are so easy at that age. It gets a lot more complicated as they get older. I never imagined I'd see Sophie homeless at thirty-eight.'

'She seems to be coping well, though.'

'She's been incredible. Her first few days in work have gone well. She's better off busy. When things are hard, having too much time on your hands isn't good for you. You don't need to think and analyse. You need to keep busy, keep your mind occupied. Otherwise you'll get depressed.'

'True, but then you can be too busy as well.' I sighed. 'Working and trying to be a mum is harder than I thought.'

'Louise, I've been telling you for years to slow down. You'll wear yourself out and, believe me, no one in that office will thank you for it. Your priority now is your baby.'

'Yes, Mum, but I also need to provide for her.'

'Well,' she sniffed, 'if the father was around, you'd have less pressure.'

'Not necessarily. Look at Sophie. Jack's completely dependent on her now.'

'That's true, but it's only temporary. He'll get a job soon, a bright lad like him.'

'It might take a while. It's tough out there.'

'Don't say that to me. I'm praying every day that he gets a job. And your brother needs one too. If he doesn't find something soon, your father's going to kill him.'

'I helped Gavin with his CV and he's sent it out to a lot of recruitment agencies. Something should come up. At least alternative energy and the climate-change crisis is a growth area. He's in the right field.'

'That's good to hear, but he needs a proper job in an office. I want him to stay away from those unhygienic tree-huggers. I can tell you, Louise, you never stop worrying about your children, no matter how old they are. By the way, have you been talking to Julie? She seems down in the dumps. I called her the other day and she sounded very fed-up.'

The last thing I needed was the third degree from Mum about Julie. 'I'm sure she was just tired. The boys are a handful.'

'That's true. They get more boisterous as they get older. The sooner they go off to primary school, the better. Poor Julie needs a break – it hasn't been easy for her.'

'No, it hasn't. Well, I'd better go and put Clara down. Thanks for being enthusiastic about her tooth.'

'Call me any time she does anything. I'm a very proud grand-mother.'

I hung up and went to put on my pyjamas. I took Clara into bed with me. We snuggled up and she drank her bottle while I finished off some emails. When she had finished, I held her up on my shoulder to burp her. She fell asleep, her left arm curled around my neck, her face snuggled into my shoulder. I watched her little body rise and fall as her breath caressed my neck.

My heart skipped a beat and I finally stopped fighting it. I stopped suppressing it. I stopped denying it. I stopped resisting it. I jumped off the cliff, feet first, and allowed unconditional love for my baby girl to sweep over me.

It was exhilarating and terrifying.

36

Sophie

After a couple of weeks it was obvious that I could book the models directly, without further training, so Quentin let me start earning commission earlier than anticipated. Some of the PR people I had worked with when I was modelling were still at the same companies and they remembered me, which was nice. It reminded me that I had been a person in my own right before I married Jack.

I had spent so much time and energy being the perfect wife that I had forgotten who I was. For six years I had focused on being Mrs Jack Wells. Now I was Sophie Devlin again. I had decided to use my maiden name for work, the same one I'd had as a model, and it felt great. I was me again. It was also nice to be busy. From nine until five I didn't have time to think about anything but work. All my worries about Jack, Jess and our situation were put aside for eight hours. I was busy, I was dedicated, and I worked my backside off.

The models seemed so young. They were gorgeous, and some were very sweet, but among them there were a few over-confident girls with an overblown sense of importance. Avril, who was one of the more successful models, was a nightmare. She was dating a soap star and clearly thought they were the Brangelina of Ireland. She turned up late for photo shoots, and the previous Thursday she had got drunk at the opening of a new nightclub she was there to promote. Instead of PR photos of her looking beautiful and having fun, there were tabloid shots of her staggering out of the door, with her dress undone and a nipple on view. The PR rep was not happy and refused to pay for her time. Quentin had freaked and wanted to get rid of Avril, but I told him to give her a break: I had seen girls like her when I was modelling. A little success went straight to their heads and they thought they were invincible. I felt she deserved a second chance. After all, we all make mistakes.

I booked her for a marketing campaign at a new DIY shop that was opening in Dublin. It was a very successful UK firm that wanted to expand into Ireland. Their PR guy, who was very pushy, said they wanted Avril because she had a profile – people knew who she was. For the campaign, they wanted her to dress up in a boiler suit with oil on her face and hands. They didn't want anything overtly sexy because it was a mum-and-dad store.

'I'm not dressing up in some baggy boiler suit,' she snapped, when I told her. 'I don't starve myself for my body to be hidden under guys' clothes with oil on my face.'

I took a deep breath. 'It's a big UK company that's planning to open up lots of stores here, if this one is successful. They're paying top rate for you. Don't blow it.'

She flicked back her long wavy bleached hair. 'Tell them I'll wear short, tight dungarees and a push-up bra and stand beside a hunky guy in a boiler suit – that way I look hot and they'll still get the whole DIY message.'

'Avril, they've been very specific about what they want. If you won't do it, I'll get someone else.'

'Fine. Get me something decent. I like doing club openings – find me one of those.'

'After your last performance, the phone hasn't exactly been ringing off the hook,' I reminded her.

'They got loads of publicity.'

'Bad publicity of you falling out of their club.'

She frowned. 'You're new here and you obviously haven't a clue how this works. If you knew anything about this business, you'd understand that there's no such thing as bad publicity.'

I leant across the desk. 'Avril, I was Quentin's number-one model for almost ten years. I know exactly how this works. Bad publicity will destroy your career.'

'Maybe back in your day, but in the modern world, all publicity is good. Look at Kate Moss, for God's sake. She got loads of amazing contracts after those pictures of her snorting cocaine came out.'

Sadly, she had a point. Bad publicity did seem to work for some people. Depending on how you handled it, it could enhance your career. What kind of a world was my daughter growing up in? There was no way in hell Jess was ever going to model. Now it was all about celebrity and notoriety and less about hard work, beauty and charisma.

Avril was only twenty-one. She thought she knew it all. She thought she was so street-smart and sassy, but she was clueless. I felt sorry for her because she wouldn't last a year if she didn't change her attitude. Ireland was a village. Everyone was cutting their budgets and people promoting their businesses wouldn't consider an unprofessional model. 'Listen to me, Avril. We live in a very small country and people are not going to book someone who turns up late, gets drunk or refuses to wear what they're asked to. You're a gorgeous-looking girl with a potentially great career ahead of you. Don't blow it with a bad attitude. Take my advice. The more professional you are, the more in demand you'll be and the more money you'll make.'

She reapplied her lip-gloss. 'Look, Sophie, I have a mother. I don't need your advice. I know exactly what I'm doing. Maybe, like, forty years ago when you were a model everyone was a tee-totaller and a virgin, but nowadays women can vote and it's not considered a sin to have fun. I didn't get into modelling to have crappy photos of me wearing overalls. Call me when something decent comes in.' She flounced out of the office in her micro-mini and wedge platforms.

I somehow resisted the urge to follow her out and slap her arrogant face. I called the PR guy and said Avril wasn't available, and suggested Fiona, one of our other models who looked like Avril but was sweet and eager to please. I knew she'd wear anything they wanted and would be a pleasure to work with.

'No,' he said. 'We want the saucy one who's always in the papers. We can change the date to suit her.'

I then had to explain, as tactfully as I could, that Avril wasn't keen on wearing a boiler suit and wanted to wear dungarees.

'She's right,' he said. 'She should get her tits out. OK, find me a male model with big muscles and we'll run with Avril's idea. I'll sell it to my boss. Let's face it, it's mostly men who go to DIY shops and we blokes like a sexy bird.'

I hung up and sighed. For the first time in my life I felt old. I, who had prided myself on looking ten years younger and always considered myself to be young at heart and 'cool' for my age, was completely out of touch with the modern world.

Things at home weren't good. Jack and I were still fighting a lot, although I have to confess he was great with Jess. At first he seemed at a loss as to what to do with her, but Jess told him which parks she liked, what programmes she watched and which food she ate, and he began to find a rhythm. I came home one day to find them cooking pancakes together – there was flour everywhere. I didn't like Jess eating pancakes because they were full of butter, but she was blissfully happy so I bit my tongue and even ate one myself.

Jack took her to the zoo, played football with her and was trying to teach her how to cycle without stabilizers. He now knew the words to all of her favourite songs from *The Princess and the Frog*. He knew what stories she liked, that her favourite colours were pink, purple, red and yellow, and that she was afraid of spiders and snails. He found out that she could colour really well, hardly ever going outside the lines. He could tell that she was tired and needed to go home when she started twirling her hair. He knew she liked to go to sleep with her princess lamp on. He was even able to put her hair into a ponytail without causing her too much pain.

Sometimes when I came home from work in those first few weeks I felt jealous. I was envious of the time they were spending together, of them having fun together while I worked. I missed being with my daughter. I only saw her in the evenings when she was tired and at her worst.

But the biggest problem was Jack spending my money. He asked for money to meet up with old colleagues or potential employers or just to 'network'. I resented giving him my hard-earned cash to go drinking or out to dinner while I stayed at home and ate porridge. Things came to a head when he told me he needed my credit card because he was going to dinner at Le Manoir with one of his UK contacts.

'No way,' I said. 'It's the most expensive restaurant in Dublin. We can't afford it.'

'Jesus, Sophie, it's important. This guy is looking to set up a fund here and wants to discuss it with me.'

'You said the same thing last week. Nothing came of it and you spent thirty quid on drinks. Le Manoir will cost a fortune.'

'He's the best shot I've had at getting a job.'

'So let him pay for the meal.'

'He probably will, but I can't get caught out. I have to be able to offer to pay. I don't want to look like I'm desperate. I'm trying to give an impression of confidence and self-assurance. I can't do that if I'm sweating about the bill all night.'

'Why can't you go for a drink instead?'

'Because he asked me to book a table there. He heard the food was fantastic.'

'But if you end up paying for dinner, it'll cost a week's wages. We have bills to pay.'

'I'm aware of that. I paid all of our bills for years, remember?'

'Well, you haven't contributed anything for months and if this guy wants to hire you, if he's really interested in you, he can meet you for coffee. Wining and dining in fine restaurants is not on and I'm not funding it.'

Jack's face reddened. 'I never begrudged you anything,' he snapped. 'While I was working fourteen-hour days, killing myself so you could have everything you wanted – the big house, the clothes, the jewels and the shoes – I never complained. You spent the money as fast as I made it. And when you wanted a forty-thousand-euro kitchen, I said, "OK, honey," and worked harder. I gave you everything and now that I need a little help you're saying no.'

'We don't have the money,' I reminded him. 'You lost it all, remember? And I gave up work to be the perfect wife for you because Jack Wells wanted his wife on call. He wanted his wife to look good, smell good, dress well, be skinny, beautiful, manicured, pedicured, waxed, buffed, groomed, shiny, bright, happy, available for sex and to accompany him on work trips whenever he needed her.'

'Oh, boo-hoo. Poor Sophie had to look pretty for her husband. What a chore that must have been, shopping and getting your nails done regularly. And can you *please* stop blaming me for my company going bust? I feel shit enough as it is. I don't need you constantly making me feel worse. Give me a break. Be a supportive wife for a change.'

'You selfish bastard!' I screamed, all of my pent-up anger bubbling to the surface. 'Because of you needing me to be perfect after Jess was born, and getting impatient and grumpy when I wasn't back to myself a week after giving birth, I had to take Prozac for a year. Yes, Jack, because of you and your expectations of perfection I ended up on anti-depressants. And now we're homeless and you want me to tell you how great you are?'

Jack stared at me, open-mouthed. 'What the hell are you talking about? Anti-depressants? I don't –'

'Don't understand? Of course you don't. You were far too busy conquering the world to notice that I was having a meltdown after Jess was born. You didn't like me crying and looking wrecked with leaky boobs. You made that very clear.'

'I never said a word to you.'

'You didn't have to. Your disapproval was written all over your face. You liked your life the way it had been and you didn't want our baby to change anything. Well, guess what, Jack, babies change everything. I was so low I could barely get out of bed, but you

384

arranged for us to go to a black-tie ball a few weeks after Jess was born and I was expected to fit into my dress and look amazing. I never wanted to end up on Prozac, but I had no choice. I wasn't allowed to work through my blues. You didn't support me or help me. You just presumed I'd get on with it and get back to normal. So I did.'

Jack was shocked. 'Jesus, Sophie, why didn't you say something?'

'Why didn't you ever ask me how I felt?'

'Because you seemed fine.'

'Exactly.'

'Oh, for God's sake, I'm not a mind-reader. You should have told me.'

'I was too depressed!' I shouted. 'And you should have noticed, but you didn't want to know.'

'You're not so great at being supportive yourself. Do you ever ask me how I feel? Have you once asked me if I'm OK? Shattered? Devastated? Is my confidence trashed? Do I feel like I've let down everyone I love? Am *I* depressed? Do I find it hard to get out of bed in the morning?'

'Gee, I'm sorry, Jack, but there isn't much time in my day to fit that in – I'm working full-time to make money to keep a roof over our heads and in my "spare" time I'm trying to make sure our daughter is OK now that everything in her life's been turned upside-down.'

'Jess is fine. She's a very happy girl. She has her mum and her dad and that's all kids need to feel secure. The rest is just material stuff. I think when we get sorted and I'm working again we should really focus on having another child. Jess told me she'd love a baby sister.'

'I don't think so,' I said.

'Maybe we should see someone to check that nothing's wrong. It's been three years and you haven't got pregnant.'

I threw my head back and laughed. 'And why do you think that is, you idiot? Why do you think we haven't had a child?'

He looked at me, confused.

'Because I never came off the pill, Jack. Do you honestly think I'd dream of having another child with a man who refuses to under-stand that babies change your life – that they don't fit into your schedule? Or who doesn't understand that a woman should be allowed to breast-feed for as long as she wants without her husband staring in disgust at her boobs? Or who doesn't see that some days his wife might be too tired to get dressed and shouldn't have to face reproving looks from him when he comes home from work? A husband who doesn't understand that his wife might not want to leave her kid every time he wants her to accompany him on a work trip or go to black-tie balls just after she's had a baby, or have sex for months after giving birth because it hurts? There's no way I'm going to have another baby because I know I'd end up getting depressed, that the pressure from you would be too much and I'd end up back on Prozac.'

Jack sank down into the couch. 'Why didn't you talk to me? All this time I thought we were trying for a baby and you were lying to me. Why didn't you just tell me? I had no idea you felt this way. I'd no idea you were so bad after Jess. I never meant to make you feel pressured. I just thought we should try to get our lives back to normal and not turn into one of those couples who live only for their children and forget about each other. I wanted to put our relationship before our kids. You were always my number-one priority and Jess was a very close second. I didn't mean to pressure you and the only reason I booked that ball was so that you could get out of the house and have some fun. I thought you seemed down in the dumps and needed a night out. You loved getting dressed up and going to balls. I thought I was doing something nice for you, cheering you up. Obviously I got it all wrong. I'm sorry, I really had no idea.' He put his head in his hands and looked like he was going to cry.

I sat down opposite him. Suddenly my anger was gone, leaving me feeling tired and lonely. 'It's OK. I should have told you, but I was ashamed that I couldn't handle motherhood and be a good wife. It should have been straightforward, especially as I had Mimi to help, but when I had Jess I found it hard to cope and eventually I realized I was depressed and needed help.' I sighed and looked down at my hands. 'Anyway, it's all in the past now.'

'But what about having other children? I don't want Jess to be an only child. I promise I'll be more supportive this time.'

I looked out of the window. 'Jack, I'm just about managing to muddle through the day at the moment. I can't even think about getting pregnant. Maybe in a year's time, if everything is calm and sorted out, I'll consider it, but I'm not sure. I have a lot to figure out and I can't make any big decisions now. All I want from you is that you get a job so we can rent a house and give Louise back her apartment.'

'I will, Sophie. I'm very good at what I do. I made millions for the fund. We'll be back on our feet soon and you can give up work, get back to having a nice lifestyle, meet up with your old pals.'

I snorted. 'Old pals? Those shallow bitches have barely bothered to get in touch. We're out, Jack. We're no longer welcome in the jet-set. We're losers, has-beens. Anyway, I don't think I'll ever give up work again. I want my own life, my own money, the security of knowing that if something goes wrong again, we won't lose our home.'

'I always thought Victoria was an awful pain in the arse, to be honest. She was so self-obsessed. To hell with them all. We'll make new friends, real friends. And I promise I'll never lose my job again.'

'You can't promise that, Jack. Your job is up and down, highs and lows, people get laid off all the time, funds collapse all the time. I understand that now, so I want to be able to help. I don't think all of the pressure to earn and support us should be on your shoulders. Besides, I was getting bored with my life and I like working. I like feeling that I'm doing something worthwhile. I do miss spending time with Jess, but if you get a job maybe I could work part-time. I want Jess to see the world as it is. I've been really stupid and filled her head with nonsense about money and diamonds. I want her to be realistic and understand that money doesn't grow on trees and that you have to work hard to make a life for yourself. I want her to go to college and have a good career.'

Jack held up his hands. 'Hang on a minute. I don't want her to think that success is all about intellectual ability. I want her to know that you can be successful in lots of ways – not just by going to college and getting a degree. I don't want her to feel stupid, like I did, if she doesn't get into university to study medicine – or learn to play chess or the violin. I want her to choose a career that makes her happy. I love my job – thank God I didn't go into medicine because I'd have been a terrible doctor. I just want Jess to know she has choices.'

'Well, neither of her parents is an intellectual genius. With our DNA, chances are she won't be a rocket scientist.' I smiled.

'She might have my brother Roger's brains.'

'Or Louise's.'

'So she could be a rocket scientist.'

'Or a neurosurgeon.'

We laughed . . . It had been months since we had spoken to each other civilly, not to mind laugh. It felt strange.

Jack looked at his watch. 'Shoot! I need to go. I'm meeting Harvey in twenty minutes. Look, I know it's hard for you to give me money for all this networking, but I promise it'll be worth it. I'll do my very best not to pay for anything, but I really do think something could come out of this dinner.'

I fished out my credit card and handed it to him. 'I hope so, Jack. I really do.'

37

Julie

Marian said she'd take the triplets for the two days I was in Paris, which was incredibly generous of her. I asked Mum to look after Tom, but when I told her to say nothing about it to Harry she got a bit suspicious. So I told her that he was going on a work trip and I was going to surprise him by joining him over there. She said she thought it was an excellent idea, and that I looked in desperate need of a break.

I had got hold of Harry's laptop and found the email where he told Christelle the details of his trip. He was staying in Hôtel Jean Baptiste, rue Everett, and his Métro stop was St-Michel. Christelle told him to meet her at eight o'clock in the Café Le Petit Pont.

Marian and I Googled the hotel on her computer.

'Two-star – it looks like a dump,' Marian said.

'Well, he can't afford anything else. We had to cancel my birth-day trip to Paris, but now he's going over to see his mistress. It's the ultimate insult.' I sobbed.

'Julie, you've got to stop crying. Your eyes are going to fall out of your head. Seriously, if you stopped bawling and put some makeup on, Harry'd be gobsmacked. You've lost stones and your shorter hair takes ten years off you. I want you to look your absolute best when you confront the bastard. I'm going to lend you my skinny clothes. I only kept really good stuff after I had the kids because, realistically, I knew I'd never fit into it again, but now you've been on the misery diet, you'll get into them. At least one good thing came out of this. You got your figure back.'

'I wish I was twenty stone and happily married,' I wailed.

'OK, stop with the waterworks – I don't want to drown. Come on, try some of these clothes on. I was a fucking knock-out in my early thirties.'

I wriggled into a red halter-neck dress. It was size twelve and it was even a little big.

'You cow! It's stunning on you. With some makeup and heels, you'll drive the French men wild. Now what about this?' She handed me a slinky black sequin dress with a very low back.

I tried it on. It fitted perfectly. I was so shocked by my figure that I actually stopped crying for five minutes. It looked really good on me.

'Jesus, you're a super-model.' Marian whistled.

Liam came into her bedroom. 'OUT!' Marian roared. 'No small people allowed upstairs.'

'I just want to ask Mummy something,' he said. Then, he stopped, open-mouthed. 'Mummy, you look weird.'

'Good weird or scary weird?' I asked.

'Just weird.'

'Do you like the dress?'

'I dunno, it's a bit shiny. But your eyes are funny. Are you still sad about your friend who died?'

Marian looked at me quizzically.

'The boys were wondering why I was crying a lot, so I told them about my friend who died,' I explained.

'Oh, yes, that was so sad. Your poor mummy's been very upset.'

'She has sad eyes a lot now,' Liam told Marian. 'But she always makes them look nice before Daddy comes home. She doesn't want him to be sad for her.'

Marian bent down. 'Your mummy is a saint. Your daddy on the other hand is a –'

'Marian!' I warned her. I wasn't going to slate Harry to the boys – yet.

'I was just going to say your daddy is a very lucky man. Not everyone gets to marry a wonderful person like your mummy.'

'Is Greg lucky to marry you?' Liam asked.

'Luckiest day of his life,' Marian said. 'Although he might describe it a little differently if you asked him. Now shoo.'

'Hold on,' I said to Liam. 'What did you want to ask me, pet?'

'What are Ghostfreak's special powers again?'

'He can pass through walls and become invisible, and he's the creepiest looking of all the *Ben 10* aliens, which scares the criminals too.'

'I forgot the invisible part. Thanks, Mummy.' Liam scampered off.

'How the hell do you remember that stuff?' Marian asked. 'I can never tell who's who – there are so many bloody aliens.'

I smiled. 'I have four boys. You either learn about all these alien guys or you get totally left out. I've kind of got into it.'

'You're a legend. Those boys are very lucky to have you as their mum.'

'Well, I'll need to keep up to speed as a single parent.' I began to cry again.

Marian handed me a handkerchief. 'Please let me kill Harry. I can't stand seeing you so upset. You should put a stiletto through his thick head when you see him in Paris.'

'I keep wondering what she looks like. You know, is she blonde or brunette? Is she much younger? Is she very sexy? Does she smoke and pout like all beautiful French women do? How can I compete with some young sex-bomb? He's going to leave me, Marian. Confronting him isn't going to change anything. Harry's going to leave me and I don't want to be alone.'

'You're gorgeous, you look younger than you are and you're skinny now. You'll have men queuing up.'

'We both know I won't.'

Marian forced me to look her in the eye. 'Julie, I have seen a woman waste her whole life waiting for a man who was never coming back. I will not let you end up like my mother. If Harry's going to leave you, then it's going to happen no matter what you do. And you're not going to spend your life crying about it. You'll have a shit year and then you'll pick yourself up and dust yourself down and get out there and live your life. You have four children. You don't have a choice. You have to get on with your life. You have to hope that someone else will come along. You have to live. I saw my mother give up living. It was horrible growing up in that environment. I won't let it happen to you or your kids.'

I hugged her. 'Thanks for being my friend and my lifeline, and for being the only person in the world who would offer to look after the triplets.'

We both cried and went down to our kids with 'sad eyes'.

Four days later I was sitting in a bar in Paris with my two sisters. The trip had been organized by Louise with military precision. When Harry told me he was going to Paris for work, I didn't flinch. When he left that morning, he hugged me tight and told me he loved me. I was numb from head to toe. As soon as he left, I rushed the boys over to Marian's with a suitcase of clothes for them. They had no idea what was going on: I hadn't told them I was going away because they would have said something to Harry.

'But where are you going, Mummy?' Leo asked, looking upset.

'I have to go away for just two sleepies. It's very important, but I'll be back very soon.'

'But Daddy's away too. Who will mind us?'

'Marian – I told you.'

'But Marian shouts and says bad words a lot.'

'Yes, but she's also a great friend to Mummy and you know you'll have fun with her.'

'Don't go.' Liam clamped himself to my leg.

I had to get out of there, drop Tom to Mum's and get to the airport by eleven. I was already running late, so I used the oldest trick in the book: bribery. 'I'll bring you back treats.'

'Sweeties?' Leo asked.

'Chocolate?' Liam wondered.

'Toys?' Luke looked excited.

'All of them. Sweets, toys and chocolate. Now I have to go. Be good for Marian.' I hugged my little boys and squeezed them tight.

'Ouch! Mummy, you squashed us,' they complained.

'Sorry, I just love you so much.' A tear rolled down my cheek.

'Right! That's it, you lot. Get into the playroom.' Marian stepped in. 'Julie, get into that car and get on that plane.' She frogmarched me to the car. I put Tom in his seat and turned to hug her.

She waved me off. 'Good luck, and don't make it easy for the cheating bastard.'

I dropped Tom to Mum's and started crying when I saw him waving his little hands and shouting, 'Bye-bye, Mama.' I ran back to hold him.

'Go on – you'll miss your flight.' Mum nudged me out of the door. 'Don't be getting upset. You deserve this break and Tom will be fine. Now go and have some fun with your husband.'

I arrived into the airport with minutes to spare. Sophie rushed over. 'Come on, Julie, I've been having a heart attack. We need to run.'

And now here we were, the three of us sitting in the bar in the lovely hotel Louise had booked, drinking wine, looking out on to the Seine. After we'd arrived, Sophie went to take a long bath and Louise worked so I'd spent a couple of hours in the Shakespeare and Company bookshop, which was only a short walk from our hotel. I had always wanted to go there and it didn't disappoint. It was as old and quirky as I'd imagined. Looking out on to the river with a view of Notre Dame, it was the most perfect setting to inspire writers and a wonderful way for lovers of books, like me, to potter about, wiling away an hour or two reading Hemingway or Proust or Joyce . . .

I bought a second-hand copy of Hemingway's *A Moveable Feast*, which was recommended by one of the students working in the shop. He told me it was Hemingway's memoir of his years living in Paris in the 1920s, spending time with F. Scott Fitzgerald, Hilaire Belloc and James Joyce, among others. It sounded so carefree and glamorous. I knew reading it would take me away from my miserable life for a while.

I walked back to the hotel, soaking in the beauty and majesty of Parisian architecture. It was even more stunning than I had imagined. I should have come to live here and not London after college, I should have travelled and explored and been more adventurous. I berated myself for settling down too quickly with Harry and getting overwhelmed by children. There were so many things I'd wanted to do, so many places I'd wanted to see, but I'd done and seen none of them. I'd stopped thinking about what I wanted and focused only on what my family needed. And for what? To find myself dumped at forty.

So here we were, the three sisters, sitting on the terrace of the hotel bar, on a beautiful balmy evening in Paris. I was wearing Marian's black sequin dress with no back. Sophie had done my hair and makeup and made me look a lot better than I could ever have managed.

'You look incredible, Julie,' Louise said. 'I know it isn't going to make you feel better, but you really are gorgeous.'

'The best I've seen you in years,' Sophie agreed. 'The dress is perfect and your hair is so much nicer shorter.'

'Thanks, guys. And thanks for being here to support me on . . . um . . . you know . . . this, um . . .'

'No tears,' Sophie ordered. 'You are not to ruin your makeup. After we've confronted them you can sob your heart out, but I want Harry and his mistress to see you looking beautiful.'

'Have you thought about what you're going to say?' Louise asked.

I shook my head. 'I can't think straight. My heart's thumping and I think I'm going to get sick.'

'Deep breaths and more wine,' Louise said.

Sophie looked around. 'Who would have thought this time last year that all of our lives would change so dramatically? I certainly never could have imagined I'd be penniless and homeless and working full-time. And I know Julie never thought Harry would cheat on her and, Louise, you never thought you'd be a mum. How did this happen?'

'Life throws you a curve ball when you least expect it,' Louise mused.

'It stabs you in the heart,' I muttered.

'It pulls the rug from under your feet,' Sophie agreed.

I let out a huge sigh. 'I'm forty. I've got four kids. I'm too old and tired for this. I haven't the energy to be out in nightclubs trying to meet a new man. I'm going to be on my own for the rest of my life and that terrifies me.'

'You're not old,' Louise snapped. 'Forty is young and you look great. You don't need a man to make you happy. You just need lovers to have sex and go out for dinner with. As far as I can see, husbands are more trouble than they're worth. Look at how they've let both of you down.'

I didn't like Louise slating Harry. 'To be fair, until recently Harry has been a brilliant husband. He's always made me feel great about myself, helped out with the kids, and he's never been the type to dump me with the boys on Saturday afternoons so he can watch rugby matches with his friends, or abandon me on Friday nights for drinks after work. He was great, but now it's all gone horribly wrong. I guess I put on weight and let myself go and the sex became sporadic at best and he lost interest in me.'

'Hold on,' Louise barked, banging her glass down on the table. 'You were an amazing wife to him. You gave him four healthy sons, you looked after them day and night – even though it's bloody difficult – and when he came home with salary cuts, you never complained or made him feel bad, you just budgeted even more. You have no time for yourself – you're a bloody slave to your family. Harry may have been a great husband but you are an unbelievable wife and mother, so don't put yourself down and blame yourself for his affair.'

'She's right, you know,' Sophie added. 'You're brilliant – I don't know how you do it. Your life always seemed such a struggle to me. There I was with one child in Montessori and a full-time housekeeper and you had no help at all. You have literally given up your life for your family and I admire you for it, but I think you lost yourself along the way. After Jack's business went bust, I saw that my life was a bit empty and soulless. Don't get me wrong, I loved being wealthy, I really did, but my whole identity was wrapped up in money, in being Mrs Jack Wells, in being part of an élite set, in appearance, clothes, the house I lived in and the car I drove. I definitely lost myself and I think you have, too, Julie, but in a different way. You're so selfless. You never have time to yourself to do things outside being a mum and a wife. I think you need to try and find something for yourself that has nothing to do with the kids.'

I nodded. 'Yes, I've morphed into a mum. That's all I am. And I love my boys, but my life is like bloody Groundhog Day and it's getting me down. I honestly haven't had time to do anything for myself because we can't afford help so the childcare is entirely up to me. But when the boys go to primary school next month, I'm going to try and find something I can do, something that feeds my soul. Because I'm drowning in motherhood, and the weird thing is that, although I never have a second to myself, I find it very lonely. Do you?' I asked my sisters.

Louise shook her head. 'Because I spend so little time with Clara during the week, I love being with her all weekend. I cherish our time together. I don't find it lonely and I'm single.'

'I was very lonely in the beginning. When Jess was small and I wasn't coping very well, before I went on Prozac, I used to –'

'*What?*' Louise and I stopped drinking and stared at her.

'Oh, God.' She put her hand over her mouth.

'You were on Prozac?' I was shocked. Sophie was always so together, so perfect, never a hair out of place, and Jess was an angel child.

Sophie blushed and fiddled with her ring. 'Yes – I was on it for a year after Jess was born. She was quite colicky in the beginning and Jack didn't understand. He thought the baby would just slot into our lives and nothing would change. I found trying to be the perfect wife and mother really difficult. I got depressed and was crying all the time and even getting dressed seemed like a huge ordeal, so I went to my GP and he put me on Prozac.'

'Why did you never tell us?' Louise asked.

Sophie shrugged. 'I guess I was embarrassed. You've never needed help for anything, Louise – you're so bright and smart and capable – and Julie was bringing up triplets and not having to take anti-depressants. I had just one child and was unable to cope.'

'Oh, Sophie, I wasn't coping well at all. I wish I'd taken Prozac – it would probably have made the first year more bearable,' I admitted.

'After three months of hell with Clara crying all night, I would definitely have ended up on Prozac if I hadn't got her sorted out,' Louise said.

'No, you wouldn't,' Sophie said. 'Look at you now with Clara. You're still doing your high-powered job and managing to juggle it with motherhood.'

'I'm not really managing,' Louise said. 'I never knew how needy and all-consuming babies are. I'm struggling – I'm not at my best in work any more and I'm missing out on seeing my baby all week.'

'What's the solution?' I asked. If anyone had one, it was Louise.

'I'm trying to figure it out. I love my job and I've worked so hard to get where I am that I don't want to give it up. Besides, I need to work to support Clara. But I miss her. A lot of the time when I leave in the morning she's still asleep and then when I come home she's usually asleep too. I hate that. I love being with her – she's so adorable now, all smiley and cooing and gorgeous.'

Sophie and I grinned across the table at each other.

'I think someone's in love,' I said, squeezing Louise's hand.

'Yes, I am, completely and utterly,' she said, her eyes filling. 'It kind of crept up on me and then, *bam*, I was besotted with her. Suddenly it wasn't all about trying to stop her crying or what time she needed to be fed, it was about staring at her beautiful face and cuddling her and smelling her and going for naps with her in my bed and watching her sleeping and thinking my heart was going to burst.' She took a gulp of her wine.

'Welcome to motherhood.' I hugged her.

'But what am I going to do?' she asked. 'I want to spend more time with her.'

'What would your ideal set-up be?' Sophie asked.

Louise thought for a moment. 'To be able to do what I do but with more flexible hours. To be my own boss, I suppose.'

'Well, could you set up on your own?' I asked.

Louise shook her head. 'There's too much competition in London. I'd have to work twice as hard to bring in clients. I'd never see Clara.'

'What about in Dublin?' Sophie wondered.

We all looked at one another in silence.

'That's a *great* idea,' I burst out. 'Come back and let Clara hang out with her cousins and her aunties and Gavin and her grandparents. I'd love it if you did. We could be single parents together.'

Louise looked shocked. 'I've never considered coming back to Dublin. I don't know why, I suppose because I consider London my home. I'm not sure, though. How much work would I get as a solo corporate lawyer? I'd have to find a niche market I could tap into. It wouldn't be easy – I don't have a profile in Dublin but I have a big one in London.'

'Don't rule it out, Lou,' I said. 'Just think about it. It would be so great to have you home, and really good for Clara to have close family around.'

'I'd love her to get to know her cousins and grandparents better, but I'm not sure about the career side of things in Dublin.'

'Louise, if anyone can make it work, you can. It probably won't be easy but when has that stopped you doing anything?' Sophie asked her.

'Tell you what, I'll look into it, put some feelers out and see what happens. Who knows? It could work.' She raised her glass to us.

'What would your ideal situation be?' I asked Sophie.

She looked down at her wine. 'To stop hating Jack. To stop blaming him for losing all our money when it wasn't really his fault. To be a good role model to Jess, which I now know I wasn't. I was filling her head with rubbish about money and diamonds. It was completely unintentional, but she was watching the way I lived my life and soaking it all in. I'm ashamed of some of the things I said to her. So I suppose that's one good thing to come out of this fiasco. I'm showing my daughter a more realistic version of life and teaching her proper values. I'm also enjoying being independent. I'm finding myself again. I'm stepping out of Jack's shadow, which is quite liberating, actually. The downside is that we're getting on incredibly badly. I wish we could get back to how we were. I do still love him, but there's a lot of resentment and anger in me and I need to let it go. It's poisonous and it's ruining our marriage.'

'What about you, Julie?' Louise asked.

I looked at my sisters. 'I used to wish for a bigger house, a nicer car, to be thinner, to have money in the bank, for the boys to be in school until six p.m. every night, and for Harry to get a big promotion and a huge salary rise. But now . . . all I want is my husband back. I want the man I married, my children's dad, my Harry to come home to me.'

'But what would you like for you – for yourself?' Sophie gently probed.

I sat back and thought about it. 'I think I'd like a part-time job and to make enough money so I can treat the kids to new bikes, pay for a family holiday every year, buy myself some new clothes and get a decent washing-machine.'

'What kind of a job?' Louise pushed me.

'I don't know. Something to do with books or writing. Maybe I could be a librarian . . . or write a blog or a column or something. I don't know. I'm not qualified to do much – I haven't worked for years – but I do love writing.' I blushed. It felt strange to admit how much my writing had meant to me these past few months. 'Anyway, they're all pie-in-the-sky dreams – who would hire me?'

'If I can get a job, anyone can,' Sophie said.

'I'll help you with your CV,' Louise offered.

I held up my glass. 'Thanks, guys. I honestly don't know what I'd do without you. Thank God I have sisters. You've been so supportive and helpful and kind and generous, coming here with me to hold my hand. I really appreciate it.'

Sophie raised her glass too. 'If it wasn't for you two, I'd be living on the street and back on Prozac. You've both helped me get back on my feet.'

Now Louise picked up hers. 'And you both helped me get through the first months of having a baby and managed to keep Mum from finding out Clara is the product of a one-night stand. So I'm really grateful too.'

'To sisters,' I said, and we clinked glasses.

Louise looked at her watch. 'Shit! It's seven forty – we need to go.'

I stood up, but my legs crumpled. Sophie and Louise caught me. They tucked an arm each around my waist and half carried me out to a taxi.

Ten minutes later we were sitting in a corner in the Café Le Petit Pont. We were the only people inside – everyone else was on the terrace enjoying the warm night. We had a perfect spot from which we could watch everyone outside without being seen.

'Do you think that's her?' Sophie asked, as a tall, willowy girl with short black hair and a lot of black eye makeup sat down at a table on her own. She was the only person not in a group. It was ten to eight.

'It can't be. She's too young and she's no *femme fatale*,' Louise said. The girl was wearing jeans and flip-flops with a plain white T-shirt.

'Oh, my God, *that's* her!' Sophie squealed.

We looked around and saw a stunning blonde woman of about thirty, walking a poodle, approach the café. She was wearing a red sundress. It was tight and really sexy and her pert, perfectly round boobs were peeping out of the top. She had red lipstick to match and really high red shoes. Every man in the café turned to stare at her. She sat down at a table on her own and plonked her pooch on the chair beside her.

There was a deathly silence at our table. 'I think I'm going to be sick,' I whispered.

Louise and Sophie grabbed my hands. 'She's nothing but a tart,' Louise hissed.

'She looks cheap,' Sophie huffed.

'She's trying way too hard,' Louise added.

'She's stunning,' I sobbed.

Sophie grabbed a napkin and tried to stop my tears. 'Don't cry yet.'

Then Harry walked around the corner and my heart stopped. He looked around. I could see he was nervous. When he clapped eyes on the sexy woman, he smiled shyly and walked towards her.

'*Noooo,*' I wailed.

He didn't sit down with the sex-bomb. He went over to the table behind her, where the girl in the jeans and T-shirt with the short hair was sitting.

'Bastard! She's young enough to be his daughter,' I said, jumping up and bolting out to the terrace, followed by my two sisters. 'HARRY!' I shouted, and all the people on the terrace turned to stare. 'YOU ARE A PIG! HOW DARE YOU CHEAT ON ME WITH THIS CHILD? WHAT'S WRONG WITH YOU? WHAT DID I DO TO DESERVE THIS? I WAS A GOOD WIFE AND I'VE PUT UP WITH A LOT OF SHIT, BUT NOT THIS, HARRY, *NOT THIS*. YOU ARE NOT GOING TO CHEAT ON ME WITH SOME FRENCH . . . PIXIE. I WON'T BE MADE A FOOL OF.'

Harry was paralysed. 'Julie? How did you –'

'HOW DID I KNOW?' I roared. 'I'LL TELL YOU EXACTLY HOW I KNEW. YOU'VE BEEN DISTANT AND GRUMPY AND SECRETIVE AND A REAL ARSEHOLE TO LIVE WITH, THAT'S HOW I KNEW, AND THEN I SAW THE TEXTS AND THE EMAILS.' I turned to the girl, shook my finger in her face and bellowed, 'OH, YES, MISS *CHRISTELLE*, I KNOW ALL ABOUT YOU AND YOUR SECRET MEET-ING AND I WANT YOU TO KNOW YOU'RE A HOME-WRECKER. DID HE TELL YOU HE HAS FOUR CHILDREN? FOUR CHILDREN UNDER THE AGE OF

FIVE? DID HE MENTION THAT? DID HE TELL YOU THAT I HAVE BEEN A LOYAL, LOVING AND DEVOTED WIFE – OK, I ADMIT I HAVE ALSO BEEN VOLATILE AND HORMONAL AT TIMES, BUT, COME ON, WHO WOULDN'T BE WITH TRIPLETS AND A TODDLER TO BRING UP?'

'*Triplés?*' the sex-bomb in the red dress said. '*Elle a bien dit triplés?*' she asked Louise.

'Yes, she has triplets and another small boy.'

'*Mon Dieu!*' she exclaimed. '*Et ça c'est la maîtresse de son mari?*' She looked surprised.

'Yes, that's his mistress,' Sophie told her.

'*Mais c'est un enfant!*' a man at another table huffed.

'Yes, she is very young – we're shocked too,' Sophie agreed.

Everyone in the café began to talk about the situation, and soon they were shouting, mostly at Harry. There was lots of '*idiot*' and '*imbécile*' and '*crétin*'. One man even said, '*Il est fou – sa femme est magnifique.*'

'Did you hear that, Julie?' Louise said. 'That man said you were magnificent.'

'*Merci*,' I said.

Harry grabbed me by the shoulders. 'Julie,' he said, trying to get my attention as the French people shouted their support to me and abuse at him. 'Julie! I can't believe you think I'm having an affair.'

'What would you like to call it, Harry? A liaison? A – a – *tryst*?'

'Christelle isn't my mistress.'

'Oh, my God, she's a prostitute?'

'I certainly am not.' Christelle was highly offended.

'JULIE!' Harry shouted to get my attention. 'Christelle is my daughter.'

My chin hit the floor. 'WHAT?'

'Daughter?' Louise and Sophie exclaimed.

'*Elle n'est pas sa maîtresse, elle est sa fille,*' the sex-bomb in the red dress informed the terrace.

'Ah.' They nodded, intrigued.

'DAUGHTER!' I stared at Harry and then at Christelle, who was glaring at me.

'Yes, you crazy woman. I'm Harry's daughter.'

I turned to Harry. 'But . . . how?'

'Nineteen years ago I spent my college summer holidays in New York and I had a relationship with an American girl. Christelle is the result. But I had absolutely no idea she existed until a few months ago when she tracked me down. Her mum moved from New York to Paris eight years ago, and when Christelle turned eighteen, she decided to find me.'

'*Je ne comprends pas.*' The sex-bomb tugged Louise's arm.

'Um, Harry had *le sexe avec une fille* when he was a teenager *et Christelle est le bébé de la fille.*'

'*Ah, d'accord.*' The lady in red translated for the others and they all threw their hands into the air, smiled and nodded.

'So you're not cheating on me?' I asked Harry.

'I would never cheat on you, Julie. I love you. I always told you I felt as if I'd punched above my weight when I married you.'

'You did. Julie's amazing,' Louise piped up.

'One of a kind. A gem,' Sophie added.

'Jesus, Harry,' I groaned, 'why didn't you tell me? I've been so upset – I've been heartbroken.'

'I'm sorry, I wanted to meet Christelle in person before telling you. I didn't want to land this on you without knowing what she was like and if she even wanted to meet my other kids. I wasn't sure how she'd react to it all.'

'I've been so miserable,' I bawled.

Harry wrapped his arms around me. 'Julie, you're my life, I'd never hurt you. I'm sorry about all this.' Then, turning to my sisters, he said sternly, 'And as for you two, I would have thought you'd have had the decency to give me the benefit of the doubt. How could you think I'd cheat on Julie?'

'The evidence against you was very damning,' Louise retorted.

'You've both known me for eighteen years – you must know I'd never hurt Julie. I was trying to protect her from this until I had it sorted out. I'm still reeling from the discovery myself.'

'If you'd been upfront and honest with her, there wouldn't have been any misunderstanding.' Louise wasn't one for backing down easily.

'But we're sorry,' Sophie added, ever the peacemaker. 'We're very sorry for doubting you. We know how much Julie means to you.'

While Harry turned back to hug me and kiss away my tears, Sophie and Louise introduced themselves to my new step-daughter.

'Hi, I'm Louise. I guess I'm your step-aunt.' Louise shook Christelle's hand. Sophie did the same. 'We're actually a fairly normal family most of the time,' she added.

I pulled away from Harry and looked at his daughter. 'I'm sorry. I've completely ruined your first meeting with your dad.'

She shrugged in that French way. 'I've waited a long time. I can wait a few more minutes. Besides, since I moved to France from the States, I'm used to drama. They thrive on it here.'

I reached over and hugged her. 'I'm Julie, Harry's insane wife. Welcome to the family.'

Everyone on the terrace clapped and cheered. It seemed that even the French were suckers for a happy ending.

38

Louise

We stayed in the café until three in the morning, talking, laughing, listening and, in Julie's case, crying. People kept buying us drinks and coming over to congratulate us and hear the details of the dramatic story. Harry refused to let go of Julie's hand all night. It would have melted the hardest heart to see them together.

Julie felt awful about causing a scene at Christelle's first encounter with her father, so we made a big fuss of our new step-niece and she turned out to be a pretty cool girl. She was very together, very independent, smart, bright and ambitious – in fact, she kind of reminded me of myself at that age. After the initial awkwardness we all got on like a house on fire, and Julie showed her new step-daughter pictures of the boys and insisted that she come and stay with them before she started college in three weeks' time. You could see Christelle was relieved that Julie was actually a lovely, warm, welcoming person and not the raving nutter she had first seemed to be.

I woke up early the next day, despite my hangover. My flight back to London wasn't until six that night. We sisters had planned to spend the day together, but Julie had gone back to Harry's hotel and Sophie was sleeping soundly beside me. I knew I couldn't wait until this evening to see my baby. I had never been in a different country from her. I had never left her on her own for a night. I felt too far away physically. I yearned to see Clara. I ached to hold her and kiss her chubby little cheeks.

I went into the bathroom and logged on to my computer to see if I could catch an early flight home. There was one at eleven. I booked it, threw my clothes into my bag and left Sophie a note explaining that I'd gone home early, that the hotel bill was paid and that I'd left her some spending money in her wallet.

I looked out of the taxi window as Paris whizzed by. The old me would have spent the morning in the Louvre or the Musée d'Orsay, then had a leisurely lunch and later gone to the ballet at the Opéra. But now all I wanted to do was go home and hang out on the couch with my baby girl. My heart pounded the whole way home. The closer I got to seeing her, the more emotional I became. I had never felt this way about a man. This love was in a whole different stratosphere.

I charged into the apartment, giving poor Agnes the fright of her life, as she was expecting me home much later. Clara was lying on her play mat, kicking her legs in the air. I swooped in and picked her up, nuzzling my face into her neck. I sat down with her on the couch and cried tears of utter joy, love and gratitude that life had given me this gift, this bundle of joy, this angel.

Agnes patted me on the back, kissed the top of my head and left, saying, 'You going to be great mummy.'

I spent the day playing with Clara, making her laugh, taking her for a walk, having a bubble bath with her, lying in bed together while I read her stories and she slapped the pages of the book. I wasn't lonely, I wasn't bored, I wasn't lost. Clara had made my apartment a home and filled my life in a way I could never have imagined. We were a team, a pair, a match, a couple. She was my soul-mate.

Over the next few weeks I investigated moving back to Dublin and opening up my own office. There appeared to be a niche for a securitization specialist, which was an area of corporate law that I was all too familiar with – I'd worked on mortgage-backed securitization for years. I decided that the best option was to try to head up my own department within a law firm. I'd have more security that way and none of the costs of starting up alone. I called the top five law firms in Dublin to discuss the possibility of setting up a department and was flattered when they all tried to head-hunt me. They had all heard of me, knew about my success at Higgins, Cooper & Gray and were very keen to have me work for them.

I had underestimated the legal field in Ireland. They had their finger very much on the pulse and knew all the movers and shakers in London. My reputation had preceded me and it was really refreshing to know that all those years of hard work had paid off and that I was considered a prize catch for the legal firms in Dublin. As a result, they were willing to match my current salary, which was a very welcome surprise to me. The move would not be a step down: it would be a new and exciting challenge and one over which I would have complete control.

After looking at lots of different options and interviewing with the five top firms, I decided to go with Price Jackson. They had offered me free rein and a generous budget to set up my own department, specializing in securitization. I would be in complete control of selecting my team. I made it very clear that I would often be working from home. Nothing had ever felt so right. I knew this was the best decision for both Clara and me.

In London, Clara only had me. Back in Dublin, she'd have a big extended family with cousins and grandparents, aunts and uncles. She had no father, so family was extra important, and I wanted her to have positive male role models in her life – Dad and Gavin, Harry and Jack would be her surrogate fathers.

I was dreading telling Alex I was leaving. He had mentored me from my first day at Higgins, Cooper & Gray, and had encouraged me and supported me over all the years. On the day I was due to hand in my notice, he called me into his office.

'Have a seat,' he said. 'As you know, Dominic behaved inappropriately in New York and is office-bound for the time being. He's going to have to prove he can be trusted to behave in a professional manner at all times and that's not going to happen overnight. Now, I need you to go to our sister office in Chicago for three weeks. There's a –'

'Alex,' I interrupted him. 'I can't go to Chicago for three weeks now or ever. I have a baby girl who needs me. She sees very little of me as it is and there is no way I could leave her for three weeks.' I took a deep breath. 'I'm very sorry to say that, after a lot of soul-searching, I've decided that my time at Higgins, Cooper & Gray is at an end.' A lump began to form in my throat. I was very sad to be leaving. This had been my whole life until Clara had come along.

Alex said nothing.

I cleared my throat. 'I've loved working here. It's been a privilege and a pleasure to have you as a mentor, and I owe you a deep debt of gratitude for all you've done for me over the last twenty years. I'm very sorry to be going, but I cannot keep working to the intensity and level that I have been with a baby at home. I tried, Alex, I really did. I really wanted it to work and I was sure I could make it happen. But I've discovered that I no longer want to live in the office. I no longer want to work harder and more diligently than everyone else. Having my daughter has changed me in ways I never thought possible and I can't fight it. I'm making myself and her miserable by trying to maintain this pace. For my happiness and hers, I need things to change.'

Alex smiled sadly. 'Oh, Louise, I thought if anyone could do it, you could. I saw how you struggled in the beginning, but you seemed to have worked everything out and got back into your stride. I believed you were on top of the situation. I'm very sorry to hear you're giving up on your career. You're so talented.'

'Oh, no, Alex, I'm not giving up. I'll never give up my job because I love what I do. I'm just changing the way I work. I'm moving back to Dublin to be close to my family and I'm going to set up a securitization department at a law firm there called Price Jackson.'

Alex reached over to shake my hand. 'I'm very glad to hear it. You'd be a great loss to the profession. Price Jackson are very fortunate to get you, Louise. I've immensely enjoyed watching you soar at this company. You're a bright, hard-working and loyal young woman. We'll miss you and your sharp legal mind.'

I fought back tears. 'Thank you, Alex, I appreciate that. I'll make sure everything's in order before I leave.'

'I know you will. You can pass any files that you don't manage to close by the time you leave to Dominic.'

'Dominic? I thought he was in legal Siberia.' I couldn't believe this.

'He is, but he can come in from the cold now that you're leaving. He did a very foolish thing, which I know from speaking to his father at golf last week he truly regrets. He's certainly delayed making senior partner by several years, but when all this dies down, if he's proven himself to have matured, we can review the situation.'

And there it was – the thing I could never compete with. Dominic was from an upper-crust family Alex admired and looked up to. He wanted to hang out playing golf in his posh club with Dominic's family. Dominic had an edge I'd never have, a safety net I couldn't create. It was time to go and set up my own department, be my own boss, hire my own staff and march to the beat of my own drum.

The news of my imminent departure spread like wildfire, and Meredith was the first to come and see me. 'Are you sure?' she asked, sitting down opposite me and getting straight to the point.

I nodded. 'Yes, I am. I can't do it any more, Meredith. I'm not happy. I feel guilty all the time. When I'm here I want to be with Clara, and when I leave early to see her before bedtime, I feel guilty for that too. Besides, I've always wanted to be my own boss, so this could work out very well.'

'I wish you'd stay. I need other women, other mothers, to shatter the glass ceiling with me. It's not easy being the only female senior partner.'

'I'll be breaking the ceiling, just in my own way, in my own time. I'm not giving up my career, I'm readjusting it to fit my daughter in. And, in a strange way, it's all fallen into place. I'm not even taking a salary cut – the Irish firm is paying me the same salary and I get to run my own securitization department.'

Meredith looked surprised. 'My God, that's great. And do you get to set your own hours?'

'More or less. They know me by reputation, so they're aware that I'm hard-working. When I told them I'd be working from home quite a bit, they were fine about it.'

Meredith sat back in the chair. 'Good for you. To be honest, Louise, I couldn't do this without my husband's support. He ferries Hermione to and from crèche every day, and when she's sick, he takes the day off work to look after her. I'm going to miss having you around as a fellow journeywoman, but you seem very happy and relieved, so your decision must be the right one for you and Clara.'

'I really think it is. Clara's only got one parent, so I really need to spend time with her – and she'll grow up with her cousins and grandparents around. I'll have a support network that I just don't have here.'

'And you need it. We working mums need support to be able to do what we do. It sounds like a great set-up – I'm tempted to move there myself.'

'No way! You have to keep flying the flag at this male-dominated firm. I'm sorry I won't be beside you – I tried, Meredith, I really did, but it just wasn't working.'

'Life's too short to make yourself miserable. Besides, it sounds like you're going to be a very big fish over there in Dublin.'

'It's a much smaller pond, but it'll be interesting and challenging, which is good – and lucrative, which is also important.'

Meredith grinned. 'Hell, yes! We don't do this for the good of our health.'

'Do you think women will ever be able to have it all, the way men do?'

'Yes – but only if we can park the guilt. The problem is, we're programmed to feel guilty about everything. Do you think a man feels guilty if he eats a cream cake? If he doesn't ring his mother for a week? If he gets drunk and raucous at the Christmas party? If he doesn't tuck his kids into bed every night? If he doesn't cook dinner for his kids or forgets to buy their favourite yoghurts? If he's ten minutes late to pick his kids up from a birthday party? No! Men don't feel guilty and it frees up their time and energy to focus on work.'

I nodded. 'I'd never really felt guilty about anything until I had Clara. Now guilt is ever-present in my life and it's exhausting.'

'We need to extract it from our DNA,' she said. 'Well, speaking of guilt, I need to go and do some work. Good luck, Louise. I'll miss you.'

I went to hug her. 'Good luck to you, too. Don't stop being a trail-blazer and watch out for the sharks coming up behind you.'

'I will.' Meredith walked back out into the corporate world we had both studied and worked so hard to succeed in. I was sure she'd end up as managing partner of the firm. I really hoped she would – we needed role models like her for our daughters to know that anything is possible.

Later that day, Dominic slithered into my office, smiling broadly. He had been keeping a very low profile since returning in shame from New York. I had barely seen him, which had been wonderful.

'Louise,' he said, throwing his arms up in the air in mock horror, 'I've just heard the news. I can't believe it. Is it true? Are you really leaving us?'

I continued working on my computer. 'Yes.'

'So you're moving back to the old sod.' He sat down in the chair opposite me.

'If you're referring to Dublin, yes, I am.'

'From the dizzy heights of London to the third largest firm in Dublin. It'll be quite a change.'

'Aren't you happy, Dominic, that with me out of the way there's a vacancy? Oh, sorry, I forgot. You screwed a client's daughter and lost the business – that's not quite senior-partner material, now, is it?'

Dominic's face reddened. 'We all make mistakes, Louise. Don't forget how furious Hanks and Alex were with your purchase-price fuck-up.'

'I think Hanks was probably slightly more annoyed with you for having sex with his baby girl.'

'She was eighteen.'

'Only just.'

Dominic crossed his legs slowly and sneered, 'Alex has got over it now. He played golf with my old man this weekend and said it was water under the bridge.'

I smiled at him. 'I wouldn't get too comfortable, Dominic. Alex reckons you've set yourself back a good five years. I hope Hanks's daughter was worth it.'

He leant forward in his chair. 'Don't you find it sad that after all those years of study and hard work you're ending up back in Dublin changing nappies? It's a big come-down.'

I continued typing. 'I don't see running my own department as a come-down. Call me crazy, but a come-down to me would be something like getting sent home from New York in disgrace for sleeping with a client's daughter and having that client break your nose.'

Dominic sighed dramatically. 'Ah, Louise, I'll miss our lively banter.'

'Me too. It's always such a joy to spend time with you.'

'Well, I'd better go and do some work. I'll need to clear my files so I can deal with your clients when you go home to push a pram around.'

'Do me a big favour and try not to have sex with any of their children. Keep it in your pants, there's a good boy.' I grinned as he stormed out of my office.

Later, when I'd tucked Clara into bed, I called Julie for an update on what was going on at home. Christelle had come to stay with them for a week and I was dying to know how it was going.

'How's your new daughter?' I asked.

'Great,' Julie gushed. 'I swear, Lou, she's a really lovely person. She's not at all needy or awkward. She arrived yesterday to the mayhem that's our home and just slotted in. She seems to like the madness. She said that, being an only child, she'd always wished for siblings and now she has four lunatics.'

'What do the boys think of their sister?'

'They don't really understand the sister part. I knew they'd get confused if I tried to explain that she was their half-sister so I just said she was a very special friend who's like a big sister. But the brilliant thing is that they love her and do everything she says. She tells them what to do in her gorgeous French-American accent and they obey. She even gave them their bath tonight and there was no flooding. I'm thinking of asking her to move in permanently. And Tom just follows her around staring at her adoringly because she reads him books and pays him attention, which he so rarely gets. He's completely besotted with her.'

'What about Harry?'

'He's still a bit shifty. He's not sure how to be a dad to a teenage girl he's never known. It's a difficult role to know how to fill, but he's getting better. And the fact that the rest of us get on well with her makes it much easier for him. It's actually lovely to have another female in the house.'

'I'm thrilled it's working out.'

'How are you? Did you tell work you're leaving yet?'

'Today.'

'Oh, my God, what did Alex say?'

'He was really nice about it – he said he'd miss me, was sorry to see me go and all that. I'm so relieved it's over. I was dreading it. But now it's out and everyone knows. There's no going back. I hope I've made the right decision. It was really hard telling Alex – I actually felt quite emotional.'

'Hardly surprising. It's been your life for twenty years. But you *have* made the right decision. It's going to be brilliant having you home and Clara will love having cousins to play with. What did Dominic say?'

'He tried to wind me up but I nipped him in the bud. I won't be sorry to see the back of him.'

'The great thing about your new job is that you get to hire your own staff, so no more snakes like Dominic.'

'Alleluia.'

'How's Clara?'

'Angelic, as always. By the way, have Mum and Dad met Christelle?'

'Oh, yes. They had us over for lunch today – and this will give you a laugh . . .' Julie told me what had happened.

When Mum opened the door, she took Christelle's hand, led her into the lounge and shouted loudly and deliberately, 'Welcome to Eye-ur-land. I hope the journey was not too long.'

'Mum!' Julie tried to get her attention.

'Hold on, Julie, I'm talking to Christelle. Paris is a very bee-ooo-ti-ful city.'

Christelle looked at Julie. 'Is your mum OK?' she whispered.

'Mum!' Julie snapped.

'*Bonjour*, Christelle.' Dad came into the room wearing a red beret. '*Je suis le papa de Julie. Je suis un* big admirer of *la France. Allez les* blues.'

Christelle smiled politely. '*Bonjour.*'

'*Tu es très* welcome in our *maison.*' Dad looked very pleased with himself.

'*Merci,*' Christelle said.

'*Je pense que* Sébastien Chabal is the best rugby player *dans le monde.*'

Harry arrived in from the car with the boys. 'Why is your dad speaking bad French to Christelle?'

'I've been trying to tell them,' Julie explained.

'*Voulez-vous un* cheese puff?' Mum held out a plate to Christelle.

'*Non, merci,*' she said.

'Mum, Dad,' Julie said loudly, 'Christelle spent the first ten years of her life in New York. Her English is perfect.'

'Well, why on earth didn't you say so?' Mum fumed.

'You might have let us know.' Dad took off his beret.

'Why don't we eat?' Julie suggested.

'Did someone say food?' Gavin came in.

'Nice of you to get up,' Dad said, tapping his watch. 'Until I retired I'd half a day's work done by this time.'

'You must be Christelle.' Gavin ignored Dad and went over to shake her hand.

'Yes, hi.'

'Welcome to the family. They're all slightly mad, as you may have noticed, but they don't bite.'

She giggled. Harry glared at Gavin.

'I've made beef bourguignon for our guest,' Mum said.

'I'm very sorry, Mrs Devlin, but I'm a vegetarian,' Christelle announced.

'Me too,' Gavin said, as Harry choked on his wine.

'Since when?' Julie asked.

'Since ages.'

'Was that not a burger I saw you stuffing down your neck yesterday?' Dad smirked at his son.

'Yes – a veggie burger.'

'Gavin seems to go through phases of not eating meat, depending on whose company he's keeping,' Dad told Christelle.

'What do you do? Are you a student?' Christelle asked.

'Yes, Gavin, what is it that you do exactly?' Dad asked.

'I'm in the process of landing a job in climate change.'

They all roared laughing – well, everyone except Christelle and Gavin.

'What does looking for a job imply to you?' Dad asked Christelle. 'Because to Gavin here, it seems to mean posting out a few CVs and then sitting around on your arse waiting for the phone to ring.'

'Well, you do have to wait around to hear back from companies,' Christelle said. 'Actually, I'm about to start a science degree. I'm hoping eventually to work on alternative energies.'

'Wow! That is so cool. Alternative energy is where it's at. I spent the summer in London protesting the new terminal at Heathrow and everyone was talking about how alternative energies are the only way forward.'

'Really? I'd love to hear more about that protest.' Christelle looked impressed.

'Why don't we go for a drink later? I'll tell you all about it,' Gavin suggested.

'No way,' Harry hissed in Julie's ear. 'Do something! Gavin is her uncle.'

'He isn't related to her,' Julie pointed out.

'That won't be possible,' Harry said loudly. 'Christelle is staying in with us tonight.'

'Cool. I'll call around. We could babysit and let you guys go out if you like.'

'Great,' Julie said.

'No, thank you. We'll be staying in.' Harry was adamant.

'Harry,' Christelle turned to her father, 'I'm not going to have sex with him. I just want to hear about the protest.'

Dad, Harry, Mum and Julie spluttered into their drinks while Gavin looked disappointed.

Julie and I roared laughing at that bit.

'You know the French, Lou – they're so upfront about sex. None of us knew where to look. I thought Dad was going to have a heart attack.'

'I wish I'd been there.'

'Harry's turned out to be really strict. He won't let Christelle out of his sight.'

'Poor her. By the way, how's Sophie?'

'I haven't seen her in a couple of weeks. I spoke to her on the phone and she sounded OK. Jack still has no job, which is hard, but she seems to be doing really well – she said she made lots of commission this month, which is great, and her stuff is still selling on eBay. She's made forty-two thousand on it.'

'Good for her.'

'She's looking at apartments to rent. Apparently one has come up in the building next to your block. She's thinking about taking it so she'd be nearby to help you settle back in and for Jess to spend time with Clara.'

'I'd love that.' It'd be great having Sophie so close by. 'Well, I'd better go.'

'OK, talk soon.'

I hung up. That had been the first conversation I'd had with Julie in which none of her kids was interrupting her or trying to kill themselves. Christelle must be a miracle-worker.

39

Sophie

Quentin was waiting for me when I got into the office, hopping from one foot to the other. 'Thank God you're here! We're in deep trouble.'

'What's happened?'

'Six of the girls have called in with food poisoning. They all went to that new Japanese restaurant in town, ate raw fish and spent the night bloody well throwing up. None of them can do the show in Harvey Nicks today. And you know what that PR bitch Veronica is like. I do *not* want to lose the account. Parkers PR pays very well.'

I put my hand on his arm. 'First, you need to calm down. We'll sort this out. Who was booked for the show?'

'Natasha, Alicia, Nadia, Rose, Georgia and Chloë. They're by far the best runway girls we have,' he wailed.

His mobile rang. 'Shit! It's her – it's Veronica from Parkers! What'll I say?'

I grabbed his phone. 'Good morning, Beauty Spot model agency.'

'I want to speak to Quentin.'

'He's not available. My name is Sophie Devlin. I'm one of the bookers. Can I help?'

'I want to confirm that your girls will be here in fifteen minutes for fittings and a run-through of tonight's show,' she snapped.

Quentin was flapping his arms and hyperventilating. I decided to be direct. 'I'm very sorry, Veronica, but the six girls we booked for you are out with food poisoning.'

'*What?* Are you joking? Do you have any idea how big this show is? I will never –'

'Veronica,' I cut across her, calmly but firmly, before she blew a fuse. 'Parkers PR and Harvey Nichols are our most valued clients. If you can give me one hour, I will personally deliver six models to you. I'll stay with them all day, make sure they know the running order backwards and help dress them for tonight's show. In addition to which we will, of course, be giving you a fifteen per cent discount for the forty-five-minute inconvenience caused this morning. Does that seem acceptable to you?'

'Well, I'm not sure I –'

I jumped in: 'Because if it is, then I'd better go and pick up the girls right now so as not to waste a minute more of your valuable time.'

'You have one hour,' she said, and hung up.

Quentin hugged me. 'You were amazing, so strong and assertive and calm. My God, Sophie, where did it come from?'

'I don't know.' I laughed. 'Since Jack lost his job and I became the breadwinner, I feel like this protective tigress who has to save her family or something.'

'Well, I love the new arse-kicking you. You handled that witch so well.'

'Now I just need to go and get six models out of bed, dressed, into my car and over to Harvey Nichols in an hour. Come on, Quentin, you start calling them and I'll drive over to their houses.'

I scribbled down their addresses and grabbed my keys.

Jess was due to start in a new national school in ten days' time. She had been very brave about it. Jack and I had broken the news to her together and I had set up an appointment for her to meet her new teacher. Jack had taken Jess to the meeting, answered her questions and put her mind at ease. He'd even met a mum in the playground whose daughter was starting in the same class and had set up a play-date for Jess to get to know the little girl.

I was impressed with how he was handling being a full-time dad. He was so good with Jess now. They had fallen into a nice rhythm and each day they had their little routine. He had made her less scared of everything, and under his care she had grown in confidence. Instead of always saying, 'Get down, you'll hurt yourself,' like I did, Jack let Jess climb walls and go on the big slide in the park. He'd take her to the beach and run into the freezing sea with her, then sit on the damp sand making sandcastles with her for hours. Things I had never done.

I still occasionally felt a pang of jealousy when Jess told me about all the fun she and Daddy had had that day while I was at work. Jack was getting all this time with our daughter while I worked long hours to pay the bills. But, deep down, I knew this was a good thing for Jess and Jack. They needed to get close. They needed to spend time together. I just hoped he'd get a job soon so that the pressure on me to earn and budget, scrimp and save would be relieved a bit. I have to admit I missed having money. I missed being able to shop and eat out and even go to the cinema without having to save for a month. But I was enjoying work and I liked having my own money and independence. Even if Jack did get a job I wasn't going to give it up.

Jack and I were still not getting on very well. So far his networking hadn't generated a job and he had spent more than three hundred euros on it. Nowadays that was a huge amount of money to us. So, when he came to me and said he had to go to London for a job interview, I wasn't happy.

'Why can't you do it over the phone?'

'Because they want a face-to-face. It's important – I think this could be the one. I've a good feeling about this company. They're a very well-established fund and I know one of the main guys there.'

'How much will it cost?'

'I can get flights for eighty euros return, but I'll need money for the tube and taxis and to buy them a drink if need be.'

'We can't afford taxis. I walk everywhere or get the bus. You'll have to do the same.'

'I will, but if my flight is delayed or the guys take me for a nice lunch, I'd like to be able to pay for the cab.'

I sighed. 'OK, but I need money for Jess's uniform and she needs new shoes too. Please try to keep your spending to a minimum.'

'I always do,' Jack muttered.

The night before he was due to fly to London for his interview, his brother phoned. He hadn't told his family anything and initially I'd agreed with that decision. They had never been nice to us and I didn't want them belittling him any more than they did already. I knew Jack was embarrassed and ashamed. They had always dismissed what he did, and now if they found out his company had blown up in a Ponzi scheme, they'd never stop going on about it.

Not telling them had been easy because they had never called into our house so they had no idea we had moved. They only phoned occasionally, so Jack had just told them everything was fine. We only ever saw them at Christmas, on Jess's birthday or when his father or Roger wanted us to buy a table at a fundraising ball for their hospital.

'Hi, Roger,' I heard Jack say. 'Oh, right – is it this year? . . . I see . . . A party sounds like a good idea . . . You want to go splits on the bill . . . Uhm, OK. When do you need the cheque by? . . . Oh, tomorrow. I could have done with a bit of notice . . . Twelve hundred euros isn't a drop in the ocean to anyone, Roger . . . I'm not saying I won't pay for our parents' anniversary party . . . I just think a few days' notice would have been nice . . . Of course they deserve it . . .'

My head snapped up. I looked at Jack. He was pacing the room. He caught my eye. 'No way,' I mouthed. 'We're broke. You have to tell him.'

Jack shook his head and turned away. 'I won't have it for tomorrow . . . Sorry, Roger, I just . . . No, I'm not being difficult . . . I know they've been great parents . . . I want to give them a good party too . . . It's not . . . I can't . . .'

I watched Jack struggle as Roger demanded money from him.

How dare he call and put Jack under pressure? How dare he insist that the money be given the next day? How dare he only ever call when he wanted something? The years of seeing him belittle Jack boiled up inside me. I grabbed the phone.

'Hi, Roger, it's Sophie. Here's the thing. I need you to stop harassing Jack for money because we don't have any. We've lost everything – house, cars, paintings, jewellery, clothes, the lot. Our house was repossessed and we don't have a penny to our names, so instead of giving your brother a hard time, why don't you try and be supportive for once in your life?'

'What? But I had no idea,' Roger blustered. 'Why on earth didn't he call? Was I supposed to guess? How could –'

I cut straight across him: 'Of course you had no idea. You only ever call Jack when you're looking for something – money for your hospital charity balls, money for a new machine for the obstetrics department, money to pay for your parents' parties or to tell him about some new promotion you've had. You never, ever call him to see how he is. To ask how he's doing. And all he ever does is support you, tell you how delighted he is when you do well, cheer on Grace when she wins her chess competitions and fork out money over and over again whenever you come asking. Well, Roger, it's time for you to be supportive. Do you think you can manage to get your head out of your arse for five minutes and be nice to your brother? My family have helped us out – my family have given us everything they could. They've given us the roof over our heads and helped us slowly get back on our feet. Because that's what family does, Roger. They care for each other. They don't just use each other for donations or praise.'

'How was I to know? You should have called me. Of course I would have helped out. How did this happen? Where did all the money go? I always said he was excessive with his spending – he should have put some away in solid investments instead of spending all his earnings like a madman.'

'Jack's fund invested in something that crashed. So did lots of the other top hedge funds in New York.'

'Dad and I told him it was a very unstable business. We urged him to get a steady profession, something proper, solid, not flighty hedge-fund management.'

'Well, he really doesn't need to hear that now, thank you, Roger. We all know that you doctors think you're demi-gods, but let me tell you what I've found out over the last few months. It doesn't matter what you do, how many lives you save or how much money you make, it's how you share it with others when they're down that matters, and Jack is the most generous person I know. When he had money he loved nothing more than to spend it on his family and my family. He never said no when you came looking for money for your hospitals and charity events. When you had five tables of ten people left last year and the ball was going to be a disaster, Jack paid for them all and filled them with our friends. He always made you look good by buying expensive auction items at those charity balls – even though all you've ever done is sneer at his profession and consider your own to be far superior. I can tell you, Roger, that Jack is a much nicer human being than you'll ever be.'

'Calm down, Sophie. Now that we know Jack's lost all his money, of course we'll help. How much do you need? Would five thousand be enough?'

'Thanks for the offer, but I'm working and Jack's going to London for an interview tomorrow. He'll probably get the job because he has a very good reputation in the business.'

'Put my brother on,' Roger barked.

I handed the phone to Jack, who was beaming at me. 'Hi, Roger . . . Didn't want to trouble you with it . . . Bit of a mess . . . All coming together now. Sophie wasn't being rude, she's just had a stressful few months. She's been amazing, I'm so proud of her . . . She's working full-time and supporting us all . . . No need to write a cheque . . . Thanks for the offer . . . Yes, I'm going to continue trading . . . No, I don't think it's irresponsible . . . I'm actually very good at what I do . . . Just one bad decision . . . Bad timing . . . No, there's no need to call in, we're doing fine now, the worst is over . . . No, I'll phone Dad and tell him myself . . . OK, fine, I'll let you go and help Grace practise her chess for the competition . . . 'Bye for now.' Jack hung up and exhaled loudly.

I knew I'd gone too far. 'Sorry, I just lost my temper. He's such an arrogant pig. How did you turn out so normal from a family like that?'

He grinned. 'There's no need to apologize. I liked being defended. Feel free to do it any time.'

'Well, there was no way I was going to let him bad-mouth you or your job or any of the choices you've made. He's such an intellectual snob it makes my blood boil.'

Jack sat down beside me on the couch. 'I should have told them.'

'Why? They're useless. All they would have done was make you feel bad.'

'They're still my family. I've been lying to them for months. God, now I have to tell my father – and you know what he'll be like.'

I patted his arm. 'I'll call him for you. I have no problem telling him what's happened and giving him a piece of my mind while I'm at it. Family is so important, and your father has been so unsupportive of you your whole life just because you weren't as intellectual as Roger. It makes me sick. And your mother's a bloody doormat.'

'Well, you're certainly not.' He chuckled.

I giggled. 'Was I awful? Did I make a show of myself?'

He kissed my cheek. 'No, you were magnificent. I've never been prouder of you.' He looked at me intently, then leant over to give me a deeper kiss, and for the first time in months, I didn't push him away.

Two days later a breathless Jack called me from London – he'd got the job with a big UK-based hedge fund. He was going to be working in London from Monday to Thursday and from home on Fridays. It wasn't ideal, but it was a job and it paid quite well. It was a low basic salary with high performance-related incentives, but it would be a huge relief to have two salaries coming in. We would be able to breathe and even go out for dinner to celebrate.

I called Louise the next day to tell her. '. . . so I wanted you to be the first to know because you've been so amazing to us. Honestly, Lou, I don't know what we would have done without your advice and your generosity in giving us your apartment. You're the best sister.' My voice quivered.

'Hey, come on, Sophie, you would have done the same for me. That's what sisters are for. Besides, you can pay me back by telling me where to go and what to do with Clara when I get home. I need information – the best doctors, playgroups, parks, the best agencies to hire childminders from, the best schools, places to buy girls' clothes, kid-friendly restaurants, the works. I have no idea where to go in Dublin with a child, so I'll need your help.'

'I'll have a list typed up for you when you get home. I'm having Mini Maid come in to spring-clean the apartment when we move out on Saturday so it'll be pristine for you when you get back next week.'

'You didn't need to do that.'

'Now that Jack's got a job, I'm allowing myself to spend a little more.'

'What's your new place like?' she asked.

'It's nice, actually. Two bedrooms, a lovely big sunny living room and a small kitchen that fits a table and three chairs, which is all we need. I've just booked Jess into after-school care until four every day. And I asked Quentin this morning if it was OK for me to leave at four from Monday to Thursday if I work through lunch. He's fine with it and on Fridays, when Jack's working from home, I can work late.'

'It sounds like you have it all organized.'

'Well, I had to sort it out this morning. We move into the new apartment this weekend and Jess starts school on Monday.'

'Any update on Gavin trying to get Christelle into bed?' Louise asked.

'I slagged Harry about it and he got really pissed off. He's taking his fatherly duties very seriously.'

'Julie told me he flipped when he saw Gavin flirting with Christelle.'

'Apparently nothing happened, and now that she's back in Paris, they're on Facebook to each other all the time. Gavin keeps saying he's always wanted to go to Paris so he might pop over and visit her. Dad said the only place he was popping was down to Tesco to pack shelves if he didn't get a job soon. He's had a few interviews, but nothing's come of them yet.'

'Something will turn up – all that hard-core protesting will stand to him. It actually reads well on his CV. I beefed it up a bit and worded it to make him look very committed and passionate. Well, I'd better go – I'm in the middle of packing up twenty years of belongings. I'll see you next week, neighbour.'

'Are you excited about moving?'

'Excited and nervous.'

'Well, we're all thrilled you're coming back. It'll be great.'

On my way home from work the next day I felt lighter, freer, less burdened. Now that Jack had a job, things were going to be easier. I was swinging my arms and enjoying the end-of-summer sun when I passed a boutique I used to shop in. I couldn't afford anything in it, but I stopped to admire a dress in the window that was way out of my new price range and saw a familiar face peering out at me. It was Victoria. Since Jack had lost his job she had phoned into my voicemail twice and texted me three times. She'd never invited me over or asked to meet me. Initially I was hurt and then I realized I didn't miss her.

I took a deep breath, opened the door of the boutique and went in. Saskia was there as well. They were both golden brown from a summer in the Spanish sun. I was pasty from a summer in rainy Dublin. They were trying on full-length ballgowns. I was wearing a high-street dress I'd bought for twenty-five euros.

'Hi, girls,' I said brightly. 'How are you? Long time no see.'

Saskia came over and pecked me on the cheek. 'Oh, Sophie, I'm so sorry about your financial difficulties.' She whispered the last part, repeating word for word the only text she had sent me.

'How are you?' Victoria placed her hand on my arm and tilted her head to the side, as if she was talking to someone who had recently lost a loved one.

'Great, thanks.' I beamed. 'So, are you getting new dresses for a ball?'

'Well, the Pink Ribbon Ball is coming up in two weeks,' Victoria said.

'Oh, yes, of course, that'll be fun. It's always a great night. Last year was a hoot.'

'I was going to invite you to be at our table, but then I thought it would be too awkward for you to see everyone after what happened.' Victoria sighed.

'Jack's company went bust. It happens to people all the time. I don't feel awkward at all,' I said loudly.

'Oh – well, I just assumed you would.' Victoria examined herself in the mirror.

'Is it true you're working now?' Saskia asked, round-eyed.

'Yes! I'm a booker at my old modelling agency. It's fantastic. I'm really busy and I love it.' I was determined to smother them with positivity. 'We live in a rented two-bedroom apartment five minutes from here. Jess is starting at the local national school next week and Jack is going to be working in London for a while. I think that's pretty much all my news.'

'Poor Jess must be devastated not to be going back to Mrs Holland's school,' Victoria said. 'Those national schools can be very crowded.'

'Actually, she's fine about it and the national schools are streets ahead of the private schools academically,' I replied. The cow wasn't going to make me feel bad about sending my girl to a national school. 'What's new with you guys?'

'We're just back from Marbella – it was such fun. Everyone came down this year,' Saskia said, and then she blushed. 'Sorry, Sophie, I mean everyone except you guys.'

'Sounds great,' I said.

'Now Jack has a job, I presume you'll give up work?' Victoria turned to admire her backless dress in the mirror.

'Are you mad? I love earning my own money and not relying on a man to buy me things. I could never stop work again. I like the security of it – I like being a person in my own right and not just Jack's wife. Seriously, girls,' I winked, 'you should try it.'

Victoria glared at me. 'You've changed your tune. You always said you loved not having to work and having a husband who earned lots of money so you could buy fabulous clothes.'

'Yes, I did, and I'm ashamed of myself. I got carried away with it all. I was an idiot and a really bad role model for Jess.'

'There's nothing wrong with being happy that your husband is successful and enjoying a nice lifestyle, Sophie,' she snapped.

'No, there isn't. Neither is there *any* shame in your husband losing his job and you having to go back to work to support your family. Well, I'd better go. By the way, Victoria, I don't think that colour does anything for you – it's very ageing. *Ciao*.' I left the shop and laughed the whole way down the street.

How had I ever been friendly with silly women like them? I must have been a bit brain-dead myself. Despite all the misery and shock and upset that losing our money had caused us, I preferred the person I was now. My life was more honest, more realistic, fuller, more equal and personally fulfilling. I liked the new me, the straight-talking, no-bullshit, upfront me. I had spent most of my life sitting on the fence, avoiding confrontation, peacemaking, ducking out of awkward conversations, changing the subject if people began to argue, not thinking my opinion mattered very much because I was just a model and then just a housewife. But now I was a working woman, supporting my family, paying the rent, putting food on the table, and my opinion did matter. I felt strongly about lots of things and I was no longer afraid to say it, no longer afraid to show my emotions. I was, finally, no longer afraid of being imperfect.

40

Julie

I now have a daughter. How weird is that? Paris was the most draining, emotional, exhausting, devastating, wonderful, happy and exhilarating weekend of my life. I went from thinking my husband was cheating on me to finding out I had a step-daughter in the space of about twenty seconds. The relief and joy of discovering that Harry, my Harry, wasn't a two-timing snake! I felt the weight of the world lift off my shoulders. We even got a standing ovation from the terrace when the translation of the situation was complete.

Louise and Sophie were amazing. They were my rocks, my support group, my therapists, my best friends . . . I couldn't have got through those last few weeks without them. Sitting in that bar in Paris, confessing to each other what we really wanted in life, had been really special. We'd never been so open or honest with each other and we'd never been closer. I'd always appreciated them, but the older you get, the more you realize that family is the most important thing and that blood really does run thicker than water. Those two women were my best friends in the world and they'd do anything for me, just like I'd do anything for them.

And Harry . . . It was like we were teenagers again. We couldn't keep our hands off each other. The idea of losing what we had had shown us how much we loved each other and how lucky we were. Harry was really worried about how I'd react to Christelle, but it was fine. She was an adult; she lived in Paris; she was studying there; she didn't want to move in with us; she didn't want Harry to move to France; she just wanted to get to know him. And the best part was that she was a lovely girl and I got on really well with her.

When she came to stay for a week she was brilliant with the kids and it was lovely to have female company in the house. The triplets were in awe of her. She has that kind of rock-chick look – her nose is pierced and she wears lots of black eyeliner and T-shirts with safety pins in them. The boys thought she was very cool and a little bit scary. They did exactly what she told them and she even babysat one night for us, although Harry insisted we went home after one drink because Gavin had called over to hang out with Christelle.

'Harry,' I said, 'they're just chatting.'

'Julie, I was a twenty-three-year-old boy once and I met a girl I "chatted to" and Christelle is the result of that.'

'They're not going to have sex on our couch when they know we could come in at any moment.'

'It only takes five minutes,' Harry said. 'I'm not having my daughter pregnant by her step-uncle.'

I giggled. 'When you put it like that, it sounds very *Jerry Springer*.'

'Drink up, we're going home.'

'Harry, you have to relax – she's eighteen.'

'Look, until recently I didn't have a daughter. Now I do, I have no idea how to behave. But I know one thing for sure. She's not going to get pregnant on my watch.'

When we got home, Gavin was sitting on the couch beside Christelle. They both had all their clothes on. No ruffled hair, no lipstick marks, nothing. They were watching *An Inconvenient Truth* and debating climate change.

Harry looked around suspiciously. I didn't know what he was looking for – a bra? Boxer shorts? 'What are you up to then?' he asked.

'We're just talking about how climate change isn't a political issue but a moral one and we can't ignore it,' Christelle said, and Gavin nodded.

'Well, it's time Gavin went home.' Harry motioned for him to get up.

'But the movie's not over,' Gavin complained.

'Take the DVD with you,' Harry said.

'There's only ten minutes left, Harry,' Christelle pointed out.

'It's almost eleven o'clock – time for bed.'

'I'm eighteen, not twelve,' Christelle reminded her father.

'Let them watch it.' I dragged Harry out of the room.

He spent the next ten minutes with his ear glued to the door.

'What do you think you're going to hear? Grunting?' I smirked.

'Ssh, I can't hear.'

The door opened and Harry fell into the TV room.

Gavin chuckled. 'Seriously, dude, I'm hardly going to try and have sex with your daughter when you're sitting in the next room.'

Harry hustled him out of the door and came back in.

Christelle turned to him, hands on hips. 'Come on, Harry, I'm not some innocent virgin – I know how to look after myself. Gavin is a cool guy, but I don't feel sexual towards him. If I do decide to have sex with someone while I'm here in Ireland, I'll tell you so you won't have to waste your time hiding behind doors. I know you're trying to protect me, but it's a little bit late for that. *Bonne nuit.*' She headed off to bed.

I patted his shoulder. 'Close your mouth, Harry, you'll catch a fly.'

'Is that the way eighteen-year-old girls talk?'

'Not any I know, but the French are more open about sexuality and sex than we are. They're miles ahead of us in that regard, so she was probably brought up being upfront about it.'

'She's not to meet any boys while she's here. I don't want her feeling "sexual" towards anyone until she goes home to her mother. Jesus, Julie, thank God we have boys – I can't handle this at all.'

'Boys do seem to be more straightforward,' I agreed.

'Come on, let's go to bed. I'm worn out worrying about Christelle and she's only been here three days.'

'Too worn out for sex?' I grinned.

'Did you just offer me sex?'

I nodded.

'Without me having to get you drunk, bribe you or beg?'

I nodded.

'I think I could rise to the occasion.' He whooped.

A couple of days later, Marian called in. I hadn't seen her in almost a week, which was really unusual. She was alone, which was also unusual, as she always had at least one or two children with her.

'Give me a large drink.' She threw herself into a kitchen chair.

'It's eleven, will a brandy-coffee do?'

'Fuck the coffee. Just give me the brandy.'

'What happened?' I handed her a glass.

She knocked back the contents. 'I've spent the last week getting my mother moved into a home and I've just left her there,' she said.

I sat down beside her. 'Was it awful?'

'Horrendous. It was the first time she'd left the house in thirty years. She was completely hysterical. The people from the nursing home were brilliant. They were really gentle and reassuring, but they had to sedate her to get her out. They brought her in an ambulance and I raced ahead and put the final things into her room. I'd spent the week making it look like her bedroom at the house. Same paint, same curtains, same duvet, same towels in the bathroom, same bathmat. Today I set out her personal things in the same places and made up her bed in the sheets she likes, put the picture of my dad on her bedside locker and hung her clothes up before she arrived.'

'What happened when the sedative wore off?' I asked.

'She was OK. She knew it was different, but she couldn't really figure out why. She's got dementia now, so her memory is kind of banjaxed anyway. Once she saw all her things were there, she was fine. I got her a room with a window that looks out on to a road, so I left her sitting in the same chair looking out of the window, waiting for Dad. And you know what she said to me when I was leaving? "Don't worry, Marian, he'll be home soon."'

'That's so sad.'

'Tell me about it, but I have to say – and I know this is going to sound harsh – I'm so relieved she's in that nursing home. Every time I called into her at the house, I thought I'd find her dead on the floor. At least now she's safe. I was finding it hard cooking her meals and doing her cleaning every day as well as looking after the kids. I was going a bit mad with it all.'

'You've had so much to deal with – this is a really good thing and it'll take a lot of the pressure off you.'

Christelle walked in.

'Marian, this is Christelle, Harry's daughter.'

'You're a ringer for Debbie Harry with black hair.'

'I love Debbie Harry.' Christelle smiled.

'Well, you could be her daughter.'

'CHRISTELLE,' the boys roared, 'CAN WE COME OUT NOW?'

'Not yet. You need to count to one hundred,' she shouted back.

'What are you playing?' I asked.

'Hide and seek.'

'Even Tom?' He never played: he got bored after three seconds.

'Yes, he was very enthusiastic.'

'And you're making the triplets count to a hundred?' Marian laughed. 'You're a genius. How'd you do it?'

'I told them that when I was naughty my mother pierced my nose with this ring and tied me with a rope to my bedpost. And that's what happens in France if you don't do what you're told.'

'Hard-core. I love it.'

I wasn't sure how thrilled I was. It was a bit frightening for them. I didn't want them having nightmares.

As if she was reading my mind, Christelle said, 'Don't worry, Julie, they know I'm joking – kind of.'

'Do you have any rock-chick friends in Paris who want to come and live in Dublin and look after – or should I say terrify – children?

I need an au pair and I want a really scary one to discipline my kids. Do any of your friends have mad tattoos on their faces or anything?' Marian asked.

'Let me think about it and get back to you,' my step-daughter said.

'ONE HUNDRED!' the boys roared in unison.

'I'd better go.' Christelle left to go and play with the boys.

'Julie, she's a legend,' Marian said. 'Why the hell couldn't Greg have got someone pregnant when he was a student? Useless git.'

'Well, it wasn't so great when I thought Harry was having an affair,' I reminded her.

'I know, but you've had a good result. You lost weight, you cut your hair, which turned out nice, thanks to my hairdressing skills, and you've inherited a super and scary nanny.'

'I suppose when you put it like that . . .' I laughed.

Marian got up and put on her coat. 'I have to shave my legs. It's Greg's birthday so he'll need his birthday shag. See you tomorrow.'

A week later, Christelle had gone back to France and the triplets were starting their first day at big school. After much chasing, shouting, wrestling and threatening, they were finally lined up, dressed in their new uniforms – grey trousers, white shirt, navy jumper and red tie. They looked adorable.

I had been waiting for this moment since the minute I'd found out I was having triplets and everyone had kept saying, 'You won't see daylight for five years'; 'You won't come up for air for five years'; 'You'll only get your life back when they go to proper school.' Now here we were. The day had finally arrived and I felt sad, nostalgic, emotional and guilty for having wished it would come so soon.

I crouched down to take a photo. 'Say cheese.'

Liam stuck his tongue out, Leo crossed his eyes and Luke did bunny ears behind Leo's head.

'Well, boys,' Harry said, coming into the kitchen in his suit, 'this is a big day. Your first day in real school. Are you excited?'

'I hate school,' Leo complained.

'It's so boring,' Luke moaned.

'I want to go back to bed,' Liam whined.

'Well, this is a very proud day for me,' I said. 'Now please just stand close together in front of Daddy and Tom and smile, just for one second. If you do I'll give you all a jelly.' They did. I took the photo of my husband standing holding little Tom, and in front of him our three boys, our tearaways, our wrestlers, our angels, our babies.

'Mummy, why are you crying?' Leo asked, munching his jelly.

'Because I love you all so much. I'm so lucky to have this amazing family. And this is a really big day and you're the best kids in the world and I know I don't tell you that enough. But I really do love you and I'm so proud right now that my heart is bursting.'

'Is it going to explode and loads of blood will come out?' Luke asked.

'Like a big tub of tomato ketchup?' Liam sniggered.

'Are you going to die?' Leo looked excited at the prospect.

'OK, that's enough. Get your coats on.' Harry ushered them to the front door. I'd asked him to take them because I knew I'd make a show of myself at the school gate, bawling.

I hugged them all and kissed their clean, shiny faces. 'Have fun and try to be good. I love you.'

I picked Tom up and we waved the triplets off to their new school, to a new chapter in their lives . . . and mine.

Threescompany:

Hi, everyone,

Sorry I've not been in touch for ages. So much has happened since my last message. Thanks for all your support by the way. You won't believe it – my husband wasn't cheating on me after all. He actually had a daughter he didn't know existed, who lives in Paris, and they were meeting up for the first time. He didn't want to say anything to me until he had met her himself.

Anyway, I followed him to Paris with my two sisters, who have been so supportive, and we confronted him and then we realized the whole thing was a complete mix-up. Honestly, it was just like in the movies – only more dramatic! But it's all sorted out now, so I didn't lose a husband, I gained an eighteen-year-old step-daughter. You couldn't make this stuff up.

She's a lovely girl, grown-up, independent, mature, not needy or troublesome at all. She came to visit and it went really well. The boys were mad about her and followed her around the house like adoring puppies.

The triplets started school today. I was an emotional wreck, but I know it'll get easier and that in no time I'll be waving them off with glee. It's funny – I've been living for this moment since the day they were born and now that it's here I feel a bit sad and nostalgic. No wonder men find us difficult: we women can be so contrary!

My younger sister, whose husband lost all their money, has got a job and is doing really well. I never thought I'd see the day when she was supporting her family, but she is and I'm really proud of her. The whole situation has put a huge strain on their marriage, but hopefully in time they'll work it out. It's amazing the way the dynamic shifts in a relationship when one person stops earning and the other becomes the bread-winner. It's like a shifting of power. They've been through a lot, but I honestly think she's a better person now. She'd got very wrapped up in her jet-set lifestyle and lost sight of what's really important in life.

My other sister is moving back to Dublin to set up her own legal department so she can spend more time with her little baby. She's happier than I've ever seen her. Becoming a mother has mellowed her and she's a much more content person. Her career will always be incredibly important to her, but having a baby has forced her to stop and smell the roses.

Life has changed for all of us. I think we really grew up this year.

Anyway, that's all for now except to tell you that something exciting might be coming my way. Something I hope you'll be able to share with me. I'll keep you posted when I know for sure . . . Sorry to be cryptic, but it's not definite yet.

41

Louise

Moving back to Dublin had been so much easier than I imagined. Mum and Dad collected me from the airport. Dad carried my bags to the car, and Mum held Clara. They had a lovely lunch waiting for us when we got back to their house. Mum gave Clara her bottle and put her down for her nap. She then offered to look after her for the afternoon while I went to sort out my apartment and unpack my boxes.

Sophie and Julie came to help me. They brought wine and music, and we had fun doing it. I had only ever moved and unpacked alone before. They helped me make up the beds, put together Clara's cot, hang up my pictures, then flattened all the boxes and left them outside my front door. Dad collected them and brought them to the dump for me. I barely had to lift a finger. It was fantastic.

That evening, when I went back to pick up Clara, Mum had fed her, bathed her and put her into a gorgeous new pair of pyjamas she'd bought for her. When I got home to the apartment and put her to bed, I discovered Sophie and Julie had packed my fridge and cupboards full of groceries and formula milk, nappies, wipes and all the other things I needed. I curled up on my couch with a glass of wine and smiled. It felt good to be back. I had made the right decision, I just knew it.

Work wasn't quite as straightforward, however. Some of the partners at Price Jackson were very cool towards me. They had found out the salary I was on – which I discovered was second only to the managing partner's – and they weren't too pleased about the 'blow-in' from London being so highly paid.

I had to prove myself to them, but that was nothing new to me. I'd been proving myself all my life. I did what I'd always done: put my head down and worked incredibly hard. It took me six weeks to hire my team: two were internal appointments and two were from outside. They were bright, ambitious and keen to get ahead, but they knew who their boss was and they respected me. As the clients rolled in and the other partners realized I wasn't some prima-donna with an over-inflated ego, they began to pay me a grudging respect until, after a couple of months, I became 'one of the boys'. Interestingly, of the twelve senior partners at Price Jackson, five were women and three of them had children. It seemed as if more glass ceilings were being smashed in Dublin than in London.

As for Clara, she was thriving. Mum's friend's daughter had a fantastic nanny she no longer needed as she had given up work after her third child so I inherited the wonderful, capable, cheerful Suzie from Sydney. She was lovely with Clara and I trusted her completely. Sophie had left me a list of playgroups for them to go to, so Suzie took Clara to all the happy-clappy ones I'd have absolutely hated, and everyone was happy.

I worked from home every Friday, so I had a leisurely breakfast with Clara, then went into my home office (a desk in my bedroom), while Suzie took her off to a playgroup. At two o'clock, after Clara's nap, Suzie left and I spent the afternoon with my little girl. Granted I spent half the time on the phone, but I was still with her physically, so it was a big improvement on my old job.

At weekends we went to Mum and Dad's for family lunch on Sunday and Clara got to see all her cousins, uncles and aunts. I loved those days – long, leisurely and lively.

Moving home had been a fantastic decision. I felt safe, supported, loved and genuinely happy. Clara was getting tons of attention and love – every time we drove up to Mum and Dad's house she'd squeal with joy and wave her arms.

Last Sunday at lunch, Gavin announced he had something to tell us.

'This'd better be about a job,' Dad muttered.

'You know the way I've always been really into animals?' Gavin asked.

'No,' we all answered.

'I have,' he replied.

'No, you haven't,' Julie said.

He frowned. 'I used to take Toby for walks when none of you would.'

'Only because you could have a smoke while you were doing it,' Julie retorted.

'You were fifteen – tell me you weren't smoking!' Mum pleaded.

'Thanks a lot, Julie,' he drawled. 'I actually loved that dog.'

'Well, how come you forgot to feed him for two days when Mum and Dad went away and you were supposed to be looking after him?' Sophie grinned.

'I was busy in college. Anyway, I was really sad when he died.'

'Were you?' Mum asked. 'You told me you were too busy playing football to say goodbye to him the day I had him put down.'

I roared laughing. 'Yes, Gavin – if I remember correctly you said of Toby's demise, "It's no harm, he was banjaxed anyway."'

'I'm not good at showing my emotions, OK? Anyway, can I get to the bloody point without being interrupted, please?' Gavin snapped.

'Go on. I can't wait to hear this.' Jack grinned.

'My money's on a new tree-hugging expedition in the Amazon.' Harry chuckled.

'I'm betting on save the whales.' Jack snorted.

'Ssh – let him speak,' Sophie scolded them.

Gavin carried on oblivious: 'So, I've been offered an internship programme with the NWF.'

Everyone stared at him blankly.

He looked at me. 'Come on, Louise, you're in bloody Mensa, you must know them.'

I let him sweat for a minute and then piped up, 'It's the National Wildlife Federation. They're very well regarded – and I'm impressed

440

you got on their programme. It's really competitive. Seriously, well done.'

'Of course he got on. Sure he's brilliant,' Mum said, patting Gavin's back.

'What exactly does this mean and how much is it going to cost me?' Dad was less enthusiastic.

'Nothing, except my flight to Washington DC.'

'America?' Mum looked upset.

'Are you telling me you're going to get paid on this internship?' Dad was suspicious: he was looking for the catch.

Gavin nodded. 'Yes, Dad, you're off the hook financially. It's not exactly millions, but it'll be enough to live on. Eighty people applied for the internship and I got it. They were very impressed with my on-the-ground campaigning.'

'It looks like the tree-hugging paid off.' Julie winked at him.

'So is this it, then?' Dad asked. 'This is where you want your career to go?'

Gavin shrugged. 'It's a great opportunity. I'm not saying I'll stay with the NWF long term, but I'll see how it goes, see if it lights my fire.'

'Oh, to be young and carefree and have choices,' Sophie said.

'Footloose and fancy free.' Julie sighed.

'Feckless and clueless,' Dad muttered.

'Well done, Gavin. You've done yourself proud,' Mum said. 'I'll miss you, though. It'll be lonely here without you.'

'When do you go?' I asked.

'January the third.'

Mum looked relieved. 'Oh, good, so you'll be here for Christmas.'

'It'll do you the world of good to get out there and stand on your own two feet,' Dad said.

'Do your own laundry,' I added.

'Cook your own meals,' Julie said.

'Pay your own bills,' Sophie noted.

'Get away from you three witches.' Gavin grinned.

I was pleased for him. Going to America, looking after his own finances and working with new and diverse people would be good for him. He was ready to leave home. He needed to cut the apron strings. Mum spoilt him and it was time for him to assert his independence and be his own man.

When things had settled down in work, I took Sophie and Julie out to a nice restaurant for an early Christmas celebration and to thank them for having been so great in helping me settle back home.

We all dressed up and, I must say, we were a fine-looking bunch. Sophie had put on weight and looked much better for it: her face had lost that pulled look now that she had stopped getting Botox. Julie had kept off the weight she'd lost and glowed with happiness and contentment. I was back running every day and felt fit and healthy. I was also much less stressed and I could see it in my face.

We ordered our food and sipped our wine.

'It's such a treat to get dressed up and go out after a long week at work,' Sophie said.

Julie and I looked at each other and laughed.

'What?' Sophie asked.

'You used to go out for dinner three or four nights a week,' Julie reminded her.

Sophie looked surprised. 'God, you're right. I did and I never appreciated it. It was just the way my life was. Now I consider it a huge treat.'

'Dinner in a fancy restaurant was always a big deal for me,' Julie admitted, 'but instead of spending an hour trying on clothes that didn't fit me and feeling crap about myself, I threw this dress on and ran out the door. It feels great.'

'And I left my angel baby without feeling guilty – I've spent all afternoon with her, which would never have happened in London. I was lucky if I got to kiss her goodnight on a Friday.'

'Well, Lou, it looks like things have worked out well,' Julie said. 'Did you ever think this time last year that you'd be living back in

Dublin, running your own department, madly in love with your baby and getting on so well with Mum?'

'Not in my wildest dreams. I have to say, since I had Clara, Mum has been brilliant. We never argue any more – it's like we have a completely different relationship.'

'It's because you've let her in,' Sophie said.

'What do you mean?'

'You've always been so independent and capable. Never needing any help. In fact, if any of us was in trouble we'd go to you for advice. There was no space for Mum to mother you. She had no role in your life. But then Clara came along and you let her in. It's made her so happy – she loves being closer to you.'

'I'd never thought about it like that.'

'Did you ever think you'd be working and supporting a family?' Julie asked Sophie.

'Not in a million years.' She laughed. 'Me – working? This time last year I was out Christmas shopping, spending horrendous amounts on presents no one wanted. Buying clothes I didn't need. Going to endless parties. This year it'll be a quiet one at home with Jack and Jess, watching movies, eating home-made popcorn and being a family.'

'Do you miss it? The high life?' Julie wondered.

'Occasionally I miss the buzz of going on a shopping spree, and I do miss the amazing holidays, but mostly no. And when I do buy myself something, it's really special because I've saved up for it and worked hard for the money to buy it. So, no, I don't miss it and I'm a much better mother. Even though I'm working, the time I spend with Jess now is quality time. Instead of dropping her off at endless activities, I'm properly focused on her when we're together. And I'm giving her a realistic view of life and instilling good values into her sweet little head, not filling it with rubbish about diamonds and money. I also like being good at something, having my own life – Sophie Devlin, head booker at Beauty Spot. It's nice. It makes me feel important in my own little way.'

'How are you and Jack getting on?' I asked.

She lifted her nail to chew it, but stopped and put her hand back down. 'In a way it's been good that he's working in London. When he comes home on Thursday night I'm glad to see him. I've missed him. It's almost as if we're dating again. It's by no means perfect and we have a long way to go. Our life has been completely pared back and it's just us. No bells and whistles, no five-star hotels or glitzy balls, just him and me in our apartment. I'm still nervous about him losing his job again, but I'm not angry any more. What happened is in the past. It's over. We are where we are and, overall, it's turned out to be a good thing.'

'What about you, Julie?' I asked.

'I made it.' She grinned. 'I made it to the triplets going to school. It was the longest marathon in the history of the world, but I did it and I didn't kill them or harm them. I got them to school and now Tom goes to play-school two mornings a week and life is suddenly clear again. The fug I've been in for so long, where I couldn't see past piles of laundry, has gone. I'm finding myself again. The old Julie is coming back and it feels really great. And you know what? I was getting into a rut of feeling sorry for myself – poor me, with four kids and no help, poor me, with no spare cash, poor me, I can't lose weight. And then the thing with Harry happened and it jolted me right out of my self-pity party and made me see how lucky I am. How blessed I am. How I have everything I've ever wished for and didn't know it. I'm more appreciative of everything now and I've even inherited a long-distance daughter. Actually, guys, I have a bit of exciting news.'

'Jesus, you're not pregnant again?' I asked.

'Louise,' she said, 'if I was pregnant again, I'd stick this fork in my eye. My news is that a while ago I started posting comments, an online stream-of-consciousness really, on this mums' website and I got a big reaction to what I was saying. Anyway, the *Evening Herald* picked up on it and they want me to write a weekly column about motherhood and marriage – just rant about life, really.'

My sisters' mouths dropped open and they looked at me with admiration.

'My God, that's fantastic.' Sophie hugged her.

'Well done, Julie.' I kissed her.

'Stop, you'll make me cry. It's not that big a deal and the money is crap, but it's something for me. My own little thing.'

'It *is* a big deal,' I said. 'You've devoted your life to those kids and it's great that you now have this outlet for yourself – and, of course, a means to make a bit of extra cash.'

'We can give you plenty of material,' Sophie said.

'You'd never be stuck for content with this family.' I laughed.

'It's pretty amazing how this year has changed us, though, isn't it?' Julie said. 'Even Gavin's grown up, although I'm not sure how long the wildlife career will last.'

'Remember how he flushed Goldie down the loo and overfed Skipper so we found him floating and bloated at the top of the fish bowl?' Sophie giggled.

'I give him six months, tops,' Julie said.

'I give him five,' I said. 'Unless Mum moves out to Washington and does his laundry for him.'

'Are we being a bit harsh? Were we so mature at twenty-four?' Sophie asked.

'Yes, we were,' I reminded her. 'We were all working and living in our own apartments.'

'I envy him, though. America will be great. I wish I'd travelled more,' Julie said.

'I wish I'd never given up work,' Sophie said.

'I wish I'd moved home years ago,' I confessed.

'So, we're not perfect.' Julie laughed.

I looked at my sisters. 'You know, the strange thing about moving back is that all the things I ran away from are the very reasons I wanted to come home.'

'How do you mean?' Sophie asked.

'I ran away because Dublin was too small. I wanted a big city, bright lights, the best college, the top law degree, the finest law firm. I wanted to be independent. I wanted to get away from Mum constantly trying to mother me. I wanted to get away from being one of the Devlin sisters. I wanted to live my own life without having to answer to anyone. And you know what? It's not all it's cracked up to be, but it took having a baby to make me realize that I love having Mum to fuss over me, I love family lunches – and that if my dishwasher breaks down all I have to do is call Dad and he'll come over and fix it. I love the fact that Clara will grow up surrounded by family. But, most of all, I love being one of the Devlin sisters.'

We raised our glasses and toasted ourselves.

Threescompany: MY FINAL MESSAGE

Mums,

I have some very exciting news. As of 10 January, you will be able to read my views and comments in the *Irish Evening Herald* every Thursday. I have you all to thank for that. Your response to my ramblings has helped me land a dream job. I'm absolutely thrilled, so thank you all very much.

I'll be writing as Threescompany. I've decided to remain anonymous so I can be truly honest without hurting anyone's feelings – or causing a family feud!

The triplets are now in school until one thirty every day – bliss! And my toddler is in play-school two mornings a week from nine till twelve, so I now have six hours a week to myself. You might think I'd use the time sensibly to get on top of my laundry, washing and cleaning. Sod that! I step over the mess, go back to bed and read my book with a cup of tea because, ladies, that is what makes me happy. I've waited over five years for these precious hours and I sure as hell am not going to spend them hoovering.

Am I Zen now that I have this time to myself? No. I wish I could say I was. I wish I could say I was more patient, less snappy with the boys, but I'm not. What I am, though, is happier within myself and I see now how important that is. Being a stay-at-home mum

447

is the most challenging, thankless job there is. We mums need to 'feed our souls'. I know it sounds a bit hippie-dippy but it's true and it's important. We need to find one thing that we can call our own, whether it's planting tomatoes in the garden or going for a walk by the sea or working in a soup kitchen. It doesn't matter what it is, it just matters that we find it and allow ourselves the time to do it.

Taking the time to do something for ourselves doesn't mean we love our children any less. It doesn't mean we're not great mothers. It just means we know we need something too. We're people. We exist as individuals. We're not invisible.

The other thing I've learnt over the last year is how important family is. I wouldn't have got through it without my sisters. I've given out about them in the past, and there were times when they drove me mad. But this has been a defining year for all of us. We always slag our little brother for not growing up, but we girls needed to grow up too and, thankfully, we have. The three of us have overcome big obstacles this year and have survived, bruised and battered, but the better for it.

I know that I for one am a better person since the whole palaver with my husband and the non-affair. I was becoming dissatisfied with my life, picking holes in it, wanting more, wanting a better life, a different life, a nicer life. Well, Mums, I know now that I have the life I always wanted. Is it perfect? No. Are there still days when I want to book a one-way flight to Brazil? Yes, plenty. But every night before I go to sleep, I peep into the boys' bedrooms, and as I watch their little bodies rise and fall as they dream, I thank God for what I have and I really mean it. I wouldn't change a thing.

Acknowledgements

I would especially like to thank Rachel Pierce, my editor, whose help and advice were invaluable to me; Patricia Deevy, for all her enthusiasm and support; Michael McLoughlin, Cliona Lewis, Patricia McVeigh, Brian Walker and all the team at Penguin Ireland for making the publishing process so enjoyable.

Thanks also to all in the Penguin UK office, especially Tom Weldon, Joanna Prior and the fantastic sales, marketing and creative teams; to my agent Marianne Gunn O'Connor who is a pleasure to know and work with; to Hazel Orme, as always, for her wonderful copy-editing; to Anwen Hooson for her hard work on the publicity front; to Mark White for his insight into the world of corporate law.

Thanks to my friends for being so honest and often hilarious about the trials and tribulations of motherhood; to Mum, Dad, Sue, Mike and my extended family for their unwavering support and loyalty. It means so much. This book is dedicated to Mike, the best brother in the world.

Thanks to my nephews, Mikey, James, Jack, Sam and Finn, and to my nieces, Cathy and Isabel – all unwitting muses for this book; to Hugo, Geordy and Amy, my inspirations and the loves of my life.

And, saving the best for last, thank you, Troy.

Finally, to all the mothers out there, I salute you!